DEATH BY VILSMEIER

OTHER TITLES by HENRY D. SCHREIBER

The Treasure Keepers (2020)
Stolen Blessings (2021)
The 4th Beast (2021)
Mohlers Loop (2021)

Death by Vilsmeier

A NOVEL

Henry D. Schreiber

YELLOW HYDRANGEA BOOKS

DEATH by VILSMEIER: A NOVEL
by Henry D. Schreiber

First Edition: March 2022
Printed in the United States of America
ISBN: 978-1-7347785-3-3

Cover photograph of Anton Vilsmeier at Erlangen, from "Der Mann hinter der Reaktion: Anton Vilsmeier (1894-1962)" presented by Christoph Meinel before the Faculty of Chemistry and Pharmacy of the University of Regensburg on 12 June 2012. [Christoph Meinel, "Ein Mann und seine Reaktion," *Nachrichten aus der Chemie* **60** (2012) 1187-1190.]

Back cover painting of the Peruvian Rainbow Frog copyright © by Helen P. Irvine. Used by permission.

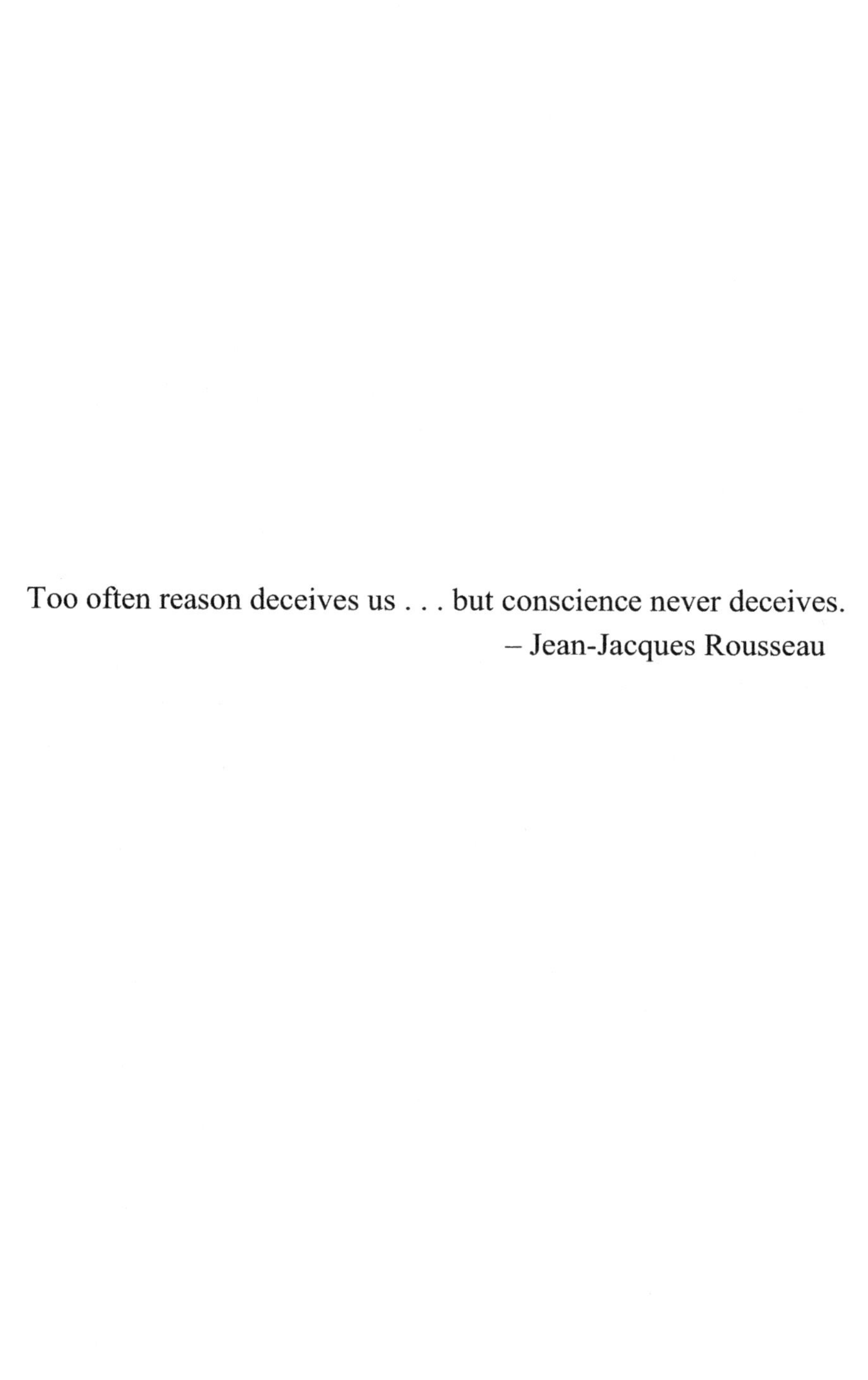

Too often reason deceives us . . . but conscience never deceives.

– Jean-Jacques Rousseau

PROLOGUE

EAVESDROPPED

Evalina paced back and forth. Her eyes kept staring at the decorative ceramic tile squares of the hallway floor. She fidgeted with her keys in one hand, and in her other held a cell phone tightly to her ear.

"But you promised," she suddenly shouted. "You promised you'd leave her!" She kicked the leg of the nearby china press; the plates and glasses clattered. Catching her breath, she continued, "You keep telling me you love me. And I love you like I've loved no other. Now all I hear from you are excuses, excuses, and more excuses."

Lum stood motionless in the kitchen, out of sight of his daughter. He shuddered, clearly hearing every one of her words.

Evalina's frustrations exploded. "I'm just so, so tired of sneaking around, always in the shadows."

She took a few deep breaths, momentarily listening to a calming voice.

"I know about your career. But I want you all the time, not just when it's convenient for you." Her voice started to quiver. "And accusations of improprieties would be the least of your worries."

Now enraged, she launched her keys at the front door.

Lum heard only the scuffing of Evalina's shoes for a minute; then, no movement. He peeked around the corner. She was leaning against the wall, next to a framed print of *The Last Supper*, paying rapt attention to the voice on the phone.

Evalina changed moods and sobbed uncontrollably. "I'm so sorry. I love you. I'd never tell anyone. I just let myself get so worked up, saying things I don't mean."

Following another reply, her mood reversed yet again. "You need to do what you promised," she yelled. "No more stalling!"

She smacked the phone to disconnect the call, stomped down the hallway, snatched her keys from the floor, and slammed the front door behind her – all without realizing her father had eavesdropped on a very private exchange with her lover that Saturday afternoon.

Moments later, Lum heard his daughter's car start. The tires squealed as if the car had donned her anger. Tears welled in his eyes. He wished he'd stayed working in his home's backyard. All he'd wanted was a drink of ice water, not to hear his daughter's outbursts and confessions. He slipped into a seat at the kitchen table, ignoring his ice water. He gazed intently out the window without focusing on anything in particular.

He tried to keep his emotions in check, but rapidly worked himself into an internal frenzy. Thoughts spiraled. He linked what Evalina said on her end of the phone conversation to what he imagined must be happening with Turville. It was hard enough for him to envision inappropriate hugging or kissing, much less a full-fledged affair. The latter, though, would explain nights Evalina didn't spend at home, and the tense irritation she exhibited when questioned about her mysterious nighttime activities. Lum had quickly learned these things were better left unasked in order to keep peace in their house.

Only a few days earlier, several co-workers at PAYNE Pharmaceuticals told him they'd observed Evalina angrily storm out of Turville's office. She appeared disheveled with make-up smeared and hair a-kilter. Her unsettled emotions came across as more personal than professional. His lovely Evalina should've known better than take up with a married man.

Lum slammed his fist on the table. "That pig Turville!" he snarled.

It made sense. All the pieces of the puzzle fit together. Obviously, that "playboy" Turville had been pursuing Evalina –

with her flowing blonde hair, hazel eyes, elegant stature, and movie star looks – in clear violation of work policy. The annual training sessions at PAYNE Pharmaceuticals made it quite clear. Supervisors couldn't make romantic overtures toward their employees. Such was *de facto* sexual harassment and would result in the automatic firing of the supervisor.

Lum felt knots in his stomach.

He stared at the array of pictures magnetically attached to the nearby refrigerator. They showed Evalina in various stages of her life: childhood, beauty queen, graduation from high school and college. He focused on the most recent picture, a five-by-seven inch photo of her being presented an employee-of-the-month certificate by Turville. He studied the picture, seeing whether it hid anything more than just an award presentation. How did his beautiful daughter become involved with her low-life of a boss Turville?

Lum started to question whether he'd misinterpreted her professional approval of him for personal admiration. Dr. Mason Turville admittedly possessed a strikingly handsome physique. Many women at PAYNE Pharmaceuticals swooned as he passed by their desks or work stations. Now, Lum wondered – when Evalina had paraded up to her boss after church services, was she simply acknowledging his presence, or was she more subtly flirting with him, not resisting his advances?

Disgust and anger overwhelmed Lum. He stood and knocked his chair away from the table. Slamming the kitchen door, he traipsed outside. He wandered about the patio with a balled fist. He couldn't get it out of his mind – Turville, married with a couple of kids, close to twenty years her senior, messing around with his daughter. For many years, rumors had swirled around PAYNE Pharmaceuticals that Turville was a skirt chaser. He knew the gossip wasn't just gossip, but a fact. He knew the scorned women. Evalina, though, had hid underneath his radar.

Overcast skies turned to drizzle, adding more gloom. Lum's wheelbarrow, hoe, and trowel sat next to the flower bed.

"Let'em git wet," he mumbled.

PART 1

PRELUDE TO REVENGE

Chapter One
LUM BAUMGARTNER

Columbus "Lum" Baumgartner stood only five feet five inches tall. He tipped the scales at barely 110 pounds when fully dressed. During his upbringing, his older brother and sisters referred to him as the runt of their family's litter. His looks – a pointy, gnome-like head with ears too big, nose too small, and mouse-colored hair – only added to his torment. In school, others routinely bullied this scrawny kid, always picked last in gym class games. He garnered even less respect on the playground. Just on sight, most guys figured he could be whooped with little effort. But he learned at a young age to fight for his survival, scratching and clawing instead of using brute strength. Still, he donned a slight limp and a scar on his cheek, as evidence of his rough childhood.

○ ● ○ ● ○

Nowadays, Lum worked as the maintenance supervisor for PAYNE Pharmaceuticals, a manufacturer of generic drugs, specializing in those controlling pain. PAYNE Pharmaceuticals used the cheapest procedures to make the active ingredient in pain-killing medicines no longer having patent protection. Its sales team then marketed these drugs for a fraction of the cost charged by the major pharmaceutical firms. The founder of the company, Jim Payne, often quipped, "PAYNE controls pain." Jim hired Lum nearly 35 years ago, a few days after Lum graduated from the local high school. Now Lum worked for Jim Payne, Jr., whose personal mantra echoed and extended that of his father's: "There's money in pain, so profit for PAYNE."

PAYNE Pharmaceuticals sat on sixty acres on the outskirts of the small town of Millikan in West Virginia. Jim Payne established his company there for the abundant cheap labor. Surrounded by several abandoned coal mines in the heart of the Appalachian Mountains, PAYNE offered one of only limited employment opportunities for Millikan's residents. Lum had been one of the first employees of PAYNE, and knew, or knew of, essentially all the employees. He worked his way up the ranks, starting as janitor. He was promoted to subsequent jobs by apprenticing with the person he eventually replaced.

Lum had become invaluable to the company, even though he supervised only three janitors and one mechanic working the night shift. Repairing or jury-rigging everything from the fabrication machinery to research instrumentation to plumbing to HVAC systems, among others, established the norm for Lum each night. All equipment was up and running for the fully-staffed day shift. Production lines hummed along smoothly, in large part due to Lum's mechanical wizardry. In addition, Lum doubled as the unofficial security guard, albeit an unarmed one, on his shift. He kept an eye on the goings-on at PAYNE Pharmaceuticals. In essence, nothing occurred during the night, and indirectly throughout the entire day, at PAYNE Pharmaceuticals that wasn't quickly known to Lum.

○ ● ○ ● ○

Lum had been married to Partie, his wife of more than thirty years, until losing her to an aggressive form of lung cancer the previous year. He always marveled at his good blessings to have found a wife who saw past his shortage of physical attributes. He was a loving husband, providing Partie with all her worldly needs, and with nary a wandering eye. Likewise, he'd been just as devoted to, as well as protective of, their only child, Evalina, named for Partie's maternal grandmother.

Lum's hobbies were few, just hunting and fishing. But even those interests subsided with his aging body; mostly he'd evolved to just talking about hunting and fishing.

The family for many years consisted of only Lum, Partie, and Evalina, until about ten years ago. A cat – plain gray, smallish, cut on his shoulder, and walking with a slight limp – appeared at their doorstep. Evidently he'd been dumped nearby and chose them as his adoptive parents. Lum named him Possum. Not only did the cat look the part, but he often feigned sleep. Possum, playing possum, didn't use the ploy defensively but as a surprise attack upon his prey or even an unwary visitor.

Lum was also a God-fearing Christian, quite concerned about the need for a religious education for all children in Millikan as well as the direction of his church, the Goose Creek Lutheran Church. His church regularly elected him to leadership positions, until a little more than a year ago. Dr. Mason Turville orchestrated a takeover in the control of the governing church council from Lum and those who thought like Lum. Rumors swirled that Turville wanted to replace their current pastor with one of his own choosing. No longer was Goose Creek Lutheran Church a bastion for traditional Christian services. Instead, the present church resembled a boisterous and informal congregation that would've been barely recognizable to Lum's ancestors.

• • • • • • •

That Saturday evening, Lum ate an early supper. He fried himself a hamburger patty and baked some frozen fries in the oven. A paper plate served as his dinnerware, the local news reporter on television as his eating companion. Evalina had texted she'd gone out with a friend. She wouldn't return home until past her father's bedtime.

After dinner, Lum bumbled about his empty house, then drifted outside to the patio in back. The drizzle and clouds had given way to a mostly clear and warm evening. He nursed an ice cold can of Bud Light.

He admired the pink carnations he'd planted a few hours ago as a centerpiece to the flower bed. They were Partie's favorite flower and color. She never tired of repeating the legend that these carnations grew from the Virgin Mary's tears as she watched Jesus carrying the cross. Lum planted them every year on the anniversary of his and Partie's first date. His smile transformed to a tear.

He sighed. He'd put the wheelbarrow and tools away tomorrow.

The rumble of trucks traveling the main highway a few blocks away created a constant background noise. Wafts of some sulfur-containing chemical spewed by the PAYNE Pharmaceutical stacks mildly irritated his throat. The company timed the gaseous release for the weekend when EPA inspections were more lax. Jim Payne always said, "Push the limits; cleaning up emissions costs money." Lum coughed, spit the bad taste from his mouth, and took a swig of Bud Light.

Possum joined Lum next to his lawn chair and proudly presented him with a mauled field mouse. Lum gently petted Possum. "Perhaps you could bring Turville to me in the same way." He smiled. "Do ya do contract killings?" Possum purred, but took off through the backyard. "Guess not," Lum cynically chuckled.

Lum jumped into his aged, blue Ford Ranger pickup truck. He drove onto Millikan's Main Street. Empty store fronts outnumbered those occupied by the Dollar Tree, Thrift Shop, Harvey's Hardware, and C.C.'s Mexican Cafe. He headed to a back road. After crossing a set of railroad tracks, he traveled through the mountainous hollows toward the neighboring town of Colebrook. A little over halfway there, he turned into the Hickory Grove development, the exclusive estates for the ever dwindling upper crust of both Millikan and Colebrook. He cruised slowly down Birch Lane by Turville's house, a mini-mansion with an immaculately manicured yard and landscaping on its five acre lot. The house had multiple levels and Cape Cod dormers. Lum had heard the more changes in rooflines, the higher the price of the house – Turville's had the most except for a couple others, like that of Jim Payne, Jr., higher up the ridgeline on Chestnut Lane. Lum parked at Birch Lane's *cul de sac.* Several signs advertised lots for sale at prices higher than the assessed value of Lum's house. He parked far enough away from Turville's house not to cause notice, but close enough to spy on the house.

Turville's garage sat open. Turville's car, a metallic blue Volvo SUV, wasn't there, only his wife's red Cadillac sedan. Lum waited, angry at himself for not bringing along a cooler with some Bud Lights. He stewed. He pounded on the steering wheel, then got out of the truck and leaned against the hood. How could he have missed the affair between Turville and his daughter? He prided himself in knowing everything that happened at PAYNE Pharmaceuticals. He'd previously tussled with Evalina's boss, Dr. Mason Turville, not only at work but also at church. He didn't like Turville before the afternoon's phone call. Now he utterly despised him.

At nightfall, lights were turned on in the house. A woman came outside and sat on a deck chair. She appeared to carry a wine glass, filled to its brim, and have a phone to her ear. She was laughing, enjoying a good time. Lum wondered whether Shelley, Turville's wife, knew of her husband's past and current shenanigans.

Chapter Two
EVALINA VAIL

Both Lum and Partie doted on their daughter Evalina. In Evalina's early years, her parents as well as relatives and friends fully recognized her picturesque beauty. Evalina also loved to sing, with her naturally melodius voice, even at this young age. When combined with charm and poise, she easily won local pageants such as Little Miss Millikan.

As a teenager, she continued in this tradition by being named queens of numerous community carnivals, festivals, county fairs, and parades. At her mother's suggestion, Evalina eventually entered these teenage competitions under the name Evalina Vail instead of Evalina Baumgartner.

When Partie first proposed the use of "Vail" in the car on the way to a pageant, Lum was shocked. He disgustingly sputtered, "Evalina's a Baumgartner. It's not even a subject for discussion."

"But Vail is Evalina's middle name, as well as my maiden name," Partie calmly offered. "Evalina would be using the surname of my parents. It'd just be her stage name."

"Our daughter is a Baumgartner, plain and simple," Lum protested. "I see no need to change her name."

Partie rested her hand on Lum's shoulder. "Look at it from the viewpoint of the pageant judges. Vail evokes a vision of scenic beauty – think of Vail, Colorado." She continued with a wink of an eye to Lum. "When a woman wears a veil – same pronounciation but different spelling – it adds a bit of mystique."

Lum scowled.

Partie hesitated a moment, then persisted, "On the other hand, to a pageant judge, Baumgartner might spur notions of farmers or laborers." She placed her hand over her mouth, regretting her decision to comment on this connotation as soon as it slipped out.

"What?" Lum angrily squawked, "Baumgartner is a solid German name. I don't see why you feel the need to distance Evalina from her heritage?"

"But, daddy, your job is simply a glorified janitor," a young and naïve Evalina blurted. "I don't want to be that kind of Baumgartner." She clearly sought to distance herself from such a demeaning occupation in her mind.

Lum sat speechless. He glared at Partie too long. The car drifted onto the gravels on the shoulder of the road.

Partie cried, "Lum," as she reached for the steering wheel.

Lum quickly corrected, pushing Partie's hand aside. He tried to hold back tears.

"Oh, Lum, Evalina didn't mean that as it came out," Partie said. She gently stroked and massaged Lum's shoulders. Then, she sweetly added, "Let's just try it this once. Just once, I promise."

Evalina won that pageant. The concluding comment from the judges proclaimed: "Even her name evokes beauty, magic, and charisma!"

Despite Lum's sulking and pouting, Evalina not only used Vail as her surname in subsequent beauty pageants but also in high school, and then for all her identifications. In fact, many lost track of the father-daughter relationship between Lum and Evalina in her teenage years because of this disconnect in surnames as well as in appearances. Some, who didn't know Evalina from birth, started to question whether Evalina was the adopted daughter of Lum.

○ ● ○ ● ○

Evalina's voice, a perfect soprano, sent warm chills up listeners' spines. She started singing in the Goose Creek Lutheran Church's choir at five, and sang anthem solos before the age of ten. The worshippers loved her renditions of standards such as

"Amazing Grace," "Holy, Holy, Holy," "Beautiful Savior," "Seek Ye First," and "Great Is Thy Faithfulness." And singing Christmas carols such as "O Holy Night" and "O Come All Ye Faithful" often brought spontaneous and thunderous ovations from an admiring audience. Members of the congregation boasted that she sang as though she were filled with a musical Holy Spirit, touching the hearts and souls of all.

Although Evalina dabbled for a time in country music, especially those with religious overtones, she always returned to her roots – the traditional church songs as her favorites.

At the age of fourteen, Evalina started private voice lessons under the tutelage of Reverend Adam Clarke, the newly ordained pastor of Goose Creek Lutheran Church. Reverend Clarke was both recently married and freshly graduated from the Lutheran seminary when he began at Goose Creek. He often sang hymns, and accompanied himself on the piano, with his booming baritone voice during the church services. He'd considered singing professionally before going into the ministry. Listeners compared his passion and voice to a gospel-singing Elvis Presley. Under his keen ear, piano accompaniment, and gentle direction, Evalina's singing blossomed. The congregation at Goose Creek considered it a spiritual treat when Reverend Clarke and Evalina sang duets of, for example, "How Great Thou Art," "Old Rugged Cross," and "Wonderful Grace of Jesus," as well as "Because He Lives" (originally sung by Bill Gaither and his sister).

Evalina, to her credit, never lost sight of academic aspirations. She was on the honor roll from elementary through high school, graduating in the top five of her class at Millikan High School. Her interests and proficiencies were science and mathematics. She particularly excelled in chemistry her junior year in high school. Putting atoms together to form a molecule and seeing how its resulting structure controlled its reactivity totally fascinated her.

And, unlike many other teenagers, Evalina wasn't rebellious. She did her chores without complaint or sass, always arrived home before curfew. Although she had many boys as friends, she never had one who was considered a boyfriend. She looked forward going to school every weekday and to church on Wednesday nights and Sundays – and doing her homework and her singing practices and lessons. Lum and Partie felt blessed.

○ ● ○ ● ○

During her senior year in high school, Evalina strained her vocal cords a week before an upcoming beauty pageant. She'd practiced singing "You'll Never Walk Alone" with guidance from Pastor Clarke for its talent competition. But, instead of withdrawing from the pageant, she decided to switch to presenting a chemical demonstration on the stage. The organizers weren't happy. Chemicals could spill and make a mess; and how would her talent be judged against the singers, musicians, gymnasts, and dancers? They begrudgingly acquiesced.

Evalina looked absolutely glamorous dressed in a white lab coat, while wearing safety glasses in front of a table sprinkled with glassware, chemicals, and molecular models. The week before the pageant, her father helped her construct some styrofoam models of different colors and sizes in the shape of oversized Lego blocks.

To start her demonstration, Evalina added separate scoops of reddish-purple cobalt chloride crystals to two large test tubes. One contained water and the other isopropyl, or rubbing, alcohol. As she held up the test tubes, one in each hand, she proudly announced, "Cobalt ions dissolved in water result in a pinkish red color, while in isopropyl alcohol they create a brilliant blue coloration. Two different solvents, two different colors – why? It's all a matter of the size of the water molecules versus the alcohol molecules. Let me show you with my models. The white blocks represent cobalt ions, the small pink ones represent water, and the larger blue ones represent alcohol. The positive cobalt ion is attracted to the negative oxygen atom on both the water and alcohol molecules."

Evalina then joined six pink water blocks in a spherical array around the central white cobalt block, but could only fit four of the larger blue alcohol blocks around its cobalt block. "Gee, it's all about size. Basic chemistry – size matters. If you build a structure with six units around the cobalt ion, you get red; but if you build it with only four units, you get blue. Now let's go back to our solid cobalt chloride. It's actually cobalt chloride hexahydrate, meaning that it has six water molecules within its solid structure."

She then heated the solid in the test tube with a butane torch. The solid cobalt chloride turned blue. She confidently continued, "Once again, a color change – why? The dark red solid has six water molecules around a central cobalt ion. Six means red. Upon heating the solid, the water is expelled or essentially boiled out of the solid. Only four chlorides fit around the central cobalt. Four means blue. So we can control the color of this material by both temperature, or by water content."

In the audience, Lum nudged Partie. He beamed. "That's my girl!"

Partie quietly responded, "She explains things so anyone can understand."

To conclude her demonstration, Evalina added hydrochloric acid to the pink solution of cobalt in water. Holding the test tube up to the crowd, she proudly proclaimed, "Once again a red to blue color change – Why?" But the solution stayed pink. She stared at the test tube, then added more acid. It remained pink. Taken aback, she rubbed her hand over her chin.

The audience rustled in their seats.

Exasperated, Lum turned to Partie and whispered, "Why didn't it turn blue? It's supposed to turn blue!"

Partie removed her glasses and cleaned them with a tissue.

Pastor Clarke, who'd tagged along with Lum and Partie even though Evalina wasn't singing, held his head in his hands.

Evalina added more acid. Still pink. She looked at the acid bottle, then smiled. "Oh, well. It would've helped to use the right chemicals. I picked up dilute hydrochloric acid instead of the concentrated form. The concentrated acid would've added enough chloride ions into the system to replace the six waters with four chlorides, just like the heating of the cobalt chloride hexahydrate."

Evalina was cool under pressure, not becoming rattled or upset. She analyzed what went wrong. She knew her chemistry as well as she sang hymns.

Only polite applause followed after this demonstration, though, not the standing ovation she'd been accustomed to after some of her singing performances. The judges praised her gracefulness and composure, but awarded her no trophy that night.

Evalina took the loss in stride, saying, "It was a learning experience!"

"You might want to stick to singing," quipped Pastor Clarke with a wink of the eye. "It's easier to hide a missed note than a wrong reagent."

○ ● ○ ● ○

As Evalina applied to colleges, she struggled about whether to major in chemistry or music. Lum and Partie waited impatiently for her decision. Her father asked of her plans every night for a week at the dinner table.

One day, Evalina laughingly responded, "An architect."

"I didn't realize that was an option," her father replied with a puzzled look on his face. "What happened to music and chemistry, or maybe physics or math?"

Evalina rose from her chair and lovingly hugged her father. She whispered in his ear: "Not just any old architect, but a molecular architect."

Her father remained bewildered and clueless. She added, "A molecular architect, that is, a chemist. Much like an architect designs buildings from bricks and mortar, a chemist designs molecules from atoms and bonds. My ambition is to build molecules." Her fascination with chemistry had flourished with the understanding that what happened at this molecular level manifested itself in the physical and chemical properties of a substance. In a sense, atoms were simply tiny Lego blocks, or spheres, that could be used to build molecules, much like bricks could be used to build buildings of different forms and structures.

"Ah-Ha," Lum replied, smiling. "You're just so clever!" he added with a smidgen of sarcasm.

○ ● ○ ● ○

Evalina received a partial academic scholarship to attend Keaton College, a nearby undergraduate school in West Virginia. Within her first year, she was immediately attracted to organic chemistry, a field in which the chemist assembles molecules from building blocks of mostly carbon atoms.

○ ● ○ ● ○

During her undergraduate years, Evalina continued to enter beauty pageants, culminating in being crowned the runner-up in the Miss Academic America - West Virginia competition during her senior year at college. She caused a minor stir as well as generated much publicity at the state pageant for refusing to cover her small tattoo "Jesus Loves Me," in the motif of a cross, which was quite visible on the back of her shoulder. She claimed that covering the tattoo would've made her a hypocrite for her Christian faith. Some argued she would've won the competition, but for this tattoo. In the talent preliminaries, she sang lovely, stirring renditions of the gospel songs, "Go Tell it on the Mountain" and "His Eye is on the Sparrow," in addition to the classic patriotic song "God Bless America," all of which led to rousing applause from the audience. To further impress the judges, Evalina sang a medley of her original compositions, "From Manger to Cross," "Faith, Hope, and Love," and "My Race to Grace," in the finals. Newspaper accounts of her talent described her performances as truly inspirational, with a vocal range comparable to that of a young Whitney Houston.

Although Evalina minored in music and joined the choir at Keaton College, Pastor Clarke continued to give her voice lessons throughout her time in college. Evalina returned home at least twice a month to visit her parents as well as to garner instruction and direction from Pastor Clarke for her pageant singing routines. Her voice professor at Keaton College insisted she focus on classical music and operatic singing. The professor considered such her strengths. But those weren't Evalina's interests. Pastor Clarke, not college professors, always traveled along with her parents, Lum and Partie, to pageants to provide support at the competitions.

In addition to beauty and talent, the Miss Academic America competition judged the contestants on their academic achievements and stated platforms. Evalina emphasized a "Chemistry is Cool" theme. During her reign as runner-up to the state crown, she continued to soar not only in popularity but also in controversy. In order to generate interest in science and empower young girls in chemistry, she traveled to public schools throughout West Virginia to present a program including several chemical demonstrations as well as songs about chemistry. For example, she often sang "The Elements," which incorporated the names of all chemical elements up to number 102 on the periodic table, and made relevant by the musical humorist and lecturer Tom Lehrer. Evalina's combination of awesome beauty, eye-popping chemistry, and passionate singing captured the students' interest during her typical half-hour time slot. But then, she also started to sneak songs with catchy tunes and Christian overtones such as "More Precious than Silver" and "I Believe in Jesus," to the tune of "I Believe in Music," into her routine. This provided even more publicity for Evalina, as the media highlighted her use of Christian songs.

In an interview with a newspaper to publicize her appearance at a local school, Evalina emphasized, "Christians have rights. There's nothing wrong with religious songs being sung in schools."

The reporter argued, "But many public schools have backed off from inviting you into the classroom in order to avoid controversy. So isn't that counterproductive?"

"I haven't let anything hold me back," Evalina proudly asserted. "I haven't let others bully me with respect to my religious choice – after all, our Bill of Rights says 'freedom of religion' not 'freedom from religion.' No one has complained about my singing Christian tunes except the media."

"You might have a point," the reporter chuckled. "The students seem to be entranced by your program of both chemistry and singing."

"Students should be able to break barriers by experimenting with science, singing their own types of song, professing their faith, or doing whatever they are good at," Evalina adamantly exclaimed.

With her background of academic and musical knowledge, along with being the focal point on stage when competing in beauty pageants, and traveling throughout the state talking to students, Evalina blossomed into a profoundly confident and independent young woman.

• • • • • • •

That Saturday, after her father overheard her phone conversation, Evalina killed some time by driving around the streets of Millikan before stopping at Hillside, a small local park. As usual, no one was there. It had been in a state of disrepair for years. Even after the closing of the coal mines, the omnipresent coal dust still seemed to settle on the grass, rocks, and playground equipment. She stayed in her gray Honda Accord, music blaring and windshield wipers intermittently removing the drizzle.

She then drove to Goose Creek Lutheran Church. Its lot was empty and nary a light burned inside. She parked in the back, just outside the choir room. The door didn't require her key, as it'd been left unlocked. She felt relief. She passed through the choir room, down the hall, and peeked into the church office. No one was there. She drifted into the unlit sanctuary. A vase of pink carnations sat on a pedestal next to the front stage. She smiled – her mother's favorite. Her eyes immediately darted to the large cross displayed in the front of the sanctuary. She wiped a tear from her eye – her mother always told the story of a mother's love, the Virgin Mary's for Jesus. Would her mother understand her actions – not just what was happening but also what was about to happen? Evalina sat on the front row, praying to God for forgiveness and guidance. Would her Father forgive her, still love her?

She traveled the fifteen miles to the larger town of Colebrook, big enough to support a WalMart and strip mall, where she grabbed a burger and fries at the Golden Arches. She caught an early showing at the local movie theater. She was one of only eight patrons to watch the showing of a critically-panned action flick. The movie reviewers had been correct in their assessment of the readily forgettable movie.

Now under to cover of darkness, she drove into a quiet residential section of Colebrook. Her heart beat faster and faster as she neared the rented efficiency apartment. It was essentially a renovated motel room with a television, pull-out sofa, a table and chairs, and a small bathroom. But it was at a perfect location; its entrance and parking were in the rear, hidden from view from passing motorists on the road.

She turned into the driveway, hoping he'd be there.

Chapter Three
ANTON VILSMEIER

While at Keaton College during both the academic year and summers, Evalina became involved in chemical research under the direction of Professor Quinn Stanton, or the "Q-Dawg" as dubbed by the students. Even though he worked at an undergraduate college, Q-Dawg had acquired an international reputation as an expert in the use of the Vilsmeier reaction in organic synthesis. The Vilsmeier-Haack reaction, commonly called just the Vilsmeier reaction after the German chemist Anton Vilsmeier, prepared a specific organic product, a vinamidinium salt, from a potful of reagents "cooked" under specific conditions – time, temperature, and solvent. Within the field of organic chemistry, there're a multitude of reactions, each named after their discoverer. These named reactions are also explicit in their syntheses of very specific molecules built mainly from carbon atoms strung in straight chains, branched chains, or rings. The carbon frameworks then possess attachments with arrangements of other atoms such as hydrogens, oxygens, and nitrogens.

The design and construction of such substances in the laboratory satisfied Evalina in her dreams of molecular architecture. During a visit with her parents in which they toured the research laboratory, she excitedly rambled, "I experience the real life of a scientist with all of its joys as well as frustrations in trying to get things to work. I get to design and synthesize molecules that no one else has ever made. Sometimes I make what Q-Dawg and I predict we should, but mostly it's just trial and error with good guesses. When I try a procedure that should work, but doesn't, I keep changing the reaction conditions until I get it to work. But even when I end up with the wrong stuff, sometimes it's more interesting than the desired stuff."

Q-Dawg's research group applied the Vilsmeier reaction to a witches brew of chemicals, typically an organic acid (a molecule possessing the $-CO_2H$ group), dimethylformamide (DMF, a common solvent for organic reactions as well as a contributor of nitrogen-containing groups), and phosphorous oxychloride ($POCl_3$, a very potent chemical that can decompose to choking fumes of hydrogen chloride in the presence of water). Upon adding sodium perchlorate ($NaClO_4$, normally a stable chemical, but also known to explosively decompose to oxygen in certain situations) at the completion of the reaction, the solid vinamidinium perchlorate precipitates from the liquid solution in very high yield and purity. In essence, the Vilsmeier reaction almost magically replaces the $-CO_2H$ group on the reactant with a larger array of atoms connecting carbon and nitrogen atoms in an established bonding arrangement called the vinamidinium group. Imagine different shapes and sizes of Tinker-Toys connected by glues of different strengths; such is analogous to the world of pulling apart one structure and putting together another to create different organic molecules. Q-Dawg's research group didn't stop with the formation of these vinamidinium salts. They used these molecules to transition to a variety of heterocyclic compounds – combinations of rings made of both carbon and nitrogen atoms, not just carbon atoms. In particular, they focused on a family of heterocycles called pyrazoles.

Q-Dawg's research group also introduced another twist to their manufacture of vinamidinium salts, in that they cleverly put a second organic acid group onto the opposite end of their starting reagent. Accordingly, they achieved the formation of a molecule possessing two vinamidinium groups, as shown by the following chemical equation:

CO_2H

CO_2H

1)DMF, $POCl_3$

2)$NaClO_4$

$Me_2\overset{\oplus}{N}$ NMe_2

$Me_2\overset{\oplus}{N}$ NMe_2

$2\ ClO_4^{\ominus}$

A Vilsmeier reaction to produce a symmetric pattern of two vinamidinium groups. "Me" represents the methyl, or $-CH_3$, group.

Subsequently in a second reaction, they produced heterocycles called dipyrazoles. But these weren't the only final products possible. Employing these procedural schemes, Evalina and her student colleagues facilitated the synthesis of a wide range of unique chemical compounds.

Evalina was repeatedly enamored by being the first, and perhaps only, person ever to manufacture a never-before-made substance, and by understanding how to tinker with the conditions, such as reagent amounts and temperature, to improve the yield and purity of that product.

○ ● ○ ● ○

Evalina enthusiastically advocated Q-Dawg's research program to all who'd listen. For example, Grover Brabham, one of her classmates, stopped by the laboratory on an afternoon during their junior year. He claimed he was interested in doing research with Q-Dawg's group.

He nonchalantly asked, "What do you like best about your project?"

Evalina exhuberantly replied, "I get to design my own molecular world. Such is the power, or I might say the beauty, of the Vilsmeier reaction."

"I don't think I've ever described a reaction or a molecule as beautiful," Grover deadpanned, rolling his eyes in disbelief.

Evalina quickly sketched one of her dipyrazole Vilsmeier products on scrap paper. "Look at that symmetry and its aesthetically pleasing structure." She pointed to the molecule.

"That's not only beautiful but also majestic. Can you imagine anything more beautiful?"

"I guess you have a point." He nodded in mock agreement. His glance, though, quickly drifted to eyeballing Evalina's figure from head to foot. He seemed more interested in the beauty of Evalina rather than her sketched molecule. Even in blue jeans and an oversized sweat shirt, her attractiveness couldn't be denied. He scooted closer to Evalina under the pretense of getting a better view of the drawn structure.

Evalina directed him to the ventilated hood behind which she had the Vilsmeier reaction apparatus assembled and ready to go.

Grover took an exaggerated sniff of the nose. "I can't really say the smell of a Vilsmeier, though, is beautiful." He laughed.

Through the rest of their conversation, it became abundantly clear that Grover was more interested in Evalina than Vilsmeier. He'd stopped by the laboratory under pretense of doing research, but wanted to ask her out on a date. Not successful. Grover was momentarily taken aback. His popularity with the college girls had been firmly established – handsome stature, good grades, and the star shortstop on the baseball team. Seldom had his advances been spurned.

○ ● ○ ● ○

Dr. Quinn Stanton and his students synthesized their novel compounds with the goal of using them someday for the treatment of cancers. Evalina, along with the Q-Dawg and other students, published several journal articles outlining the use of the Vilsmeier reaction to produce novel pyrazoles and dipyrazoles, which were then clinically tested by others as possible anti-cancer pharmaceuticals.

In addition to the hard work and long nights worked by Q-Dawg's students in their pursuit of their next potential cancer-curing drug, Evalina and co-workers found ways in which to have fun in their undergraduate research. Q-Dawg instituted a celebration with cake and ice cream every June 12th during the summer program to honor Anton Vilsmeier's birthday. In a parodied ceremony presided over by Dr. Stanton, each student presented a vial containing a novel compound produced by that student through use of the Vilsmeier reaction to their memorial shrine, which was an internet picture of Anton Vilsmeier in poster form. Each vial was a symbolic gift to Vilsmeier.

During the summer after her junior year, Evalina also composed a song to honor the Vilsmeier reaction and its importance to Q-Dawg's research group for this annual celebration. To the tune of "Rudolph the Red-Nosed Reindeer," she sang *a cappella* –

You know Grignard and Diels-Alder,
Cannizzaro and Wurtz,
You know Sandmeyer and Kindler,
Friedal-Crafts and Finkelstein,
Say, but do you recall
That most important reaction of all?

Vilsmeier the Heterocyclic Reaction,
Directed both nitrogens and carbons into a ring,
And if you ever used it,
You would even say it's the king!
But all the other organic reactions
Used to laugh and call it names,
They wouldn't let poor Vilsmeier
Join in any chemistry games.

Then for one puzzling organic laboratory,
The Q-Dawg came to say:
"Vilsmeier with your heterocyclic way
Won't you guide my synthesis today?"
Then how the students loved him
As they shouted out with glee:
"Vilsmeier the Heterocyclic Reaction,
You'll go down in history!"

Q-Dawg and the other students howled with laughter and delight, with Q-Dawg – AKA Dr. Quinn Stanton – bursting with pride for not only the chemical talent but also the musical forte of Evalina. The ditty was corny, but fun. It could've been a song right out of an episode of an academic *Hee-Haw*.

Dr. Stanton then convinced Evalina to sing her composition to an orchestral sound-track of "Rudolph the Red-Nosed Reindeer" in front of an actual Vilsmeier reaction in progress the next day. He recorded such on both sound and video. Interestingly, the percent yield and purity of her Vilsmeier product that day was the all-time laboratory best for those reaction components. It was as if Evalina's singing anthropomorphically enhanced the reaction efficiency. Afterwards, part of Q-Dawg's laboratory tradition evolved into each student superstitiously playing the song to the chemical mixture at the start of every Vilsmeier reaction for good luck.

○ ● ○ ● ○

Dr. Stanton and other faculty at Keaton College encouraged Evalina to go onto graduate school to obtain an advanced degree in chemistry. Q-Dawg effervescently confided, "Evalina, with your attributes – smart, huge amounts of energy, lots of enthusiasm, articulate, an innate desire to succeed, unabashed curiousity – you'd be guaranteed success in graduate school."

"Maybe later." Evalina shook her head. She smiled. "I'm ready to strike out on my own."

"You have the dexterous hands of a lab chemist," Q-Dawg added, "making reactions materialize others couldn't get to happen."

"Oh, I'm going to stay in chemistry," Evalina responded, "I've applied throughout the state for entry-level chemist positions. I don't really want to wander too far from home."

"With your kind, wonderful, and warm personality, you should have no trouble fitting in at any laboratory," Q-Dawg concluded.

Before graduation ceremonies, in appreciation of Q-Dawg's role in encouraging her in chemistry, Evalina presented him with a framed cross-stitch. She designed a portrait of Anton Vilsmeier, along with the chemical equation of a Vilsmeier reaction. Q-Dawg was overcome with emotion. He cherished the creation and placed it in a prominent place on the wall above his office desk in the chemistry department at Keaton College. And, of course, the framed cross-stitch replaced the poster of Vilsmeier as the memorial shrine for the annual celebration of Vilsmeier's birthday.

○ ● ○ ● ○

By happenstance as her graduation neared, PAYNE pharmaceuticals in her hometown advertised an opening for a bench chemist in their research and development laboratory. The director of the laboratory, Dr. Mason Turville, was immediately attracted to her application. One of the routine duties of that chemist would be to perform organic synthesis using the Vilsmeier reaction under his direction. Thus, upon graduation from college, Evalina began work at PAYNE Pharmaceuticals. In her three years working there, she enjoyed her job, being one of the three laboratory technicians working with Dr. Mason Turville. And staying in her old room at her parents' home allowed her to save significant money. It also allowed her to help care for her mother Partie, once her mother's rapidly spreading and terminal cancer had been diagnosed.

● ● ● ● ● ● ●

That Saturday evening, no car greeted Evalina in the driveway. No light burned outside the door to guide her entry. Only the sweet smells of a blooming honeysuckle vine infiltrating a nearby forsythia hedge welcomed her.

She plopped her WalMart bouquet of flowers on the table and searched for a vase under the sink. The flowers were rapidly wilting. The bouquet had attracted her attention, having a few pink carnations distributed among the daisies and roses. Perhaps her mother would look over her tonight.

She started the coffee pot, hopeful he'd be there soon. She microwaved a bag of Orville Redenbacker popcorn, his favorite, and dumped the buttered feast in a bowl.

She switched on the television, mindlessly surfing the available channels and nibbling on the popcorn. Such had become an all too common occurrence while waiting, always waiting, at the apartment. She watched, but didn't watch, an old rerun of the Andy Griffith Show. She grabbed a Bible from the bookshelf and read some verses from the Book of Acts, before she realized the passages weren't registering. Instead her thoughts oscillated – from disappointment, with a twinge of anger, to making excuses for him. A bath failed to relax her, after which she changed from her shorts and tee shirt to clean jeans and blouse.

After another quiet hour, she snatched her keys from the table and headed toward the door. As she reached for the door knob, she froze. Her smile radiated joy. Headlights were turning into the driveway.

Chapter Four
PAYNE ON PAIN

PAYNE Pharmaceuticals specialized in the manufacture of generic drugs for chronic pain control. Since its founding, the company experienced, as did other generic drug manufacturers, unprecedented growth in their production facilities and sales. In 1984, generic drugs accounted for less than 20% of all prescriptions in the United States; but by 2013, the percentage of generics approached 90%. Clearly, generic drugs had become integral to American healthcare. In order to remain competitive, generic manufacturers, like major drug companies, needed to become more innovative in developing ways to manufacture their active ingredients. PAYNE Pharmaceuticals, accordingly, had a research and development effort to manufacture known medications for chronic pain control more efficiently, thus more cheaply.

One of every three Americans suffers from chronic pain, leading to agony in sleeping, working, and performing daily activities. Such pain lasts from a few months to one's lifetime. The price tag for treatment exceeds $600 billion annually. PAYNE found the production of generic pain pills quite lucrative, expanding its facilities and output by 10% every year since founding.

The standard drug to treat general neuropathic or chronic pain is morphine, and other natural and synthetic opiates. Physicians usually only prescribe opiates for severe short-term pain because of its side effects such as drowsiness, dizziness, nausea, bowel disorders, and suppression of breathing. Patients then develop a tolerance to opiates, requiring higher-and-higher doses and further enhancing the side effects. In addition, paradoxically, opiate use makes a person more sensitive to pain, so their use enhances the pain in the long term, even when the drug use has ended. All of these factors, though, pale with respect to the addictive nature of the opiates. Patients develop both a psychological and physiological dependency on the drug. Despite these drawbacks, the Centers for Diesease Control and Prevention reported the sale of opiate pain relivers rose 300% in the decade starting 2000.

○ ● ○ ● ○

Instead of just copying known painkillers like other generic drug manufacturers, PAYNE Pharmaceuticals decided to invest a portion of their profits to research novel painkillers. Their market research estimated over 100 million Americans struggle in the misery of chronic pain, most often in the form of back pain, headaches, or arthritis. Jim Payne, Jr., often quipped, "There's a market for pain pills, so money for PAYNE!" If PAYNE would be lucky enough to discover the next generation of pain medication, their gamble in terms of research and development dollars would be amplified many times over. They'd have won the research lottery.

To paraphrase a leading scientist in the field, venoms from the weirdest animals seemed to yield the greatest return on finding likely molecules for potential use as drugs for chronic pain. For example, one firm's current research explored assassin flies that possess venom powerful enough to kill a mouse, while another's investigated sedentary sea anemones with venom that temporarily paralyzed fast-moving fish.

PAYNE's approach for their research program focused on isolating the nerve-numbing molecule from a single naturally-occurring venom. They gambled this molecule would be the road to their bonanza. Before the arrival of Dr. Mason Turville at PAYNE Pharmaceuticals, their research and development department spent five years studying the potential of the Asian tiger snake, but to no avail. This snake is unique in being both venomous and poisonous – releasing a venom through its bite and also storing a poison in its skin. The active ingredient of the skin's poison seemed to have possibilities as a molecule binding to a human's pain pathways. After establishing a breeding colony of the tiger snakes, though, the PAYNE scientists no longer could isolate this component from the snakes' skin. Much to the dismay of PAYNE's scientists and management, the poisonous compound came from specific toads eaten by the snakes in the wild. No longer eating these toads resulted in no poison in the snake skins.

Their current Director of Research and Development, Dr. Mason Turville, convinced Jim Payne, Jr., to redirect all their research dollars to what he called the Holy Grail of pain medicine. It was a drug called anodynol, which had been initially isolated from an extinct South American frog. This drug had no problematic side effects and wasn't addictive. Furthermore, unlike with opiates, users experienced no feelings of euphoria, limiting any potential abuse. But, although anodynol's structure had been published many years ago and its use for the relief of pain proven, its synthesis had never been accomplished.

• • • • • • •

That Saturday night, Jim Payne, Jr., returned home to Hickory Grove from a dinner with his wife at a new restaurant in Colebrook. Big John's Steakhouse indeed served a generous cut of prime rib, both tender and tasty. He immediately retreated to his den to enjoy another glass of scotch.

He picked up the current issue of *Chemical and Engineering News* on the end table next to his recliner. He read one of the magazine's lead articles, on the synthesis of batrachotoxin, the active ingredient of the poison dart frog toxin. Natives from the Columbian rain forest used the slime on this brightly colored frog's skin to tip their blow darts. Up to two milligrams are stored in their skin, enough to kill more than 20,000 mice. And scientists at one time thought it also showed potential as a pain medicine, as a sodium channel blocker. But an effective dose turned out to have toxic side effects. Batrachotoxin has a very complicated chemical structure. In this article, scientists reported a novel procedure to synthesize the chemical – taking only 24 steps to knit together several fused ring precursors. They bragged of their great improvement over the prior synthetic scheme that took more than 40 steps.

"Nitwit academic chemists," Jim grumbled, "Twenty-four freaking steps and probably a yield of less than ten percent. It'd never be useful for anyone except those in their own ivory tower."

He sat back in his chair and took another sip of scotch. He'd invested oodles of his company's money on Turville's guarantee that he'd be able to synthesize anodynol. That synthesis would be worth a veritable fortune to PAYNE Pharmaceuticals. But Turville can't even do the synthesis in 24 steps; he can't do it period. Here of late, Turville seemed preoccupied with other stuff. He used to put in extra hours at his office and laboratory, now he seemed to spend time elsewhere. It wasn't at home. His car was always gone and Shelley, his wife, complained to his wife that Turville's never home but at work. Even when he was chasing women, he always had extra time for anodynol. What's he up to? What's he spending his time on?

He threw the magazine back down on the end table. He mumbled to himself: "I need to talk to Turville next week. He's big on promises but short on results. It's time for him to refocus, or I'll find someone else who will."

Chapter Five
DR. MASON TURVILLE

Dr. Mason Turville was the current Vice President for Research and Development at PAYNE Pharmaceuticals. However, the entire research and development department at PAYNE consisted of him as supervisor and three laboratory technicians, all of whom had bachelor's degrees in chemistry, working on a variety of projects. Most of the laboratory's efforts dealt with maintaining quality control and in defining the cheapest, easiest, and most efficient way to synthesize the active compounds for generic pain pills. The PAYNE Pharmaceuticals' production facilities then manufactured these compounds for sale as medicines under labels such as CVS or Walgreens.

Turville had been employed by Jim Payne, first by father and then by son, for about ten years. After he obtained his Ph.D. in organic chemistry at the University of Wisconsin – Madison, he worked for two drug companies as their project directors for about five years. Subsequently, being promoted to a Vice President of Research and Development this quickly stroked his ego, which bordered at times on intellectual arrogance. In fact, many of the PAYNE Pharmaceuticals' secretaries would derogatorily call him "Dr. Turdville" behind his back. He would subtly make it known to them their lack of importance compared to him. But, on the other hand, he was also quite handsome and athletic at his 43 years of age, so women tended to swoon over and flirt with him to see whether they might garner some return interest.

○ ● ○ ● ○

Soon after Evalina's employment at PAYNE Pharmaceuticals, Turville assigned her to the company's special long-term research project. Calling her into his office, Turville offered Evalina a chair next to his desk.

He stated, "You've quickly acclimated to your routine development projects and analytical duties in the laboratory – and have done so quite competently. Now, you'll also be the lead laboratory chemist – under my supervision, of course – on PAYNE's project to develop a total synthesis for anodynol. This is one of the pet projects of mine as well of the big boss – Jim Payne, Jr."

"Ah . . . Um," Evalina interrupted, then almost apologetically continued, "I don't think I ever heard of anodynol. Should I know what it is?"

"Nor should you," Turville chuckled. "Anodynol is coined from the Latin 'anodynus' meaning pain relief. It's allegedly a very potent pain killer. In fact, some refer to it as the Holy Grail of pain medicines."

"But I don't remember it as being one of the drugs in PAYNE's stable of painkillers." Evalina looked confused. "And I don't even recall seeing it on the list of possible generics that PAYNE has under consideration for future production."

Turville chuckled louder, then continued, "That's not too surprising. PAYNE doesn't want it to be known to other drug companies that we're investigating the anodynol molecule. In a sense, this is our secret project."

"But, why me?" inquired Evalina, growing restless in her chair. "The other technicians have more seniority than me in the laboratory."

"Yeah, that's true – but you have one key attribute," Turville stated with conviction. "I believe the KEY step in anodynol's synthesis will be the successful execution of a Vilsmeier reaction – something where experience definitely helps. You've run several hundred in your undergraduate career, according to my phone conversation with Dr. Stanton before you were hired here at PAYNE."

"Oh, I see," Evalina proudly replied. "You're right; I've run more Vilsmeiers than I care to count. Each one always seems to be a challenge."

"And furthermore, Dr. Stanton said you achieved higher yields from Vilsmeier reactions than his other students," Turville offered. Then, with a laugh, he added, "Dr. Stanton said that you've even sung to the reactions in order to squeeze out more of the right product."

Evalina returned the laugh. "Yep, one of the traditions of our research group. Instead of actually singing, though, I now just play the recording of my Vilsmeier song. So you already know the molecular structure of anodynol – that is, the final product."

"That's right," Turville nodded. He smiled. "Its structure has actually been known for quite a while. In fact, the anodynol molecule possesses a deceptively simple structure." Turville opened a reprint, lying on his desk, of an article from a scientific journal. He showed Evalina a figure illustrating anodynol's molecular structure. Throwing his arms in the air in mock exasperation, he continued, "On the other hand, the molecule has been impossible to make in the chemistry laboratory. Its synthesis remains an enigma. After over twenty years, to my knowledge, no one has even come close to making it."

Evalina looked at the structure and thought for a few moments. She flipped back to the front of the article. "I see from the byline that the discoverer of anodynol is the group of Frank Hofmann at Cornell University." Evalina smiled, and added, "Q-Dawg, I mean –"

"Q-Dawg?" Turville interrupted quizzically with a smirk on his face.

"Oh, sorry," Evalina giggled. "Q-Dawg is Dr. Stanton's nickname, a play on his first name of Quinn, given to him long ago by students. Sometimes he even calls himself 'The Q-Dawg.' Q-Dawg told us stories about Hofmann. Evidently, he was an intellectual giant as a natural products chemist, but also eccentric beyond belief."

Turville nodded his head in agreement. "I think everyone has heard stories of Hofmann's escapades. Even though he was a renowned chemist, he was just as famous for collecting weird and bizarre animals and plants. He went to all the remote locations in the world. Then, in a sense, he did chemical prospecting on these animals and plants – finding all sorts of unusual and novel chemicals, or natural products, excreted or produced by the critters."

"Q-Dawg said he once went to a chemistry convention where Hofmann gave the keynote speech," Evalina excitedly remembered. "Supposedly, he'd just gotten off a plane after returning from a couple months exploring the jungles of the Amazon basin in western Brazil. As he was giving the speech, he started to have spasms in his head. Finally, he beat the side of his head with his hand. To the astonishment of the crowd, he pulled a foot long worm out of his ear. But he never missed a beat in his presentation. His only comment was that he'd been worried that he'd picked up this parasite in the jungle from eating a local delicacy – and that the worms find their way into their host's brain cavity. After finishing his talk, he calmly said he needed to head to the hospital to take care of the worm infestation, instead of answering questions."

"Yep, that's definitely an occupational hazard for a collector of his ilk." Turville shook his head and laughed quietly. "In this case, Hofmann was in northern Peru on one of his adventures. He heard about a folk remedy for pain relief handed down from generation-to-generation by an indigenous tribe there. The natives simply rubbed the Peruvian Rainbow Frog on their painful area, or killed the frog and ate it to alleviate internal pain. So, Hofmann collected a few of these frogs and sent them back to his laboratory." Turville got up from his desk and pointed to one of the many pictures of frogs on his office wall. "This frog was quite unusual in many ways. It's tiny, less than an inch in length. It has a toxic slime as a skin coating. And it belongs to the class of glass or transparent frogs, such that you can see its internal anatomy in stunning X-ray detail, revealing its beating heart and bones. Oddly, its bones are green, not white, due to an accumulation of biliverdin, a metabolic by-product. Furthermore, the backs of these frogs had splotches with concentric circles of different colors, from which its rainbow moniker was acquired. And instead of making croaking noises like other frogs, this species burped a squeaking hiccup."

"Wow, that's one weird frog," Evalina concluded, enamored with the story.

"The toxic slime on the frog's skin allegedly kept predators from eating 'em, but not sufficiently toxic to kill humans," he added, returning to his desk. "Hofmann and his minions back in the laboratory isolated and discovered a molecule, which they called anodynol, as the active ingredient in the frogs' toxic slime. Anodynol was a new compound – never before identified in nature. Its extraction and identification was truly a feat of heroic proportions by Hofmann."

"Yep, I read somewhere that the stranger the critter, the more likely they produce bizarre chemicals," Evalina replied. "However, I scanned through the paper here – but other than the mythology, source, isolation, and structure determination, they never indicated they did any testing of anodynol for painkilling ability."

"Ha . . . Once again, an interesting story – or actually several stories in one," Turville enthusiastically added. "One of the technicians in Hofmann's lab group had arthritis in his hands. So he rubbed one of the frogs all over his hands. Amazingly, the arthritic pain in his hand and knuckles subsided greatly. Hofmann evidently became visibly upset with the technician for performing an unauthorized and potentially dangerous experiment, and also because the group had to wait for the frog to regenerate its skin slime. On the other hand, he told others he was glad that the technician provided more anecdotal evidence to support the Peruvian folk remedy. Then, supposedly, rumors and unsubstantiated reports from Hoffmann's laboratory related they discovered that anodynol was very effective in the relief of generalized chronic pain and was devoid of addictive potential – in essence the perfect pain therapy."

"Wow! That's amazing," Evalina exclaimed. Then she queried, "Why only stories and non-published accounts? Why didn't they publish their evidence?"

"Hofmann was a friend of my graduate advisor. They talked quite a bit," Turville admitted, as he rocked back in his chair. "Hofmann told him that his group had isolated and characterized anodynol, then determined its molecular structure, before realizing the true potential of the chemical as a pharmaceutical. Further, he was only able to purify a few grams of anodynol from the frogs before the Peruvian government listed the frog as an endangered species. The frogs also didn't survive in captivity for very long. Unfortunately, there was only a short burst of harvesting the frog to obtain their trace amounts of anodynol. Extravagant compensation was promised to any natives willing to poach these frogs, but went uncollected simply because no frogs were to be found. In essence, the frogs went from abundant, to endangered, to assumed extinct in a blink of the eye. All of this was in the space of a couple years back almost before you were born."

"Yeah, I did notice that the date of publication on Hofmann's paper was actually my birthyear," Evalina admitted with a grin.

He continued, "Nevertheless, these quantities of anodynol, according to laboratory tales, were enough for Hoffmann – in unauthorized trials – to successfully test anodynol's potency on his grandfather who suffered from painful pancreatitis and on his great-aunt who had tremendous back pain. A drug company supposedly working with Hoffmann also did some select tests using tablets with the remaining amount of anodynol and convinced the FDA to approve it as an effective drug without any known side effects. Then, Hoffmann made his fatal mistake. He rushed to patent the molecular structure of anodynol, anticipating pharmaceutical companies would readily be able to synthesize the compound. He wanted to protect his discovery, anticipating a payoff of millions."

"Well, I guess his prediction didn't come to fruition, because I don't see anodynol on the pharmacy shelves." Evalina shook her head.

"That's right," Turville agreed, with a nod. "Anodynol delivered remarkable relief, much better than any known pain pill. But no one had any more of it. Even though the molecular structure of anodynol was known, the core of which is a dipyrazole, the drug companies just couldn't design a reaction scheme to synthesize it. And its extraction from natural sources was no longer an option with the demise of the Peruvian Rainbow Frog. Other natural sources for anodynol weren't discovered despite extensive efforts to do so. Now, with the expiration of the original patent, others entered the fray to try to synthesize and market anodynol without paying patent royalties to the discoverers' estate."

"I saw the dipyrazole functional groups in the molecule. Dipyrazole containing molecules – Geez, those are amazingly beautiful molecules. I used to prepare them for Q-Dawg via the Vilsmeier reaction. I'm starting to see where I fit into your scheme," Evalina joyfully surmised.

"Well, I'm not sure about 'em being beautiful, but definitely could be very profitable," he laughed quietly. "A few years ago, when the patent on anodynol expired, the boss – Jim Payne, Jr. – and I decided to see whether we could synthesize it. Technically, anodynol is a generic drug, even though it hasn't ever been marketed. The one difficult part of our synthesis is the generation of the dipyrazole ring at the proper location in the molecule. I'm firmly convinced that the use of the Vilsmeier reaction to generate the precursor vinamidinium salt is the crucial step to circumvent these difficulties in both positioning and imparting the dipyrazole ring on the anodynol template. Despite several years of research, and although we've gotten closer to its total synthesis, we haven't yet succeeded. But, with your ability to manipulate Vilsmeier reactions, I'm confident that PAYNE Pharmaceuticals will!"

Evalina smiled from ear to ear, looked at the picture of the molecular structure of anodynol again, and reiterated, "And it's such a beautiful molecule too. Look at its unique symmetry, especially the arrangement of its methyl groups in addition to the dipyrazole locations."

Turville was momentarily taken aback, but recovered and kiddingly said, “It’ll only be beautiful once we make it!”

○ ● ○ ● ○

Along with Evalina, Turville designed the necessary experiments for Evalina to identify the necessary reagents, concentrations, and reaction conditions. Turville was incredibly confident that his proposed synthetic scheme for the manufacture of anodynol would eventually succeed, making this research an investment with modest risk but the possibility of a gigantic pay-off. If PAYNE Pharmaceuticals became the sole manufacturer and distributor of anodynol, Jim Payne, Jr., and Dr. Mason Turville anticipated the value of PAYNE Pharmaceuticals would skyrocket. They then imagined the subsequent acquisition of the company by a major drug manufacturer for hundreds of millions of dollars, if not several billion, just on the basis of becoming the sole producer of anodynol.

In the meantime, Evalina initiated her boss, Dr. Turville, and the others in the research and development laboratory to the commemoration of Vilsmeier’s birthday on June 12th, continuing the tradition started with Q-Dawg at college. Evalina impressed Dr. Mason Turville, like Dr. Quinn Stanton before him, with her rendition of “Vilsmeier the Heterocyclic Reaction” sung to the tune of “Rudolph the Red-Nosed Reindeer” in the merriment of the day.

The next celebration of Vilsmeier’s birthday in the PAYNE Pharmaceuticals research and development laboratory, during her second year of employment, Evalina presented a bronze bust of Anton Vilsmeier to Dr. Turville. Evalina had commissioned her college roommate, a mixed-media art major and now teacher, to create a hollow life-sized cast of Vilsmeier’s head from the few remaining pictures available of Anton Vilsmeier. Dr. Turville cherished this gift, not only because of his admiration for the Vilsmeier reaction but also because it was probably the only bust of Vilsmeier in the entire world. Vilsmeier’s bust subsequently sat in a place of honor in the front center of Turville’s office desk. When Turville would sit at his desk thinking, he claimed that having Vilsmeier staring back at him always helped with his creativity in developing the next attempt at the scheme to synthesize anodynol.

The third year of remembering Vilsmeier's birthday brought yet another gift from Evalina to Dr. Turville, in addition to once again singing the Vilsmeier song. This time Evalina had commissioned her artistic friend to craft a hanging mobile based on a design prepared by Evalina. The bottom level of the mobile had a ball-and-stick molecular model of anodynol fashioned therein, the middle level contained a similar model of the presumed vinamidinium salt intermediate, and the top level possessed molecular models of the proposed reactants being used in the central Vilsmeier reaction to produce anodynol's dipyrazole core. Wires connecting the levels also showed the reaction conditions needed to go from the top to the middle level and from the middle to the bottom level. An ecstatic Turville treasured the mobile, hanging it from the ceiling in his office so that everyone entering would see it.

More importantly throughout these three years, Turville appreciated Evalina's scientific knowledge, laboratory skills, enthusiasm, and efforts in experiments to synthesize his long-sought anodynol. And, even in the chemistry laboratory, the beauty of Evalina captivated all, including Turville, with their glances and stares, as it did previously in pageants.

• • • • • • •

That Saturday night, less than an hour before Lum's survellience mission, Mason Turville sat down with his wife Shelley and two children for a dinner of pizza. Shelley had thrown the frozen DiGiorno's entrée into the oven after polling the kids for their choice. Once Turville prayed the blessing, his daughter announced she no longer wanted pizza. She wanted a hot dog. Shelley hopped up to put a pot of water on the stove. His son whined that the pizza had nasty pepperoni circles on it. The kids got on his nerves. Shelley sat back down at the table, reminding him to fix the wobbly leg on the one kitchen chair. He mumbled, "I need to trade her in on a younger model," under his breath. He grabbed a few bites of the pizza before retreating to his home office.

Turville took a deep breath and stared at some papers scattered over the top of his desk. After a few minutes, he smiled. His thoughts identified a new approach to solve the problem that had created a bottleneck in his project.

His son ran into his office with a book waving in hand. "Daddy, read to me."

Turville swept his papers into his briefcase. On his way to the side door, the one to the garage, he told Shelley he needed to go back to work at PAYNE Pharmaceuticals – that Jim Payne, Jr., was being a pain to get some stuff done. He wouldn't return until late.

She rolled her eyes, guilted him by telling him the kids were expecting him to read to them that night. "What's more important, your work or your kids?"

"Get off my back," he snarled. "The work supports you in this lifestyle. I'm close to a breakthrough."

"Yep, you're always close to a breakthrough," Shelley snickered. "What's this, your tenth breakthrough this week?"

Turville stomped out the door. But Shelley knew where he was going – not to PAYNE Pharmaceuticals. She'd followed him several times. She'd also rifled through his brief case and his home office, unbeknownst to him or so she thought. She knew all about his extracurricular activities outside PAYNE. But she actually relished his absence. It gave her the opportunity to make a phone call later.

As he rolled out of the Hickory Grove subdividion in his spic-and-span Volvo, he turned right toward Colebrook, not left to Millikan and PAYNE Pharmaceuticals.

Chapter Six
SPATS

Evalina and Lum worked different shifts at PAYNE Pharmaceuticals. Evalina worked the day shift in its research and development laboratory, Lum the night shift in maintenance. Because of this disconnect in job schedules, they had minimal contact with each other week days, though they lived in the same house. Then, on weekends, Evalina usually socialized with her "friends," as she evasively described such to Lum. When Lum and Evalina attended Goose Creek Lutheran Church on Sunday mornings, they drove separately. Evalina was in the choir and practiced the hour before the services.

The only time Evalina reserved for Lum was dinner each weekday evening. Lum suspected this was simply because Evalina didn't want to cook. Lum had dinner waiting when she returned home from work each day.

After the death of Partie, Lum quickly learned not to talk to Evalina about her personal life during this one-on-one time. Being fiercely independent, Evalina politely changed the subject when Lum asked what she did at night, who or whether she was dating, and even who her "friends" were. Her confidante for such topics had always been her mother. Now she spent hours on the phone discussing women-type things with her Aunt Melody, Partie's sister, who lived in Virginia about two hours east of Millikan.

Evalina often visited her Aunt Melody, or so she claimed, for the weekend. But several times when Lum called Melody on such weekends to relay a message, Melody proclaimed Evalina unavailable. All sorts of vague and elusive excuses were provided for Evalina's absence. When Lum once confronted Evalina about his suspicions that she hadn't even visited her aunt, Evalina exploded in anger that her father was checking up on her, even though she was over 21 with her own job. She threatened to move out of the house and get her own apartment. Lum realized such were only idle threats.

He always felt Evalina was somewhat ashamed of her father. As she once blurted out innocently many years previous, he was nothing but a glorified janitor. Those words stung at his heart and soul. Lum believed Evalina still had such lingering thoughts, although she'd matured enough not to say them out loud anymore. He also noticed Evalina never volunteered to tell strangers that he was her father. Many, who didn't know Evalina from childhood, didn't immediately make the father-daughter connection because of their two different surnames. Lum even suspected that many in PAYNE's research and development laboratory, including Turville, weren't aware that Evalina's father was Lum, also working at PAYNE Pharmaceuticals on the night shift. Many of the newer members at his church were likewise unaware, as Evalina would get upset when Lum boastfully offered "That's my daughter singing the solo in the choir" or "That's my precious Evalina singing the duet with Reverend Clarke." Lum learned that to avoid conflict with his daughter, he just needed to be inwardly – and not outwardly – proud of her achievements.

○ ● ○ ● ○

The one safe topic of discussion for the dinners Lum spent with Evalina was her research work. In particular, they seemed to drift into talking about Vilsmeier reactions.

Evalina once relayed a little personal history about Anton Vilsmeier. His father Wolfgang was a mill owner; and his mother's name was Philomena. He fought with the 11th Bavarian Infantry in World War I before being taken prisoner by the

British after the Battle of Somme. Lum often wondered why his daughter was drawn to Vilsmeier as a good German name, but not to Baumgartner. He left that query unasked.

Another night, while adding a dollop of ketchup to her serving of meatloaf, Evalina eagerly revealed, "I ran another Vilsmeier reaction today. This one looks more promising than the ones last week. I've gotten into the routine of running a Vilsmeier every Tuesday and Thursday, usually taking the entire morning to complete the reaction and the afternoon to separate the product from the unwanted stuff. Then I do the analyses on the off days – as well as my other tasks."

"So, you waved your wand, said the right words, and 'shazaam' today," Lum laughed, as he helped himself to a second helping of meatloaf.

"Yep . . . the reaction goes 'shazaam.' Just like magic, only real." Evalina smiled, and excitingly continued, "I just mix the chemicals together in the right order and at the prescribed temperature. And boom, the product forms . . . or, at least, something forms."

During these mealtime conversations, Evalina imagined herself as the teacher wanting to convey knowledge to her father as student. She appeared to escape into her own private world of molecular architecture. Without being condescending to Lum whether he could comprehend the chemical concepts with his limited education, she taught Lum as though she talked chemistry to Dr. Stanton or Dr. Turville. She was not only a valued employee at PAYNE Pharmaceuticals but also highly enthusiastic about her work with Turville.

"Well, did you get the product you wanted, though?" Lum questioned, as he sipped from his glass of iced tea. "You said your 'shazaam' reaction seemed promising today – but was it also successful?"

"Oh, sort of . . . from just looking at it, I would guess I got some of our desired product. But it'll be mixed in with a lot of other stuff we don't want." She paused as she took another bite of ketchup-smothered meatloaf, then one of mashed potatoes. "It'll be tomorrow before I start identifying the exact composition of the products. So, I'm probably one step closer – though the conditions aren't quite optimal and need some tweaking – and still a ways off from completion."

Lum laughed, as he reared back in his dining room chair. "So, no 'shazaam' – you haven't made the anodynol yet. Maybe it's your encantations that need tweaking."

"It's amazing," Evalina sighed. "The synthesis of anodynol is supposedly a secret project, yet everyone who's worked more than a year at PAYNE knows about it. It's definitely not a well-kept secret." She spooned the last remaining bit of creamed peas from her plate.

"I've known about the first attempts at making anodynol in the laboratory before you even arrived at PAYNE," Lum related, as he cleared the kitchen table of plates and silverware. "Jim Payne, Jr., tells everyone who listens how they're eventually gonna hit the jackpot – a real financial boon for the company. But other than you and Turville, no one else is working on it. You would think the boss would spend some more of his money to invest in the effort."

"Well . . . it's not much use assigning more people to the task until the key Vilsmeier step succeeds – they'll just be spinning their wheels." Evalina knew that the design and completion of this key step in the synthesis of anodynol was a definite bottleneck for the research.

"So what are you gonna tweak – the temperature or the concentration or try another starting point." Lum understood much more than what Evalina could ever have imagined after a lifetime of working at PAYNE Pharmaceuticals and being acclimated to its production facilities.

"I think I need to keep the temperature a little cooler. The reaction was a little more exothermic, –"

"Exothermic, generating heat . . . seems like it always does." Lum interrupted. He grasped the concept completely when Evalina said the Vilsmeier reaction was very exothermic, that is the reaction generated a lot of heat.

"Yep, the Vilsmeier reaction gives off so much heat it is like a hot pack of chemicals on steroids. So, we need to control the temperature at a relatively low temperature in order to keep the chemicals from burning into a lump of charcoal. Usually I keep the primary Vilsmeier reaction at 0°C (or 32°F) in order for the reaction to operate efficiently and safely."

"Doesn't the system freeze?"

"No; there's no water in the reaction flask. At temperatures above 10°C we get tar; and at 0°C we got products that look promising, but not quite. We're gonna see whether we can get the right stuff without getting to tar. It's great to be running the reactions at PAYNE. Back at Keaton College with the Q-Dawg, we ran the reaction in a round-bottomed flask full of reactants, which in turn set in an ice bath. The reaction container was in a large trough full of ice and water so that the reaction temperature stayed at 0°C, the temperature at which water and ice co-exist. We couldn't easily control the reaction at other temperatures back there. Now, at PAYNE Pharmaceuticals, I have the luxury of better equipment. A synthesis workstation has the reaction flask surrounded by a mechanical heat sink so that the desired reaction temperature can be punched into an electronic controller."

"Sounds neat."

"This workstation is sort of like a refrigeration unit enveloping the round bottom flask. It leaves a portion of the glass flask exposed so that I have a line of sight into the happenings inside the flask. Thus, I can now tweak the synthesis temperature to be, for example, 4.0°C, 6.5°C, or whatever, instead of being fixed at 0°C. Temperature control is important because different reaction products and yields of a specific product form at different temperatures, even if they differ by only a single degree."

"When I peek in the lab at night, I see your set-up in a laboratory fume hood, why not just on one of the lab benches."

"For safety reasons," Evalina emphasized. "The reaction is always done behind the laboratory fume hood. It's vented directly to the outside. It has a protective plastic sash that shields me, but yet allows visability – sort of like bulletproof glass – for protection."

Lum found himself both fascinated by the complexities of building molecules as well as captivated by the level of chemical knowledge achieved by his daughter. "Sometimes I worry about you working in the chemistry laboratory, something could go wrong."

Evalina indicated both Turville and Q-Dawg emphasized safety when performing the Vilsmeier reaction. Both had initially supervised her in her techniques before each allowed her to perform the reaction by herself.

Lum smiled at the thought of his daughter performing reactions solo at work as well as singing solo at church. But he persisted in his concerns. "But exactly what could go wrong?"

"Oh, daddy, you worry too much." Evalina giggled. "Q-Dawg always told me any number of things could go wrong in running a Vilsmeier reaction – from incorrect concentrations, to adding things in the wrong order, to not controlling the temperature properly. Temperature is always of paramount importance. He made sure I had enough ice in the ice bath at Keaton College. Or here at PAYNE, Dr. Turville frets about dialing the wrong temperature on the synthesis workstation. As a consequence, the Vilsmeier reaction is performed in a laboratory fume hood with the sash closed."

Lum pressed further. "But what bad things could happen if the reaction goes awry."

Evalina shrugged. "The Q-Dawg always stressed never to let these bad things happen. But he never really identified the bad things that would result. I never witnessed any bad happenings. I assume the worst that could happen is a fire or a mini-explosion in the reaction flask. The phosphorous oxychloride used in the reaction is especially nasty in catalyzing such concerns."

"Interesting."

Evalina smiled. "My general chemistry instructor at Keaton College would add a very tiny chunk of sodium metal to water. Immediately it would explode with a pop. Sodium rapidly reacts with the water in an exothermic reaction to produce hydrogen gas, with so much heat being generated that it self-detonates the hydrogen in an explosion. During my summers at Keaton, Q-

Dawg disposed of his scrap sodium metal by throwing the sodium metal into a sewer manhole behind the chemistry building. An audience of summer researchers observed intently. The very loud bang of the subsequent explosion resonated throughout the parking lot and enthralled the students. However, in my senior year at Keaton, Q-Dawg halted the tradition. He used a little too much sodium and blew off every manhole cover in the city to the delight of the students and to the irritation, to say the least, of city workers. I can speculate doing the Vilsmeier reaction incorrectly might result likewise in explosions beyond my imagination."

• • • • • • •

During the Saturday evening of Lum's stake-out at the Turville home, the minutes became a half-hour, then a full hour. No traffic moved on Turville's dead-end street, and only a handful of cars were seen coming in and out of the Hickory Grove subdivision. Shelley, Turville's wife, drank wine and stayed on the phone. She appeared happy and upbeat. Eventually she went inside and put the kids to bed.

Turville had yet to return.

Lum muttered, "Still out messing with my Evalina."

But the sounds and smells of the night air relaxed him. The crescendo of the katydids provided background noise for the croaking of the frogs around the drainage pond next to the *cul de sac*. Perhaps he'd return one night to gig a few frogs – perhaps also to gig Turville. Lightning bugs were out in full force. An owl hooted. Lum's adrenaline, and his desire to confront Turville that night, crashed. He felt exhausted. Good sense replaced his emotions. Turville had the advantage on him in terms of height, weight, youth, and athleticism. Perhaps he should've brought along his hunting rifle.

Back in his truck, Lum yawned and closed his eyes. He woke a half hour later. His watch showed it was a few minutes past eleven o'clock – still no Turville. Only a single bedroom light burned in Turville's house. Lum needed to return home and get some sleep. Church service would come much too fast in the morning.

He headed out of Hickory Grove, back to Millikan. His truck windows were open, blowing a cool breeze on his face to keep him awake.

About two miles down Muddy Hollow Road, Lum saw it in his headlights. He slammed on his brakes. The body lay on the edge of the road surface. A set of beady eyes also reflected in the truck's lights and stared at him.

Chapter Seven
SKIRMISHES

About a month after Dr. Mason Turville started work at PAYNE Pharmaceuticals, he marched, clearly upset, into the office of Jim Payne. "You need to fire Lum Baumgartner."

The company's owner looked up from his cluttered desk disconcerted. "Good morning to you as well, Mason," he deadpanned.

"It's not a good morning when I show up for work with my office trash cans overflowing and the lab's floor not mopped," Turville snarled. "The janitors aren't doing their jobs. And this isn't the first time they've been slipshod."

Jim Payne stewed for a few moments. He took a deep breath and calmly stated, "Last night, Lum and his crew fixed the roller compactor on the #5 production line. Its feed screw was clogged. A large chunk of binder had gotten stuck and had thrown the screw mechanism out of whack. They not only repaired the damage done by the jam and realigned the roller, but also readjusted the particle size control for the incoming powder. The #5 production line was up and running for the day shift. I guess they didn't have time for your trash cans."

"So I get to empty my trash cans myself," Turville griped.

"That's one way of putting it." Jim Payne chuckled as he shuffled some papers on his desk. "You know what it would've cost the company to get a repair technician here ASAP in the backwoods of West Virginia, all the time having the production line not cranking out tablets?" He paused, then continued, "Perhaps more than your annual salary."

Turville quickly retreated, recognizing it wasn't useful, nor would it ever be useful, to complain directly to the big boss about Lum.

Jim Payne also worked late that same night so he could track down Lum who had just started his shift. He caught up with Lum just outside the company's break room. "Hey, Lum – I need you to do me a favor. For the next month, empty only one, never both, of the trash cans in Dr. Turville's office each night." He hesitated, then laughed, "In fact, always empty the least full one."

"Consider it done," Lum chortled. "I guess I shouldn't ask what he did to tick you off."

"Just think of it as a lesson in humility for a new employee, appropriate for a vice president."

Because one worked during the day and the other at night, Dr. Mason Turville and Lum had essentially no face-to-face interaction at PAYNE Pharmaceuticals. The strained relationship between the two consisted of continuous and contentious sniping. Turville would leave notes almost weekly for Lum complaining that the floors of his research laboratory weren't being cleaned adequately. Such notes would be formally typed by Turville's secretary, and simply signed with his initials "MT." Upon receipt, Lum would shake his head in disbelief and mumble, "Something must be wrong with Turville's fingers. It'd be just as easy for him to handwrite a note or leave a voice mail for me." Then, in a tit-for-tat, Lum would sarcastically leave messages that Turville's workers needed to dispose of their broken glass in the clearly marked glass disposal bins, not in the wastebaskets – or for the lights in Turville's office to be turned off after he left for the day. The strings of back and forth persisted with Turville grousing that the nighttime janitorial staff disturbed some reaction vessels on the laboratory benches; and Lum retorting that chemicals had been spilled on the floor and not cleaned, with him not knowing the identity of the chemicals for waste clean-up. Their exchanges were mostly petty bickering. Neither of them ever backed off completely.

About a year into Dr. Turville's employment, he formally requested Lum deliver some full nitrogen gas cyclinders from their storage shed to his laboratory that night. As always, he signed the typed note "MT." Previously, a lab technician working for Turville would do the gas cylinder transfer. But Turville was upset with Lum for some reason, demanding him do more to satisfy his needs. Lum, though, got the last laugh. Turville arrived the next morning to a dozen gas cylinders, all labeled "MT," sitting front and center in his lab. Lum taped a note to one of the cylinders – these were all the nitrogen cylinders in storage labeled as belonging to MT." Turville stomped into his office. He angrily scribbled a note, which he gave to his secretary to type to Lum: "As any scientifically literate person should know, MT written on a gas bottle means empty – not my initials. Are you dumb or something?" Turville's secretary shook her head and smiled, knowing full well that Lum was messing with her boss. Henceforth, Turville's notes to Lum were always signed with his full name.

They never did call a truce. The bad chemistry between the two became entrenched, albeit with ebbs and flows.

Every year at the employee picnic for PAYNE Pharmaceuticals, the company presented its annual "Achievement Award" to one of its many workers. The year before Evalina was hired, Lum heard through the grapevine he'd been nominated for this award in honor of his many years of dedicated service to the company. In fact, he was the most senior employee at PAYNE Pharmaceuticals. The citation was to praise him for performing whatever had been asked of him, and for doing things on his own for the betterment of the company without being formally assigned the task. On one hand, Lum was humbled to be considered for the award, but on the other hand felt as though he definitely deserved it. Lum readied himself the day of the picnic to be recognized by the management at this special occasion. He dressed accordingly in slacks and a button-down shirt instead of his usual jeans and pullover. But Dr. Mason Turville received the award. For the next week, Lum moped around with his personal disillusionment and dismay for the lack of appreciation. Company gossip corroborated Lum's belief that Turville "stole" the award from him. Turville had gone to Human Resources and vetoed Lum's nomination, then browbeat the award committee to present it to him.

○ ● ○ ● ○

Although Evalina seemed happy in her job at PAYNE Pharmaceuticals and often told Lum that she admired Dr. Turville as a wonderful and caring boss, company chatter got back to Lum of the not-so-happy meeting between Evalina and Turville. Less than a week before Lum overheard the private phone conversation of Evalina, she'd met with Turville in his office behind closed doors. Gossip-mongers reported Evalina left his office clearly upset and in tears for an early lunch – with some describing the incident as a purported lover's spat. Lum initially discounted such interpretations because of the jealously of those office workers for Evalina's beauty and work ethic. Furthermore, Evalina supposedly returned to the laboratory that afternoon as if nothing had happened out of the ordinary. A couple days later, Lum questioned Evalina about the meeting with Turville. As Lum should've expected, Evalina chewed his head off, saying disgustingly that it was no business of his. Turville had just been upset that she'd run a Vilsmeier reaction under the wrong conditions and wasted some valuable chemicals. After many years as a parent, though, Lum could tell that Evalina was lying, that the conversation with Turville had definitely been personal and not professional. In addition, there were the mystery telephone calls that Evalina would receive on her cell phone on the weekends. They were always secret. Evalina never told Lum who was calling. But one of either two outcomes resulted: Evalina's mood quickly transformed sour as she sulked around the house, or she left the house smiling from ear-to-ear with the disposition of an angel. Unbeknownst to Lum's consciousness, suspicions already had been swirling in his mind for quite awhile before that Saturday afternoon.

• • • • • • •

That Saturday evening, Lum slowly drove around the smushed opossum. The possum was a mother, as babies with their black eyes and tiny pink noses skittered all about the dead body.

About twenty yards past the body, Lum braked, then hesitated a moment before putting the truck into reverse. He parked on the road's shoulder a few feet from the fresh road kill. After dumping the empty cans of Bud Light from their cardboard box into the bed of his pickup, he herded the baby possums into the box. He dialed the number for Ida Kay Hall on his cell phone's contact list.

"Ida Kay, sorry to be calling you so late at night," Lum apologized.

Ida Kay indicated she'd just gotten to bed. She hadn't fallen asleep yet. She'd just returned from rescuing a wayward possum. A woman had called 9-1-1 earlier to report she'd caught a possum in a cat trap. Phyllis Taylor, the 9-1-1 dispatcher, had called her instead of bothering a deputy. Ida Kay rambled on about the possum, that it was one very mad critter. It showed its teeth, hissed, growled, spit, and puffed. The possum had already used one of its last lines of defense – squirting green gook out of its butt and smelling of death. Then it laid down motionless. The woman freaked out, thinking the possum had committed suicide in the cage in her backyard. Ida Kay tried to explain that all those actions were part of a possum's *modus operandi*. Possums just play dead. It's all just an act. Ida Kay rattled on, "The possum is just so misunderstood!" Five minutes after her story had started, she finally asked Lum why he was calling so late on a Saturday night.

"I should be pulling into your driveway in less than five minutes. I have a litter of ten young-uns. Mother met her demise on Muddy Hollow Road."

Ida Kay was known throughout that region of West Virginia as the "Possum Lady," a rehabilator of orphaned and injured opussums and other wildlife. This would be the second visit for

Lum today. She also operated the specialty greenhouse where he purchased the carnation plants for his garden that Saturday morning. She was the same age as Lum, having graduated in the same class from Millikan High School. Lum wasn't quite sure of her marital status – widowed, divorced, or separated – as her husband mysteriously disappeared five years ago. One rumor was that he was at the bottom of a coal mine shaft one county over, a statistic of him being an illicit drug entrepreneur. Another was he ran off to Mexico with his mistress.

Ida Kay, looking like an old hippie, greeted him in her driveway. Bib overalls with the peace symbol stitched on its bib had been thrown over her nightgown. Bright yellow mud boots were on her feet. A smile, as always, covered her face. She had spiked gray hair and stood a couple inches taller than Lum. Although her face showed lots of wrinkles as a testament to a hard life lived outside, such did not detract from her inherent attractiveness.

Lum jumped out of the truck and grabbed the box of possums from the pickup's bed.

"Hey, Lum," Ida Kay teased, "Seeing me twice in one day. People will think you're a courting me."

Lum blushed. He tried to ignore the comment. Instead he plopped the box into Ida Kay's outstretched arms and turned. "Gotta go. It's way past my bedtime."

Ida Kay grabbed Lum's shoulder, chuckling. "Not so fast, fellow. If I'm gonna stay up late mothering these li'l critters, you are too. You're gonna be the assistant nanny."

Lum took a deep breath. He'd hoped on the way to Ida Kay's that he'd be able to avoid the expected duty. With a grin on his face, he snorted, "I have a fishing date tomorrow morning – leaving before daybreak."

Ida Kay looked around at the multitude of fireflies popping light flashes. "You know as well as I do – when the fireflies are out, there aren't any worms for the digging. All the worms have turned into lightning bugs. So whatcha gonna fish with?"

"Was worth a try," Lum kidded.

"You'll just be going to church, as always, in the morning," Ida Kay bellowed. "I'll let you go before then."

Lum obediently took the box and followed Ida Kay to a large shed behind one of her greenhouses. Over the course of the next hour, the two of them started the ten baby possums in their rehab. They threaded a small tube down each of their throats to mimic their mother's long nipples in her pouch, placed them in tiny specially-made hammocks in a couple of cages, and fed four at a time – a bottle in each of their hands.

In an adjacent inside/outside run were five more orphaned possums, all scurrying about. Ida Kay said they were two months old, another two months before they could be released to the wild. She plopped some food, looking like a smoothie, in a bowl. The possums came a running. Ida Kay offered some of the food to Lum – she said a mixture of dog kibble, carrots, strawberry yogurt, quail eggs, leftover corn pudding, and herbs. Lum declined.

On the one wall of the nursing room were framed pictures of baby animals. Ida Kay indicated they were but a smattering of those she'd saved. She told Lum of Oscar, the grouchy raccoon, and Pooh, the sweet bear cub, and Dinky, the albino skunk. Other photographs displayed rabbits, squirrels, foxes, and lots and lots of opossum babies. She pointed out Stuart, her pet possum who now lived under another of her sheds, in a picture of eleven babies.

"How do you know that one's Stuart?" Lum deadpanned, "They all look the same."

Ida Kay responded as though offended. "Each one has its characteristics – not only in looks but also in mannerisms. I'll have each of the ones in your litter named within days."

All the time, Ida Kay kept spewing animal trivia nonstop to Lum who couldn't get a word in edgewise. She told him about wombats, marsupials like possums, being unique in that they poop in cubelike nuggets. A sesame-seed sized mite living in pavement cracks in Southern California is the fastest animal in relation to body size. The speedy arachnid was clocked at 322 body lengths per second, the equivalent of a human running 1300 miles per hour. Then, also, the Alfort jumper rabbit doesn't hop. It lifts its back feet above its head in a handstand and walks upside down on its front paws. And that a rooster's crow can register over 140 decibels, as loud as standing 100 feet from a running jet engine. She asked Lum why roosters then don't go deaf from their own ear-piercing crow. She answered before Lum even had a chance to think about an answer. When roosters open their beaks, their ear canals close, protecting their ear drums while they crow.

"Fascinating," mumbled Lum.

"And then do you know the loudest known mating call of a bird?" Ida Kay snickered.

Lum shrugged and kept bottle feeding his twosome.

"125 decibels, by the Brazilian white bellbird. It lives in the Amazon. For comparison, that's louder than a chain saw. The male bellbird stands face to face with the female and gives two staccato blasts of his air horn."

"I guess that'd get her attention," Lum chuckled.

"How loud might I expect your mating call to be tonight?" Ida Kay giggled.

Lum blushed and glanced at Ida Kay incredulously. But then, feeling playful, he replied, "Not gonna happen tonight; don't wanna wake up 'Toad.'"

Lum had met Norris "Toad" Crabbler that morning. He was staying in Ida Kay's small apartment on top of the possum nursery. He'd been released from jail the week before. Ida Kay was well known for giving humans a second chance, not just animals. As Ida Kay was want to say: "I take in strays."

"Can't use that as an excuse," Ida Kay laughed. "I kicked him out this afternoon. He'd gotten into Tequila – against the house rules. The apartment's empty."

Lum rolled his eyes. "Oops!"

But just as quickly, Ida Kay was well onto her next chain of thought, telling Lum that possums are no bigger than bees at birth and that the wee ones claw their way from the birth canal to their mother's pouch where they stay for two months. That possums are good for the environment, eating vermin and trash – mice, rats, cockroaches, dead animals, rotten fruit, slugs, and voles. They even eat up to five thousand ticks per season. And since they're immune to snake venom, thanks to a single protein in their bloodstream, they keep the native copperheads in check. Some scientists were developing an antidote for snakebites, relying on a sequence of eleven amino acids in this protein.

Lum had just about put all his worries aside when Ida Kay asked, "How's Evalina doing?"

Chapter Eight
BATTLES

Both Mason Turville and Lum Baumgartner were fixtures at Goose Creek Lutheran Church. For all ten years in Millikan after being hired at PAYNE Pharmaceuticals, Turville attended and greatly contributed to the activities of the church. Lum had been a devout member his entire life. In fact, Lum's great-great-grandfather was a founding member of Goose Creek Lutheran Church. Every one of Lum's ancestors had been elected to leadership positions in the church. Accordingly, Lum also felt a responsibility to be a leader in the church. Lum served on the twelve-member church council at Goose Creek for consecutive four-year terms over the course of 28 years. In particular, Lum had been instrumental in recruiting the current pastor, Reverend Adam Clarke, to the pulpit of Goose Creek. Lum also chaired the property committee, being just as multitalented in the mechanical workings – plumbing, heating, kitchen repairs, and carpentry, among others – of the church, as he was in maintaining equipment at PAYNE Pharmaceuticals. Turville, on the other hand, was a recent addition to the church council, just having started his second four-year term. But he'd already been elevated to a position of power, having been elected the chair of the council.

Turville's vision for Goose Creek Lutheran Church diametrically opposed that of Lum's. Whereas the tit-for-tats between the two at PAYNE Pharmaceuticals were but minor skirmishes, the encounters of Turville and Lum during council meetings were outright dog fights. The battle lines were clearly drawn. Lum argued for maintaining the *status quo* in the church services, to keep Sunday mornings at church pretty much the same as it had been since the days he'd been raised by his parents in the church. Turville and his followers, many being recent additions to the church roster, wanted dramatic transformations in the church. Turville convinced the council to switch some of the traditional church hymns in the worship services to modern songs with a more upbeat tempo. A smattering of these songs could be considered Christian rock. Other changes pushed by Turville included showing pictures, Scripture verses, presentations, movies, and web-access on screens in the sanctuary before, during, and after services; encouraging congregants to clap, raise hands, and sing Hallelujahs; replacing wine with grape juice in holy communion services; and mandating a certain quota of women and minorities in the composition of the church council.

To say there was resulting congregational friction or division was an understatement. After church services, Lum's friends often flocked about Lum, fussing.

"Do I have to be upset every Sunday?" griped Beatrice Conley. Like Lum, she'd grown up in the church. She wore a light green dress with matching shoes and handbag. "These changes are destroying the way we talk to God in our worship service."

Myers Epperly, wearing the only sports coat and tie he possessed, chimed in: "I just don't like coming to church anymore. It doesn't feel solemn and churchlike. People are making too much noise and having fun!"

"My parents and grandparents would be rolling over in their graves, if they knew what is now happening in the church!" echoed Donna Lynn Bowman.

On the other side of the congregation, followers of Turville described the worship at Goose Creek as having been stale, stuffy, and lacking energy.

"Must I continue to sit through services designed in the last century," complained Roger Ross. Roger's wife nodded in agreement. Both wore jeans and tees.

Nelda Graves, blonde and thirty-ish, gave Turville a hug. "Thanks for all you do!"

At the next council meeting, Lum was particularly disillusioned with Turville's successful proposal to have joint worship services with neighboring Pentecostal, Evangelical, Baptist, and Presbyterian churches for Thanksgiving, Christmas, and Lent. Lum reasoned his church practiced Lutheran doctrines. Why should they associate with these other sects who didn't worship like them?

And at the next meeting, Turville wanted to replace the old wooden picket fence, which had been erected by Lum's grandfather, in front of the church. The two sides, then, quibbled over the color of the new carpeting in the church sanctuary, as well as changes in the placement of the pulpit and choir chairs.

The congregation had become so polarized, full of strife, and infighting that the two factions even sat in separate cliques in the church during services as well as Sunday schools.

○ ● ○ ● ○

Pastor Clarke preached for several weeks on biblical passages in Corinthians. The apostle Paul wrote about his role as an intermediary for heated arguments between two divisions in the early church at Corinth millennia ago. The pastor used as the basis for his sermons Paul's admonitions –

> *1 Corinthians 3: 1-9*
>
> Brothers, I could not address you as spiritual but as worldly – mere infants in Christ. I gave you milk, not solid food, for you were not yet ready for it. Indeed, you are still not ready. You are still worldly. For since there is jealousy and quarreling among you, are you not worldly? Are you not acting like mere men? For when one says, "I follow Paul," and another, "I follow Apollos," are you not mere men?

> What, after all, is Apollos? And what is Paul? Only servants, through whom you came to believe – as the Lord has assigned to each his task. I planted the seed, Apollos watered it, but God made it grow. So neither he who plants nor he who waters is anything, but only God, who makes things grow. The man who plants and the man who waters have one purpose, and each will be rewarded according to his own labor. For we are God's fellow workers; you are God's field, God's building.
>
> *2 Corinthians 12: 19-20*
>
> Have you been thinking all along that we have been defending ourselves to you? We have been speaking in the sight of God as those in Christ; and everything we do, dear friends, is for your strengthening. For I am afraid that when I come I may not find you as I want you to be, and you may not find me as you want me to be. I fear that there may be quarreling, jealousy, outbursts of anger, factions, slander, gossip, arrogance and disorder.

Pastor Clarke emphasized that the squabbles in this early church mirrored those currently happening in Goose Creek Lutheran Church. The church in Corinth had rifts between the older and younger church leaders. Discord flared up when a group of younger church leaders ousted the older leaders. As a consequence, the church disintegrated into groups beset with strife and bickering. Paul wanted the leaders of the church to repent and rid themselves of the internal rivalry, envy, and disruption. Instead of working to the detriment of others, all leaders needed to submit to the will of God, working together in harmony and peace. In particular, the younger leaders needed to respect the experiences of their elders. Likewise, Pastor Clarke surmised the two factions at Goose Creek had been battling over trivial matters in the overall scheme of the worship of God and their savior Jesus Christ. Accordingly, such led to slander, gossip, and polarization of the congregation into two camps.

After identifying the problem, Pastor Clarke then continued with solutions, perhaps most pointedly provided by Paul in the biblical passage –

> *1 Corinthians 13: 2-7*
>
> If I have the gift of prophecy and can fathom all mysteries and all knowledge, and if I have a faith that can move mountains, but have not love, I am nothing. If I give all I possess to the poor and surrender my body to the flames, but have not love, I gain nothing.
>
> Love is patient, love is kind. It does not envy, it does not boast, it is not proud. It is not rude, it is not self-seeking, it is not easily angered, it keeps no record of wrongs. Love does not delight in evil but rejoices with the truth. It always protects, always trusts, always hopes, always perseveres.

Thus, Pastor Clarke attempted to smother the disagreements and battles within his church. He tried to keep his church members from missing the point of the worship services, with one side not demanding that the other side agree with them but instead opening their arms to those that disagree with them. He chided that their worship was about God, not about individual preferences. The worship services started with God's loving kindness, and then followed with Scriptures (Christian stories) as exhortations of praise and thanksgiving. The heart of the service focused on the confession of individual sins and the sacrifice of Jesus Christ to wash away the sins of the believers. A worship service established an encounter between a Holy God and unholy people, NOT between two sets of unholy people. But, as Pastor Clarke continued, it was hard to surrender to Christ when refusing to love other Christians with whom we disagree. The pastor chastised those in the congregation who continued to complain once a decision had been made, which indicated personal selfishness. Individuals shouldn't be concerned about the type of worship that he or she liked, wanted, or desired; but what the group wanted. Individual wants were simply foolish pride, caused by envy. Individual members should care less about themselves, focusing instead on the needs of others. Pastor Clarke emphasized the love for God must be translated into the love for all other church members, not just a selected portion of those members.

The two factions of the church, though, heard only the portions on which they agreed within the pastor's sermons. Lum interpreted Pastor Clarke's messages as telling the younger leaders – that is, Turville – to accept and submit to Lum's traditional views. On the other hand, Turville thought that the pastor's messages justified the changes, otherwise Lum and his followers were just being selfish. Neither faction heard the underlying need for love! The internal strife at Goose Creek Lutheran Church instead exploded, with a lack of acceptance of the worship changes by the older members and previous leaders of the church.

Both sides, surprisingly, maintained their support for Pastor Clarke. Pastor Clarke, without argument, instituted the changes decided by church council. Lum believed Pastor Clarke did so begrudgingly, that the pastor actually agreed with his conservative views on the church operations.

Pastor Clarke continued to be a mentor for Evalina in her singing. That was one constant throughout the changes – Pastor Clarke and Evalina continued singing duets of traditional hymns.

• • • • • • •

It was no longer Saturday evening, instead the wee hours of Sunday morning. Evalina pulled into the driveway next to Lum's truck. Her headlights lit up Possum, their cat, stalking potential prey under a nearby bush. He hobbled with his distinctive limp to greet her on the front porch, flopping on his side as she approached. Evalina gave him a quick belly rub. He wanted more, swatting his paw as she tried to remove her hand. She smiled. As she scratched his belly some more, she whispered, "Possum, do you ever worry? Do you dream about anything other than future belly rubs? Will my dream of yesterday be my hope of today, and the reality of tomorrow?"

She quietly unlocked the front door and tiptoed to her bedroom. Unbeknowst to her, her father was still awake, but barely, having arrived home only a few minutes before she. He'd been too tired to even have the Bud Light he'd wished for most of the night.

Evalina felt a sense of euphoria overcome her as she looked out the window of her bedroom. Moon beams shone on her. She focused on the highs, not the lows, of the day.

She pulled a suitcase from her closet and opened it on her bed. She neatly folded a red dress into the suitcase.

Chapter Nine
WORSHIP WAR

The battles at Goose Creek Lutheran Church erupted into a full-scale worship war. Turville and his supporters were adamant in their belief that the church needed to change in order to compete with the independent churches that were thriving in that area. The transformations instituted by Turville became more-and-more entrenched. Many of those who sided with Lum, though, showed their disapproval of the changes with their feet. They simply walked away and transferred to other churches. Others left the church because they got tired of the continuous squabbling. As an unintended consequence, Goose Creek Lutheran Church started to have financial problems because the deep-pocketed conservatives who had previously tithed large amounts of money to the church were those who drifted away.

Church council meetings became even more raucous. Verbal insults even spilled out into the parking lot after one particularly contentious meeting. The council had voted to replace the old wooden cross in front of the sanctuary with a new, metallic gold-plated one.

As Leonard "Bud" Light walked to his car, Dirk Havens snarled, "What a waste of time! It took almost an hour, instead of five minutes, to vote to get rid of the trashy cross."

Bud swirled around. "My grandpappy made that cross."

"He obviously wasn't a very good carpenter," Dirk laughed.

Bud clenched his fists and started towards Dirk.

Dirk growled, "It probably looked as bad fifty years ago as it does today."

Calmer heads prevailed as friends redirected them to go their separate ways. Bud resigned from council, never to return to Goose Creek Lutheran Church. He was replaced on council by one who thought like Mason Turville.

Soon thereafter, over a year before that Saturday night, the election for Goose Creek's church council became the final battle in the war. A candidate who supported Turville's reforms ousted Lum from his long-serving position. Many of the new church members at Goose Creek had considered Lum an impediment to the apparent improvements being established in the church. Lum and those who thought like him were now in the clear minority. Lum's side had been defeated. They had lost power as well as a voice in church politics. Even more lifelong members left Goose Creek Lutheran Church.

○ ● ○ ● ○

Although many times caught in the cross fire between the two clashing factions, Reverend Clarke survived as pastor by his willingness to follow the wishes of the majority. Lum felt a betrayal, in a sense, because he believed the pastor needed to follow the direction of the Holy Spirit, not the whims of the congregation. Furthermore, once off church council, Lum sensed Reverend Clarke ignoring or avoiding him because of Lum's now minority status in church politics. But Lum rationalized that the pastor, like he, firmly supported conservative practices, but only instituted the changes imposed by Turville in order to keep his job. Lum envied the attention that Pastor Clarke now directed toward Turville, not him, almost as though God was selectively choosing another instead of him to speak for the people.

Many of Lum's conservative friends also thought Reverend Clarke supported their traditional views, but then perceived him as a turncoat who much too readily adapted to the changes brought about by Turville. Although the pastor preached of acceptance and love, they thought Pastor Clarke hypocritical in that only Turville's views were now accepted at Goose Creek Lutheran Church.

Rumors ran rampant that Turville now wanted to force Reverend Clarke to resign in order to replace him with a minister with more liberal views.

○ ● ○ ● ○

Lum maintained his support for Pastor Clarke, primarily because he was a friend. He believed in the pastor's passion for goodness, and in being a caring and compassionate individual. The pastor had helped with Evalina's practices and pageants – and had spent many extra hours with Evalina in teaching the holy gospel, tutoring her singing in pageants, accompanying her singing as a pianist, and teaching her guitar and piano to accompany herself in pageants.

The day before Lum overheard Evalina's private telephone conversation, Lum had dropped by the church to repair a leaking pipe in the men's restroom. He had planned to stop by Pastor Clarke's office afterwards to say "Hi." But, as he turned the corner of the hall, he saw Turville quietly entering the office. Lum waited in a classroom down the hallway, as what Lum surmised as a private meeting between Pastor Clarke and Turville convened. After only about ten minutes, Turville angrily stomped out of the Reverend's office and slammed the exterior door shut, clearly upset with the happenings of the meeting. After a while, Lum did indeed stop by Pastor Clarke's office, but the pastor was quite sullen and not talkative. In fact, Lum thought the pastor was about to shed a tear at times. Such confirmed Lum's initial thinking that Turville was indeed trying to force Pastor Clarke out of the pulpit so that Turville could finally hire a preacher of his own liking.

Lum's dark thoughts about sexual liaisons between Evalina and Turville, after the eavesdropped conversation, were now accentuated by his unholy thoughts of what Turville was doing to Pastor Clarke. Turville was doubly despicable in Lum's mind!

● ● ● ● ● ● ●

Ida Kay Hall had set her alarm for 5:30 am that Sunday morning. It had been a long night. Every two hours the baby possums needed to be fed. She grabbed an hour's sleep, without even taking off her bib overalls, on the couch between feedings.

She toasted herself a half-stale onion bagel, spread some cream cheese on it, and took a bite. After pulling on her boots, she headed for the shed. It was dark – the moon having set and the sun having yet to rise. But she didn't need a flashlight, having made the trek many times.

When she opened the shed door and flicked on the light switch, she dropped the half-eaten bagel and stared at the floor. Her framed picture of a rescued baby squirrel had fallen off the wall. Pieces of glass littered the plywood floor.

Her hands covered her mouth. She gasped, "Someone's gonna die!"

PART 2

REVENGE

Chapter Ten
DEPARTURES

Despite the early hour, Ida Kay telephoned Buck Fowler, the detective in Millikan County's undermanned and underfinanced sheriff's department. She had called his direct phone number often over the course of the past five years. He was the case officer investigating her husband's disappearance.

A bleary-eyed Buck answered on the fifth ring, grumbling to himself about being awakened on the one day of the week he could usually sleep late. Without even saying hello, he gruffly warned the caller. "This better be important."

"Buck, this is Ida Kay. And it is important."

Buck rubbed his eyes and glanced at the clock. He sighed. After taking a deep breath, he flippantly teased, "What? Did someone kidnap Stuart, your possum?"

"Stuart is doing just fine – thank you," Ida Kay responded, trying to sound insulted. "But someone's gonna get himself killed."

"And exactly how do you know this?" Buck muttered as he walked to the bathroom.

"You know how," Ida Kay fussed, and indeed Buck did know. "Just like your daddy always told you – When a picture falls from a wall, someone's gonna die."

"I know how the saying goes, you don't have to remind me," Buck said.

"Have I ever been wrong before?"

With an ounce of sarcasm, Buck kidded, "And which picture was it? That of Dinky the skunk, or Oscar the raccoon, or –"

"No," Ida Kay interrupted, "It was the picture of a rescued squirrel named –"

She heard the dial tone before finishing the sentence.

○ ● ○ ● ○

Lum, still in his pajamas, sat at the breakfast nook sipping on orange juice and nibbling a lemon-filled doughnut. He felt exhausted after his short, mostly sleepless night. He'd lain in bed fretting about Turville's affair with Evalina, now sitting and doing the same during breakfast. Rays of sunlight periodically streaming through the kitchen window did little to brighten his mood. He needed to talk to Pastor Clarke, to solicit some guidance and advice – perhaps he could corral him before worship service that morning.

On his way to shower and change into his Sunday's finest, Lum gently rapped on Evalina's still closed bedroom door. No response. He knocked again and leaned into the door. Bedsheets rustled.

"Good morning, Dear," he softly said. "You might wanna roll on out of bed. You're gonna be late for choir practice."

A few moments passed, enough time for Evalina to check the clock on her nightstand. "I'm tired. I'm gonna skip church and sleep a little longer."

As Lum quietly started to walk away, she added, "The choir doesn't have any anthems planned for the service today."

Lum couldn't remember the last time Evalina had missed church.

○ ● ○ ● ○

Lum tried to locate Pastor Clarke when he first arrived at Goose Creek Lutheran Church for Sunday morning worship service. No luck. Instead, Lum traipsed to his regular seat near the back of the left side of the sanctuary. He bowed his head and prayed silently. Upon opening his eyes, he did a double take. On the front stage sat a distinguished gentleman, probably in his eighties, next to Dr. Mason Turville. No Pastor Clarke – Lum was confused.

Turville introduced the Reverend Coolidge Spangler. The pastor looked so frail that a good breeze could blow him away. He would be the supply preacher for that day's service. Turville, as chair of the church council, then read a letter of resignation, which had already been accepted by a called meeting of the church council, from Reverend Adam Clarke effective immediately. The resignation cited philosophical differences in the direction of the church between Pastor Clarke and the council. The congregation stirred.

Every muscle in Lum's body tensed. His legs pranced in place. His hands clasped shut into a fist, then opened. In one regard, Lum felt vindicated that Pastor Clarke resigned in protest of the direction of their church. The pastor must've supported Lum's conservative view of church policies all along. But on the other hand, Lum was embittered that Turville had forced Reverend Clarke from pastoring his flock at Goose Creek Lutheran Church. Lum's face turned red, seething in anger.

Turville announced that Pastor Barney Bennington would be in the pulpit next week. Pastor Bennington would assume the position of interim pastor, while the church council started its search for a new full-time pastor. With every additional word that spewed from Turville's mouth, Lum's blood boiled with even more ire.

Lum mumbled to himself: "Turville did it!" The resignation of Reverend Clarke and his quick replacement must've been orchestrated by Turville and his followers – as he'd previously suspected was Turville's main objective all along.

Lum recalled little of the service that morning, other than Pastor Spangler had a surprisingly strong voice for an old geezer and was bald as a billiard ball. On his way out the door, Lum groused to one of his friends: "Turville got rid of a good man. He chased off Pastor Clarke."

With a tear in his eye, his friend nodded in agreement. "It's a sad day for the church."

○ ● ○ ● ○

Lum was still in a daze when he pulled into his driveway. He skulked from his truck to the front door. Before Lum realized what was happening, Evalina stood in front of him in the hallway with several suitcases, her guitar, and laptop computer.

Lum stopped, speechless and mouth agape.

"Daddy, I'm going to be spending a couple months with Aunt Melody," she calmly announced, as if she'd been practicing that statement all morning.

Lum was blindsided. He remained silent with a deer-in-headlights look on his face. After a few moments, he gasped, "But . . . but why? . . . All of a sudden."

"I've actually been thinking about doing something different for quite a while."

"What . . . What about work?" Lum sputtered.

"I resigned Friday afternoon. And, daddy, you don't have to worry. I've saved up quite a bit of money over the past three years." She smiled. "I appreciate living rent free here."

Lum leaned back onto the door knob for support. He could find no words.

Evalina stepped forward and hugged him. She whispered that she appreciated all his help in taking care of her while she was working at PAYNE. She emphasized her move didn't have anything to do with him. She wanted to consider other career choices such as singing instead of doing chemistry. As she kissed him on the cheek, she firmly stated, "I love you."

Lum stood like a block of stone. Although Evalina seemed sincere in her decision, he was aghast at the suddenness of the announcement. He thought to himself: What's happening? Pastor Clarke's here one moment, and gone the next. And now Evalina's here one moment, and will be gone the next. He also knew the futility of trying to convince Evalina to stay. Once she made up her mind, there was no turning back for her.

He mumbled, "It's all Turville's fault."

Evalina denied Dr. Turville had anything to do with her decision. Lum detected, though, a certain uncomfortableness in her disavowal, as she teetered from one foot to the other. She quickly left, saying she'd call when she arrived at her aunt's house.

Lum waved from the front door. After standing there for several minutes, he realized he hadn't told her that Pastor Clarke had resigned – also Turville's fault.

○ ● ○ ● ○

Lum skipped lunch. Instead he sat on the patio with an open can of Bud Light. His wheelbarrow and gardening tools still needed to be put away. He stared at the pink carnations planted just 24 hours earlier. As he looked upward, he shaded his eyes from the sun. "Partie, what's happening?"

He looked back at the carnations. "In the course of one day, both our daughter and our minister have left us for elsewhere."

Possum, his cat, came out of nowhere to rub against his ankles. Lum mindlessly petted him, then scratched his belly as he flipped on his side. Lum wondered how the rescued baby possums were doing at Ida Kay's. She'd left him a voice mail on his phone that morning. He played it – the babies were all doing fine. Then, she babbled on about a flea-sized spider – the peacock spider. The male of the species has vivid coloring and flamboyant dance moves. In the springtime, he flips up his iridescent fan-like abdomen, waggles a pair of legs in the air, and jerks back and forth as if doing a zig-zag moonwalk. His courtship then switches to swinging abdominal vibrations. Shimmering mosaics of scales clash reds and yellows against blues, reflecting sunlight to create rainbow hues. All of this is to show a female he's the most amazing and worthy mate. Ida Kay ended by reminding Lum it was springtime and she hadn't seen him dance since high school.

Lum looked at Possum. "Who's crazier? That woman . . . or whoever watched those spiders dance?"

His thoughts quickly returned to Turville for being the source of all his troubles. He gritted his teeth and kicked at a nearby rock on the patio. Foremost, Lum blamed Turville for defiling his daughter Evalina. He just couldn't understand why she didn't turn on him, to report him to Human Resources at PAYNE. But Turville must've paid her money to go away and not ruin his marriage and his position. Lum also blamed Turville for forcing

Reverend Clarke from the position of pastor at Goose Creek Lutheran Church.

Possum rubbed again against Lum's ankles.

Lum scowled, "Turville just wanted the power to run Goose Creek his way, without interference from Pastor Clarke. And in doing so, he ran off and ruined a good Christian man!"

Possum saw a bird flitter in a nearby bush and fly away.

Lum stewed in anger, until a quick phone call disturbed his self-fueled pity pot. Evalina announced her arrival at Aunt Melody's.

He picked up the hot Bud Light and crushed the still full can in his hand. Beer spilled over his pants and onto the patio. But he hadn't succumbed to temptation – drinking neither on Sundays nor on days on which he worked the night shift.

Chapter Eleven
REVENGE

That Sunday afternoon Lum needed to get a few hours sleep. The night shift at PAYNE Parmaceuticals started at 11 o'clock. He doubted sleep, though, would come – he was right. Adrenalin freely flowed through his body, continually stoking his fury and wrath toward Turville.

That night, a pipe spewing hot water had already flooded the boiler room at PAYNE when a tired Lum arrived for work. His crew cut and rethreaded a new piece of three-inch galvanized pipe, then exchanged it for the broken one. They also replaced a leaky valve. It was wet and exhausting work. All the while, Lum imagined ways in which he could garner revenge on Turville – poisoning him, filleting him with a fishing knife, throwing acid on him, shooting him with his hunting rifle. Turville needed to have his disgusting life ripped away. Lum figured the momentary smile on his face would be worth spending the rest of his life in prison to exact this satisfaction. But he needed a plan. For that night, though, not emptying Turville's trash cans would have to suffice.

○ ● ○ ● ○

Before he started dinner the next day, Lum confidently opened his Bible and turned to the index in back. Two biblical passages commented on "revenge." Neither pleased Lum. Both Moses and the apostle Paul spoke the same message – Do not seek revenge; love, or live in peace, with your neighbor. Let God take care of the ones who wrong you. Lum slammed the Bible shut.

He needed to talk to Pastor Clarke. The pastor didn't answer his cell phone. Pam, the pastor's wife, picked up their house phone, between sobs said "Hello," then promptly hung up on him. Lum sighed. He should've realized the pastor and his wife would be upset about his being fired.

Lum's phone rang – Ida Key's number. He debated whether to answer. He did.

Ida Kay wanted him to visit his possum family. The babies all had been named. She called the nine boys Cleatis, Clyde, Cecil, Butchie, Freddie, Bruce, Redford, Newman, and Clint. And the one girl was a real spitfire – she was Dinah. Ida Kay also told him of the other possum rescued from the cat trap that same night; he, Claude, was doing fine. Interestingly, Claude seemed to have a unique smell about him. Then, Ida Kay rattled on about how the males of Alaskan crested auklets produced a citrusy scent to attract females. These birds had the most intense smells of all birds. In fact, the males exuding the strongest odor, actually a pleasant blend of lemon and tangerine, got the females. The females found this bird cologne intoxicating. And, by the way, when Lum had come to visit, Ida Kay had picked up a uniquely exhilarating smell about him.

Lum shook his head in disbelief. He promised to "try" to visit his possum rescues later that week. But, for now, he needed to take a shower, get the work smell off him, and try to get some sleep.

Instead of showering and sleeping, or even eating, Lum went back to his Bible. He tried other key words – affair, adultery, kill, retaliation, retribution, payback, among others – in the index. None provided biblical passages he found satisfying. He looked up the word "defile." Its reference was to Genesis, chapter 34, the story of Dinah.

Lum gasped, "Dinah!" He walked around the room, then into the hallway. He stopped at the picture of *The Last Supper*. "Maybe God is talking to me," he mumbled. Dinah was the only daughter of Jacob and his wife Leah; all their other children were sons.

Lum read Genesis 34 several times. Shechem had defiled Dinah, lying with her against her will. Jacob and Dinah's brothers were filled with grief and fury. They wanted revenge. But they were greatly outnumbered, basically immigrants living in the land occupied by Shechem's people. So Dinah's brothers tricked Shecham – consenting to Shechem's marriage to Dinah if he and his men would agree to be circumcised. Then, while all the men were in pain from their circumcisms, two of Dinah's brothers, Simeon and Levi, killed Shechem and his men.

"Sweet revenge," Lum smiled.

The story continued. Jacob wasn't happy, saying his sons gave him a "stench," which the people living nearby could smell. He chided Simeon and Levi. The two sons, though, argued otherwise. As recorded in the last verse of the chapter, they proclaimed, "Should he [Shechem] have treated our sister like a prostitute?"

Lum closed the Bible. He raised it in his hand. He looked upward, then spat, "Should Turville have treated my daughter like a prostitute?"

"NO!" Lum yelled. This biblical passage was the Word spoken directly by God. God was telling him to go ahead, like Simeon and Levi, with his plans for revenge. And to use trickery to exact it.

While grinning with his newly found self-satisfaction, Lum turned on the television. Time to relax. The classic movie channel popped on the screen. Trailers for *The Sting*, starring Robert Redford and Paul Newman, advertised the upcoming movie. Lum's eyes opened wide. He mouthed "Redford" and "Newman," two of possum Dinah's brothers and shook his head at the eerie coincidence.

Lum recalled this movie detailed a specific type of revenge on your enemy: to gain the revenge subtly, without the target even knowing what's happening. If done successfully, the victim doesn't even realize he's been "stung." Likewise, that could be his strategy, to inflict pain and torture slowly so that Turville's good life would be destroyed without him realizing it's being taken away. Lum licked his lips, deep in thought. Could this be the second part of God's message – not only is it proper to seek revenge, but to do so in an unsuspecting fashion? He'd jerk the rug out from underneath Turville. Lum wouldn't be identified as responsible for Turville's demise. Lum smiled. He danced a Texas two-step in joy.

○ ● ○ ● ○

Over the course of the day, Lum hatched his plan. What could be a better way to disgrace Turville than to discredit him as a chemist! One of the worst humiliations a lab researcher could encounter would be to have government agencies clamp down on him for a safety violation and bury him in paperwork. Turville would never be able to get anything done, in particular completing the synthesis of his precious anodynol. Such would be especially demeaning to Turville. Turville always claimed to be preaching safety first in the laboratory. Lum plotted – he could rig a safety breach in Turville's laboratory, then call OSHA (Occupational Health and Safety Administration) inspectors anonymously on their hotline to come and investigate. After a slew of such accidents and complaints centered in Turville's chemical laboratory, OSHA might even shut down his work because of his lackadaisical attitude about safety concerns. Maybe, if Lum was lucky, Turville or one of his lab workers might be slightly injured because of safety problems, further upsetting the OSHA inspectors. Lum smirked at the mischievous nature of his planning. Everyone at PAYNE Pharmaceuticals and beyond would identify Turville as a hypocrite for claiming to preach safety but not practicing laboratory safety himself. Eventually, Jim Payne, Jr., might even be so disgusted at the problems that he'd fire Turville.

"Having Turville out of my life and disgraced as a chemist," Lum chuckled to himself, "and Turville would never know I did it to him. Afterwards, maybe I could anonymously send him a Bible with a bookmark at chapter 34 of Genesis. Maybe even write on the bookmark – 'Should you have treated her like your prostitute?'" A sense of peace overwhelmed Lum. But such was only fleeting.

Lum paced around the room in further thought. He stopped. His expression brightened. His first laboratory disruption should be in honor of Evalina, to have Vilsmeier contribute to the downfall of Turville. Lum laughed out loud. In an additional play on irony, he could stage the first accident on the 12th of June, Vilsmeier's birthday, a little over a week away.

He took a few more steps around the room. Plans for the first safety accident came to him just as quickly, as if God through the Holy Spirit was directing his devious but blessed thoughts – much like God must have directed Jacob's sons to seek revenge on Shechem.

Lum recalled Evalina telling him the importance of temperature control for the Vilsmeier reaction. One never wanted the temperature to be too high. Bad things, perhaps a boil over or a fire, might happen. An uncontrolled chemical spill, or a small explosion, in the laboratory's fume hood might certainly spark an OSHA investigation, especially if reported due to safety oversights. Lum figured he could sneak into the research and development laboratory one night. No one else would be there. How hard could it be to have the temperature controller reading one temperature but actually being at another? Evalina indicated to him, in one of her teaching sessions over dinner, she periodically calibrated the synthesis workstation's controller to exactly 0.00°C by putting the temperature sensor in an ice-water bath. She said that the controller would get out of calibration with time, but usually by no more than a fraction of a degree. That was easily corrected by tweaking the calibration control or, in other words, turning the designated knurled screw to bring the temperature into calibration. All he had to do was adjust the calibration control!

○ ● ○ ● ○

Indeed, that night, Lum had plenty of time to root around Turville's laboratory under the guise of helping the janitor on duty empty the trash cans in the laboratory. He emptied only one of the two in Turville's office. Lum scrutinized the synthesis workstation's temperature controller in the fume hood, which was once Evalina's work space dedicated to running Vilsmeier reactions. An arrow above the calibration control even indicated to turn the screw counterclockwise to increase the temperature. He simply needed to twist the calibration screw counterclockwise a few rotations to cause his mischief.

Lum had heard rumors around PAYNE Pharmaceuticals that Turville was close to perfecting the synthesis of his miracle pain-killer, anodynol. Employees were thrilled about the possibilities of prosperity for the company. Turville had even gotten into the laboratory, running a key Vilsmeier reaction himself. Lum smiled. When Turville thought he was running the Vilsmeier reaction at say 0°C, the temperature would actually be 2°C, or 5°C. And perhaps the apparatus would go boom! Lum was anxious. It'd be hard to wait until Vilsmeier's birthday to do the deed.

Lum had also started rumors that Evalina Vail, Turville's top assistant in anodynol's synthesis, quit PAYNE Pharmaceuticals because Turville had been cutting corners with safety in order to push the project too quickly. Of course, Lum refused to disgrace his daughter by telling others what he had actually surmised: Evalina quit because Turville had been having a romantic liaison with her, and she wanted to get away from him and start anew after a contentious break-up.

He slammed the door to the laboratory – and cackled, "Should he have treated my Evalina like a prostitute?"

Chapter Twelve
REPLACEMENTS

By mid-week, Lum discovered Turville and PAYNE Pharmaceuticals had already hired a replacement for Evalina. He was astonished that PAYNE moved so quickly to find a new laboratory scientist. Such confirmed the rumors Turville neared a total synthesis of anodynol and needed someone to perform the day-to-day Vilsmeier reactions. The new hire was Ron Austin, a West Virginia native. Like Evalina, Ron Austin graduated from Keaton College. He had even done research doing Vilsmeier reactions under the direction of Dr. Quinn Stanton, Q-Dawg, during his undergraduate days. Austin then obtained his Masters degree in organic chemistry, having used the Vilsmeier reaction routinely in many of his procedures at the University of Wisconsin – Madison, Turville's alma mater. The gossip at PAYNE Pharmaceuticals spread word Austin had started his work towards the Ph.D. degree, but Turville lured him with the promise of his completing the key steps in the synthesis of anodynol – and sharing in the potentially big pay day. More PAYNE chitchat added that Turville made a deal with Austin's graduate advisor to have Austin return to Wisconsin for the Ph.D. degree after he finished the synthesis of anodynol at PAYNE, using the synthesis as the work for the degree.

Lum was shocked to learn that Austin would be making about fifty percent more in salary for doing the same job as Evalina, further fueling his distaste for Turville. Lum's sources told him that because of Austin's experience, he'd already started to perform solo Vilsmeier reactions his third day of work at PAYNE Pharmaceuticals. Lum surmised that Turville was pushing hard, real hard, to accomplish the synthesis of anodynol, quickly approving the work techniques of Ron Austin in addition to going over the laboratory policies and protocols.

○ ● ○ ● ○

During the week, Lum kept trying to contact Pastor Clarke. No answer. Pam Clarke refused to talk to him – hanging up on his phone calls as well as not opening the door to the parsonage. Moving boxes were stacked on their porch.

Every night as part of his passive-aggressive retaliation plan, Lum emptied only one, never both, of Turville's office trash cans. And, while cleaning Turville's laboratory, he spent time investigating and tinkering with the Vilsmeier set-up in the lab hood.

He never did visit Ida Kay and the rescued possum babies. Most of his free time was spent imagining Turville getting his due. He envisioned taking that smug smile off his arrogant face.

○ ● ○ ● ○

As the week ended, Buck Fowler stopped by Ida Kay's greenhouse. He wanted to pick up a hanging basket of petunias for Phyllis, the 9-1-1 dispatcher. She was retiring after forty years in the sheriff's department.

Buck also brought Ida Kay up to date on a recent development, or rather dead end, on her husband's disappearance. A deputy had arrested Hubert Kiser, a known drug dealer, for larceny and possession of stolen property. Buck related how Hubert had a backhoe in his front yard. The backhoe had been stolen from the West Virginia Highway Department earlier in the day from a road construction site.

"Yep, I read about that in the newspaper," Ida Kay laughed. "He claimed he didn't know how it ended up in his yard."

"Despite the fact that several people saw him driving the backhoe," Buck said, as he shook his head in disbelief. He chuckled, "But there's more to the story than the paper printed. The deputy showed up at Hubert's house because his live-in girlfriend called 9-1-1. She reported hearing a strange noise coming from the end of the driveway. She thought someone was stalking her. The funny part is the noise was coming from the windshield wiper sweeping across the back window of her SUV in the driveway. She didn't realize she'd turned it on."

"Unbelievable," Ida Kay howled, "Some things you can't make up – from a clueless, probably drugged-out, girlfriend to Hubert not even trying to hide the stolen property."

"Anyhow, as my daddy used to say – Common sense isn't a flower that grows on everyone's tree."

Both Buck and Ida Kay shared a good laugh.

"Once arrested, Hubert tried to make a deal," Buck continued. "He'd tell us where your husband's body is hidden in exchange for a reduced charge. He conveniently couldn't remember who had told him about the body."

"I suspect Hubert was just running his mouth," Ida Kay interjected.

"Indeed, he gave us two places, neither panned out." Buck then got a mischievous smile on his face. "By the way, I checked out your lead on someone dying. On Monday, old man Elmer Hylton died at the nursing home – he was older than dirt, I think 97. And two days later, Cissy Atkins died; she was only 88, but in bad health for the past ten years."

Ida Kay stuck her tongue out at the detective. Buck doubled over in laughter.

"I got a new frame for the picture and put it back up on the wall." Ida Kay spit out. "Mark my words. It won't be a laughing matter."

After Buck left, Ida Kay went into the possum nursery. It was time for the babies' feeding. The reframed picture of the rescued squirrel was once again on the floor, shattered glass and shards everywhere.

Ida Kay mumbled, "It's gonna happen. Someone's gonna get killed."

○ ● ○ ● ○

The next Sunday, Dr. Mason Turville introduced the Goose Creek Lutheran Church's congregation to their new interim pastor, Reverend Barney Bennington. Lum's reaction combined anger and sorrow. The unveiling of Pastor Barney, as he wished to be called, was a frontal attack on Lum's way of worship. Pastor Barney had long scraggly hair, sported an unkempt beard, wore peace beads, dressed in blue jeans and a beach shirt, and proclaimed to be an ex-hippie. Further, Pastor Barney displayed his musical talent by screaming what was billed as Christian Rock but sounded like heavy metal. Lum fully expected the youth of the church to organize into a mosh pit at the front of the church. Pastor Barney accompanied his screechy falsetto voice with a banjo. Lum immediately likened Pastor Barney to a bad imitation of Tiny Tim playing his ukulele, but "Crunching through the Tulips" instead of "Tiptoeing through the Tulips." Lum thought Turville was making it too easy for him to foment a revolution at the church. He did some rabble-rousing of the members of his church clique after the services. But surprisingly to Lum, many of the younger and newer members of the church appreciated the candor and excitement generated by Pastor Barney.

Perhaps, Lum thought, it was also time for him to now drift away from the church of his ancestors, as the church was no longer his church. Besides which, God now spoke directly to him. God helped him formulate the plans to destroy his Satan, who went by the name of Turville. So, he really didn't need to attend Goose Creek in order to communicate with God. But perhaps, he should stay. After Satan's (AKA Turville's) downfall, he'd return triumphantly to lead the rebuilding of Goose Creek Lutheran Church.

○ ● ○ ● ○

After church, Ida Kay called Lum. She was disappointed he hadn't visited her or the possums that week. As usual she jabbered on about different animal facts. One of her stories told of young sea slugs. They can pull their heads free of their bodies. These crawling heads then regenerate a new body. Strange, but true. The leaf-cutting worker ant coats its body with a thin, but tough, layer of armor made of magnesium-rich calcite. The armor protects this small ant from being killed by the more aggressive and much larger enemy soldier ants. Then, monarch butterfly caterpillars fight each other to eat milkweed leaves, their favorite food. They lunge at each other, knocking their opponents aside. They even resort to head butting. Ida Kay laughed, as she transitioned to a story about fig wasps, which are no larger than jelly beans.

"Male fig wasps spend their whole life on a single fig," she related. "They don't fly away. These male wasps grow humongous mouthparts that look like a pair of scissors. Their goal is to decapitate as many other males as they possibly can. The last he-wasp crawling has no competition to mate with the female wasp on the fig."

Lum smiled, thinking of a giant fig wasp slicing and dicing Turville. Much like Dinah's brothers slaughtered Shechem and his men in the biblical story.

"You know, Lum, both you and I have spent our whole lives in the Millikan area, and –"

"Don't even go there," Lum howled. He chuckled, but not about fig wasps. June 12, Vilsmeier's birthday, was two days away. It was time for him to activate his sabotage on Turville and Turville's laboratory. Turville wouldn't be the last man crawling!

Chapter Thirteen
RON AUSTIN

On the night of June 11, or more accurately the early morning hours of June 12, Lum helped the other janitors empty trash cans and clean floors. No emergencies needed his attention. All machinery and equipment were up and running.

In particular, Lum swept the floors of the research and development laboratory. He peered into the lab fume hood containing the apparatus in which Evalina, and now Ron Austin, used to run the Vilsmeier reaction. The chemicals were already in place. It was clear Ron Austin would be performing a Vilsmeier reaction the upcoming work day. Lum turned the calibration screw five complete revolutions counterclockwise, believing that the 5°C increase would be sufficient to cause trouble in the synthesis. When Ron Austin dialed to his reaction temperature, it would actually be 5°C higher than the controller indicated.

Lum imagined chemicals spewing from the top of the reflux column, maybe all 250 milliliters of reagents in the reaction flask, and flowing out of the hood onto the floor. What a mess it would make. Or, maybe even a minor explosion, the best case scenario.

Lum had already heard the rumors return back to him that Turville was cutting corners and performing reactions quickly instead of safely. In fact, one person told Lum that he'd heard Turville now just gave a wink-wink to safety; Turville wanted results and would look the other way in terms of staff wellbeing.

Even if the temperature change didn't cause a spill or explosion, fiddling with the reaction temperature should assure, if Lum remembered Evalina's dinner-time teaching correctly, a collection of unexpected and different products. At the very minimum, this mischief should lead to confusion and problems for Turville. His next action, then, would be a few more twirls of the calibration knob, an even higher temperature.

His musings were suddenly interrupted by his work phone buzzing. John, the night shift's loading dock supervisor, needed him immediately. An incoming tractor trailer had backed into a chemical storage tank.

○ ● ○ ● ○

The next day, the Director of Operations at PAYNE Pharmaceuticals woke Lum from a deep sleep with a phone call. An explosion had occurred in Turville's research and development laboratory. Lum smiled – June 12th, Vilsmeier's birthday, time for celebration.

"The explosion killed the new guy, Ron Austin, instantly," the Director gasped.

Lum's smile quickly departed. He took a deep breath and frowned. "That's terrible," he cringed. "I didn't know him."

"Don't go anywhere today," the Director ordered. "You'll be on call in case things need to be cleaned up."

"I'll be right here."

"The deputies have closed off the laboratory for now. The crime scene unit looks like a bunch of white-suited aliens bumbling about. Supposedly, OSHA investigators have been dispatched."

"I guess it's like a mad house."

"Indeed," the Director spoke as though out of breath. "You know, rumors have been rampant about Turville's lax safety standards. Austin had only worked here less than a week. I've heard he hadn't been properly trained by Dr. Turville. I'm sure OSHA's gonna focus on improper training or a lack of safety procedures by Turville in his supervision of the new employee."

After the phone call, Lum wandered out to his patio with a glass of ice water and a Kit Kat candy bar. His hands shook –

What had he done? He didn't know whether to be happy or sad. His plan was meant to create minor injuries at the worst, not death – and, in particular, not to involve a person other than Turville as collateral damage. Possum meowed to catch his attention. Lum returned to the kitchen and put some milk in a bowl. He sat next to the planting of pink carnations as he watched Possum lap up the milk as though starved.

"It's okay, Possum," Lum said, "Remember Jacob's sons killed not only Shechem, the perpetrator in defiling Dinah, but also every male in the area." He thought for a few minutes, then continued, "The death of Austin, likewise, must've been orchestrated by God's will. I was only the catalyst for such action. It's all in God's plan."

○ ● ○ ● ○

Buck Fowler had been on his way to the next county to interview a suspect in a recent burglary. The dispatcher redirected him to PAYNE Pharmaceuticals – an explosion in the laboratory, and a guy by the name of Ron Austin killed.

Fifteen minutes later, Buck arrived at PAYNE with siren blaring and blue lights flashing. He glanced at his beeping cell phone. A text message from Ida Kay Hall. He read the text and gulped. News traveled fast around the county.

Squirrel's name in fallen picture was AUSTIN!

Chapter Fourteen
THE ACCIDENT

The local rescue squad pronounced Ron Austin dead at the scene. They found him in a pool of his own blood. The cause of death wasn't hard to ascertain. An inch-long glass shard stuck out of Ron Austin's neck. Large amounts of blood had flowed from this single wound. The other technicians working in the laboratory didn't disturb the scene other than turning the body over to see whether they could stem the flow of blood and resuscitate Ron Austin.

Such attempts were futile with the catastrophic eruption of blood from the caratoid artery in his neck.

Flashing blue lights identified the arrival soon thereafter of local deputies, then detective Buck Fowler, of the Sheriff's Department. On the surface, how the accident happened was just as easy to determine. Evidently, Ron Austin had been performing an experiment in the laboratory fume hood. The flask in which the reaction was occurring exploded. Unfortunately for Austin, the fume hood was not fully closed, but was slightly ajar with a gap of about two inches at its base. Austin must have been sitting on a laboratory stool watching the reaction and writing in his laboratory notebook. Then, he must have bent down slightly. In the worst case of bad luck for Austin, the one, and only, piece of glass blown out of the side of the round-bottomed reaction flask flew perfectly through the two-inch opening and scored a direct hit. The caratoid artery had spurted blood with every beat of his dying heart. Buck Fowler mulled a hired assassin couldn't have done the job any more efficiently.

After his inspection of the accident scene, Buck Fowler interviewed the two, now traumatized, lab technicians present when the explosion occurred. Both were at the opposite end of the laboratory at the time of the accident. They claimed not to have disturbed the apparatus, only pulling the electrical cords plugged into the outlets on the outside of the laboratory fume hood. Neither technician could explain why the lab hood wasn't completely closed. It would've contained the flying glass. And neither one heard anything Ron Austin may have said; just a pop – not even a loud explosion – followed by Austin hitting the floor. The pop sounded like a balloon bursting. They volunteered that Ron Austin had been performing a Vilsmeier reaction. The procedure was somewhat "dangerous" in that the reaction used potent chemicals and was quite exothermic. But they walked back their characterization of "dangerous," describing it much like a knife is dangerous in the wrong hands. Austin had been well-versed in performing the reaction even before he'd started working at PAYNE Pharmaceuticals the past week.

Buck Fowler grumbled at the use of jargon such as Vilsmeier and exothermic, but did pick up the fact that Austin had been assigned the job of doing a potentially risky reaction during his first week of working at PAYNE Pharmaceuticals. Red flags went up in Buck's mind as to whether Austin had had proper training to do the experiment . . . and whether, as it apparently seemed, the death of Ron Austin was just a tragic accident, one better suited to be investigated by OSHA than the local sheriff.

The last entry in Austin's laboratory notebook, though, puzzled Buck. Austin wrote: "Reaction going too fast. Temperature seems to-----------." The explosion apparently interrupted his writing as the ink trailed off into a wobbly line. The bottom of the notebook page was covered in blood.

Buck meandered from the laboratory to the office of a distraught Dr. Mason Turville. Turville's eyes were red, as if he'd been crying. Turville identified himself as the immediate supervisor of the research and development laboratory in which the accident happened. Buck continued to stand as he surveyed the office, immediately being drawn to the bust front center on the desk, a cake with candles next to the bust, the mobile with lots of different colored balls and sticks hanging from the ceiling, and a wall filled with framed pictures of frogs.

Trying to put Turville at ease, Buck pointed to the bust. "I don't recognize this guy."

"Nor should you," Turville said, softly. "He's Anton Vilsmeier. Even an organic chemist who knows the name probably doesn't know what he looks like."

"So, I would guess the Vilsmeier reaction, the one Ron Austin was doing, is named after him." Buck stared at the bust for a moment. Oddly, he realized there wasn't a picture of Turville's wife or family on the desk, the shelves, or walls – just this bust of Vilsmeier. He then glanced at the cake.

Turville read Buck's puzzled looks. "We were going to celebrate Vilsmeier's birthday today in the laboratory. It's an annual tradition."

Buck rolled his eyes.

Turville redirected him to the hanging mobile. "That's a molecular representation of the reaction. Somewhat complicated. But as you can probably surmise, you combine some smaller things into a big molecule."

"But is it also a dangerous reaction?"

"I'm not sure what went wrong," Turville groused. "The Vilsmeier reaction uses potentially nasty reagents. But, when performed according to the laboratory protocol, it's as safe as any other experiment. Ron had done the reaction many, many times without incident at Keaton College and Wisconsin. He'd done it perfectly as I watched over him here last week."

Buck walked to the wall of framed pictures. Turville followed. Buck pointed to one. "What's the fascination with frogs? Seems odd for a chemist." Buck's attention was drawn to the photograph of a frog looking like a blob of black, brown, and white. "Now that's one odd looking frog, as well."

Turville half-laughed. "Indeed, that frog is strange. It's commonly called the bird poop frog. It masquerades as a large pile of bird droppings so that snakes and other animals don't eat it."

"So why do you have pictures of not just this frog but also others?"

"Part of our research, here," Turville seemed to relax significantly. "Certain toxins from frogs might be the active ingredients in the next generation of pain medication."

"Are you serious?" Buck was momentarily fascinated – first Possum Lady texted him a few minutes ago, and now Frog Man in the flesh.

Turville drew Buck's attention to a picture of a large yellow-skinned frog. "This one's called the Brazilian Greening's Frog. You might see the small spikes on its head. It discourages predators with its venomous head butts. Its poison is 25 times as powerful as a pit viper's." He then pointed at another yellow, but more golden colored, frog. "And this one's the Columbian Poison Dart Frog. It carries enough venom to kill ten humans." Turville then described the three foot long, eight pound Goliath Frog from Cameroon, the Bat Frog, the Krokosua Squeaker Frog from Ghana, the Strawberry Poison Dart Frog from Central America, the Starry Dwarf Frog, and the Costa Rican Glass Frog, before Buck put a halt to the lecture. He shifted the interview back to the accident.

In order to explain why the sash on the fume hood was found slightly open, Turville could only surmise that Austin may have been trying to open the fume hood to stop the reaction just before the explosion. "He should've left it closed," Turville groaned. "It was a fatal mistake."

The temperature was being controlled at 3°C, a little above the freezing point of water. That was also the temperature that the technicians had seen blinking on the temperature controller when they'd pulled the electrical plugs to the instrument. So, Austin's entry in his notebook didn't make any sense to Turville, as Austin was running a duplicate of an experiment at the exact same temperature as the day before. There shouldn't have been any problems with the reaction and, in particular, with the temperature.

Buck also queried Turville about Austin performing a dangerous reaction when he had only started work at PAYNE Pharmaceuticals less than a week previous. Turville assured him that he'd spent the first couple days on safety protocols with Austin, and that Austin had been doing the Vilsmeier reaction for the last five years, dating back to Austin's undergraduate schooling at Keaton College.

Buck then closed up the laboratory after Austin's body was removed by the coroner's office. He told the remaining deputies and crime scene technicians to secure the laboratory until the state officials and federal OSHA inspectors had a chance to view the scene.

On his way out of PAYNE Pharmaceuticals, Buck stopped to talk to some workers he knew at the plant to get background information for his investigation. He heard the upsetting rumors that Turville had been cutting corners with respect to safety in his quest to push for the completion of the synthesis of a new pain-killing drug. But no one could supply specifics. In fact, the laboratory technician, Evalina Vail, who Ron Austin replaced, had quit supposedly because of concerns for her safety. The week before her resignation, she'd been seen crying and upset as she left Turville's office.

○ ● ○ ● ○

Buck, being a life-long resident of Millikan, knew almost everyone in Millikan and the surrounding county. He was a second grader in the Millikan school system when "Lum" Baumgartner was a senior many years ago. They rode the same school bus. Buck still remembered Lum as his savior that year when Lum protected him from a bus bully. They'd bump into each other periodically at the local diner. They were friendly but not friends. He knew Evalina was Lum's daughter – and often wished he was twenty years younger when he'd see her. On his drive back to the station, Buck called Lum to get Evalina's phone number. Lum coyly confirmed he'd heard the same rumors about safety concerns in the research lab, but Evalina had never shared those thoughts with him. In the next breath, though, Lum volunteered that Turville was a mean, arrogant, back-stabbing, womenizing low-life. He didn't blame Evalina for leaving Turville's laboratory.

Strangely, after Buck called Evalina, she claimed she resigned for personal reasons, in fact to explore changing her career from chemistry to music. She wasn't aware of any safety problems in Turville's laboratory in particular, or at PAYNE Pharmaceuticals in general. Buck deemed that Evalina was quite stand-offish about Turville but compassionate for what her other co-workers were going through. She was clearly quite upset, to the degree that their conversation halted intermittently because of her sobbing, that her replacement in the laboratory died in an accident. Under further questioning by Buck, Evalina repeated that her leaving upset from Turville's office the week before she quit was for personal reasons that had absolutely nothing to do with the laboratory or work at PAYNE Pharmaceuticals. She refused to elaborate further. Once Buck hung up, he wondered whether Evalina had been having an affair with Turville. Maybe, at least some monkeying around. Evalina was an extremely attractive woman. And Turville had been called a womanizer or skirt-chaser by others at PAYNE Pharmaceuticals.

OSHA inspectors arrived at the scene by late afternoon, started their interviews, and began their examination of the accident scene. They sealed their active probe site that night with large "DO NOT ENTER" signs, and yellow "ACTIVE ACCIDENT INVESTIGATION SITE" tape draped over the door frames of the laboratory. Nary a soul guarded the laboratory or the area during Lum's work shift that night. Lum readily entered the laboratory without disturbing the tape. If perchance someone happened by the laboratory, he'd profess ignorance. He needed to do his job, to empty the trash cans. Lum quickly and confidently strode over to the fume hood and turned the calibration screw on the temperature controller five complete revolutions back clockwise to undo his deed the previous night. He left the laboratory undetected. There were no security cameras in this section of the PAYNE Pharmaceuticals complex. Lum smiled. He'd performed the perfect sabotage on Turville's research program. Not only had he upended Turville's status in his profession, but he also did so anonymously without any personal credit.

Lum had exacted his revenge, like Simeon and Levi had done to Shechem, with God's blessing.

Chapter Fifteen
SUSPICIONS

A couple days later, Ida Kay convinced Lum to visit "his" baby possums at her animal rehabilitation facility. Lum had another reason for the visit. He wanted to pick up some pink geraniums to add to his patio garden. It was a mild, sunny day and he was in a good mood. OSHA investigators had absorbed most of Turville's time ever since the accident, and by all accounts, would do so for many more days. Turville's research had been stymied. The big boss, Jim Payne, Jr., wasn't happy with Turville, blaming him for the first deadly accident since the founding of PAYNE Pharmaceuticals. Evalina had also telephoned her father that morning. Except for feeling sorrow about the death in Turville's laboratory, she sounded upbeat and happy with exploring a new direction for her life.

Ida Kay sat in a lawn chair next to her driveway. Lum shook his head in amazement as he parked his truck. She wore a pair of pink crocs, polka-dotted socks, baggy orange shorts, torn multicolor-striped tee shirt, brilliant red bonnet, and aviator sun glasses – definitely not a trendsetter in fashion.

She shushed Lum, mouthed "Be Quiet," and motioned him over to her chair.

She watched a crow hop around her yard. It seemed to have something in its mouth. It would periodically flit in and around nearby bushes and trees. Everytime Lum tried to talk, Ida Kay shushed him. He smiled – It was the first time in his recent memory she'd been quiet for more than a minute. After about five minutes, a larger crow dive-bombed from its perch and chased the first away.

Once again, Lum tried to talk and got shushed. The second crow seemed to follow some of the path of the first. Finally, it cawed several times and angrily flew away.

Ida Kay giggled and stomped her feet. "Well, I'll be a monkey's uncle!"

Lum stared incredulously at her. "Have you lost your mind?"

"I did that a long time ago," Ida Kay laughed. "I'd read an article about crows and decided to do an experiment. Boy, are they clever!"

Lum looked at the yard, now void of either crow. "Clever? They both flew away."

"I put a peanut on the picnic table and waited. Poe, the first crow, came and picked it up. Moe, the other crow, was up in the big oak tree over there watching Poe." Ida Kay took off her bonnet and fanned herself for a moment. "Poe must've known he was being watched. He faked burying the peanut under the rhododendron bush, which was in clear sight of Moe. Then he actually buried it under a piece of scrap wood, but only after he was hidden from Moe's view. Moe chased Poe away and immediately went to the rhododendron bush to get the peanut. He appeared to be mad the nut wasn't there."

Lum laughed. "So that's how you spend your time?"

"Yep," she returned the laugh. "The author of the article said crows are smart – not only thinking for themselves, but also thinking about what other crows are thinking. Poe faked out Moe, feigning where he buried the peanut, then hiding it somewhere else. Supposedly, Poe will come back later and retrieve the peanut. He'll remember where."

"So you're instigating crows to play games like hide-and-seek," Lum kidded.

Ida Kay smiled from ear to ear. "Yep, just like you play this game where you hide your underlying affection for me."

Lum blushed and shuffled his feet. He turned away from the crow's playground. "Let's see how Dinah, Redford, Newman, and gang are doing."

The babies had more than doubled in size since he'd last seen them. All scurried about their cages when they saw Ida Kay, probably correlating her presence to food. All seemed healthy.

"Why do you do it?" Lum blurted.

"What do you mean?" Ida Kay was caught off guard. "Do what?"

"Rehab critters like possums – give 'em a second chance. Critters most people don't give a care about. They call 'em varmints and pests."

"Every one of God's creatures deserves a chance at life." She smiled. "After all, one of these possums might be your superior in your next –"

The door to the possum nursery squeaked open. A pretty woman in her late twenties peeked into the room. She was petite with long brown hair. Her outfit was dark brown, matching the color of her hair. She was the polar opposite of Ida Kay in terms of fashion sense. Lum noticed, though, she seemed to have sad eyes. Ida Kay introduced her as Sara Austin.

"Ida Kay was so nice to reach out to me. She offered me her apartment rent free and bought my plane ticket." Sara tried to smile as she combed through her straight hair with a hand. "She took care of me while I took care of my husband's affairs these past few days."

"I didn't know he had a wife," Lum struggled to whisper. His knees felt like they were going to buckle and his head swirled.

Ida Kay needed to drive Sara to Charleston to catch her plane back to Wisconsin. She told Lum to pick out some geraniums in the greenhouse. He could pay later.

○ ● ○ ● ○

Upon Ida Kay's return from the airport, Buck Fowler was waiting in an unmarked car in her driveway. Both Buck and "Toad" Crabbler jumped out of the car. Buck briskly strode over to greet Ida Kay, while Toad shuffled along behind him.

"Toad appreciates you giving him yet another chance," Buck smirked. "The judge was going to send him back to jail unless someone gave him a roof to live under."

Toad looked at his feet. He sheepishly mumbled, "Thanks, Ms. Hall. I promise I'll behave myself this time."

Ida Kay sent him onto the apartment. But first he had to listen to Ida Kay lecture him on the house rules again. Then, he had to promise to work from sun-up to sun-down in her greenhouses, the animal houses, fields, and gardens. Ida Kay told him she'd keep him so tired from working he wouldn't even think about straying back to the bottle. For tonight, he could heat up one or two microwavable dinners from the freezer. She'd meet him in the possum nursery in an hour to show him the feeding routine.

Buck also thanked Ida Kay for taking care of Sara Austin while she was in Millikan. It was a difficult situation for her. She grew up in West Virginia, albeit on the other side of the state, and married Ron their last year at Keaton College. They'd been planning to start a family after she followed him to Millikan. She had stayed behind in Wisconsin to pack their belongings. All that changed; her life had been upended.

Buck shook his head. "It was a tragic accident. Ron Austin definitely had bad luck that day. The odds of that glass shard shooting through the small opening in the lab hood and hitting him perfectly in the caratoid artery was probably something like one in a billion. No one has yet figured out what caused the flask to explode."

"So no one was to blame," Ida Kay bemoaned. "Sara said he had no life insurance. And PAYNE had hired him so fast, he hadn't completed all the paperwork to be formally employed. PAYNE says he was still a Wisconsin student, and Wisconsin says he was a PAYNE employee. Sara fears it'll be a legal quagmire. The lawyers may end up with some money, but she isn't expecting any. He was the love of her life."

Buck shared that he still had some loose ends to tie up in his investigation. He should have paid more attention in his chemistry class years ago. The cause of the accident was probably due to some quirk of the reaction's chemistry.

“I hope you pin the accident on that scumbag Turville,” Ida Kay grumbled.

“Didn’t even know you knew Dr. Mason Turville,” Buck chuckled.

Ida Kay groused, “It’s a long and crazy story.”

“Well, if you’re in it, it has to be crazy,” Buck teased. He told her he was still on the county’s timeclock, to talk away.

And she did. About four years ago, Jim Payne, Jr., went into Dr. Mason Turville’s office and saw a new addition. Turville had hung pictures of frogs on one wall. Jim told Turville about the rare “West Virginia Barking Swamp Frog,” a reclusive frog known to exude a toxin potent enough to kill a dozen rattlesnakes. And that the frog had recently been found in a location just outside Millikan.

“I never heard of such a critter,” Buck frowned.

Ida Kay laughed, “It’s about as real as Big Foot or Sasquatch . . . or going snipe hunting in the dark of the night. Jim knew Turville was captivated by poisonous frogs. He just made-up the tale, and told it flippantly to jerk Turville’s chain.”

“But Turville believed him?” Buck chuckled.

“Yep,” Ida Kay continued. “Turville was gullible. He fell for it hook, line, and sinker. Jim told him that this mountain woman by the name of Ida Kay Hall knew where to find the frogs. That she had caught a few. And that the frogs only came out at night.”

“I see,” Buck howled. ”So you took him on a wild goose chase.”

“Jim gave me a couple hundred dollars to have fun with him. We sloshed around the mud at Maple Swamp under the light of the moon and flashlights for quite a while, following the barking sound of the frog.”

“I guess you had someone holding a dog nearby, probably over on Bryant’s Ridge,” Buck interjected dryly.

“Of course, but Turville turned the tables,” Ida Kay snarled. “It became clear after a half hour that Turville had lost interest in tracking the frog. Instead, he got all grabby-like and propositioned me. What a jerk!”

"If I had to put my money on you or Turville in the woods, I'd put it on you."

"Let's just say I made Turville quickly change his mind," Ida Kay scowled. "I hear it didn't stop him from chasing women, though."

○ ● ○ ● ○

The OSHA preliminary statement, released several weeks after Ron Austin's death, corroborated Buck Fowler's suspicion of an unfortunate accident. The coroner's report confirmed he died by a glass shard rupturing and severing his caratoid artery. And, despite many attempts to prove otherwise, the OSHA officials simply could not find evidence of lax safety procedures at the PAYNE Pharmaceuticals research and development laboratory. There seemed to be no problems. The lab technicians routinely discussed safety updates with Turville. In fact, Ron Austin in his brief time at the laboratory had already instituted a new safety practice. He placed "Safe Operation Cards" on the fume hoods. These note cards communicated who was running the reaction, what reaction was being run, the chemicals involved, the conditions, and associated hazards; in essence, repeating what was in Austin's laboratory notebook for all to quickly see.

In a perusal of Austin's lab notebook, the OSHA officials labeled it every investigator's and administrator's dream. He clearly identified adequate safety training in his notebook, plainly noting the warnings about the Vilsmeier reaction and his experience in performing Vilsmeier reactions. He also discussed his training in laboratory protocols, and had been supervised by Turville in running the Vilsmeier reaction. He had completed a couple Vilsmeier reactions without any problems under the watchful eyes of Dr. Turville before doing the explosive one solo. All the chemicals and their concentrations were correct; and the apparatus, in particular the temperature controller, seemed to be operating as it should. The temperature was indeed set at 3°C, the target temperature displayed when the controller was plugged into the electrical outlet. The calibration, though, did seem to be off by a fraction of a degree. Such would've been of no consequence. Thus, it appeared to the OSHA inspectors there were no safety deficiencies in the laboratory, and that the most likely cause of the explosion was operator error. Perhaps Ron Austin simply mixed the chemicals in the wrong order or the wrong amounts, even though his notebook recorded otherwise.

The OSHA inspectors suspected that Austin made the fateful mistake of opening the laboratory fume hood's sash in order to correct that unknown mistake. It was indeed a mystery. Nevertheless, OSHA slapped Turville's laboratory with several weeks of mandatory safety training, followed by administrative safety forms to complete weekly for the next year.

Lum had a wide grin on his face when he heard through the rumor mill of these OSHA actions to bury Turville with paperwork.

○ ● ○ ● ○

The PAYNE Pharmaceuticals research and development laboratory had been cleaned and the lab technicians back at work when Buck Fowler returned to the facilities to tie up some loose ends. He tended to obsess on certain details of every investigation. He thought of himself as a hound dog honing in on the scent of relevant clues. It was like a sixth sense on his part. Although his boss, the sheriff, and even the district attorney told him to report the death of Ron Austin as the accident it was, two main things kept haunting him about the case.

The first was Ron Austin's last written words before the explosion. Austin seemed to express concern about the temperature of the reaction. Buck even traveled to Keaton College to interview a Vilsmeier expert, Dr. Quinn Stanton, who he'd identified from the common undergraduate background of Evalina Vail and Ron Austin. Dr. Stanton, or as Buck later learned Q-Dawg, had taught Evalina and Ron to run Vilsmeier reactions and had complete confidence in their abilities. Q-Dawg claimed they were two of his finest students he had the privilege of teaching in his career. Buck spent a whole afternoon learning the finer points of Vilsmeier reactions, the potential for problems if protocol wasn't followed, and in particular that the reaction generated lots of heat. Temperature control was a key component in doing the Vilsmeier safely. Q-Dawg willingly volunteered to do anything necessary in helping Buck with the case.

The second concern of Buck was the reason why Evalina quit her position in Turville's laboratory and whether it had any connection to the death of Ron Austin. Buck was prone to say to his colleagues in the police department when they complained of his obsession to certain details: "My daddy always said it was better to do it right than do it fast!"

Buck, in his inspection of the temperature controller for the synthesis workstation in Ron Austin's lab hood, couldn't find anything even remotely amiss with the instrument. But he was far from the expert. Nothing of any consequence was obtained by Buck's follow-up interview with Turville about temperature problems. At Buck's suggestion, Turville readily agreed to have Buck contract with Dr. Quinn Stanton to perform a Vilsmeier reaction in the hood using the same stock chemicals, temperature controller, and synthesis workstation that Ron Austin had used in his fatal reaction. The only piece of equipment that needed to be replaced was the round-bottomed glass flask whose side had blown out. Turville even offered to use PAYNE Pharmaceuticals' funds to pay Dr. Stanton to perform this duplicate Vilsmeier reaction, as such would confirm all was okay (and aid in jump-starting Turville's research into anodynol synthesis once again). Buck indicated that the sheriff's office would allocate funds to pay Dr. Stanton's expenses. Such would avoid any appearance of improprieties. The openness of Turville to allow the test, though, showed he didn't seem to have anything to hide. Q-Dawg solved the dilemma; he'd do the experiment at no charge.

Turville was much more reticent to tell Buck about the nature of the conversation he had with Evalina the week before she left the employ of PAYNE. He shrugged his shoulders. "I just can't tell you. It was confidential."

Buck rephrased the question. Same answer. Buck tried again. Same answer.

Buck studied Turville's body movements. Turville kept squirming in his seat, kept his arms in constant movement – clearly uncomfortable.

Buck slowly and deliberately crossed his legs. He calmly asked, "Were you having an affair with Evalina?"

"No," Turville replied emphatically.

They sat in silence for probably a minute. Turville had been taken aback. He seemed to be in deep thought.

Turville sighed, then confided, "I asked Evalina about her relationship with Reverend Adam Clarke, the preacher at Goose Creek Lutheran Church. I'm the chair of the church council there."

Buck's eyes opened wide.

"I'd been quietly investigating accusations of sexual misconduct by the pastor," Turville continued. "Pam, the pastor's wife, had told me she 'knew' her husband was having an affair for quite a while with Evalina . . . and that he'd asked her for a divorce."

"I, of course, will keep this information confidential," Buck nodded

"An accusation of a sexual affair between a pastor and one of his parishioners is particularly disturbing." Turville closed his eyes. His squirming had calmed, but only slightly. "Such is not only morally frowned upon but also *de facto* sexual harassment. I asked Evalina about it in my office that day as a church matter, not as a work matter." He took a deep breath. "Evalina exploded on me, said it was none of my 'blankety-blank' business, and stomped out of my office crying. Within a few days Evalina told me she would be leaving to explore other career choices. She had appreciated the opportunity to work under my supervision in her wonderful time at PAYNE Pharmaceuticals."

"So, she never did answer your question," Buck prodded.

Turville grimaced. "The next day, confronted by the church council, Reverend Clarke confessed his affair with Evalina and promptly resigned to try to keep his reputation as a pastor somewhat intact. Evidently, the two had been in love for several years, dating back to her college years. Maybe, even before. I then picked up Reverend Clarke's resignation letter personally on a Saturday. He left town at the same time as Evalina."

Although intriguing and scandalous, Buck wondered what this would have to do, if anything, with Ron Austin's accident. Buck also fretted. He'd heard no rumors of this affair. Usually, he heard everything. Evalina and her pastor certainly knew how to keep their love for each other a secret. He questioned Evalina's choice of a lover. Whereas Buck would have rated Evalina a definite "11" on a 1 to 10 scale of beauty, he'd give Reverend Clarke only a "5," and even that was generous, on the same scale for handsomeness. And the pastor was more than ten years her senior.

○ ● ○ ● ○

The next week, Dr. Quinn Stanton arrived at PAYNE Pharmaceuticals to perform a Vilsmeier reaction on center stage. When Dr. Stanton entered Dr. Turville's office for introductions, the eyes of Q-Dawg were drawn like lasers to the bust of Vilsmeier on the desk. Turville commented that while Q-Dawg wasn't the first to admire the bronze bust, he was the first to recognize the bust as that of Vilsmeier. Meanwhile, Buck Fowler failed to comprehend why anyone would want, much less show pride, in having or seeing a bust of Vilsmeier – "Crazy scientists!" That the Vilsmeier bust was a gift to Dr. Turville from Evalina led to small-talk among the men about her fascination with the Vilsmeier reaction.

While Buck Fowler watched intently, Q-Dawg duplicated the fatal Vilsmeier reaction while he gave full explanations at each step. Buck directed that under no conditions would the sash for the fume hood be raised during the reaction. The reaction went smooth as silk, with absolutely no problems. In particular, Q-Dawg encountered no problems with the temperature or the control of the temperature at the synthesis workstation. Turville was elated. He could now resume his research program and his push for the synthesis of anodynol. On the other hand, such didn't help Buck Fowler in his quest for answers in what went wrong during Ron Austin's deadly attempt running his Vilsmeier reaction.

Buck shared with Dr. Stanton his obsession with Ron Austin's last written words that something was amiss with the temperature.

"Well, detective," Dr. Stanton responded. "There might be a way to tell the exact temperature during Austin's experiment. I still use ice-water or similar baths to control the temperature of the Vilsmeier reactions in my lab at Keaton. But this limits my ability to vary the reaction temperature." His blue eyes lit up. "I've recently received a grant to upgrade my apparatus to use the new-fangled, and quite expensive, temperature-controlled synthesis workstations, like here at PAYNE. They'll give me more flexibility in my syntheses. Just last week at a conference and exposition, I met with a salesperson for these workstations. Her sales pitch showed me many of the features of the instrument. I now remember one in particular, and I wondered at the time why I would ever need the feature. The instrument recorded a chronology of the temperatures controlled by the instrument."

Buck tried to keep from yawning.

Dr. Stanton smiled, realizing he was losing Buck in his technical explanation. "If I attach the instrument to a computer, I can download the actual temperature profiles as a function of time. Much like a history of phone calls can be downloaded from a smart phone, the history of temperatures controlled can be likewise downloaded on the computer."

Buck's eyes now sparkled with interest.

"The instrument retains in its memory what temperatures were used and what changes were imposed – with a time stamp when any change was made," Dr. Stanton said.

"Can you do it?" Buck excitedly asked.

The Q-Dawg hooked up his laptop computer to the temperature controller of the synthesis workstation. For the most part, the computer showed nothing out-of-the-ordinary.

Suddenly, Q-Dawg exclaimed, "Wow, here it is! At 2:05 am on the morning of 12 June, the temperature calibration was increased by 54.1°C. Then at 3:16 am on the morning of 13 June, the calibration was lowered by 53.3°C."

Evidently, the five revolutions that Lum assumed would be 5°C were closer to 50°C.

"What does that mean?" Buck rubbed his chin, trying to concentrate.

"Ron Austin must've thought that he was operating the reaction at 3°C, but he was actually running the Vilsmeier at about 57°C. That's just a crazy-high temperature for a Vilsmeier. You have to cool the reaction, not heat it. The controller was telling him it was three degrees, but it was lying to him since it was way, way out of calibration. At 57°C, no wonder the reaction spiralled out of control," Dr. Stanton gasped.

"So the words after 'the temperature' that Ron Austin must've been getting ready to write were 'too high,'" Buck concluded.

The Q-Dawg nodded.

Within a matter of a couple minutes, Buck's probe of this accident took a dramatic turn. Someone must've intentionally changed the temperature calibration, then covered his or her tracks by returning it close to its original setting. Several key questions now bombarded him. Who tampered with the temperature controller? Who covered his or her tracks? Who had opportunity in the wee hours of the morning? Who had a motive to kill Ron Austin; he'd only been ay PAYNE for less than a week? Was the accident a murder?

Buck snickered – If Ida Kay had a vote, she'd pin it on Turville. But what would be his reason for booby-trapping his own laboratory, to stop his own research in its tracks? He, too, had only known Ron Austin for a week.

His snicker turned into a grumble. PAYNE Pharmaceuticals didn't just have lax security at its plant, it had essentially none. No cameras in any labs or buildings, none at doorways, none even at the parking lot. Its one security guard, old man Galen Rigney, only worked the day shift and was known to have his eyes closed much of the time. Sometimes he closed the gate to the parking lot at five o'clock, but most times not. And the gate was never locked. The unofficial night watchman at PAYNE was Lum. Buck knew it was time to pay him another visit.

Chapter Sixteen
REVELATIONS

At the same time Q-Dawg uncovered the sabotage of Ron Austin's Vilsmeier reaction, Lum had just awakened. After his night shift, he usually slept until about two in the afternoon. Sleep had been fitful. He'd been having nightmares, always centered about Sara Austin's sad eyes. The guilt was overwhelming – him being the cause of her being a widow. Prayers didn't help. He retreated to Dinah's story in Genesis 34. He found only momentary relief. Simeon and Levi in their revenge on Shechem and his men would've also left many widows in their wake. He doubted Simeon and Levi felt any remorse. They, as well as he, were doing God's will. His rationalization, though, did little to comfort his conscience.

Lum took a peanut butter sandwich and a coke to his patio. He sat near the planting of pink carnations and tried to force Sara Austin from his mind. Possum had joined him, sunning himself at his feet. Today started as a replay of the past few weeks. He sat alone brooding for hours at a time on the patio.

"It's Turville's fault," Lum bellyached to Possum. "He, not I, did it to Sara."

Possum yawned, stretching his front legs.

"That's right," Lum thought out loud. "I need to be thinking of my next revenge on Turville." Lum considered loosening some pipes in the restroom above Turville's office at PAYNE, creating a water leak. Turville would be greeted with a flood in his office when he showed up for work. Papers, documents, books, and computer files would be ruined.

But thoughts of Sara Austin quickly returned. Just yesterday he'd visited Ida Kay to try to escape those piercingly sad eyes. Ida Kay had been watching her crows again – the escapades of Poe and Moe had expanded to stories about Joe, Woe, Row, and Go. Ida Kay surmised, "Crows know what they know and can even ponder the contents of their own mind." Poe, by far, was the smartest. He quickly adapted to rule changes in her games. As she changed the box color containing a peanut from red to blue, Poe then changed likewise his behavior. Poe also used a hooked stick to reach peanuts she'd hidden under stones. Because "Toad" Crabbler had been doing many of her chores, she had more time for her crow experiments on problem-solving. A dragonfly flew by. She told Lum they're one of the fastest insects, zipping along at speeds over 50 miles per hour. And did he know that the intricate patterns of veins on their wings are like human fingerprints. No two are the same. Then, she spoke of the cuttlefish, a sea-borne mollusk that can also "think" much like a crow. If they knew they'll have a dinner of their favorite food, shrimp, they'll eat less for lunch to save room.

Lum and Ida Kay strolled to the possum nursery where the rescue possums were growing like weeds. These had been joined by two other baby possum families the previous week. Afterwards, the two startled Stuart, her free-range possum living under one of her sheds. He fell on its side and stayed motionless, playing possum, for ten minutes.

"Hey, Lum," Ida Kay spouted. "Have you ever heard of an olm?"

"Nope, but I'm sure you're gonna tell me," Lum chuckled.

"An olm plays possum much better than possums. They're small, cave dwelling salamanders in Europe." She elbowed Lum in his ribs. "One stayed motionless for seven years."

Lum shook his head. He thought to himself: "Who's crazier? This woman . . . or whoever watched this salamander for seven years?"

Ida Kay laughed at Lum's feigned disbelief. She teased, "Is that how long I'm gonna have to wait for you to make your move on me?"

Lum blushed. He changed the subject, telling her of his disillusionment with Pastor Barney and the ruling church council at Goose Creek Lutheran Church. She couldn't understand his need to attend church. She communicated with God by taking walks through the woods adjacent to her property. She felt His love through the sounds, smells, and sight of nature; that's the peace God showed her.

"And when I want to hear a sermon on Sunday morning," she confided, "I turn the television to the Holy Trinity Network and listen to the televangelist Danny Einstein."

"Never heard of him." He laughed, "Any relation to Albert?"

○ ● ○ ● ○

Lum was still sitting on his patio later that afternoon when he was visited by Buck Fowler. It had been over a month since the death of Ron Austin. Possum was still stretched out next to Lum. His sandwich was only half-eaten, his coke warm. Lum was surprised that Buck hadn't closed his investigation into Ron Austin's accident.

Buck queried him whether he saw any suspicious activity, or any visitors, at PAYNE Pharamaceuticals in the early morning hours of June 12 and June 13 – that is, the night before and the night after Ron Austin's death. Lum quickly indicated that he didn't remember anyone or anything out of the ordinary those nights.

Lum tore off some bits of his sandwich and tossed them in front of Possum. The cat batted them around a bit before nibbling. The discussion strayed to some small talk about the hot, humid weather. Possum pounced onto Buck's lap, swatting at his pen, wanting some attention. Buck kept moving his pen, allowing Possum to be entertained by this novel toy.

"Oh, I just remembered," Lum interjected. "There was something on the night before Ron Austin's accident. A tractor trailer delivering boxes of vials was backing up to the loading dock. He hit a storage tank – claimed he slid on the wet blacktop.

You might remember there'd been a 'toad strangler' thundstorm that night. So everything was still wet – and foggy. But slid, I don't think so."

"Why not?" Buck leaned in to hear the story.

"Beer. You could smell it on the driver's breath."

"Did you report it?"

"No. It didn't take too long to get the trailer straightened out. It only dented the storage tank support poles. So no harm, no foul, and his company paid for the damages." Lum smiled. "He was sober when he left, unloaded him re-eeeee-al slow and loaded him up with coffee."

Lum wondered why Buck would be interested in that time frame. He thought the police had concluded Ron Austin's death was an accident.

Buck readily volunteered that someone sabatoged the temperature controller for Ron Austin's Vilsmeier synthesis workstation the night before the accident, then returned it to normal the night afterwards. Someone fiddled intentionally with the calibration control so that the higher temperature resulted in an out-of-control Vilsmeier reaction, leading to the explosion, and ultimately to the death of Ron Austin.

Buck noted that, although Lum responded with an unemotional poker face as if he didn't understand these details, his color seemed to betray his true feelings. His face turned white, as if the blood seemed to drain from it.

Once his wits returned, Lum gulped, "Ya think the truck accident might've been a diversion for someone to fiddle with the controller?"

Possum jumped back off Buck's lap, having lost interest in the pen.

"What can you tell me about Evalina and Reverend Clarke?" Buck asked.

"Whatcha wanna know?" Lum scowled. "Don't know what you're asking?"

"What can you tell me about their love affair?" Buck casually followed up.

Lum just stared at Buck, wide-eyed and open-mouthed.

Buck noted this time Lum started to tremble and then, without saying a word, became physically ill. Lum quickly excused himself and ran inside to the bathroom. Buck readily picked up the distinct smell of vomit when he let himself inside the house. Upon Lum's return from the bathroom, Buck somewhat sarcastically said, "Obviously, you weren't aware of that!" Buck tried to comfort the visibly shaken Lum, but without much success.

A few minutes of awkward silence followed. Lum stared off in the distance in a zombie-like trance. He kept mumbling, "God lied to me! God lied to me! God lied to me! God lied to me!"

Thinking that Lum refused to accept that his daughter not only had an affair with but also ran off with her pastor, Buck showed himself out of Lum's house. Lum continued in his dumbfounded state.

○ ● ○ ● ○

Buck returned to pondering who monkeyed with the temperature controller of the synthesis workstation and why. Lum's lead on the tractor trailer driver was a dead end. No one ever saw him leave the loading dock area or even go inside any of the buildings. Evidently, if no one came in or out of PAYNE Pharmaceuticals those nights, the tampering must have been an inside job. But if so, what could Ron Austin have done in one week to cause someone to sabotage his equipment? And furthermore, Lum definitely reacted weirdly to the information that Buck had advanced. Lum hadn't even been on Buck's radar screen. Lum disliked Turville. But he hadn't even met Ron Austin. The only thread connecting Lum to Ron Austin's accident, or now killing, was Evalina, Lum's daughter, as the employee that Ron Austin replaced. Buck readily surmised that Lum had the opportunity, but definitely not the expertise, to tamper with the temperature controller. He could easily do so without being detected on his night shift, but had no apparent motive. Buck snarled at himself – too late to fingerprint the controller, everyone and his brother had touched the device since it'd been fiddled with.

○ ● ○ ● ○

About an hour later, Lum thought about whether to call in sick for his shift that night. His stomach was still mighty queasy. His mind was spinning a mile-a-minute with a pounding headache from the revelations sprung on him by detective Fowler. Lum was disturbed – "What have I done?"

The front door opened. No one had knocked.

Lum heard the gleeful sounds of Evalina coming down the hallway. He turned to face not only Evalina, but Evalina hand-in-hand with Pastor Adam Clarke. Both effused joy and happiness. Lum responded only by uncontrolled crying with his face in his hands. The first time since his wife Partie died. His crying was fortunate, because such forced him to keep from saying things he may have regretted later, especially in his current confused state. Both Evalina and Pastor Clarke were pretty much oblivious to Lum's state of mind. They interpreted Lum's crying as expressions of his uncontrolled happiness to see them. Lum remembered Evalina giving him a hug and several kisses on his cheek. Pastor Clarke shook his hand passionately as if two good friends had been reunited after a long separation.

Evalina proudly announced to her father that Adam had legally separated from his wife, and that she and Adam planned to marry as soon as his divorce was finalized, probably in the next few months. Pastor Clarke did interject he should have asked Lum for his daughter's hand in marriage before Evalina revealed their plans; but Lum likely realized that what Evalina wanted, Evalina would get anyhow. Furthermore, Evalina confessed that Adam had gotten into lots of trouble with the ruling bishop because of Turville's report that they had been having an affair while he was still pastor at Goose Creek Lutheran Church. Evalina now claimed this accusation was no longer of any concern. They had lived together at Aunt Melody's for the past month. And they had enough money saved for their living expenses for another.

"Daddy, we had it all planned," Evalina's voice spewed excitement and delight. "Adam and I are going to be Christian singers."

Lum nodded, still wiping tears from his eyes. He forced a smile.

"We'd intended to go from church to church as a duo called "Adam and Evalina," or maybe "Adam and Eve-alina." Evalina giggled. Her future husband joined in. "And to live off free-will offerings collected at each place."

Lum remained in a state of shock.

"But God intervened, and blessed us. He sent us in a slightly different direction." Although Lum thought it not possible, Evalina got even more excited. "It was a long shot, but we interviewed with the television evangelist and personality, the Reverend Danny Einstein of the Quantum Christian Church. He's affiliated with the HTN, the Holy Trinity Network. He needed lead singers for his worship services and telecasts. He hired us on the spot."

"Danny Einstein?" Lum mumbled, astounded at hearing this name so soon again.

Evalina continued, "You can't believe the money that Reverend Einstein is paying us for doing what both Adam and I love. And besides which, we will be working and living together, praising the Lord together, singing together." Evalina bubbled on, "My God is an awesome God! He has blessed Adam and me with the start to a wonderful life in revealing the work of the Lord through our singing!"

Lum couldn't help but smile at Evalina's enthusiasm.

"Reverend Einstein was just so encouraging," Evalina professed. "He told us of a quote from Kurt Vonnegut – the author of the novels *Cat's Cradle* and *Slaughterhouse Five* among others. 'The only proof needed for the existence of God is music.' Music is a vital part of Pastor Einstein's ministry."

In her effervescent happiness, she hadn't given her father much of a chance to even say anything, much less her now fiancé Adam to contribute much. Lum, still in emotional shock, thought it interesting that Evalina had confided more to him in the past hour about her personal life than she had total for the several years previously.

Lum did call in to Human Resources at PAYNE Pharmaceuticals. He needed to take personal time off that night. He spent the evening treating the couple to dinner at a local restaurant in order to celebrate the betrothal of his daughter. Evalina effused happiness with the change in her life. Lum couldn't help but feel happiness also for her engagement, even though he felt deceived by her future husband and his prior pastor. But if it meant Evalina's happiness, he'd put his concerns and doubts about Pastor Clarke aside.

While Evalina and Adam spent the night at his house, Lum didn't even get a hint of sleep. He just stared at the ceiling. In his nightly prayers, he got no further than asking God, "Why had You lied to me? Why did You direct me to seek revenge on the wrong person? I killed an innocent person in the course of my revenge." Oddly, Lum felt little remorse for the death of Ron Austin, just felt spiritually drained because of his betrayal by God. Lum simply failed to cope with his belief that God had led him astray.

The joyful couple left early the next morning for Dallas, Texas, to start work for Reverend Danny Einstein as part of his television evangelism.

○ ● ○ ● ○

A few weeks later, Buck Fowler re-interviewed Lum, albeit without success, to see whether he could make a connection between Lum and Ron Austin. Buck fully identified bad blood between Lum and Turville. But he also recognized that Lum knew Austin, and not Turville, would perform the Vilsmeier reaction that fateful day. Coworkers of Lum told Buck that he was mechanically minded, even being able to fix sophisticated machinery. But would Lum even know the role of the calibration screw on the lab's temperature controller? Lum admitted to knowing his daughter routinely ran Vilsmeier reactions, but claimed he knew nothing of the reaction details. Buck slammed against the proverbial dead end in his investigation. Not being able to connect the dots in this case, Buck remembered the words of his daddy, when frustrated, who used to quip: "I'm so mad that it makes my butt want to chew tobacco, knowing full well it can't spit!"

Chapter Seventeen
QUANTUM CHRISTIAN CHURCH

Danny Millikan earned his bachelor's degree in quantum physics at MIT. Four years later, he became The Reverend Doctor Danny Einstein by receiving a doctor of divinity degree from Liberty University. At first glance, the degrees might seem to be in disparate fields. The pastor, though, often preached that he dedicated himself to the infinite, spanning the range from the infinitely tiny world of quantum to the infinitely large universe of God.

When in divinity school and already dreaming of the Quantum Christian Church, Danny legally changed his surname from Millikan to Einstein. This name change allowed Reverend Einstein to introduce himself as the Einstein, Danny not Albert, of Christianity. Even at this age, the future Reverend Einstein possessed visions of *grandeur*, comparing his eventual importance in the theological world to that of Albert in the scientific world. While the genius of Albert Einstein is indelibly linked to his General Theory of Relativity, Danny Einstein declared he'd formulate the analogous Spiritual Theory of Relativity. In fact, busts of Albert Einstein with his trademark unkempt hair and of the Reverend Danny Einstein with his military style crew-cut stood on pedestals side by side in the vestibule of the Quantum Christian Church. Both greeted churchgoers with enticing smiles.

Interestingly, the Einstein and Millikan names were linked in other ways. Although Albert Einstein garnered his fame from his Theory of Relativity, he actually won his Nobel Prize for explaining the "photoelectric effect" through quantum equations. Millikan was the surname of Robert Millikan, another pioneer of quantum physics. He experimentally proved the equations Albert Einstein developed for the "photoelectric effect," but received his Nobel Prize for determining the charge carried by an electron.

It was quite ironic, then, that Danny felt the need to change his name. He ascertained, though, that Einstein was more associated with one of great intellect by the populace than was Millikan.

Danny Einstein brought to fruition his dream of delivering the Word of God and the Message of the Holy Trinity at his own megachurch. Now, in the prime of his life, Reverend Einstein preached to a live congregation of about seven thousand each Sunday in his Quantum Christian Church. Its chapel was a renovated city coliseum. It boasted a previous life hosting everything from rock concerts to professional basketball. Einstein's megachurch complex, which also included recording studios and recreational facilities, encompassed several city blocks within suburban Dallas, Texas. The Quantum Christian Church averaged a growth rate of about ten percent each year since its founding by Reverend Einstein almost two decades previous. In addition, Danny Einstein was instrumental, and in fact the major stockholder, in the formation of the Holy Trinity Network (HTN) which broadcast Christian messages as church worship services and Bible studies in one-hour blocks 24/7. These televised activities spanned the range from traditional to modern. Quite conveniently, the offices and studios of the HTN were located adjacent to the Quantum Christian Church complex. Worldwide viewership of the Sunday morning service of the Quantum Christian Church included several million people, and growing. It appealed to a wide range of people, from a scientifically astute audience to followers of Billy Graham.

Reverend Danny Einstein was a charismatic pastor and evangelist, stirring his packed house of seven thousand congregants every Sunday morning into a religious fervor and clamoring for ever more spiritual growth. He also led Tuesday and Thursday night services at his church. He acquired a loyal following of viewers, as well as donors, in the three HTN live broadcasts and numerous re-runs each week.

○ ● ○ ● ○

Lum's curiosity about Pastor Einstein had been stimulated by Einstein's employment of his daughter and soon-to-be son-in-law. Lum decided to watch Pastor Einstein on television, instead of attending Goose Creek Lutheran Church, the next Sunday. Ida Kay had invited him to her house. He agreed after she assured him such was not a date. Besides which, Toad would be viewing with them, as one of the conditions of his rehabilitation living in her apartment. She prepared a breakfast of cheese omelets and fruit salad for all before the telecast.

Toad grabbed the recliner in Ida Kay's living room, forcing Lum to sit on the couch with Ida Kay. Instead of sitting at the opposite end of the couch from Lum, Ida Kay wiggled into the center to be next to him. They watched the one-hour show, "Quantum Theory and Quantum Christianity," broadcast each week before the live worship service. Pastor Danny Einstein explained the quantum mechanical foundation of his church.

"Before quantum physics," Pastor Einstein started the program. "Waves were waves, and particles were particles. For example, a radio wave was distinct from a billiard ball. That's common sense." Accordingly, the mathematical equations to describe the behavior of waves are different from those for particles. But quantum mechanics overturned all of that. In the quantum world, wave and particle are just words. The distinction between the two blurs. Not only can an atomic sized particle sometimes behave as a particle, and sometimes as a wave, but as both simultaneously. This amazing premise of wave-particle duality never failed to fascinate Pastor Einstein. That is, depending on one's perspective, mathematical equations describe an electron as a particle (an invisibly small billiard ball), or a wave (in a sense, a spirit), or as both simultaneously. In the same sense, light behaves as a wave but can also be described as being composed of particles. "We can extend these quantum concepts to the realm of Christian thought," Pastor Einstein argued. "Is it no less crazy to consider Jesus as human, God-like, or both simultaneously – from a wave-particle duality to a human-divine duality? And is it any less crazy to expand upon this concept to God as the Father, the Son, and the Holy Spirit – at times separate and at time the same, the Holy Trinity? Who's crazier – the scientist or the Christian theologian?"

Analogous to quantum physics operating on an infinitely-small atomic scale, Pastor Einstein envisioned Quantum Christianity functioning on an infinitely-large spiritual scale. He read the following verses –

> *John 1: 14a, 18*
>
> The Word became flesh and made his dwelling among us. … No one has ever seen God, but God the only begotten [Jesus Christ], who is at the Father's side, has made Him known.

to illustrate this atom-spirit correspondence. Pastor Einstein interpreted, "An atomic-sized bit can vacillate back and forth being a wave and a particle. God's Word, or spirit, can likewise be described as flesh, or matter." The concept is the same. Something non-tangible and non-observable, like a wave in quantum mechanics or a spirit in Christianity, manifests itself as a real thing. The pastor claimed, in these verses from the gospel of John, the Bible summarized the basis of Quantum Christianity.

"Scientists have recently photographed light waves. The proof of the pudding, so to speak, is in the picture," he preached. "The picture showed the light being made up of particles called photons, as well as being a wave and particles simultaneously. We now have direct evidence for the fundamental paradoxical nature of the world governed by quantum physics. God is Light. Likewise, the Father, the Son, and the Holy Spirit describe different manifestations of God blurring into one in the spiritual world."

The bizarre events in quantum physics don't end with wave-particle duality. Not only can an atomic particle be two things at the same time, but also that wave-particle might be in two places at the same time. Imagine you have a tiny ball. This one ball sits on your finger tip and also on your shoulder. Can you conceive of this one ball being at two places at the same time? Physicists have already demonstrated this effect for 10,000 rubidium atoms being a half meter apart at the same time. Pastor Einstein posed the rhetorical question: "Is it not a stretch then for God to be omnipresent, at all places at all times, in the parallel spiritual world?"

Quantum strangeness abounds. Particles at the atomic level can tunnel through barriers without leaving a tunnel hole as evidence of its passage. Pastor Einstein spoke of the biblical passage –

> *John 20: 26*
>
> A week later his [Jesus'] disciples were in the house again, and Thomas was with them. Though the doors were locked, Jesus came and stood among them and said, "Peace be with you!"

Once again, he proposed, "Is it any more bizarre to imagine Jesus walking through a wall at the spiritual level?"

Similarly, scientists have used this same tunneling phenomenon to be the source of adaptive mutations (evolution at the molecular level) in DNA, in which a hydrogen atom tunnels to the wrong side of its hydrogen bond in the DNA spiral helix. Or, as Pastor Einstein would offer, maybe God directed evolution with quantum jumps (plants to fish to birds to animals to man) at the macroscopic level through these quantum happenings at the molecular level. Scripture readings show –

> *Genesis 1:1*
>
> In the beginning God created the heavens and the earth.
>
> *Genesis 1: 11-13, 20-23, 24-31*
>
> Then God said, "Let the land produce vegetation: seed-bearing plants and trees on the land that bear fruit with seed in it, according to their various kinds."

> And it was so. The land produced vegetation: plants bearing seed according to their kinds and trees bearing fruit with seed in its according to their kinds. And God saw that it was good. And there was evening, and there was morning – the third day.
>
> . . . And God said, "Let the water teem with living creatures, and let birds fly above the earth across the expanse of the sky." So God created the great creatures of the sea and every living and moving thing with which water teems, according to their kinds, and every winged bird according to its kind. And God saw that it was good. . . . And there was evening, and there was morning – the fifth day.
>
> And God said, "Let the land produce living creatures according to their kinds: livestock, creatures that move along the ground, and wild animals, each according to its kind." And it was so. God made the wild animals, according to their kinds, the livestock according to their kinds, and all the creatures that move along the ground according to their kinds. And God saw it was good.
>
> Then God said, "Let us make man in our image, ..." And it was so, God saw all that he had made, and it was very good. And there was evening, and there was morning – the sixth day.

God recorded these quantum jumps as days in His biblical record. The recent discovery of the Higgs boson, often labeled the God particle, identified a particle considered a key building block of the universe. This fundamental particle is crucial in showing how other particles acquire mass, or by analogy to the spiritual realm how God might have created matter and created substance out of nothingness.

"But there's even more similarities," Reverend Einstein proclaimed. He strutted about the stage.

Yet another example of wacky behavior in the quantum world, two particles are connected, or entangled, in some fashion, no matter how far (even light years) apart they are. This connection allows two or more particles separated by vast distances to behave as a single entity. Pastor Einstein stated, "One could likewise consider God always entangled with each individual. He knows every hair on each of our heads."

Einstein blended quantum theory into his brand of fundamental Christianity not to detract but to enhance belief in the Holy Trinity and biblical teachings. Anyone struggling to choose between science and faith would be relieved to hear that it's possible to embrace both. Agnostic or atheist scientists, who professed disbelief in the impossibilities within the biblical record and Christian thought, astounded Pastor Einstein when they then fully embraced the even more inexplicable happenings in quantum physics. These scientists hid behind the correctness of the mathematical formulas of quantum physics without questioning its strange results.

"Perhaps," Pastor Einstein summarized, "Quantum theory is fundamental to the properties of molecules as well as to the presence of the Holy Trinity!" He claimed the culmination of this science explained both the physical world and the spiritual world. "Particles or waves at the atomic scale are virtually invisible. You can't see them, but only describe them as images, or as parables, or by mathematical equations. Similarly, phenomena at the infinitely large scale are inconceivably immense. You can't see them, but only describe them as spiritual happenings. I am well on my way to developing the mathematical equations for the spiritual world as my namesake did for the physical world."

He took a deep breath and spread his arms in the air. "The great quantum physicist Niels Bohr once said, 'The opposite of a great truth may well be another profound truth.' A great truth of scientists is quantum theory. The profound truth, the opposite in terms of scale, is Quantum Christianity."

The show flipped to Pastor Einstein telling his televised audience how and where to send donations to the Quantum Christian Church ministries. Ida Kay turned down the volume.

Lum looked at her. "My mind is blown!"

"I think every time I watch this introductory hour," Ida Kay giggled, "I learn a little bit more about both science and Christianity."

"I don't think I understood but a fraction of what I just heard," Lum scratched his head. "It does seem to make some sense."

Toad interjected, "Makes as much sense as the gobblygook a lot of pastors spout."

"Ain't that the truth," Ida Kay and Lum replied in concert.

Ida Kay rushed to the kitchen to get drink refills for all as they waited for the worship service to begin. Once resettled on the couch, she chuckled. "Pastor Einstein's sermon last week dealt with George Carlin's premise of 'The Big Electron.' You might remember him as the comedian famous for his 'Seven Dirty Words You Can't Say on Television.'"

"George Carlin – are you serious?" Lum appeared puzzled.

"Yep," Ida Kay replied. "Evidently, George Carlin said 'The Big Electron' is a higher order of wisdom that mere mortals would never understand. This Big Electron just is! He also described 'The Big Electron' as a force, sort of like threads of fate, interconnecting the lives of family members. The pastor compared this to quantum entanglement at the atomic level, as well as God, the great 'I am,' being entangled in our lives."

Toad laughed. "And he didn't say any of the seven dirty words."

○ ● ○ ● ○

Pastor Einstein's Sunday morning service of the Quantum Christian Church was billed as "The Holy Event" on HTN and had the highest ratings of any show on the network. "The Holy Event" opened with a scene showing the two side-by-side busts of Albert Einstein and Danny Einstein as the cameraman entered the sanctuary. The picture frame momentarilly froze at the captions underneath each bust: "Theory of Relativity in Physics" and "Theory of Relativity in Christianity," respectively. It started as a formal worship service. Pastor Einstein stood in the front of the cavernous sanctuary. He smiled and stated, "In the Quantum Christian Church, we profess fundamental Christian truths. We embrace the existence of the Holy Trinity, Jesus Christ dying to save all from their sins, and the presence of God's steadfast love and grace. What do we believe?"

The congregation recited the Apostle's Creed –

> I believe in God, the Father Almighty,
> maker of heaven and earth:
> And in Jesus Christ, His only Son, our Lord,
> who was conceived by the Holy Spirit,
> born of the virgin Mary,
> suffered under Pontius Pilate,
> was crucified, died, and was buried.
> He descended into hell.
> On the third day He rose again from the dead.
> He ascended into heaven,
> and sits at the right hand of God the Father Almighty.
> From thence He will come to judge
> the living and the dead.
> I believe in the Holy Spirit,
> the holy Christian Church,
> the communion of saints,
> the forgiveness of sins,
> the resurrection of the body,
> and the life everlasting. Amen.

The service continued with prayers, Scripture readings, songs, and liturgies. Lum found it extremely inspirational in the traditional sense.

Pastor Einstein jumped into his sermon. He described a particular incidence of quantum strangeness. Scientists envision a cat trapped with a deadly radioactive atom, with a 50-50 chance of decay, in a closed box. This cat, called Schrödinger's cat after the originator of the thought experiment, has a 50-50 chance of being alive or, in other words, a 50-50 chance of being dead. Theoretically – according to the mathematical equations – the cat is both alive and dead at the same time. Pastor Einstein's namesake Albert imagined an unstable keg of gunpowder, instead of a cat, in the box for the same bit of weirdness. After a while, the gunpowder would be both exploded and unexploded simultaneously. But until the box is opened, we don't know the fate of the cat or the gunpowder. The cat is in the superposition of both dead and alive states. Common sense might dictate such an observation as not real. Werner Heisenberg, a quantum physicist called it "in the middle between an idea of a thing and a real thing."

The pastor asked whether a person could likewise be dead and alive at the same, and read from the Scripture –

> *John 11: 32-35, 41-44*
>
> When Mary reached the place where Jesus was and saw him, she fell at his feet and said, "Lord, if you had been here, my brother [Lazarus] would not have died.
>
> When Jesus saw her weeping, and the Jews who had come along with her also weeping, he was deeply moved in spirit and troubled. "Where have you laid him?" he asked.
>
> "Come and see, Lord," they replied.
>
> Jesus wept.
>
> . . . So they took away the stone. Then Jesus looked up and said, "Father, I thank you that you have heard me. I know that you always hear me, but I said this for the benefit of the people standing here, that they may believe that you sent me."
>
> When he had said this, Jesus called in a loud voice, "Lazarus, come out!" The dead man came out, his hands and feet wrapped with strips of linen, and a cloth around his face.

Pastor Einstein pondered out loud: "Could not Lazarus also have been in the netherland of alive and dead before Jesus raised him from the dead?" An accepted happening in quantum physics is a miracle for Jesus.

"Let me now follow this up with the resurrection of Jesus from the dead," he continued. "Jesus could have been in this same simultaneously dead and alive state in the time period between his resurrection and his ascension to Heaven."

Luke 24: 1-7, 50-51

> On the first day of the week, very early in the morning, the women . . . went to the tomb. They found the stone rolled away from the tomb, but when they entered they did not find the body of the Lord Jesus. While they were wondering about this, suddenly two men in clothes that gleamed like lightning stood beside them. . . . the men said, "Why do you look for the living among the dead? He is not here; he has risen! . . ."
>
> . . . When he [Jesus] had led them [his Disciples] out to the vicinity of Bethany, he lifted up his hands and blessed them. While he was blessing them, he left them and was taken up into heaven.

Once complex quantum systems have interacted, they are forever entwined, no matter how far apart. This could be a particle with a wave, a body with a spirit, or a human with a God. Albert Einstein called such, "Spooky action at a distance."

Pastor Einstein laughed. "God uses His same equations to describe our interactions with Him as He does to model atoms. Amen."

"The Holy Event" then concluded each week with the "Pastor in a Box," a five minute segment in which Pastor Einstein faced off with someone who had a particular question or concern. Scientists in the congregation or in the television audience grinned at Reverend Einstein's playfulness. He named this part after the theoretical construct called the "particle in a box" in elementary quantum physics. The set-up for the "Pastor in a Box" consisted of two chairs on center stage with Reverend Einstein faced toward the congregation (and the cameras), while the person giving testimony faced away from the audience (and cameras). Such protected the identity of the member, so that he or she could provide his or her story anonymously, if so desired. The cameras did not reveal the identity of the person, because often times those persons were confessing to things that might upset their neighbors. Reverend Einstein's assistants sifted through the thousands of e-mail queries posted to the Quantum

Christian Church's web site each week, then sent the top five to Pastor Einstein for his final selection, in order to choose the person giving testimony, asking questions, or unloading concerns in this bit of "The Holy Event."

The person that went one-on-one with Pastor Einstein was often flown to Dallas from elsewhere in the country to have his spiritual problem or question resolved. What made the "Pastor in a Box" so attractive to the congregation and viewers was that it was clearly unscripted. Reverend Einstein met the questioner face-to-face live with no rehearsals. The spontaneity generated the belief, fueled by Pastor Einstein, that the Holy Spirit spoke through his words.

This week, Pastor Einstein sparred successfully with a well-known academic biochemist, Dr. Joyce Brower, who claimed "Jesus was NOT God" so "Christianity is a fraud."

He ended that day's service with an update on his development of mathematical equations to relate quantum mechanics, the infinitely small, to the Holy Trinity, the infinitely large. He would eventually be the one to give the mathematical proof of God.

Ida Kay clicked the television off.

Lum took a deep breath and tentatively spoke, "I never knew a cat could be both dead and alive at the same time in science. And yet atheist scientists think Christians are loco for believing Jesus is human and God at the same time."

Ida Kay invited Lum and Toad to stay for lunch. She had a roast in the oven. Toad quickly accepted. Lum looked off in space as though he hadn't heard a word of Ida Kay's.

○ ● ○ ● ○

When Ida Kay walked with Lum to his truck after lunch, she pointed to Poe watching from a nearby oak limb. Moe perched in a maple tree farher away.

"Your pet crows?" Lum kidded. "Must be waiting for their daily ration of peanuts."

"Probably are," laughed Ida Kay. She said Poe was the smartest crow of her bunch. He figured out how to drop stones in a water filled tube to bring a floating peanut to within reach of his beak. "Something even kids can't do until age seven."

"Wonder what Pastor Einstein would say about the intelligence of crows," Lum wondered out loud.

"Maybe relate to something weird in quantum physics," Ida Kay chuckled.

Lum scooted into the truck. Before he shut the door, Ida Kay caught him on the arm. She told him about the wrinkle-faced bats which live in the Costa Rican rain forest. The male bats have a flap of skin used as a mask with which they can cover their face. These bats convene at a spot in the forest where they hang upside down with their masks raised, sing ultrasonic tunes not audible to humans, and constantly rustle their wing tips. In this cluster of masked males, the female shops for the right one.

"At the dramatic moment, when the female chooses," Ida Kay smiled, "the selected male drops his mask." She paused, then grabbed Lum's hand. "Just wondering when you're gonna drop your mask?"

○ ● ○ ● ○

The Quantum Christian Church's future services – a mixture of worship, entertainment, and religious education – included the duo of "Adam and Evalina," or sometimes introduced by Reverend Einstein as just "Adam and Eve," the first couple of Christian music. And "Adam and Evalina" delivered; being for Reverend Einstein what George Beverly Shea was for Billy Graham. Adam Clarke and Evalina Vail sang beautiful music together, or at times separately as soloists, from the traditional hymns to more modern melodies to their original compositions. They walked the fine line of performing their songs as if they were the stars of the show, but yet uncannily being able to use their singing to direct attention to their employer and the real star Reverend Einstein. They used him as the focal point to glorify God and the Holy Trinity. Evalina, in a link to her previous career, liked to emphasize that "Adam and Evalina" developed a holy chemistry with Pastor Einstein. Furthermore, the pastor bestowed Evalina with adjectives such as angelic and beautifully innocent, and compared her singing to the purity and gentleness of fresh fallen snow.

Chapter Eighteen
ANODYNOL

Lum no longer planned any mischief as revenge against Turville. His mission was completed. He never acted on his plans to flood Turville's office.

But his faith in God was discombobulated. He listened to God's message through the words of Pastor Barney at Goose Creek Lutheran Church and through those of Pastor Danny Einstein from the Quantum Christian Church broadcasts. He couldn't understand why God had directed him to seek revenge on Turville for an affair in which Turville wasn't involved. He felt no remorse, though, for punishing Turville. But now the guilt in his role in killing Ron Austin and widowing Sara gnawed at his spiritual fabric.

To deaden this grief, Lum sat on his patio and downed a six pack of Bud Light upon returning home every morning from his night shift at PAYNE. That was the only way he could get some sleep. Ida Kay called him sullen and grumpy when they'd get together Sunday mornings for "The Holy Event." Only Evalina's singing would bring a smile to his face.

○ ● ○ ● ○

Dr. Mason Turville and PAYNE Pharmaceuticals wanted to jump-start their quest to synthesize anodynol. It had languished for several months. They needed more experimentation in the key Vilsmeier step for anodynol's synthesis. But Turville found it difficult to hire someone qualified as a bench chemist, especially after Ron Austin had met his demise in the course of running a Vilsmeier reaction.

Turville had become acquainted with Dr. Stanton when Q-Dawg assessed the Vilsmeier apparatus at the crime site. Subsequently, he and Q-Dawg developed a professional friendship. After discussing various options with Jim Payne, Jr., Turville made Q-Dawg an offer that couldn't be refused. PAYNE Pharmaceuticals contracted with Dr. Quinn Stanton to take a faculty development leave (a sabbatical) from Keaton College and work at PAYNE Pharmaceuticals for the spring semester and following summer. Q-Dawg would have the opportunity to delve into commercial applications of the Vilsmeier reaction as well as have a key role in the synthesis of perhaps a ground-breaking drug. The offer included him bringing his two senior research students along in a funded work-study program. The salary paid Q-Dawg was two times, plus a housing and living allowance, than he would make teaching at Keaton College. The students would be reimbursed a lucrative amount, all compliments of PAYNE Pharmaceuticals.

The game-changing part of the offer, sealing the deal, was that Dr. Quinn Stanton would get a $150,000 cash bonus if he completed the synthesis of anodynol within his sabbatical time period. This obvious incentive gave Q-Dawg and, accordingly, PAYNE Pharmaceuticals a concentrated push for the completion of the anodynol synthesis.

When Q-Dawg first arrived at PAYNE Pharmaceuticals to start work, he lamented that he felt like a traveling mercenary chemist. In response, Turville joked that as a Ph.D chemist Q-Dawg was replacing an M.S. chemist, who in turn had replaced a B.S. chemist – things were getting a lot more expensive for PAYNE Pharmaceuticals. Q-Dawg then returned the tease. He wanted Turville's bust of Vilsmeier for his own desk as part of his bonus after completing the anodynol synthesis.

The Mason Turville – Quinn Stanton collaboration was symbiotically productive. Their discussions about different options for conditions and reagents for the Vilsmeier and related reactions spurred novel directions for getting at the structure of their desired product, anodynol. Within a five month period, even better than Turville had imagined, Q-Dawg and his hard-working students had completed the manufacture of milligram amounts of anodynol, and were well on their way to scaling up the reactions for larger quantities of the drug. Of course, there was nothing like the promise of a monetary bonus to provide an added incentive. Q-Dawg worked around the clock. He kidded his students: "Sleep is for the weak!"

Characterization and identification of the synthesized substance confirmed it to be anodynol. Q-Dawg and his students ran high-field NMR (Nuclear Magnetic Resonance) spectra and GC/MS (Gas Chromatography – Mass Spectrometry) patterns for their product. These instruments provided the chemical "fingerprint" predicted from the known structure of anodynol. Slight discrepancies from the NMR and GC-MS of the product were evident when compared to the "fingerprints" published over 25 years ago for the naturally-extracted anodynol. But Turville agreed with Q-Dawg that such subtle differences would be expected on the basis of more modern instrumentation and the higher purity of their synthetic material. Besides which, calculations for the spectral peaks for the target molecular structure of anodynol gave the exact NMR spectrum and GC/MS pattern obtained for the synthetic anodynol.

Within the next month, Q-Dawg and his students completed the scale-up of their synthetic scheme to prepare gram quantities of anodynol, in anticipation of its commercial production. Rumors of the successful production of anodynol spread like wildfire throughout PAYNE Pharmaceuticals. Jim Payne, Jr., hailed both Q-Dawg and Turville as corporate heroes. Both of them, on the other hand, claimed Vilsmeier was the real hero. Further, PAYNE Pharmaceuticals decided to keep the synthesis as a trade secret instead of a patent; otherwise, competing companies would just tweak the patented procedure and call it different. The patent for the actual anodynol structure had long since expired.

Q-Dawg returned home to Keaton College a month early. He waited for his bonus check, once the identity of anodynol was independently confirmed. Through his hard work, he would win a "lottery" of cash. His wife already planned the purchase of a new house, for Q-Dawg's retirement from Keaton loomed in the near future.

○ ● ○ ● ○

Buck Fowler stopped by Turville's office and the PAYNE research and development laboratory several times, usually at least once or twice a month, under the guise of keeping Turville up-to-date on his investigation. At times, Buck wondered about Turville's involvement. Turville clearly had access to Ron Austin's Vilsmeier apparatus, but had no apparent motive. Buck nosed around to see whether he could garner a hint or a clue.

Despite initially thinking Turville was a respectable guy, Buck now, after more-and-more interactions with Turville, wanted to smack Turville's arrogant expression from his face. But all he collected was interesting, albeit apparently unconnected to his case, tidbits. Clearly, Q-Dawg and his students worked like Trojans, often late into the night. On the other hand, Turville stayed around his office late as well, but not to work. Buck determined Turville was having an affair with BettyJo Burks, the assistant human resource officer who always seemed to be in-and-out of Turville's office as well as worked late the same nights. She often left work at the same time as Turville. Buck wondered whether they left for their separate homes, or whether they simply met up for a quick liaison. BettyJo was half Turville's age. Buck chuckled to himself that it was hard to ascertain whose eye and body language telegraphed the romantic relationship more. And Turville wasn't even true to BettyJo, often having one-night stands. He wondered whether Turville had put the same moves on Evalina. Turville presented himself as a Christian, being a leader in the Goose Creek Lutheran community, but was clearly a hypocrite. Buck wondered how Turville's wife put up with his shenanigans.

Another oddity that Buck once observed on Turville's office desk was correspondence between him and the Quantum Christian Church. An exchange of letters between Turville and Reverend Danny Einstein sat on a rather large manila file labeled

"Quantum Proof of the Holy Trinity." Usually the file was stuffed in Turville's briefcase. This was definitely strange, but of no apparent relevance to the case. Buck thought – Just one more confusing thing after another, or as my daddy used to say: "Who cocked up this mess?" And, the more time Buck spent in Turville's office the more he despised that ugly-looking statue of Vilsmeier's head on Turville's desk.

○ ● ○ ● ○

Buck started to watch "The Holy Event" on HTN to find out about Pastor Danny Einstein. He was pleasantly surprised to see Evalina as well. He quickly pegged Danny Einstein to be as much a smug theologian as Mason Turville was a smug scientist. They were two of a kind.

Buck watched a rerun of an interview of Pastor Einstein after one of these "Holy Events." Most of the interview seemed to be scripted. The interviewer asked Pastor Einstein: "What's new?"

"Cee divided by lambda," Pastor Einstein quickly responded.

The interviewer feigned confusion.

"Oh, you meant 'N-E-W.' I thought you meant 'N-U,'" Pastor Einstein explained.

The interviewer still looked puzzled.

"The greek symbol 'N-U' (ν), the frequency of light, equals the speed of light, c, divided by its wavelength, lambda (λ)." Pastor Einstein smiled. "It's a fundamental equation in quantum."

Pastor Einstein thought his response to be cute. The interviewer likewise encouraged its cleverness to the viewing audience.

Buck just shook his head. As his daddy used to say: "Knowledge doesn't result from the exchange of ignorance."

Chapter Nineteen
JOY FOR PAYNE

Word of the synthesis of the next generation pain-relief drug spread quickly around the drug manufacturers. Major drug firms lined up to court PAYNE Pharmaceuticals for possible acquisition in order to gain access to anodynol. In particular, the buyout of PAYNE Pharmaceuticals by NuDRUG, one of the top drug manufacturers in the United States, seemed attractive. PAYNE Pharmaceuticals and NuDRUG entered into negotiations. NuDRUG eventually offered Jim Payne, Jr., over $1 billion to purchase PAYNE Pharmaceuticals, contingent on the following conditions: (1) the anodynol samples checked out to be the reported structure; that is, NuDRUG independently confirmed the reported NMR and GC/MS analyses, (2) the synthesis procedure, using the key Vilsmeier reaction step, currently kept as a trade secret by PAYNE Pharmaceuticals actually produced the target anodynol, and (3) the anodynol produced by this method was indeed bioactive in the management of chronic pain, as expected from previous studies of the anodynol extracted from the Peruvian Rainbow Frog. NuDRUG anticipated no problems in the eventual purchase. They assigned about fifty scientists to scale-up the gram-quantity synthesis of anodynol, as perfected by Turville and Q-Dawg, to commercial scale production. Meanwhile, a similar-sized team of scientists and physicians designed a clinical human trial study to show the effectiveness of this anodynol as prescription medication for chronic pain.

PAYNE Pharmaceuticals in their pilot scale facilities had already produced tablets of varying amounts of anodynol as the active ingredient for these trials by NuDRUG. Turville kept all of the anodynol drug supply in his office to coordinate their distribution to the NuDRUG personnel for their trials. Turville quipped to Jim Payne, Jr., that the tablets of the anodynol drugs were coincidentally the exact same size, shape, and color as the blood pressure medicine he took. However, whereas a bottle of his generic blood pressure medicine was only $25, a bottle of the anodynol was worth millions. In addition, Turville boasted repeatedly to Jim Payne, Jr., that the Vilsmeier step was the key to their anodynol fortunes. Although Jim Payne, Jr., initially had some doubts, Turville just knew that the Vilsmeier reaction would eventually work its magic. Jim retorted to Turville that Turville could use a portion of the millions of dollars that Turville would net in the sale of PAYNE (part of Turville's contract was he would become a minority stockholder in PAYNE Pharmaceuticals upon successful synthesis of anodynol) to pay homage to Vilsmeier by electroplating a gold coating on that ugly bronze statue of Vilsmeier. Meanwhile, Jim Payne, Jr., indicated he and his wife had already placed a down payment on their retirement mansion in Florida, in anticipation of living the remainder of their lives in luxury. He crowed that he would never again have to stomach Turville's rants about Vilsmeier reactions or to endure West Virginia winters.

Reality, though, set in on the workers at PAYNE. The wealth gained by PAYNE would only be for the top executives. The workers would not share in the bonanza. Rumors ran rampant. NuDRUG planned to close the plant at Millikan and move the production of anodynol and other PAYNE generics to one of their more centralized and modern facilities. They all would be out of jobs. Their enthusiasm for anodynol plummeted.

○ ● ○ ● ○

"Toad" Crabbler graduated from Ida Kay's apartment to a place of his own in Millikan. He'd stayed clean and had gotten a real job as a flagger for a road construction crew. Ida Kay's apartment, though, only remained empty for three days before Wilma "Winky" Warren moved in. She'd just been released from the county jail, serving several months for breaking and entering in an attempt to support her meth addiction. She hoped for a new beginning, only 25 years old and now clean from drugs, with Ida Kay. She arrived on the same day that a brood of orphaned baby rabbits arrived for their second chance at life.

The next day, Lum watched the Sunday morning service of the Quantum Christian Church in Ida Kay's living room along with Winky. Pastor Einstein's sermon dealt with the physical and spiritual radiance given off by Jesus. The pastor related this to the quantum basis for how things glow. Neither Lum nor Winky was impressed. Winky, though, was enamored with the joy radiated by Pastor Einstein's singer, Evalina. Lum smiled, but said nothing. He was preoccupied in his own thoughts.

During lunch of fried chicken and cole slaw, Ida Kay expanded on Pastor Einstein's sermon. She'd just read about the South American polka dot tree frog. Its translucent skin was speckled with dark dots. It appeared yellow in the daylight, but glowed, or fluoresced, a lime-green color in the moonlight. Such glowing, as mentioned by Pastor Einstein, was rare for terrestrial critters.

"You know, Lum," she giggled. "These polka dot frogs have an interesting courtship ritual. Competing males will wrestle and grapple for the attention of the female. During the fight, they give off high-pitched bleats described to be like the cry of a baby." She laughed, then continued, "You used to be on the high school wresting team, didn't you?"

She looked over at Lum, expecting his typical reaction, the rolling of his eyes. He didn't appear to be listening, just staring out into space. She was worried.

Chapter Twenty
DEATH BY VILSMEIER

Lum's mind was stuck. It kept replaying, "Why did God lie to me?" He still couldn't fathom his misfortune for seeking revenge on the wrong person, and killing an innocent person. "Why had God spoken and directed him to seek such revenge?" He tried to seek counsel with Pastor Barney, the interim minister of Goose Creek Lutheran Church, but just couldn't confide his spiritual problems to someone who looked more like a drifter than a pastor.

Lum did become a devoted follower of the telecasts of the Quantum Christian Church on HTN, wondering why Goose Creek couldn't recruit a pastor that communicated and presented himself like Reverend Einstein. But many times, he failed to follow Pastor Einstein's message, as his mind wandered to his own impasse. Of course, he beamed with pride every time Evalina performed on the telecast. She indeed sang as through she was a direct conduit to praise God.

Like Lum never advancing further than his query to God, Buck Fowler's investigation languished with no new leads as to who caused the death of Ron Austin as well as why he was killed. "Patience," Buck told himself: "My daddy would say, you get the chicken by hatching the egg, not by breaking it."

Evalina enjoyed her new-found life married to Adam. Just as well, she enjoyed singing, rather than working in the laboratory. For the first time in many a year, she did not celebrate Vilsmeier's birthday on June 12th.

○ ● ○ ● ○

NuDRUG had just entered into negotiations with PAYNE when Lum submitted "Why did God lie to me?" to Reverend Einstein's website for inclusion in his "Pastor in a Box" segment. He'd become desparate. Several weeks later, an assistant to Pastor Einstein called Lum to schedule his appearance in Quantum Christian Church's worship service the next week, along with arrangements for transportation and lodging. He was to fly into Dallas late Saturday afternoon for the service the next morning. And like Adam and Evalina's first visit together to his home in Millikan, he planned to surprise them. He would appear unannounced at Quantum Christian Church, and would visit Evalina, and her now husband Adam, for a few days thereafter.

The week before his appearance at Quantum Christian Church, Lum spent many a day sitting with his Bud Lights on the patio. He talked to the pink carnations and to Possum. The Saturday morning of his flight, he dropped by to see Ida Kay to tell her he wouldn't be able to watch Sunday morning service with her and Winky. He gave her a large manila envelope with instructions to open it Sunday afternoon. Ida Kay continued to worry about Lum. He'd look at her, but his eyes were focused elsewhere.

That same week, the local weekly newspaper serving the Millikan area published a story about the hometown girl and the locally-known pastor who were rapidly becoming famous as a singing duo on the national cable television network, HTN. Buck once again tuned in to the show that Sunday, thinking that perhaps such might spur his thoughts in the proper direction in trying to solve what happened to Ron Austin. He obsessed with the fact that Evalina must be the link that connected Turville and Austin.

Lum thought that the "Pastor in the Box" segment of "The Holy Event" would never arrive as he sat nervously by himself in a backstage room. Pastor Einstein's sermon seemed to drone on forever.

Pastor Einstein spoke about walking in the Light. As the basis for his message, he used the biblical passage –

> *1 John 1:5-7*
>
> This is the message we have heard from him and declare to you: God is light; in him there is no darkness at all. If we claim to have fellowship with him yet walk in darkness, we lie and do not live by the truth. But if we walk in the light, as he is the light, we have fellowship with one another, and the blood of Jesus, his Son, purifies us from all sin.

The pastor emphasized each individual needed to walk in the light with God, not in darkness with evil. He compared the darkness to the recent discovery of Vantablack, for Vertically-Aligned-NanoTube-Array Black. A multitude of carbon nano-tubes, all positioned in the same direction, made up this material. He had the congregation imagine billions upon billions of cardboard toilet paper tubes sitting next to each other, all positioned on their ends, and all molecular sized. Its darkness results from these tubes trapping all the light photons. All light is absorbed. This substance is blacker, or darker, than any other on the face of the Earth. In fact, it's so dark scientists can't even quantify its blackness. It confounds your eye so you can't even understand what you're seeing. You think you're looking into an abyss. You lose all sense of place and time walking in Vantablack space. Imagine painting a jail cell with Vantablack, it'd be like living in Hell on Earth. If you walk in darkness instead of Light, you'd lose all sense of your moral compass.

Lum prayed – he'd been walking in a Vantablack painted existence.

Finally, with Lum sitting with his back to the camera and the congregation, Pastor Einstein shook hands with him. After the pastor took his seat, he welcomed "our guest from Millikan, West Virginia." Subconsciously, Reverend Einstein wondered whether the superposition of his given surname and his guest's hometown might have biased his choice that week. He commented that the person giving testimony today was troubled by his belief that "God had lied to him." Pastor Einstein then encouraged Lum to provide the foundation for such thoughts.

Lum confessed, "I believed my daughter had been seduced by her older boss at work. God spoke to me. God directed me to read the passage in chapter 34 of Genesis in which Jacob's sons sought revenge not only on Shechem who had defiled Dinah, their sister, but also to gain revenge on Shechem's family and friends. But, for me, all went wrong."

From backstage, Evalina looked on in astonishment as she witnessed her father providing his testimony. After all, Lum's declaractions described events that related to her, his daughter. But her father's premise wasn't correct. She was confused.

Pastor Einstein quickly responded, "You have to be very careful that it is indeed God's voice and God's call that you're hearing. And that your convictions or perspective didn't prejudice you in thinking that it's God's voice."

"Without any bias," Lum argued. "I blindly opened the Bible to this story when I was seeking guidance from God. God must've been speaking to me."

"Neither God nor the Bible would lead you astray," Einstein said. "God and the Bible talked to you, but you only heard what you wanted to hear. You wanted revenge, and that's what you heard. But if you'd heard God talking in the last verses in Genesis 34, you would've realized that Jacob was upset, to say the least, with his two sons, Simeon and Levi, who had orchestrated the revenge and had killed the Shechemites. Jacob protested their murderous acts. Both God and Jacob were displeased with their vengeful anger. God did not lie to you! God was telling you NOT to seek revenge by violence, or you would end up like Simeon and Levi. Open your Bible to Genesis 49:5-7 when Jacob on his deathbed cursed Simeon and Levi with his blessings to all his sons –

> Simeon and Levi are brothers – their swords are weapons of violence. Let me not enter their council, let me not join their assembly, for they have killed

> men in their anger and hamstrung oxen as they pleased. Cursed be their anger, so fierce, and their fury, so cruel! I will scatter them in Jacob and disperse then in Israel.

Because of the wickedness of Simeon and Levi seeking revenge on Shechem, their tribes were scattered and deprived of their numbers in the future." Reverend Einstein then continued with a question, but one for which he expected no answer. "After all, did you also do as Simeon and Levi did, and did you seek revenge by use of the sword?"

Lum quickly responded, "No, I caused death by Vilsmeier!"

Reverend Einstein was not often taken aback with surprise, but surprise definitely hit him like a sledgehammer. He shrugged, then further queried, "What's a Vilsmeier? A gun, a knife, an explosive, a poison? It's safe to say neither I nor the audience is familiar with a Vilsmeier."

"It's the name for a chemical reaction," Lum calmly responded. "And to make matters worse, my daughter's boss wasn't the one who had defiled her. So God allowed me to seek revenge on the wrong person. In the course of my revenge, I accidentally killed another."

Reverend Einstein shook his head in disbelief. He reiterated, "Once again, you cannot cherry pick the Word of our Lord out of context. In actuality, you, not God, wanted you to seek revenge . . . and now you chose to mix good and evil. For as written in Isaiah 5:20 –

> Woe to those who call evil good and good evil, who put darkness for light and light for darkness, who put bitter for sweet and sweet for bitter.

This ties in with my sermon – walking in darkness instead of Light."

Lum held his head in his hands. He softly sobbed.

"You should seek forgiveness. And through prayer throw yourself at the mercy of God in pursuing his unrelenting grace." The television producer motioned for Reverend Einstein to wrap up the segment.

Lum bowed his head and whispered, "What have I done? God spoke to me, but I only heard what I wanted to hear. God didn't lie to me, but told me to do good --- and I did evil, thinking it was good. Please, Pastor Einstein, I plead for you to gain God's forgiveness on my behalf."

Pastor Einstein stood and spread his arms. "Personal prayer is your conduit to God. You need to ask forgiveness personally not only to God but also to all those to whom you did evil."

Suddenly, Lum felt at peace. He sensed spiritual renewal. He now realized that God had not lied to him. He wondered how he could have been so oblivious to his horrendous sin. He killed an innocent victim in his act of unjustified revenge. But, yet, he felt re-energized to determine how to right his wrongs.

As the stage lights darkened and the telecast cut to a preview of the next week's service, Reverend Einstein smiled at yet another successful "Pastor in the Box" episode.

Off stage, Evalina wept.

○ ● ○ ● ○

Back in Millikan, Buck and Ida Kay, as well as most of the viewers in the population of Millikan, recognized Lum, even without seeing his face.

All the pieces of the puzzle of Ron Austin's death by Vilsmeier fit into place in the mind of Buck Fowler. Over a year and a half had elapsed since Austin had been killed – and the motive of the killer had been based on a false premise. Buck managed only a sad smile in his chair as he stared at his television screen. Instead of him solving the crime, the crime solved itself as he sat in his chair. Buck thought that it ran counter to what his daddy always told him: "that the only critter that ever accomplished anything by just sitting was a hen."

Ida Kay, upon hearing Lum's confession, put her hand over her mouth and mumbled, "What has Lum done?" She stared at the envelope on her end table with tears in her eyes.

PART 3

MORE REVENGE

Chapter Twenty One
CONSEQUENCES

After the televised Sunday morning worship service of the Quantum Christian Church, Lum thanked Reverend Danny Einstein for explaining God's Word. God had not lied to him. Lum felt relief. He now no longer had to live with his own lie, walk in his own darkness. And he'd just confessed to a crime live on a telecast seen worldwide, one that he knew would find its way back to Buck Fowler in Millikan.

Lum knelt backstage in silent prayer. He apologized to God for misinterpreting His Holy Word and for falsely accusing Him of lying. He pled for forgiveness. Evalina rushed to her father. She held him in a tight hug for several minutes, softly sobbing. She realized, though, her father was not in touch with reality. He'd escaped into his peaceful religious dreamland.

Reverend Danny Einstein pranced off stage, proud as a peacock that Lum's confession would be a great public relations coup, boosting television ratings for that week and for subsequent re-runs.

○ ● ○ ● ○

Evalina continued to cry. Clashing thoughts short-circuited her mind. She was beyond upset. Her father had unintentionally killed Ron Austin. She was the catalyst for the events that led to the killing. Then, once she warmed to her father's motives, albeit misguided, in protecting her honor, even more guilt came crushing down upon her for that thought.

Evalina put herself in the position of the biblical Dinah. Questions abounded. Was Dinah, like her, a willing lover? Did Dinah's family misinterpret whether Shecham had indeed defiled her? What if Dinah, like her, willingly loved a man forbidden to her by her family and by society? Dinah's brothers protected Dinah's honor by killing other totally innocent victims, much like her father accidentally killed the blameless Ron Austin. Evalina felt some ownership in her father's downfall. She knew her father would be upset with her running away with their pastor. She'd intentionally avoided telling him the truth. If only she hadn't kept this romantic affair secret from her father, events wouldn't have spiraled out of control and led to a death. She imagined how Dinah must've felt several millennia ago when her actions led to the massacre of not only her lover-defiler but also many innocents.

Lum's son-in-law, Adam Clarke, acted more like a stunned animal than as one who was once Lum's minister and confidante. He avoided Lum. He tried, but failed, to comfort his wife. His concerns drifted to how Lum's confession would affect his relationship with Evalina and the Quantum Christian Church.

Lum immediately took responsibilities for his actions. Even before leaving the Quantum Christian Church, he called Buck Fowler. He promised to catch the next flight home from Dallas. Once there, he'd turn himself in to the Sheriff's Office in Millikan. Lum remained true to his word, as Buck fully expected.

○ ● ○ ● ○

Back in Millikan, Lum formally confessed to Buck Fowler, as he'd done on television with Reverend Einstein, and with all the details. Having been read his Miranda Rights and being offered legal representation didn't quell his talking. All that mattered to Lum was his spiritual renewal, not his legal well-being. He refused to quibble about his role in the death of Ron Austin. He didn't mean to do it, but it happened anyway. Lum admitted he did wrong, if not evil. The Sheriff arrested Lum on a charge of involuntary manslaughter.

Later, Lum's court-appointed lawyer admonished Lum for not keeping quiet.

Lum, though, simply responded, "I'm at peace with God. I'm in constant prayer and communication with Him."

The lawyer was frustrated, but sympathetic.

Lum pled guilty to the charge with sentencing by a judge at a later date. The magistrate declared Lum could remain free on minimal bail. Lum refused to post bail, or to accept offers from anyone else to do so. He wanted to start paying his penance.

○ ● ○ ● ○

Over the next few weeks, Evalina sank into depression. She blamed herself for her father's undoing, resulting in marital friction between her and Adam. Adam argued that Lum was the one who mixed good and evil. He failed to see events from his wife's, or Dinah's, perspective. In fact, Adam tended to place most of the blame on Turville – Turville was the underlying source of Lum's internal conflicts. Adam claimed Turville set the course of unfortunate events into action by forcing him from the pulpit of Goose Creek Lutheran Church. If Turville hadn't done so, Lum wouldn't have gone on his rampage. Evalina scolded Adam to think beyond his own nose and to consider how his own actions affected other people. The main point was not about what happened to Adam; it was about her father thinking he was gaining vengeance against one who he mistakenly thought defiled her. The same biblical analogies of Dinah, Shecham, and Jacob's family plagued her now as they had previously haunted her father.

Chapter Twenty Two
SARA AUSTIN

Sara Austin had a difficult time coping both emotionally and financially after her husband's death. She'd met Ron at Keaton College, but left before she graduated to marry him and move to Wisconsin. She had switched majors at Keaton from economics to psychology to history. She hoped to finish her undergraduate work at Wisconsin. With no degree and no real skills, she worked as a clerk at a convenience store to supplement her husband's graduate school stipend. After Ron's death, she moved back to West Virginia, taking residence in her old room at her parents' rental house. There she got a part-time job as a waitress at IHOP. Her parents had no money to spare. Her father lived off his disability check while her mother picked up odd jobs, mostly household cleaning. Sara's younger brother and sister still lived at home.

Sara continued to stew about PAYNE Pharmaceuticals in general, and Dr. Mason Turville in particular. They did nothing to help her. Upon the advice of the company's lawyer, both Jim Payne, Jr., and Turville professed numerous times that neither the company nor either of them was responsible for the death of her husband. They insisted they had no liability. They claimed her husband hadn't yet officially become a PAYNE employee at the time of the unfortunate accident. He hadn't completed all the employment paperwork. Sara blamed Turville personally for luring her husband from the safety of his graduate school education to work on the synthesis of his precious anodynol. And additionally, she criticized Turville for endangering her husband by having him perform hazardous Vilsmeier reactions. Lawyers declined to work on her behalf without the benefit of a large retainer. All asserted a lengthy legal battle with an iffy, at best, outcome.

Ida Kay Hall called Sara at least once a week to check on her. She sent money, albeit anonymously. Ida Kay also visited her a couple times to try to cheer her. But Sara was still grieving and struggling – she had little to no social life. She was just stuck spinning her wheels, not going anywhere. She never was very religious, and now even less so, questioning God why He took her husband from her. It was unfair to have their future together ripped away before they had barely gotten started.

○ ● ○ ● ○

Within the hour after Lum's televised confession, Ida Kay opened Lum's envelope left in her care. His note reiterated his confession. The second part of the note instructed Ida Kay to give Sara Austin the contents of the envelope. Her jaw dropped. Lum had known that Ida Kay had kept in contact with Sara. The two women had remained close after Sara had stayed in her apartment. Ida Kay tried calling Lum numerous times. No answer. No wonder Lum had been acting strange the last week or so. No wonder he didn't want to talk to her to explain himself. Her emotions ran amok – feeling anger for what Lum had done, yet sympathy and worry for the aftermath.

Ida Kay bundled up in a heavy coat and scarf. She hiked along a mountain loop trail adjacent to her property. The wind blew quite cold. She tried to cleanse her thoughts, to reach out to her God.

She called Sara later that Sunday afternoon, as had been directed by Lum. She explained the mystery of the circumstances surrounding her husband's death had been solved. The confession of the killer was broadcast nationally during the morning service of Reverend Danny Einstein's Quantum Christian Church. Even though names and specifics hadn't been announced, enough was said to determine the admission was for Ron's death. Sara would probably hear from Buck Fowler later.

"Lum Baumgartner, the maintenance supervisor at PAYNE, evidently sabotaged Ron's reaction," Ida Kay summarized. "You met him in the possum nursery just before I took you to the airport. He wanted to get back at Dr. Turville. He mistakenly thought Turville was having an affair with his daughter."

Sara only cried. She didn't say a word. Ida Kay tried to console her.

Sara finally whimpered, "So Ron wasn't even the target."

"Wrong person at the wrong time," Ida Kay sighed.

"Turville should've been the victim," Sara moaned.

"That's right. But even Lum's motive was wrong. Turville wasn't having an affair with his daughter."

Sara sobbed. She grabbed a handful of tissues and wiped her now red and swollen eyes. She took a deep breath. "The detective said the accident was freakish. Everything had to go perfectly wrong. He said what happened had a one in a billion chance of hitting and killing Ron." She paused, then sputtered, "Now . . . now you're telling me more things went wrong – from a wrong target to a wrong reason. It's . . . it's . . . almost like an . . . Anti-Miracle." Sara sobbed more.

"I don't know what got into Lum." Ida Kay uncharacteristically teared up. "His normally good heart went astray."

"I don't see how you can say he has a good heart," Sara shot back in a growl. "He killed Ron who was innocent on many levels."

"I guess revenge overtook his senses. I don't understand either."

Sara sobbed more. She became quiet after a few moments.

"Anyhow," Ida Kay exhaled. "Lum left a few things in a sealed envelope in my care for you. He left instructions for me to open the envelope this afternoon. The note for you said, 'I'd trade my life for Ron's if I could. I'm just so, so sorry. The only things I have in order to try to make things right are my wordly possessions. That's all I can do, other than praying."

"I don't understand?"

"Lum signed over to you the deed to his house in Millikan, the title to his truck, and his bank accounts."

"Are you sure?"

"The house is probably worth about $100,000, the truck is old but in good shape, and he has about $25,000 in the bank."

"I can't believe what's happening!"

"I also talked to Jim Jones, Jr., the owner of PAYNE Pharmaceuticals, this afternoon," Ida Kay calmly stated. "I told him you might be moving to Millikan. He said you could have a job with PAYNE. They have openings for an office worker, a production line worker, and a shipping clerk. Your choice. No interview needed; you'd be hired on the spot. Millikan is close enough to visit your parents on the weekends."

○ ● ○ ● ○

A week later, Lum's Ford Ranger pickup truck returned to the PAYNE Pharmaceuticals parking lot. This time it arrived for the day shift, and this time driven by Sara Austin starting her full-time job as shipping clerk.

It didn't take long for word to get back to Dr. Mason Turville to check out the new employee. The shipping supervisor relayed, "She's real cute." He paused, then added, "By the way, she's Ron Austin's widow."

Turville slid his wedding ring into his pocket and strolled down to the shipping bays.

○ ● ○ ● ○

Later that week, Ida Kay and Sara drove to the county jail. A light snow was falling. A cold front from the northwest dropped the temperature to well below freezing. The heater blew full blast in Ida Kay's Dodge Ram pickup.

Sara was in a good mood. Her training at PAYNE was going well. She told Ida Kay of meeting Mason Turville on her first day of work. He'd been able to quickly cool the anger Sara still harbored toward him. She rambled on about working at PAYNE, but clearly she'd been enamored by the charm of Turville.

"He invited me to attend his church, Goose Creek Lutheran Church," Sara related to Ida Kay. "He's quite handsome."

"He has quite a few years on you," Ida Kay snarled.

Sara smiled, "He wasn't wearing a wedding ring. Is –"

"He's married with two kids," Ida Kay spat out, without waiting for the question.

"He made me feel so special." Sara looked out the side window at the snow falling, lost in her thoughts.

"He's a snake. Stay clear of him!"

○ ● ○ ● ○

Lum wanted no visitors. But Ida Kay knew the jailer. He fetched a reticent Lum from his cell. The guard told Ida Kay to convince Lum to eat more. Lum had lost weight, which he couldn't afford to lose, since being in jail. He just wasn't eating enough.

Lum sat across a table in his orange jumpsuit, MCP #28364, looking sullen. He remained mute.

Sara softly sobbed.

Ida Kay told Lum of the recent arrivals at her sanctuary, an injured possum named Hilda and a chipmunk named Dale. Lum had no response. He stared at the wall behind the women. Ida Kay then spoke of the bootlace worm. It's the longest animal in the world. The worms look like normal worms except for their length. They can stretch over 150 yards, longer than a football field. They also make mucus that smells like sewage and can kill cockroaches.

Lum looked down at the table.

"And, by the way," Ida Kay added, "scientists have tried to feed these worms in the laboratory. Some worms won't eat. They may eat only once in three or four years." She paused, then asked, "Lum, are you trying to outdo these worms? You need to put some meat back on your bones."

Ida Kay succeeded in getting a smirk from Lum. He glanced up, but quickly looked back down when their eyes met.

Ida Kay then transitioned into a story about the northern quolls from Australia. They're polka dotted, furry marsupials, a bit bigger than squirrels. Females live for three to five years, but the males never make it past one year. The males grow up quickly. For most of that one year, they live a happy and healthy existence, munching lackadaisically on abundant food. All of a sudden, it's like an on-off switch. The males are programmed to find and mate with as many females as possible. They run, and run some more, and run long distances in a continual romantic frenzy. They stop thinking about food. Once they find a female, they mate – then it's off to the races again to find another. Two weeks after their mating switches have turned on, they've lost their hair and muscle mass. They can barely walk and have sores all over their bodies. Then they just keel over and die.

The guard told all that time was up.

Ida Kay, without acknowledging the guard, continued, "These male quolls live for only a single, short, intense breeding season. Lum, you need to eat. You look like a sexually exhausted quoll. But I know you're not chasing me around, unless in your dreams."

The guard shook his head and snickered at Ida Kay, as he helped Lum to his feet.

Lum looked fleetingly at Ida Kay and mouthed "crazy woman." She thought she heard him mumble "thank you for coming" under his breath.

Lum coughed, caught Sara's wet eyes, and teared up. "I wish I could undo the things I did. I'm just so, so very sorry."

Lum took several steps toward the exit door before Sara responded, "Possum is doing well. And Ida Kay has shown me where to plant the pink carnations this spring."

Chapter Twenty Three
BURNT TOAST

On the day of his sentencing, Lum repeated his confession, this time to the judge. Lum, once again, felt relief.

The judge turned to Buck Fowler, who was sitting in the front row of the courtroom, and reared back in his chair. "And it's my understanding, Mr. Fowler, that without Mr. Baumgartner's unsolicited admission you probably wouldn't have solved this case."

"That's correct, sir," Buck briskly responded.

The judge waited impatiently, squirming on his chair in front of the courtroom. He looked, once again, at Buck. "No tidbits of your father's philosophy today as to why you couldn't solve the case."

Buck smiled, then shrugged. "I've got nothing today."

"I'm still following the last piece of your daddy's wisdom you spouted here two months ago. 'You don't want to approach a bull from the front, a horse from the rear, and a fool from any direction.'" The judge grinned as a chorus of laughter emanated from the handful of people in the courtroom.

Lum, along with his lawyer, was still standing at the defense table. He said, "Sir, I was a fool for what I did. Instead of seeking revenge, I should have embraced forgiveness. In my devotions this morning, I read a quote from Josh Billings: 'There is no revenge so complete as forgiveness.'" Lum continued to ramble about how he believed he had God's support for now taking responsibility for his actions. Lum confided to the judge that he'd seen the image of Jesus Christ's face burned onto his piece of toast at breakfast, right after he read his devotions. He told the judge: "Obviously, God provided me a message of forgiveness and not revenge. Jesus Christ is not only the symbol but also the pathway to the forgiveness of man's sin. God's grace offers salvation in the next life. But, in this life, I'm willing to accept my punishment."

The judge rolled his eyes and questioned Lum's lawyer in a rhetorical stage whisper, "Why didn't you plead an insanity defense?" He turned to Lum and said, "Mr. Baugartner, that's quite enough."

Lum continued to go on about he, like Jacob's sons, needed to be punished for their misguided revenge. He killed Ron Austin as collateral damage in his ill-directed revenge, for the same reason as Simeon and Levi killed all the Shechemites.

The judge ordered Lum's lawyer to shut up his client. Although the judge said he appreciated Lum's candor, enough was enough. He pronounced Lum guilty as charged.

Evalina and Adam, as well as Dr. Mason Turville, all witnessed the court proceedings and Lum's sentencing. The county prosecutor called Turville to underscore the damages to PAYNE Pharmaceuticals as a result of Lum's mischief that evolved into manslaughter. Lum's defense attorney had Evalina argue for compassion in the sentencing of her father. Lum, on the other hand, wanted no mercy from the court, only from God. And, unbeknowst to all, Ida Kay had already talked to the judge who was a regular customer at her greenhouse – giving the judge her unsolicited advice as well as the facts about Lum's restitution to the victim's widow, and conveying Sara Austin's feelings.

The judge decreed that Lum should serve a two-year sentence in the county prison, followed by five years of supervised probation. Lum would get credit for time already served.

○ ● ○ ● ○

Afterwards, Evalina talked with her old boss in the hallway outside the courtroom. Turville comforted Evalina somewhat. He indicated that, although he had spats with Lum in the past, in his opinion Lum always had a good heart. Her father just got caught up in one misguided act. Then, Turville quickly changed the topic to brag to Evalina that PAYNE Pharmaceuticals had completed the synthesis of anodynol. While polishing his crown as the one who devised the synthesis, he also admitted to the secondary role of Q-Dawg, her Keaton College professor, in the optimization of the key Vilsmeier step. Evalina didn't have much response, as she remained in shock and sorrow for her father. Vilsmeier and anodynol were no longer of any consequence to her.

Reverend Clarke felt ignored as Turville and Evalina talked. Other than some forced small-talk between Turville and Adam, Adam still resented Turville and simply scoffed at him. Adam was sick of hearing about Vilsmeier. He continuously listened to stories of Evalina's past life as a chemist and her love of the power of the Vilsmeier reaction over many of their dinners, much like Lum had heard previously. Adam thought, "Blah, blah, blah, Vilsmeier, Vilsmeier, Vilsmeier, ..." Adam further sensed that Turville looked at him as though he was a fallen minister, not as the famous singing evangelist that he currently was at the Quantum Christian Church. He also suspected Turville was subtly flirting with his wife. He continued to blame Turville for the chain of events that had his wife in her current state of depression.

The conversation broke when Lum and his prison guard departed the courtroom. Tears seemed to flow from Evalina's eyes whenever she saw her father. She told her father that she and Adam would visit with him later in the day, and the next, before they had to return to their work at Quantum Christian Church. Lum, though, seemed aloof and oblivious to her, Adam, and Turville. At that moment he seemed focused on the meaning of God's morning communication to him, that is the profile of Jesus Christ burned onto his toast. As he hugged his daughter, Lum persisted with his obsession that such was a symbol of God's forgiveness of his sins. Lum further expressed to Evalina that God was pleased with his taking responsibility for his actions, and that all would be alright.

He looked at Evalina and stated, “God speaks in mysterious ways.”

Chapter Twenty Four
PAIN FOR PAYNE

Turville returned to his office at PAYNE Pharmaceuticals after Lum's courtroom sentencing. Jim Payne, Jr., was waiting for him with the bad news. NuDRUG delivered notice they cancelled their option to purchase PAYNE. NuDRUG provided extensive evidence that the anodynol made by Turville and Q-Dawg possessed absolutely no capacity to relieve pain in humans. Their scientists, though, did say that the anodynol provided by Turville seemed to have the same molecular structure as had been reported by the original researcher who'd isolated it from the Peruvian Rainbow Frog. Oddly, the synthetic molecular structure did not have the same pain-relieving properties, or bioactivity, as did the originally extracted anodynol. Instead, in about ninety percent of the test subjects, the anodynol manufactured by PAYNE had the effect of putting the subjects to sleep quite soundly for several hours. Initially, NuDRUG thought that this drug might then be salvageable as a prescription sleep aid, because it was relatively fast-acting, making the subjects drowsy about a quarter-hour after ingestion. The drug, on the other hand, had a nasty side-effect. Almost all the test subjects awoke with stomach cramps of unbelievably excruciating pain lasting about two hours. Paradoxically, the supposed miracle pill to relieve pain instead created even more pain for the patient.

NuDRUG offered a possible explanation – the molecular structure which the original researcher reported decades ago for his extracted anodynol must have been incorrect. Different structures for the synthetic anodynol and the natural anodynol were perhaps the root cause of the NMR spectra and GC/MS fingerprints being slightly different for PAYNE's synthetic anodynol versus the extracted natural anodynol from the Peruvian Rainbow Frog. There were a multitude of places in which the molecular structure might have been slightly askew, and yet imperceptible to the instruments used to characterize the structure.

NuDRUG cited two recent incidences, both known to Turville and other pharmaceutical chemists, in which analogous bouts of confusion reigned in the manufacture of specific drugs.

The first pertained to a patent for a drug that had potential to treat certain types of cancer. The initial discoverers misidentified the molecular structure for this drug, called TIC10, in its patent application. Another company realized the error and patented the correct molecular structure. Just a subtle change in the molecular structure had dramatic effects on the use of that compound as a drug. A long legal battle ensued. The company that patented the mis-assigned structure claimed that the structural mistake was irrelevant to its licensed patent.

In another case, zolpidem, better known as the sleep aid Ambien®, was structurally similar to other imidazo compounds which were promising antituberculosis agents. Chemists reassembled pieces of zolpidem into structural isomers, compounds with the same kinds and numbers of atoms but arranged differently. One of the resulting isomers did not have the ability to induce sleep but was shown to be ten thousand times better in combatting tuberculosis. In other words, the molecular structure had to be exact in order for the drug to operate as desired – whether as a sleep aid or as an anti-TB drug.

Quite simply in the case of anodynol, Frank Hofmann, the original researcher who extracted anodynol from the Peruvian Rainbow Frog, reported the wrong structure. Without samples from the presumably now-extinct frog, the place in the molecular structure of the synthetic anodynol needing modification would be impossible to predict.

Soon after this notification by NuDRUG, Turville sent Dr. Quinn Stanton, Q-Dawg, an e-mail stating the monetary bonus for developing the synthetic scheme for the manufacture of anodynol wouldn't be forthcoming. Turville reiterated that NuDRUG reported the anodynol they had made at PAYNE Pharmaceuticals was not the "real" anodynol.

And even before the end of the day, it was fair to say that every worker at PAYNE Pharmaceuticals and most residents of Millikan were keenly aware that the expected financial bonanza for PAYNE Pharmaceuticals had imploded. Most everyone also knew by the end of the day that the anodynol tablets caused pain instead of alleviated pain.

Chapter Twenty Five
TURVILLE'S REVOLVING DOOR

The morning after PAYNE Pharmaceuticals received notice from NuDRUG declining its buy-out option, Dr. Mason Turville's day started badly. He backed his Volvo SUV out of the garage for the short commute to PAYNE. He scraped its bumper on the garage door. The overcast sky was spitting snow, typical for a February day in West Virginia. He had hoped anodynol would've been his ticket away from this cold and dreary weather. The car then beeped wildly as he continued to back out the driveway. Turville looked into the rearview mirror and saw a white coating on the paved surface. He ignored the warning signal and promptly crushed his son's tricycle under the car.

Turville remembered it was two days before Valentine's Day. He hadn't gotten anything for the women in his life, neither wife Shelley nor mistress BettyJo nor potential girlfriends on his radar. His office appointments precluded doing any shopping at the Colebrook Mall. He'd just have to call Teleflora and have flowers delivered. Perhaps they'd not remember he did the same last year.

○ ● ○ ● ○

Sara Austin stood impatiently outside Turville's office door, waiting for his arrival at PAYNE. Belle, Turville's secretary, tried to engage her in some chatter about the weather, but she wasn't in the mood. Sara was dressed fetchingly in her yellow pullover sweater and tight jeans.

Turville smiled at the sight of Sara. "Good morning, Sweetie," he warmly greeted her, as he unlocked the door. He caught a whiff of her enchanting perfume, just a hint of lavender.

Sara didn't say a word, just scowled. She followed him inside the office, not closing the door or taking a seat.

He could sense her anger. Perhaps she wasn't as smitten with him as he thought. He tried to redirect her attention. He introduced her to the bust of Vilsmeier on his office desk.

She ignored his ramblings. Hands on her hips, she seethed, "I waited at Big John's Steakhouse for you last night. You were a no-show, same as at Boccacelli's Italian Restaurant a couple days ago."

"In case you haven't heard, yesterday was a bad day," he snarled.

"Something wrong with your phone," she flippantly responded. "Life goes on. That's what you told me when I started here at PAYNE. Don't you practice what you preach?" She stomped her foot for emphasis.

"This is the wrong place and time for this discussion," he stated as he opened his briefcase and plopped some papers on his desk.

"Just like Ron was at the wrong place at the wrong time." She kicked his desk, knocking the Vilsmeier bust on its side.

"A good chemist would've never opened that lab hood," he scoffed. "I thought your husband knew how to run a Vilsmeier. I was mistaken."

Sara picked up the Vilsmeier bust and feigned tossing it at Turville. Instead, she slammed it back down on his desk. As she left his office in a huff, she turned in the doorway and shouted, "You consider yourself a high-almighty Christian because you run Goose Creek Lutheran. But you're nothing but a fast-talking con man. I hope you go straight to Hell." She paused, glared at the bust, and snickered, "And I hope you meet Vilsmeier there!"

Turville took a deep breath, still picking up the lingering scent of Sara's perfume. He shrugged off the lost opportunity, mumbling to himself: "Cross one off my Valentine list."

Within minutes of Sara leaving, Jim Payne, Jr., stormed into Turville's office. Everyone up-and-down the hallway outside the office, despite the door being closed, clearly heard Jim Payne, Jr., screaming at Turville. The PAYNE Pharmaceuticals owner unmistakenly blamed Turville for convincing him to invest company time and money to support the synthesis of a wrong molecular structure. He wished he'd never heard of the Peruvian Rainbow Frog, anodynol, and the Vilsmeier reaction. He grabbed the bust of Vilsmeier from the desk, placed his hands around its neck, and mimicked strangling the life from Turville. Jim Payne, Jr., personally stood to lose many thousands of dollars he'd already invested in his Florida mansion and property, which he could now no longer afford.

Turville, in like fashion, yelled back at his boss. It wasn't his fault! It was just a case of mistaken identity. The fault should be placed on the idiot discoverer, Frank Hofmann, who originally extracted anodynol from the Peruvian Rainbow Frog. He'd misidentified the molecular structure that corresponded to the natural anodynol.

But Jim Payne, Jr., was beyond reason. As he stomped out Turville's door, he turned to see Vilsmeier's bust staring at him. As he slammed the door of Turville's office, he bellowed to Turville at the top of his lungs: "Screw you, and screw Vilsmeier!"

Turville waved his hand in disdain, then snickered and spoke to the empty doorway. "By the end of the day, I'll be on my way to a higher-paying position. You'll be stuck here with your loser company. Screw you!" He returned to the large stack of papers on his desk, organizing and reviewing the information on them.

A little while later, Pastor Barney Bennington softly and unexpectedly knocked on Turville's office door, which had been left cracked open.

Turville looked up from his papers. Nonchalantly, he said, "I'm busy. Make an appointment for some other day with my secretary."

"I'll make it quick," pooh-poohed the pastor, confidently approaching the desk. "You can't call a church council meeting and not include the pastor. It seems like you've been doing a lot of things behind my back."

"I run the church, not you," roared Turville. "If you don't like the way things are done at Goose Creek, just resign. Take a hike." He crumbled a piece of paper and tossed it in the trash can. "That's what I think of your sermons. I should start preaching."

Pastor Barney stared at the bust on the desk. Slowly, his red face returned to its natural hue. "You know, Mason," he calmly stated. "Perhaps you might want to consider resigning from church council instead. You don't set a good Christian example by not being true to Shelley."

Turville jumped from his chair and pointed his finger to the door. "Get out!"

Pastor Barney picked up Vilsmeier's bust and looked more closely at its profile. He slowly put it back down. "Definitely German, but not Martin Luther?" Just as slowly, he left the office.

Turville hollered, "Get out, and don't come back!"

Dr. Mason Turville walked out to his secretary. "No more visitors this morning. I have work I need to get done." He turned back to his office without seeing Belle nodding her head.

A half hour later, Ida Kay Hall arrived and was greeted by Belle. Ida Kay, still in her work clothes of insulated coveralls, looked at the closed door. Belle informed Ida Kay that her boss ordered "No visitors." She smiled, knowing the message would be ignored by Ida Kay.

Ida Kay stormed through the closed but unlocked office door without knocking.

Turville scowled at her. "Get out, before I call security to drag you out."

"I have just one thing to tell you," Ida Kay shouted. "Stop leading Sara on!"

Turville chuckled. "Sara WHO?" He slid his chair back from his desk. His chuckle evolved into a full belly laugh.

Ida Kay grabbed the first thing she saw on his desk, the bust of Vilsmeier. She snarled, "Drop Sara – or your night searching for the barking swamp frog will only be the second worst night of your miserable life."

Turville stopped laughing, as Ida Kay used both hands to lob the bust at him. Startled, Turville juggled Vilsmeier before stabilizing it on his lap.

Ida Kay strolled to the doorway. She turned to face a speechless Turville. “Be wary. I may be around the next corner. You never know when you’ll come face to face with that ugly piece of bronze.”

Belle gave a thumbs up as Ida Kay hurried past her desk.

Turville replaced Vilsmeier in its proper spot on the desk, then closed his office door. He held his head in his hands. It throbbed. He kicked at his chair. He’d left his blood pressure tablets at home.

○ ● ○ ● ○

Turville rested during the noon-time hour. He nibbled on the pimento cheese sandwich and potato chips that Shelley had packed for his lunch. He closed his eyes, taking a quick nap sitting up. His headache abated somewhat. Unfortunately, he left his office door open after returning from the restroom.

Dr. Quinn Stanton arrived unexpectedly. Q-Dawg rarely became upset at anything. But when someone reneged on paying him $150,000, such got his attention. He burst into Turville’s office. Q-Dawg complained vehemently that Turville was trying to scam him out of the money he’d honestly earned.

Turville snidely told Q-Dawg to read the bonus’ contract, in particular the small print stating the anodynol not only had to be the desired molecular structure but also had to be an effective pain medicine. Whereas the latter constraint was beyond Q-Dawg’s control, that condition made the bonus payment no longer binding.

Q-Dawg accused Turville of being without honor – of being a thief, stealing his time and effort. As he got up from his chair, he grabbed the bust of Vilsmeier. “At least I deserve this as just compensation for my work.”

Turville, though, was in no mood for petty quibbling. He sneered at Q-Dawg. “Put it back down. I never promised you Vilsmeier. You get nothing. Get out!”

Q-Dawg was clearly upset when, like Jim Payne, Jr., he thundered out of Turville's office and yelled, "May Vilsmeier stare at you over your desk. And may he curse you for the rest of your sorry life."

Soon after the departure of Q-Dawg, Evalina arrived for her 1:15 pm appointment. As usual, she looked stunningly enchanting, even though casually dressed. Turville had scheduled this meeting the previous day, when both were outside the courtroom. He claimed he wanted to show Evalina the synthetic route, in particular the experimental conditions for the key Vilsmeier reaction, to produce anodynol. After all, she'd started the experimental trials, only to have her undergraduate mentor eventually complete the synthesis. At the onset of the meeting, before sitting, Evalina unconsciously straightened Vilsmeier's bust on the desk. And she expressed her empathy to Turville's situation – the sale of PAYNE Pharmaceuticals being called off. She was even more understanding of Turville's plight, once he explained the reason underlying the no-sale. The research team succeeded in making the target molecular structure. Yet because of a mistake made by Hofmann, the original researcher, the target structure was not the actual structure. Evalina, though, very quickly realized that Turville inviting her to his office to discuss the pathway to anodynol was only a guise for his real reason to see her.

Turville started to bad-mouth her husband. He surprised Evalina by saying, "Adam Clarke is nothing but a disgraced minister. He doesn't even deserve the title of Reverend. Even now, you carry the singing duo with your off-key husband."

Evalina shook her head, not believing what she was hearing.

He continued, "I've been in communication with your current boss, Reverend Danny Einstein. He's ready to fire Adam. But he'll keep you."

Evalina stood, gritting her teeth.

Turville boasted, "I'm gonna quit PAYNE Pharmaceuticals and join the Quantum Christian Church very soon. Reverend Einstein is going to hire me as his top assistant. I may be your boss once again." He gave Evalina a wink of the eye. "But my move to Dallas won't include Shelley and the kids." Turville then approached close to Evalina, telling her he knew that she really wanted him and not her fallen pastor husband. His advances were not subtle, as he pinned Evalina against the wall and popped a big kiss on her cheek. His hands wandered in exploration. Turville's arrogance, though, didn't prepare him for an unreceptive Evalina. He never imagined Evalina wouldn't be captivated by his romantic advances and wouldn't be thrilled by the possibility of his future presence at the Quantum Christian Church.

Evalina thrust her right knee upward. It hit its mark.

Yet another person that day raged out of Turville's office. Evalina exited without saying a word, and ran down the hallway sobbing uncontrollably. The office workers, and Belle in particular, thought Evalina's departure was much like almost two years previous when she ran from Turville's office after being confronted with her affair with her minister.

As Turville staggered back to his chair, he smiled. Evalina had spunk in addition to beauty. He'd have a bouquet of flowers sent to her anyway for Valentine's Day. She'd change her mind, once he turned up in Dallas.

Turville's wife, Shelley, arrived a few minutes after Evalina left his office. She exchanged pleasantries with Belle and bemoaned the bad news about the no-sale with NuDRUG. Shelly confided it was definitely a bad day for her husband to have forgotten to take his blood pressure medication. He'd called to ask her to drop off a couple doses. He'd felt his blood pressure rising that morning. Belle, the secretary, indicated that Turville had appointments scheduled later that afternoon – one at 2:30 with a Willie Mudrick; then he'd blocked out everything after 3:00 o'clock, but with no name.

As Shelley entered the office, she walked directly to the bust of Vilsmeier. She picked it up and rubbed its head. She smiled, "Does this bring me good luck?"

Her husband wasn't amused.

She quickly dropped off the two tablets of his medicine and left.

After swallowing one tablet with a swig of bottled water, Turville placed the second next to his desk pad for later that afternoon. He sat back in his desk chair and pondered, "Do I really need to send Valentine flowers to her this year? She'll soon be history."

The latest office gossip had quickly spread to BettyJo Burks – the ever-beautiful Evalina had visited Turville in his office and had taken off in a huff. The rumors just as quickly interpreted, correctly in this case, her emotional departure being due to Turville making a pass at her. BettyJo had also heard rumors earlier in the day about Turville and Sara Austin. Within fifteen minutes of Evalina's retreat from PAYNE Pharmaceuticals, BettyJo flounced into her lover's office and slammed the door shut behind her.

"Why was Evalina here?" she demanded.

"None of your business," Turville sighed.

"I think it is." BettyJo stood her ground.

"I have more pressing concerns than trying to soothe your hurt feelings," he sneered. "In case you haven't heard, the deal with NuDRUG didn't materialize. Anodynol doesn't relieve pain. It induces sleep and sickness. I should've been a millionaire by now, but events transpired to deprive me of my fortune."

"You're changing the subject," she pouted.

"I'm not staying late tonight. You might as well go home," he said matter-of-factly. He admitted he no longer desired her. He would soon be moving from PAYNE Pharmaceuticals and Millikan without her.

BettyJo did not take the put-down, conveyed in a business-like and not even a caring manner, well. She cried. Then she professed her love for him over and over again, and that her dream was to share the rest of their lives together. She begged him to give her another chance. For effect, she picked up and tightly hugged the bust of Vilsmeier.

Turville laughed and glibly proclaimed their affair was just a disappointing fling on his part. She was just a hick from West Virginia. His next wife would be a real beauty, one with a pedigree. Besides which, she was one of the many reasons he needed to take his blood pressure meds. He snatched and waved the tablet he still had to take later that afternoon in her face.

BettyJo once again confronted him, trying to guilt him. "So you're gonna throw me away, just like week-old bread."

Turville repeated his laugh. He casually replied, "Good analogy, that's whats gonna happen! Don't expect any flowers for Valentine's."

Yet again, another person that day yelled at Turville: "Screw You!" BettyJo slammed Turville's office door shut. She shed tears all the way back to her office.

Several minutes later, Belle announced that Willie Mudrick had arrived for his 2:30 pm appointment. The secretary noticed Turville rolling his eyes as if he wished he didn't have to see this next visitor. Mudrick wasted no time in lambasting Turville, not even taking time to close the office door behind him. Mudrick cursed Turville for letting him rot in a Peruvian jail for the past two years. Evidently, Turville had retained Willie Mudrick to find specimens of living Peruvian Rainbow Frogs in the jungles of northern Peru. Turville simply yawned in response.

Even during the struggle to synthesize anodynol, Turville had a back-up plan to obtain it. He wanted to acquire several breeding pairs of these frogs and raise them. He then planned to extract the anodynol from the toxin located in the mucous layer on the frogs' slimy skin. Turville also hoped that after a few weeks, the frogs would regenerate the toxin. With continuous reharvesting, the extraction of anodynol would become an on-going process. Even though other scientists couldn't find any more Peruvian Rainbow Frogs in the wild, and thus presumed them extinct, Willie Mudrick with the help of some savvy natives, who were encouraged with the promise of lots of money, succeeded in collecting a dozen living Peruvian Rainbow Frogs. Mudrick paid the natives a thousand dollars of his own money per frog. Turville promised Mudrick a more than twenty-fold profit upon delivery of the frogs. Unfortunately for Mudrick, an equally savvy customs agent identified the living specimens as Peruvian Rainbow Frogs, and not the common South American Green Frog as claimed on the export forms. Equally unfortunate, the customs agent turned the frogs over to a Peruvian wildlife official who had no idea of the frogs' value, neither scientific nor financial, and care. The frogs died in captivity in a few days.

Mudrick spent the next couple years in a Peruvian jail. He sent notes and messages to Turville to dispatch money in order to bribe the jailers to let him out. Turville ignored the requests. He claimed he never received the messages. He didn't know where Mudrick had disappeared; he thought he'd lost interest in the project.

Mudrick demanded money from Turville for his efforts.

Turville succinctly stated, "No frogs, no money!"

Murdick picked up the Vilsmeier bust from the desk. "Maybe I'll just take this. Melt it down for its gold as payment."

"You idiot," Turville laughed. "It's bronze. You might get a few dollars."

As Willie Mudrick raged out the office, he turned to confront Turville, "You'll pay one way or the other. Just like you were going to get stuff out of the frogs' hides, you're going now to get the stuff beat out of your hide. You'd better be watching your back!" Mudrick actually smirked at the cleverness of his threatening retort as he turned away from Turville.

○ ● ○ ● ○

Belle instantly recognized Reverend Danny Einstein as he walked down the hallway and announced he had an appointment with Dr. Mason Turville. The flabberghasted secretary perceived he possessed much more of an aura of awe and holiness than he exuded in his telecasts. Reverend Einstein charmed her with his presence and conversation, after which she ushered him into Turville's office. Wondering why Reverend Einstein would be visiting Turville, she left the door slightly ajar as she returned to her desk. Evidently, Reverend Einstein made a special trip, which had been scheduled several weeks in advance, to Millikan at the invitation of Turville.

On the one hand, Turville wished this meeting would've been scheduled during happier times, after a sale of PAYNE to NuDRUG. But, on the other hand, perhaps now was the best time to make the transition from chemistry to ministry.

Reverend Einstein confessed he was intrigued by the sampling of Turville's calculations and lines of reasoning he'd sent him. Einstein admitted his curiosity had been indeed piqued. But now, Reverend Einstein acknowledged he was fascinated by the bronze bust on Turville's desk. Turville proudly proclaimed the bust was that of Anton Vilsmeier. He started to tell Reverend Einstein about Vilsmeier, until he awkwardly remembered Lum's confession of "Death by Vilsmeier" during Einstein's "Pastor in a Box" telecast segment.

Einstein picked up the bust and stared into Vilsmeier's eyes. He raised his eyebrows. "Ah, the remarkable and infamous Vilsmeier!" Since Reverend Einstein had heard about the PAYNE – NuDRUG break-up between his private plane and Turville's office, he expressed encouragement that Turville would eventually be able to prepare the real anodynol.

Then, letting all the troubles of the day fall by the wayside, Turville charged, like a teacher fully engulfed and excited by the subject matter, into an evangelistic message of Quantum Christianity. And Reverend Einstein listened like a student totally captivated by the message being delivered. Turville said he'd attended a Lutheran retreat several years ago. Instead of going to the various seminars and talks, he remained in his room totally possessed by his ideas. It was as if the Holy Spirit directed his thoughts during the next few days.

Turville confided he had two interests besides making drugs at PAYNE. The first diversion was Christian theology, one consequence of which resulted in his leadership positions at the Goose Creek Lutheran Church. His second hobby was solving differential equations. Most organic chemists despise mathematics, so Turville claimed to be the oddball that actually enjoyed higher forms of mathematics. As Reverend Einstein was well aware, solutions to differential equations are fundamental to the mathematical basis of quantum physics. Turville then reviewed the teeny-tiny world, the world of atoms, molecules, and photons, well-known to Reverend Einstein. He used the Schrödinger equation, which reduces to a special type of differential equation, to solve the simple quantum physics problem of the "Particle in a Box." As a result of the mathematical solutions to this equation, quantization of the energy states for the particle follows. As one increases the complexity of the box from one-dimension to two-dimensions to three-dimensions, this simple model approximates the behavior of an electron in an atom. These quantum concepts led to the weird and strange paradoxes accepted by all scientists occurring in the quantum world, and were used for analogies in the teachings of Reverend Einstein in the Quantum Christian Church.

Turville told Reverend Einstein that in a moment of inspiration at this retreat he considered an alternate problem. Instead of an atomic-sized particle in a submicroscopic box, he viewed an extremely large wave in an infinitely-sized box. He believed that such would model the behavior of a spirit in the universe. Or, in other words, such would simulate the properties of the Holy Spirit, or God, reigning over His dominion. Over the course of the rest of the retreat as well as the next few years, Turville refined his model, developed the differential equations analogous to the Schrödinger equation, which he called the Turville equation, and approximated the solutions to these equations. Amazingly, these solutions to his wave-in-a-big-box problem provided eerily similar quantized equations as the familiar particle-in-a-small-box model. Staring at Reverend Einstein, Turville now boasted that his work gave a scientific and mathematical basis for what Reverend Einstein had been preaching for the past decade. Our God is a God describable by mathematical equations. Turville's approach to God's Holy Spirit derived equations more for the nature of a thought than a thing, and yet depicted the material order of the universe.

Turville pulled out one paper from his stack on his desk. He smiled at Reverend Einstein and said, "In this derivation, the solution to this form of Turville's equation is a summation, the sum of all the integers to infinity, $1 + 2 + 3 + 4 + \ldots + \infty$. As you probably know, this grand summation isn't infinity. Wierdly, it's negative 1/12. The result emerges through use of the Riemann zeta function – similar to its application in the atomic world. I've proven its relevance to the spiritual world as well. Notice the twelve in the denominator. This is the underlying rationalization for Jesus choosing twelve disciples."

"Fascinating," Reverend Einstein responded.

Turville pulled another paper from the stack, then folded it in half. He directed Einstein to the equation just above the fold.

$$(e^{\pi})(i) - 1 = 0$$

"Euler's identity," Reverend Einstein mused, "a crazy mix of numbers that leads to a simple result. It defies common sense."

"Yep," Turville nodded. "The endless number, e, raised to the power of pi, which in turn is multiplied by the impossible square root of negative one, i. On the rest of this page as well as the next ten or so, one finds the identity does make sense. In fact, it has enormous implications for prophecy inspired by the Holy Spirit."

"I guess you're not going to unfold that paper," Einstein groaned.

Turville smiled and put the folded paper aside. He admitted that Reverend Einstein was one of the few people in the world who would fully appreciate his abstract calculations that led to a quantum explanation of the Holy Trinity. No longer would Reverend Einstein have to use analogies to classic quantum theory and Einstein's (Albert) Theory of Relativity, there was now a direct route to a Spiritual Theory of Relativity.

Reverend Einstein was indeed inwardly ecstatic about the possibilities. He envied the reams of pages from Turville's file in front of him.

Turville bragged incessantly that just like his organic syntheses started with reagents, then followed a carefully designed pathway to the desired products, his Spiritual Theory of Relativity started with a model, described that model with mathematical equations, and solutions of those equations led to the description of a world governed by a quantized God.

Turville then dropped his bombshell. He delivered a proposal to Reverend Einstein. Turville desired a change in his career path, from chemistry to the ministry, and a change in location, from Millikan to suburban Dallas. He was open to an offer for an executive position at the Quantum Christian Church or at HTN, the Holy Trinity Network, perhaps with a title of "Vice-President of Scientific Theology" with a salary worthy of the position. In exchange, Turville would make the entirety of his theoretical foundations of the Quantum Proof of the Holy Trinity available to Einstein.

Although stunned by the suddenness of the proposal, Einstein mulled the offer for only a few moments. He declined to accept it. He flatly stated that the proposed position was unnecessary and the quoted salary exorbitant. Although the theoretical proof would be nice to have, only a handful of people would think of Turville's equations as something other than mathematical gibberish. Besides which, Einstein claimed he was close to his own Spiritual Theory of Relativity – he didn't need Turville's.

Confusion reigned in Turville's arrogant mind. Like Evalina spurning his romantic advances earlier that afternoon, how could Reverend Einstein now reject his business proposal? His astonishment, though, soon turned to threats. Turville mentioned to Reverend Einstein that, if he didn't accept his proposal, Turville would then have no choice but to start preaching himself at the Goose Creek Lutheran Church, which he planned to rename the Goose Creek Quantum Church, or maybe Turville's Quantum Church. And he'd telecast his services. After publishing his ideas and mathematics in a book, he, not Reverend Einstein, would be heralded as the true leader of the movement to connect the spiritual world to the material world via quantum concepts. He further crowed that within the next few months, he would be receiving his Doctor of Divinity Degree from an accredited on-line program. Along with his Ph.D. degree in Chemistry, his book, and his charisma from a pulpit, Turville boasted he would become a formidable foe for Reverend Einstein in tele-evangelism within a year.

Reverend Einstein abruptly ended the meeting. He stated no one threatens or tries to extort a fancy position on his ministry's staff. As Reverend Einstein turned to leave, he casually spoke, "There's a bust of me in the sanctuary of the Quantum Christian Church. I see the bust of Vilsmeier on your desk. But there will never be a bust of you – for you will be as much of a bust in theology as you were a bust in your synthesis of anodynol."

Turville seethed in anger by this calm put-down, and threw Vilsmeier's bust at Reverend Einstein as he left. "You're an idiot," Turville shouted. "You'll be sorry for not accepting my proposal. You'll be begging me for my mathematical proof."

Reverend Einstein chuckled in amusement, as Vilsmeier bounced harmlessly at his feet.

Reverend Einstein confidently told Belle to have a blessed day, as he strutted with his characteristic swagger down the hallway. He would return to Dallas later that night, very clear in his thoughts that Turville needed him much more than he needed Turville. After all, he was the only person to whom Turville's calculations and claims had any value.

After a few minutes, Belle stuck her head into Turville's office to let him know she was leaving for the day. Turville sat, angrily stewing, at his desk. Very gruffly, with a touch of sarcasm, he snarled, "Have a good night!" Suddenly, his snarl morphed into a smile. He'd have the last laugh with that fool, Einstein. He hadn't even told Einstein about the most recent refinement of his theory.

As Belle walked down the hallway, she passed Adam Clarke going the opposite direction towards Turville's office. He didn't even look at her. He seemed to be a man on a mission. She thought to herself perhaps this encounter shouldn't be missed. She turned around and went back to her desk. As she quietly rifled through her desk drawer under the pretense of looking for a forgotten item, she saw Adam Clarke almost trip over Vilsmeier's bust in the doorway of Turville's office. He picked it up.

Pastor Clarke screamed at Turville: "I should smash your head with Vilsmeier!"

"You're not man enough to do it," Turville snidely responded.

Adam then yelled, "Stay away from Evalina. She's my wife."

"You're not man enough to keep her."

"Stay away from Evalina," Adam yelled once more at Turville. He tossed the bust of Vilsmeier back on the floor, and left as quickly as he came.

When Belle left her desk for the second time, she heard a perverse laughter coming from Turville's office. Later, she would tell Buck Fowler she thought such was a right appropriate way to end the madness abounding at her boss' office that day. But the madness was far from over.

Chapter Twenty Six
PROPHECY

Ida Kay returned home from her confrontation with Turville to find glass pieces and a photograph in a bent frame on the floor. This time the fallen picture was in her living room, not in the possum nursery. The nine-by-twelve inch picture showed her dad, Dan Hall, laying bricks. He worked for the Big Foggy Gap Coal Company as a miner and, when needed, in construction. In the picture, he was helping build the coal company's office building.

She immediately called Buck Fowler. No answer. She left a voice mail: "Someone's gonna get himself kilt." No call back.

She called the County Sheriff's Office. It was important to get Detective Fowler a message – to call Ida Kay Hall, that she has information about a killing. They promised to convey the message. No response from Buck.

She sent Buck a text: *Picture fell from wall. My daddy, Dan, laying bricks for Big Foggy.*

No answer.

Ida Kay spent most of the afternoon criss-crossing the roads of Millikan County trying to track down Buck. No luck.

Chapter Twenty Seven
DEATH BY VILSMEIER

That same day, darkness had already descended when a phone call from central dispatch interrupted Buck Fowler's supper of leftover chili-mac casserole. Dr. Mason Turville had been reported dead in his office at PAYNE Pharmaceuticals. Buck looked at his watch – 6:02 pm.

Buck tried to shovel more casserole in his mouth, anticipating a long night. He also bemoaned having to listen to Ida Kay saying, "I told you so." He thought he'd successfully ignored and sidestepped the rants of that crazy lady.

With a sarcastic snicker, the dispatcher asked Buck whether he needed directions to the crime scene. And with another snicker, the dispatcher snidely added, "Oh, by the way, Lum Baumgartner discovered the body and called 9-1-1."

"Get serious, Lum's in jail," Buck groused.

"It was definitely Lum," the dispatcher reiterated.

"Why's he not in jail?"

"I'm the dispatcher. You're the detective," chuckled dispatch.

As Buck picked up the keys to his police cruiser on the way out the door, dispatch further informed Buck that the local rescue squad, the coroner, and a couple patrol cars were on the way to PAYNE Pharmaceuticals.

Buck's mind popped the question: "Unbelievable! What's Lum done now?"

○ ● ○ ● ○

Buck entered the office of Dr. Mason Turville for what seemed to be the umpteenth time. He scanned the scene. His eyes focused on Turville, his head lying in a pool of his own blood on the middle of the desk, and his body slumped over in his office chair.

A rescue squad member deadpanned, "He's dead. No pulse when we arrived. We didn't disturb anything. It's kinda obvious what killed him!"

Indeed, Buck saw the bust of Vilsmeier lying behind Turville's office chair, and the corresponding depression in Turville's skull. As he came closer to the body, Buck clearly observed the indentation in Turville's skull that looked like a mirror image of Vilsmeier's face drawn in his usually impeccably groomed hair. Someone obviously came up behind Turville and clunked him on his head with the bronze bust. Buck had to admit whoever crafted the bust did a mighty good job. There was nary a dent or crack. The one-inch thickness of bronze made a quite effective murder weapon. Whoever did this deed must've been, to paraphrase his daddy, "madder than a sittin' hen," in order to put that much force behind the death blow. Oddly enough, though, nothing else appeared out of place in Turville's office. It looked exactly the same as the many other times in the past he visited the office. The papers on his desk didn't seem disturbed. Many were neatly stacked. The papers and files were those he carried around in his briefcase, now empty, about the Quantum Proof for the Holy Trinity.

Buck caught himself in mid-thought and stared at Turville's body. By its position, it seemed as though Turville never defended himself from the attacker. Buck surmised Turville must've been sound asleep with his head on his desk when someone whacked him from behind. After a half-hour, Buck turned the office over to the crime scene unit and the coroner to document the killing.

His departing command: "Dust the bust for prints. Let's see whether we can get lucky."

The patrolman outside the office directed Buck to a nearby room where Lum was being detained. Buck immediately approached Lum and asked, "Why'd you do it?"

Lum turned white as a ghost. "It wasn't me," he gasped. "He was dead when I arrived. I just felt for a pulse. His heart wasn't beating. Then, I called 9-1-1."

"Well, it certainly doesn't look good for you. You end up in the office with the still-warm dead body of a person that you totally despised."

Lum choked up. "I didn't do it."

"Let's start from the beginning," Buck snarled. "I thought you were in jail. Did you escape just to murder Turville?"

"The jail's warden talked to the judge," Lum stated. "They gave me a four hour pass to see Evalina and Adam before they went back to Dallas. The judge said I wasn't a threat to society. Ordinarily I wouldn't have had to report to jail for a few days anyway."

Buck shook his head in disbelief.

Unperturbed, Lum continued, "Evalina and Adam were running late. So I called 'Toad' Crabbler, and convinced him to give me a ride back to jail. Since I had a little time to spare, I decided to apologize personally to Turville for my misdeeds. I stopped by his house in Hickory Grove at dusk, hoping to catch him before dinner. Turville's wife, Shelley, told me he'd not gotten home yet. She said he was probably working late at PAYNE, as he did most nights. On our way back to jail, Toad and I passed by PAYNE. We saw Turville's car in the parking lot. I thought I'd just deliver my personal apology and ask for forgiveness. He'd most likely be in his office or laboratory. When I entered the open door of Turville's office, I found the body. By the way, I hope Toad's not waiting in the parking lot. I assume y'all will give me a ride back to the jail. You might call them to tell them I'll be a bit late."

Buck shrugged and stared at Lum. "You hated Turville in so many ways. Why would you want forgiveness from your personal enemy?"

"I'm a changed man, and a true follower of the ways of Jesus Christ. I thought I was a true Christian previously, but I wasn't. God wants me to show love and forgiveness, not hate and revenge. Giving apologies might open the way for me receiving forgiveness and mercy from God."

"Just admit it," Buck flatly stated, "like you finally confessed to accidently killing Ron Austin in the laboratory next to this office. You initially denied that killing as well."

"I never denied it. I just never admitted it. But this time, I didn't have anything to do –"

"You saw Turville sleeping on his desk, and saw your opportunity," Buck interrupted, "so you picked up the bust and whomped him on the head. This time, it's murder, not manslaughter. You're going away for many years this time. Why couldn't you just leave well enough alone?"

Despite Lum vigorously professing his innocence, Buck considered having Lum open his mouth so that he could administer his daddy's test for liars. As his daddy had Buck do when he suspected his son of lying as a child: "Open your mouth and let me see those lie bumps on your tongue." Buck told the attending police officers to take Lum back to the jail, and to add a charge of suspicion of murder.

The coroner had been waiting in the hallway for Buck to finish with Lum. He informed Buck that he just couldn't leave without telling him what he was listing as the cause of Turville's death. With a perverse smirk, he announced, "Death by Vilsmeier!" He couldn't leave well enough alone, and continued, "Yes siree! Vilsmeier's head is as deadly as Vilsmeier's reaction here at PAYNE."

Buck's phone beeped – an incoming text message from Ida Kay. *Some might call a bricklayer a MASON.*

He grimaced.

Buck next encountered a quite distraught Shelley Turville sitting in a chair in the hallway outside Turville's office. After Buck offered his condolences, Shelley confirmed that Lum had indeed stopped by her house to see her husband. And that Lum had not seemed upset in any way. In fact, in Shelley's opinion,

Lum seemed quite pleasant and peaceful. Shelley sobbed. She'd seen her husband for just a few moments when she dropped off a couple of his blood pressure tablets that afternoon at his office. She hadn't seen or talked to him after, but it was not unusual for him to work late.

Then, out of left field, Shelley asked, "Can I go in his office and gather the papers off my husband's desk?"

Buck's jaw dropped. Turville's dead and bloodied head still drooped over the desk. She hadn't asked, "Who did it, or Why?" or any of the obvious questions. "Ah," was all the response he could muster.

Shelley then added, "After all, they're mine, not his."

Chapter Twenty Eight
SUSPECTS GALORE

The Millikan County Sheriff's Office asked Turville's laboratory staff and secretary to assemble at PAYNE Pharmaceuticals that evening. Buck wanted to question them about the day's events. The lab technicians rightfully proclaimed ignorance of Turville's activities for the day. Turville stayed in his office and never wandered into the laboratory once. They revealed the obvious, not only the laboratory but the entire facility was in turmoil that day. The news that the synthetic anodynol differed from the natural anodynol, and subsequently NuDRUG opting not to purchase PAYNE Pharmaceuticals, spread quickly. The lab techs had operated on cruise control; they ran mundane quality control samples. On the other hand, Belle, Turville's secretary, divulged that things were far from calm in Turville's office. She told of a steady stream of people in-and-out of Turville's office. All left on a very bad note. Most were upset to say the least, and threatening in some cases.

Belle systematically told Buck of the litany of visitors, starting with Ron Austin's widow first thing in the morning. Sara Austin was upset that Turville had stood her up on a date. As she left, she told Turville to go to Hell. Then, Jim Payne, Jr., rumbled into Turville's office, quite mad about the no sale of PAYNE to NuDRUG.

"He yelled 'Screw You' to Turville as he stormed out of the office. All that wasn't unusual." Belle laughed. "I think they yelled at each other for some reason every day or so."

Buck had Belle slow down in her rehash. He couldn't scribble in his notepad fast enough. She smiled.

"Barney Bennington, Goose Creek's interim pastor, visited for only a few minutes," Belle related. "It wasn't a pleasant conversation. It ended with Dr. Turville telling him to 'Get Out.'"

"Does the pastor visit him often at work?" Buck inquired.

"Only once before," she answered. "It was quite a while ago. And it was scheduled, not a drop in like today. Then, Ida Kay Hall showed up unannounced and –"

"Ida Kay?" Buck interrupted, expressing disbelief and not looking forward to his next encounter with her for having disregarded her message.

"Yep, I was surprised to see her as well. I'd never seen her at PAYNE," Belle stated. "But I think everyone in Millikan and thereabouts know her. She's a real catbird. Anyhow, she was mad as a hornet at Dr. Turville, told him to stop harassing Sara Austin."

"I think Ida Kay has been quite protective of Sara," mulled Buck.

"Ida Kay told him to stay away from Sara in no uncertain terms." Belle chuckled, "I, for one, wouldn't want to mess with Ida Kay."

"Nor I," echoed Buck.

When Belle returned from her lunch hours, she saw Dr. Quinn Stanton in Turville's office. It was quick and also unscheduled. She confessed she had no idea why Dr. Stanton stopped by. But he seemed to be cursing Turville under his breath when he departed. He would normally pause and chat with her whenever he dropped in to see her boss. Clearly he was preoccupied with other matters this time. Then, Evalina Vail visited with Turville behind closed doors for about a half-hour. She appeared quite happy when she arrived, but left much like she did months prior when her affair with her preacher was breaking. Belle wasn't sure what happened in Turville's office but, whatever it was, Evalina had become upset in a very personal way. Evalina ran out of Turville's office sobbing and mad.

Turville had his wife, Shelley, drop off some of his blood pressure meds. Belle indicated such was not an uncommon occurrence. When Turville had a stressful day, he often had his wife drop off his prescription medicine to lower his blood pressure. Mrs. Turville stayed only long enough to give him the tablets. Soon after, BettyJo Burks from the Human Resources Office stomped into Turville's office, but left the office in a huff yelling "Screw You."

Buck asked, "Was Dr. Turville's affair with BettyJo well-known among the company employees?"

"The affair was pretty much an open secret around PAYNE," Belle shook her head. "BettyJo sauntered in-and-out of Turville's office at her pleasure both during and after working hours." She disdainfully added. "They were always flirting, like a couple of teenagers. And before BettyJo, there was Kathleen . . . and before her, Peggy . . . and before –"

"I don't think we have to go any further back," Buck interrupted, rolling his eyes in disbelief. "Was this affair with BettyJo, or the others, known by his wife?"

"As for Mrs. Turville, I don't know." Belle hesitated, then continued, "She always seemed to turn a blind eye to her husband's affairs. I don't know whether she was intentionally or unintentionally clueless."

Turville then had an appointment with Willie Mudrick, who Belle claimed she'd never seen nor heard of previously. He wasn't the typical visitor, looking like he hadn't showered or washed his clothes in a week – smelled that way too. He had long, stringy hair and an unkempt beard to accentuate his homeless appearance. He did wear a bright red baseball cap; it looked clean. Through a slightly open office door, she confessed eavesdropping. She overheard Mudrick was upset with Turville for some screw-up about collecting frogs from which anodynol could be extracted. He demanded money from Turville. She further heard some definitely threatening exchanges between Mudrick and Turville. In fact, Murdick exhibited open hostility toward Turville as he left, telling Turville that he had better watch his back.

Turville's next visitor was Reverend Danny Einstein of the Quantum Christian Church. She had been astonished to see him. Although the three o'clock appointment had been on Turville's schedule for a couple weeks, Belle had not been privy to the purpose of the meeting – or even who the meeting was with. Turville seemed to have a quiet meeting with the minister, until the door opened about two hours later with the minister leaving. Evidently, Turville hurled Vilsmeier's bust at Reverend Einstein. But the bust was quite heavy, so it simply rolled weakly by Einstein's feet.

"What time did Reverend Einstein leave?" asked Buck.

"It was right before quitting time," Belle said, "a little before five o'clock."

"So that was the last visitor, then."

Belle took a deep breath. "I was leaving for the day, walking down the hallway. Pastor Adam Clarke flew past me toward Turville's office. Curiosity got the best of me, so I returned to the office."

"I'm glad you did," Buck intervened.

"I couldn't believe what I heard. Pastor Clarke threatened to smash Dr. Turville over the head with Vilsmeier's bust. It was still sitting in the office doorway. Words flew back and forth, but the exchange between the two lasted less than a minute. Pastor Clarke raged back out." Belle growled, "If I can put two and two together, I presume Pastor Clarke must've been riled because Turville made a pass at Evalina. I guess earlier that afternoon."

Buck nodded, keeping his pen to paper taking vociferous notes. Without looking up, he asked, "And Pastor Clarke, then, must've left around five o'clock or a little after."

"I remember looking at the clock: five minutes after five." Belle added, "I was once again preparing to leave. Dr. Turville didn't know I was still there. I heard a devious laugh, almost a cackle, from the office – much like you might hear from a bad scene in a bad horror movie. I thought it was a right appropriate way to end the madness happening at the boss' office."

"Sounds like a whole passel of people were mad at him, or him mad at them," Buck sighed. "Lots, besides Lum, wouldn't mind seeing him dead."

"Yep, take a number," Belle half-laughed. "You can add me to the list as well. Every morning when I came to work, I'd stew at some of the tasks he'd give me. Just think – today he had me polish his shoes. And every morning, first thing, he made me polish that ugly head of Vilsmeier. Have you ever heard of such a thing? I say it's poetic justice that Vilsmeier did him in." She shook her head. "I would've quit working for him a long time ago, but I needed the paycheck."

Buck smiled. "You polished the bust this morning?"

Belle nodded.

Buck gave a sigh of relief.

A deputy interrupted. He told Buck he couldn't find Jim Payne, Jr. – to tell him about Turville's death as well as Buck needing to talk to him. And his wife didn't know where he was.

Belle laughed, then volunteered, "Mr. Payne's wife knows exactly where her husband is. She just doesn't wanna tell. Mr. Payne left work around noon. Office scuttlebutt dictates that, whenever the 'Big Boss' is upset and doesn't return after lunch, he's most likely at the MeadowView Country Club bar drinking away his sorrows. I hear he's such a good and frequent customer the club has a bed in a storage room reserved just for him to sleep off his drunken stupor."

"I've heard pretty much the same," Buck shrugged.

"Tomorrow might be a better day to talk to Mr. Payne." She smiled, glancing at her watch, "Especially since it's already approaching midnight."

Most of the crime scene personnel had already departed for the night. Turville's body had been taken to the county morgue for an autopsy. Yellow tape was draped around the active crime scene just in case more needed to be investigated the next day.

○ ● ○ ● ○

After a long night, Buck Fowler persisted in his thoughts about the crime. People shuttled in-and-out of Turville's office all day helter-skelter. Buck gave a half-hearted laugh – as his daddy used to say: "They were running around like farts on a skillet." Once Lum's lawyer got hold of the cast of characters passing through Turville's office, he'd rightfully point out that there was a plethora of other individuals who might've committed the murder instead of Lum. The one and only piece of evidence against Lum was that he happened to be at the crime scene. No concrete fact yet proved Lum murdered Turville. Fingerprints on the murder weapon, the bust of Vilsmeier, should point the investigation in the right direction. As his daddy would have told Buck, it was his job to "find out which varmint had been in the chicken house." And there were varmints aplenty. Unlike the prior "Death by Vilsmeier" where Buck's investigation languished with no suspects and no motives, with this new "Death by Vilsmeier" he had lots of suspects and lots of motives. Even the murder weapon had been tossed around like a football before the actual murder took place.

Buck had a midnight snack. He thought Turville was a piece of work, leaving a trail of angry women in his wake. He made the wrong drug, resulting in a deal worth a boatload of money falling apart in the past 24 hours. Everyone blamed each other. And he succeeded in ticking off three pastors in one work day – that must be some kind of a record. His desk showed he didn't seem concerned about the billion dollar anodynol, but instead a theological treatise that may or may not have been his own.

Before Buck drifted to sleep in the wee hours of the morning, he wondered whether the use of Vilsmeier's bust as the murder weapon had any significance. He obsessed with the question: "Was Vilsmeier's bust specifically chosen for this murder to make a personal statement, or was Vilsmeier's bust simply a weapon of opportunity or convenience?" Other questions swirled. "Why did Turville not fend off the attack? Why was he apparently sleeping at his desk? Was the murder planned or one that happened at the spur of the moment?" Ironically, the first "Death by Vilsmeier" used a chemical reaction at work to settle a personal, albeit misplaced, lover's revenge. "Was this second "Death by Vilsmeier" also settling a lover's spat, or a professional dispute, or about money?" And, once again, there was a smattering of religion thrown into the mix as well. "What were Pastor Barney Bennington and Reverend Danny Einstein doing at Turville's office that day?" Buck Fowler needed some rest in order to try to unravel some of these strange twists. It'd be so much easier just to pin the murder on Lum. Buck finally fell asleep counting questions instead of counting sheep.

Chapter Twenty Nine
ALIBI

The next morning, Buck Fowler awoke conflicted about Lum's role in Dr. Mason Turville's murder. Lum definitely had motive and opportunity. Buck wondered, though, why Lum stayed around to report the crime. He could've just jumped back in the car with Toad and been back at the jail without anyone being the wiser.

Over breakfast of coffee and jelly toast, Buck called Ida Kay. No answer. A few minutes later, he called again. No answer. Over the course of the morning, he called several more times. Still no answer.

Well before noon, Buck ticked a couple suspects off his list of possible murderers. A phone call verified Jim Payne, Jr., had indeed been drinking at the country club bar at the time of Turville's demise. A bad hangover currently plagued Payne. Jim Payne, Jr., would be seeing Buck in the afternoon. After his impromptu meeting with Turville, Dr. Quinn Stanton immediately returned to Keaton College, two hours away from Millikan, to teach an organic chemistry review session from 4:00 until 5:30 the afternoon of the murder. Q-Dawg took a few moments to recover from the initial shock of hearing about the death of Turville. Once regaining his composure, he readily admitted that, during his unscheduled meeting with Turville the previous day, he vented his anger at Turville for welching on his monetary bonus for synthesizing anodynol. Buck also shared with Q-Dawg that, once again, this crime was classified as a "Death by Vilsmeier." This time the killing was done by the Vilsmeier bust instead of the Vilsmeier reaction.

And just as for the previous "Death by Vilsmeier," Buck confided one of his concerns to Q-Dawg. He mentioned that Turville appeared to be sleeping at his desk when he was bonked in the head by the bust. Q-Dawg remarked, off the cuff, he'd heard NuDRUG found anodynol put people to sleep instead of killing their pain. In fact, this misconnect in anodynol's operation was the reason why NuDRUG decided not to purchase PAYNE Pharmaceuticals. Q-Dawg offered to help Buck in any way he could. Buck already realized that he may have unwittingly provided a key piece of information in the investigation.

Phone calls by Buck that morning to the Quantum Christian Church, and to Reverend Danny Einstein, went unreturned. However, Buck finally connected with Evalina, who seemed more concerned that her father Lum was a suspect in murdering Turville than in the death of her previous boss. Buck comforted Evalina somewhat – that Lum appeared at peace behind bars for the time being and that there were plenty of other suspects. Evalina disclosed both she and her husband were on their way to the airport by late afternoon. In fact, they left as soon as Adam had returned from his outburst with Turville. When Buck questioned her why her boss, Reverend Danny Einstein, had a meeting with Turville a few hours after she visited Turville, Evalina was temporarily speechless. She confessed she'd no idea that Reverend Einstein had even been there at PAYNE Pharmaceuticals, or even Millikan, much less why he'd been there. She couldn't remember ever talking with Reverend Einstein about Dr. Mason Turville.

Evalina conceded to Buck that, although it was a terrible thing for a Christian to admit, she wasn't sad that Turville was dead. She flatly declared, "Turville was a sleazeball in the first degree." When she worked at PAYNE Pharmaceuticals, she wrongly considered Turville a kind and considerate boss. Now she knew how wrong she must've been, or perhaps Turville changed in the time since she'd moved to Dallas. Turville not only made disparaging and crude remarks about her husband, but also made sexual advances towards her, in his office that day. Her husband, Adam, just confronted Turville later that afternoon to warn Turville to stay away from her. Pastor Adam Clarke was mighty mad. Perhaps, Buck thought, the second "Death by Vilsmeier," like the first "Death by Vilsmeier," was to protect the honor of Evalina – the first by her father and the second by her husband. As a final note of disconcerting information, Evalina shared with Buck another apparent coincidence. The first "Death by Vilsmeier" occurred on 12 June, Anton Vilsmeier's birthday, while the second happened on 12 February, the anniversary of Vilsmeier's death.

Buck wished he'd never heard of Anton Vilsmeier!

○ ● ○ ● ○

Around noon, Buck tried calling Ida Kay again. No answer. He ate a bologna sandwich and drank a coke, both picked up at the HillTop Convenience Store, on his drive to Ida Kay's. Arriving there, he found Ida Kay bundled up in a heavy coat and sitting on a lawn chair at the end of the driveway. She seemed to be watching crows hopping around in her yard. He jumped out of his cruiser. Her cell phone sat on her lap. She grinned a devious smile at him.

As he approached her, he grumbled, "Why didn't you answer or return my phone calls?"

"You didn't answer or return my calls yesterday." Ida Kay stuck her tongue out at Buck. "Why should I answer your calls today?"

"So you made me drive all the way out here to see you." Buck sighed.

"That's right."

"Before the killing actually happened, had you figured out whose death was predicted?" Buck groaned.

"Nope, thought you would've been able to," Ida Kay said. "I thought a Dan or a Danny or a Hall, or maybe someone who'd worked at the Big Foggy. Like most prophecy, it only became obvious after the fact."

Buck nodded. "I hear you were at Mason Turville's office yesterday. You threatened him."

"Yep," Ida Kay responded without emotion.

"That's all you're gonna tell me," Buck took a deep breath. "You're not gonna explain?"

"I hear Vilsmeier killed him," Ida Kay snickered.

"You don't seem too upset by his death?"

"Nope," Ida Kay replied. "He was a first class jerk. Women were just toys for his personal pleasure."

"Am I gonna find your fingerprints on Vilsmeier's bust?"

"Yep," Ida Kay chuckled. She hesitated, thinking for a few seconds, then continued, "I kinda tossed it to him, sorta like a warning." She paused for a few more moments. "Did you know that koala bears have human-like fingerprints? They leave the same loopy, whirling ridges when they touch surfaces."

Buck shook his head in amazement and ignored her fingerprint trivia. "Did he heed the warning? Were you the one to bop him on the head with Vilsmeier?" Buck asked rapid fire.

Ida Kay laughed. "Whacking him on the head would've been too simple. To kill someone like Turville I would've used the strategy of the velvet worm of New Zealand. They have little glue guns on either side of their head to shoot a sticky slime at their insect prey. The slime hardens into fibers as strong as nylon, stopping the bug in its tracks. Then, while the bug is still alive but immobilized, the worm injects its saliva into the bug's body, digesting the bug's innards in place, before sucking the digested matter back out like a milkshake."

Buck rolled his eyes and made a gagging sound. "Only you could come up with something like that. I gotta ask you then – Where were you between five and six o'clock last night?"

"So I'm a suspect?"

"Gotta cross the possibilities off my list," Buck calmly stated.

"Have you talked to Sara Austin yet?"

"Nope. She's on my list for a call or visit."

Ida Kay smiled. "I met Sara at 4:30, after she finished her work shift, at Millikan Pizzeria. We both had a glass of the house Sweet Red Blend wine, then shared a medium sausage-and-mushroom pizza, thin crust. We spent most of the time bad-mouthing Turville, thinking of ways to torture him, just short of killing him. We both left around 6:30. You gonna check out the alibi with Tony, the manager, and Wanda, our waitress?"

"Yep," Buck replied. "Next time I'll answer your phone call."

Ida Kay snarled, "By the way, neither Tony nor Wanda liked Turville either."

○ ● ○ ● ○

Later in the day, Buck contacted Sara Austin. She showed no compassion in the death of Dr. Mason Turville. She didn't hesitate to tell Detective Fowler she considered Turville both arrogant and despicable. In addition, she described Turville to be the pinnacle of a hypocritical Christian – boastful of his Christian Ways but not following the Way. She repeated the same alibi as Ida Kay, and which was confirmed by Tony, Wanda, and several other diners at the Millikan Pizzeria.

When Buck met Barney Bennington at Goose Creek Lutheran Church, Pastor Barney was busy preparing for the memorial service for Mason Turville at the church. The pastor had an iron-clad alibi. He was in Charleston meeting with the regional bishop. He shared there was no love lost between he and Turville. He wasn't looking forward to eulogizing a womanizer and religious hypocrite.

○ ● ○ ● ○

Meeting with Shelley Turville the next day didn't provide any leads to Buck's investigation. Lum, by stopping by the Turville house late the previous afternoon, unwittingly had confirmed that Shelley was at her house, not at her husband's office in the time frame of the murder. Belle, Turville's secretary, had also indicated Shelley appeared clueless about her husband's professional activities. The limits to her knowledge about anodynol seemed to be that her husband had made a drug discovery that supposedly was going to make lots of money, but then two days ago the supposed purchaser of PAYNE Pharmaceuticals cancelled the sale. She confided to Buck she wasn't aware of any specifics with respect to anodynol. She'd simply been by his office that afternoon to drop off, at his request, two of his blood pressure tablets, as he thought he suffered from a headache induced by a rise in his blood pressure. Before she left, he'd taken one of the tablets, and the other was sitting on the side of his desk pad – just in case he needed one for later that afternoon. It wasn't uncommon for her to stop by the office to deliver blood pressure tablets, especially when he was stressed at work.

"You know," she told Buck, "those folks at PAYNE worked him so hard. These past few months were especially hard on him. He had to work late most nights." To his wife Shelley, Dr. Mason Turville was the perfect church-going gentlemen in her homelife. In fact, when Buck asked Shelley about what she knew about Reverend Danny Einstein visiting her husband, she claimed not to have known about the visit. She assumed it was because Reverend Einstein needed some advice about Christian theology from her husband. Since it was only two days after her husband's murder, Buck didn't want to burst her bubble by asking about BettyJo Burks. Either Shelley was indeed naïve about her husband or a mighty good actress. And she didn't appear to be in deep mourning about her husband's death.

Buck stopped by HillTop Convenience for a coffee on his drive to BettyJo Burk's house in Colebrook. He picked up a coffee for her also. Upon his arrival, BettyJo was totally inconsolable. But she did quickly drain the drink. BettyJo hadn't gone to work at PAYNE since her lover's death, nor did she intend to do so anytime soon. She confessed to Buck that she lost the "love of her life." Her darling Mason had promised to divorce his wife. She and Mason could then enjoy their perfect life together.

Buck just shook his head wondering how men are able to convince their mistresses their idyllic future together was always just around the corner, when such wasn't even remotely on his radar screen. Other than that, it was difficult for Buck to piece together anything comprehensible amongst BettyJo's blathering and crying. He left with BettyJo's empty coffee cup in hand.

Willie Mudrick remained mysterious. Belle had absolutely no contact information about him. Turville must have, for obvious reasons, wanted no paper or electronic trail to lead from Mudrick back to him. Mudrick evidently departed Millikan as quietly as he arrived, without a trace. Belle poured through books upon books of mugshots. None were identified as Willie Mudrick. She described him to a sketch artist. Buck thought the portrait looked somewhat like a male Shelley Turville, the same high cheek-bones and smallish ears – perhaps Belle had transposed some of the characteristics of Turville's previous visitor that day.

Interviews with Lum at the county jail were unproductive. Lum adamantly proclaimed his innocence. He only regretted he'd never have the opportunity to ask Turville for forgiveness. Buck wondered whether it was all an act, a cover for the murder. But Lum seemed sincere, talking for the most part without his lawyer present. He said Jesus was his lawyer. Only one interesting piece of information could be gleaned from Lum. When Lum stopped by Turville's house the night of the murder, he saw a late model black Cadillac SUV parked at the *cul de sac* of Birch Lane in the Hickory Grove subdivision.

○ ● ○ ● ○

A couple days later, the fingerprint expert for the crime scene technicians visited Buck Fowler at the Sheriff's Office.

"Lots of fingerprints on the murder weapon – the bust of Vilsmeier, or whatever the guy's name is," the expert stated, "probably at least from ten different people."

"That's what I expected," echoed Buck. "I guess one, though, was Lum's."

The expert frowned.

"Columbus 'Lum' Baumgartner," Buck proferred.

The expert shook his head. "Nope, looked and re-looked and looked again. Nary a fingerprint from Lum Baumgartner, not even anything close or matching any of the smudges."

"Well, I'll be." Buck's jaw dropped.

The expert got tickled. "What would your daddy say about that?"

"I guess he'd tell me 'experience is what you get when you don't get what you want.' Buck groaned, "So whose fingerprints did you identify?"

"None were in our database, although we had a match to the ones on the coffee cup you supplied – those of BettyJo Burks."

Chapter Thirty
DANNY EINSTEIN

Buck still harbored suspicions about Adam Clarke for the current "Death by Vilsmeier." If Lum, as he claimed, only stumbled upon a dead Turville, then Adam Clarke was the last person to have been seen with a living Turville. Adam also quite conveniently threatened to kill Turville by exactly the same means as that which killed Turville. But the timing didn't seem to work. He barely had time to catch his plane in Charleston as it was. And both Adam and Evalina were on the plane's manifest. Neither Adam nor Evalina would now talk to Buck on the phone, under advice of their lawyer.

The one time Buck connected with Reverend Danny Einstein by phone, Reverend Einstein stayed vague and evasive on answering Buck's queries, as if he didn't want Buck to know exactly why he had visited Turville that day. Reverend Einstein had already provided copies of the pilot's log for his private plane. It had landed at the small Colebrook Municipal Airport at exactly 1:57 pm, then departed for Dallas at 7:55 pm.

Nonchalantly, Buck inquired, "What did you do in the couple hours between leaving Dr. Turville's office and jumping on your plane?"

"I grabbed a bite of some fast food, then drove around a bit," Reverend Einstein said. "I like to look at the churches in the places I visit. Goose Creek Lutheran is a beautiful church."

"So you had a car?"

"Yep, I rented one at the airport." The pastor proudly volunteered, "A Cadillac Escalade."

"I didn't think the airport's car rental had but a couple Fords and Chevys," Buck kidded.

"You have to pre-order," Reverend Einstein countered.

"Black, I assume."

"Is there any other color for an Escalade?" Einstein answered, sounding offended that anyone would even ask. The phone conversation quickly ended with Reverend Einstein's secretary calling him to a previously scheduled meeting with church donors.

Buck remained curious about Turville's many pages of mathematical scribblings included in his "Quantum Christian Church" files on his desk. Turville seemed to be using gibberish in Buck's mind. What Turville called the Turville modification of the Schrödinger equation had been used to prove the existence of the Holy Spirit, and thus God and Jesus Christ. Sprinkled throughout the incomprehensible text and formulas were references to quantized states of the infinite wave in the infinite box. Buck had made copies of the reams before releasing them back to Shelley Turville. She'd emphasized the pages were valuable and copyrighted, not for release by anyone but her – or even to be seen by anyone.

Under the pretext that Reverend Danny Einstein may have important information related to the case, Buck convinced the Sheriff to spring for air fare to Dallas to interview the Reverend as well as perhaps Adam and Evalina. In actuality, Buck obsessed with not knowing the exact connection between Turville and Einstein. Surprisingly to Buck, Reverend Danny Einstein granted him an hour time block for an interview on the day he planned his trip to Dallas.

○ ● ○ ● ○

The enormity and opulence of the Quantum Christian Church overwhelmed Buck. Upon entering, the pair of Einstein (Albert and Danny) busts greeted him outside the sanctuary, just like the television audience was welcomed to the start of "The Holy Event" every Sunday morning. Thousands of padded seats ringed the spacious sanctuary. Buck finally found Einstein's office at the opposite side of the church auditorium, after walking what seemed like a mile. When Reverend Einstein's secretary led Buck into Einstein's office, Buck stood in awe at its size. The room was so big Buck's house could easily have fit inside with space to spare.

Just inside the office, Buck bumped into a display table. Some drab black chunks, arranged in the shape of a cross, were under a belljar. Reverend Einstrein, dressed in a fine suit, stood proud as a peacock nearby.

Buck pointed at the display. He chuckled, "Someone give you chunks of coal for Christmas?"

"Nope," the pastor responded. "They're crystals of samarium hexaboride, SmB_6."

Buck stared at Reverend Einstein as if he'd lost his mind. "But why? Who cares?"

The pastor laughed. "These crystals can be electrical conductors as well as insulators. That is, they possess electrons flowing freely like metal conductors, but these same electrons are also stuck in place like insulators. Conventional wisdom says it has to be one or the other, not both. Oddly, these crystals exhibit properties of both simultaneously. Some scientists theorize the weird quantum behavior of the electrons in samarium hexaboride is analogous to a higher dimensional black hole."

Once again, Buck looked at the pastor with incredulity. "Am I supposed to understand all that?"

The pastor laughed with more vigor. "Suffice it to say, the crystals might be considered God-like. They can be two different things at the same time, just like God is the Holy Trinity, three in one. They're another one of my examples for Quantum Christianity."

In person, Reverend Einstein projected a very open and affable attitude to Buck about his relationship with Dr. Mason Turville. Einstein indicated that several months prior he'd received an unsolicited packet from Turville. Turville outlined a mathematical proof for the existence of the Holy Trinity through an extension of quantum physics. Einstein admitted that he was both intrigued and impressed by Turville's approach, which was unlike anything he'd ever imagined. Turville further communicated he would like to discuss his complete proof with Einstein in person, as Einstein would be one of the few individuals who could comprehend both the scientific and theological impact of his calculations. On the other hand, Einstein expressed his concern about the motives of Turville. Turville never shared all his computations and reasonings with Einstein, just enough to pique his curiosity and attention. Einstein got the impression that Turville wanted something in exchange. But Turville wouldn't come straight out and say so. Einstein divulged to Buck that he was impressed with Turville's credentials, with Turville being a talented chemist as well as a church leader. Only after Einstein returned from his visit to Turville and Millikan, West Virginia, did he realize the connection of Turville to his singing duo of Evalina and Adam. And only after the fact did Einstein realize they were all in Millikan that same day, and all talked to Turville that day.

In retrospect, Reverend Einstein told Buck he wished he'd simply ignored Turville's initial correspondence as unsolicited junk. Once in Turville's office, Einstein quickly realized that Turville was a "slimeball" – an arrogant, pushy, boastful bully. Turville thought that, with the promise of delivering his full proof to Einstein, he could get a foothold in becoming an executive in the Quantum Christian Church. Einstein clearly understood Turville's aspirations. As the one who provided the theoretical quantum proof for the characteristics and existence of God and the Holy Trinity, Turville desired to eventually usurp Einstein as the leader of the church. Einstein readily admitted he decided knowledge of Turville's work wasn't worth the price that Turville was demanding. Near the end of the meeting with Turville, Einstein flat out told Turville that Turville needed him as an outlet for his work, more so than Einstein needed him. Turville went ballistic when Einstein rejected his proposal. Einstein would not capitulate to Turville's wants, so Turville reacted as most bullies did.

"What do you know about anodynol?" Buck finally had the opportunity to ask Einstein a question, as Einstein had rambled on in a "sermon" about the sins, deficiencies, and aspirations of Turville for close to an hour.

The pastor shrugged, "Should I know anything about it?"

"It was the supposed miracle pain-relief drug that Turville and PAYNE Pharmaceuticals developed," Buck offered. "But it didn't work."

"Oh, I'd heard that some drug hadn't panned out as expected," Einstein said. "But I'm a firm believer in the words of Rudyard Kipling, 'Words are, of course, the most powerful drug used by mankind.'" Einstein's eyes sparkled as he told Buck that the Word of God preached by him was much more powerful in healing the pain of peoples than any pill the drug companies concocted. Reverend Einstein glanced at his watch.

"Do you happen to know Dr. Turville's wife, Shelley?" Buck casually asked.

"I almost forgot," the pastor commented, "could you supply me with contact information for Turville's widow? I need to send my personal condolences."

The manner in which Einstein requested the address seemed almost rehearsed to Buck. He followed up with the query: "Have you ever met Shelley Turville?"

"When you see her the next time, tell her I might be willing to give her a good price for her husband's work on quantum physics and Christianity." Reverend Einstein rose from his chair and ushered Buck to the office door. He somewhat jokingly, but also somewhat seriously, encouraged Buck to send any suspects in this second killing to participate in his "Pastor in a Box" segment of "The Holy Event." Perhaps he could once again solicit a confession like he did for the first killing. In fact, Einstein heard Lum was also being held in jail as a possible suspect. Perhaps Buck could send Lum for another encounter in the "Pastor in a Box." He'd heard that Turville was murdered with a bust of Vilsmeier, further connecting Lum to the previous "Pastor in a Box."

Einstein confided that "The Holy Event" airing Lum's confession was the most viewed re-run on the Quantum Christian Church's website, and as such, continued to make millions in donations for the church. With that departing message, Buck wondered whether the Quantum Christian Church had become more of a business and a power trip for Reverend Einstein and less a conduit for preaching the Word of God.

○ ● ○ ● ○

Einstein's secretary escorted Buck toward the music studio - office complex of Adam Clarke and Evalina Vail. On their way there, they passed by a courtyard with what looked like the strangest and largest jungle gyms ever seen by Buck. One was a cube, about fifty feet on a side, with interconnecting red and white balls.

The secretary pointed at the construction. "It's the world's largest model for the crystal structure of salt, sodium chloride (NaCl). It'd been the project of the teenagers of the church over the course of several years. The red balls represent sodium ions and the white chloride ions. They're arranged in interlocking face-centered cubic structures." She continued, as if reciting from memorization: "Over a quarter million balls, about a hundred miles of dowel sticks, and four hundred tubes of glue were used."

"But . . . but why?" Buck asked.

"It's a perfect crystal, perfect order, no defects," the secretary said. "Perfect, just like Jesus Christ."

Buck pointed to the other jungle gym structure. It was of about the same size with the red and white balls. This time the balls appeared to be haphazardly arranged, a jumbled mess.

"It's the theoretical anticrystal for sodium chloride," the secretary answered without being asked. "It's totally disordered, not even a smidgen of order. It's the polar opposite of perfection."

"I get it," Buck nodded. "Just like the Anti-Christ."

As expected, Evalina and Adam refused to speak to Buck. Evalina, as did their lawyer, thought Buck's purpose for interviewing them was to try to collect testimony to frame Adam for the murder of Turville.

Evalina, though, did walk with Buck back to his rental car, a gray Kia. Buck got Evalina to open up a bit under the guise of discussing Vilsmeier. She readily supplied the name of her artist friend who'd created the bust of Vilsmeier. He then asked about anodynol. Evidently, Turville told Evalina of its side effects causing NuDRUG to cancel its purchase of PAYNE Pharmaceuticals. Buck reasoned that, if she knew that anodynol resulted in sleep rather than pain relief, perhaps her husband Adam Clarke knew it as well.

"How easy would it be to fix anodynol?" Buck asked as they arrived at his car in the church's parking garage.

"Not sure what you mean," she looked puzzled.

"Make the right structure like in those frogs?"

Evalina giggled, "That's way above my pay grade."

Chapter Thirty One
POW WOWS

It'd been a month since Turville's murder. Buck's investigation floundered. The Sheriff called a meeting to review the evidence, to solicit opinions on potential leads.

The coroner confirmed a generally accepted fact. Turville was soundly asleep and head lying on his desk pad when he was beaned with Vilsmeier's bust from his rear. No signs were found of Turville protecting himself from the oncoming blow to the top of the head. It was sufficient to kill Turville almost instantly. Turville's bloodwork showed nothing abnormal for the most part, although at least one unidentifiable substance was present in significant quantities. These signals from the GC/MS analysis of Turville's blood didn't exist in the legal or illicit substance databank of the crime laboratory.

The crime scene unit reported very little, if anything, had been disturbed in Turville's office, a fact confirmed by Turville's secretary. The technicians also substantiated the coroner's conclusion: there was nary a struggle before Turville's "Death by Vilsmeier." They had found, in addition to the normal trash, a single tablet had been tossed into Turville's waste basket. That tablet was identified as the medication Turville used to control his blood pressure. In addition, Turville kept a veritable stockpile of anodynol tablets in bottles stored on one of his office shelves. The bottles appeared to have been obsessively arranged in perfect order, except for one bottle that looked like it had been returned to the shelf slightly askew. This bottle contained tablets with the highest dosage of anodynol. They noted this misplaced bottle only contained 24 anodynol tablets instead of its labeled 25, whereas all others contained the labeled amounts. They also commented that the anodynol tablet, interestingly, was a dead ringer for Turville's blood pressure tablet – that is, the same color, shape, and size. The only difference was the barely perceptible letter stamped on the face of the tablet. They obtained only partial fingerprints off both the blood pressure tablet and the anodynol bottle. The blood pressure tablet had smudged fingerprints, while the anodynol bottle had fingerprints consistent with those of BettyJo Burks. But the identification was fuzzy, probably not able to stand up in court.

A whole plethora of fingerprints, smudged or not in any data base, covered the bust of Vilsmeier. Only one set, that of BettyJo Burks, was conclusively identified. As discerned by Buck, even though the bust was cleaned at the beginning of the day, almost every visitor admitted to touching that "stupid" statue at one time or another. The one set of prints expected, that of Lum's, wasn't present. And one thing never found in the trash in the office and elsewhere was a pair of plastic gloves, just in case the murderer wore them to hide their use of the murder weapon.

"But, then," Buck interjected, "Lum would've known where to stash the gloves so they wouldn't be found." He shook his head.

The technicians explained that any fingerprints on the bust seemed to be an inconclusive dead end, as was DNA evidence thereon. But they were forwarding the bust to the feds, to see whether their more sophisticated methods might be able to pick up anything.

Buck reported on the main suspects, those that squabbled with Turville that day. Jim Payne, Jr., Ida Kay Hall, Sara Austin, Dr. Quinn Stanton, and Pastor Barney Bennington all had ironclad alibis. Belle Camden, Turville's secretary, had stopped by the HillTop Convenience Store on her way home that night and talked to the clerk for quite a while. Time stamps on the video survellance cleared her.

Adam Clarke and/or Evalina Vail were likely on the way to the airport at the time of the murder, making the timing not impossible but very unlikely. If they're the culprits, they'd have to have been driving crazy fast, literally flying, on the winding West Virginia highways to get to the airport on time. Lum actually gave Shelley Turville and probably Pastor Danny Einstein alibis, by seeing them at Hickory Grove close to the time of the murder.

"I just drove through Hickory Grove yesterday," the Sheriff cut in. "A 'For Sale' sign is in front of the Turville house."

"There're some strange things about Shelley Turville," Buck responded. "She seems to want to avoid me. She really doesn't seem interested in us solving her husband's murder. And why was Reverend Einstein's car parked near her house? I think both Shelley and the pastor are being less than candid in some of their statements to me."

The Sheriff nodded. "Sounds like something fishy going on. But is it relevant?"

Buck shrugged and continued with his analysis. "That leaves the three main suspects: Lum Baumgartner, BettyJo Burks, and the mystery man Willie Mudrick. Lum, though, may have just been at the wrong place at the wrong time."

"So, who do you like for the crime?" the Sheriff asked.

"Here's my working hypothesis," Buck offered. "The murderer must've known that Turville was due for his next blood pressure medication, and switched an anodynol tablet for the blood pressure tablet. Then, after the anodynol had put Turville to sleep, the murderer in turn knocked Turville's lights out permanently with Vilsmeier's bust. This means that the murderer had to be aware that Turville was on blood pressure medication, had to know that anodynol tablets looked like the blood pressure tablets in order to make the switch, had to have ready access to roam around the office to make the switch in the presence of Turville, had to know of the side effect of anodynol to put the victim to sleep, and had to have had access to Turville's office about a half hour before the murder to make the tablet switch. Such a set of circumstances eliminates all the prime suspects except one – BettyJo Burks. Both Lum and Adam Clarke, as well as Willie Mudrick, probably wouldn't have known enough about the personal habits of Turville to make the tablet switch as well as to even know that Turville was on blood pressure meds. BettyJo had motive and opportunity. She was clearly upset with Turville because he wasn't making any movement to leave his wife, then that day he also seemed to be putting his romantic moves on Evalina. Turville's wandering eye was once again wandering. After BettyJo's initial encounter with Turville that afternoon, she must've returned to his office, but saw Adam Clarke in his office. Perhaps, like Turville's secretary hiding in her office, BettyJo lurked in the shadow of the hallways. She remained, in a sense, around-the-corner so that she couldn't be seen by the eavesdropping Belle or by Clarke. When BettyJo overheard Adam Clarke's very vocal threat to kill Turville by the Vilsmeier bust, and fueled by her own anger, BettyJo must've plotted her revenge to make Turville pay for dumping her. After Clarke left Turville's office, BettyJo might've returned to Turville's office under the pretense of apologizing for her prior outburst. Furthermore, she might have consoled him for his upsets throughout the day. Then, before she reminded him to take his blood pressure medicine, she switched the blood pressure tablet for an anodynol tablet. After waiting a bit for Turville to fall asleep, BettyJo later made it permanently 'lights out' for Turville by slamming him with Vilsmeier's bust. Soon afterwards, after the exit of BettyJo, Lum must have stumbled into Turville's office and subsequently reported the crime."

The room was quiet, waiting for the Sheriff to respond.

"Sounds reasonable," proffered the Sheriff. "But is BettyJo strong enough to deliver a death blow with the bust. After all, she's just a wee thing." He snickered, "I don't think she goes to the gym."

"That's my main problem as well," Buck agreed.

One of the crime scene technicians spoke. "It would be nice to prove that Turville had anodynol in his bloodstream at the time of his death."

"Yep, without that, the evidence is circumstantial." Buck groused, "Unfortunately, your boss asked me whether I knew how many man-hours y'all would have to put into such an effort. He said it would take days and days to develop a standard analytical procedure for determining the presence in the bloodstream of a drug unknown to 99.9999% of the world. He said 'You've gotta be kidding!' and hung up on me."

The room, especially the lab technicians, erupted in laughter. One contributed, "Sounds like our overworked and humorless supervisor."

Another offered, "But he's right, it would take years to develop a procedure."

"Could it've been someone else, someone not on your radar – other than his visitors for the day?" the coroner thought out-loud.

Buck sighed, "Always a possibility. Many others seemed to have grudges against Turville. But none would've had the inside knowledge about the tablets. Turville didn't seem to have any other active mistresses at the time. BettyJo hasn't even gone back to work at PAYNE yet."

The Sheriff rose from his chair. He growled, "Sounds like BettyJo to me. Anger can get the adrenaline flowing in your body, make you stronger than you think." He looked directly at Buck. "Now get some evidence that'll stand up in court."

Buck nodded. As his daddy would've said, he would've been "tickled stupid" to put all the pieces of the crime together. But, Buck now had to prove this sequence of events. In order to do so, he first had to prove that indeed Turville had anodynol in his bloodstream at the time of his death.

○ ● ○ ● ○

Buck Fowler arrived at the Millikan Pizzeria straight from work. He wore his standard detective garb – khaki slacks with blue button-down shirt and loosened tie, Deputy Sheriff's winter jacket, and service revolver locked and loaded in his holster. He scanned the restaurant. It was more than half-empty. He saw Sara in a booth on the far-side. She seemed to be intently watching the entrance door.

Buck strolled to the counter in the front, placed his order with Tony, then went and sat across the table from Sara Austin. Sara was dressed in jeans and a turtleneck, with a cross necklace and dangly earrings. Her hair was pulled back into a ponytail, hurriedly done as if she'd come to the Pizzeria straight from work at PAYNE. They exchanged pleasantries and bantered in some small talk, mostly about the warming weather with spring around the corner.

Sara seemed fidgety to Buck. She kept looking at the entrance. No new customers.

Within a couple minutes, Wanda, the waitress, arrived with silverware, napkins, paper cup of Pepsi for Buck, and glass of Sweet Red Blend wine for Sara. Sara looked perplexed. She quickly looked around the restaurant.

Buck smiled. "Ida Kay said the Sweet Red Blend is your preferred wine." He paused, then continued, "I'd join you with a glass, but technically I'm still on duty."

Sara scrunched her nose. "What's going on here?"

Buck emanated a confused look. "Ida Kay told me to meet you here at five o'clock, that you had information on the Turville murder."

Sara burst out laughing.

"Now it's my turn," Buck shrugged. "What's going on here?"

"Ida Kay told me to be here by five o'clock," she related, "that I'd meet the man of my dreams."

Buck shook his head. He teased, "From a detective to a man of your dreams – I guess that's a promotion."

Sara's face turned red.

"And to state the obvious," Buck continued, "I assume you have no information for me."

"That's right," Sara nodded. She looked into his eyes. They had a certain alluring quality she hadn't noticed before.

Buck grinned broadly at Sara. He got up from the table. "I guess I'm officially off-duty now. I think I'll order a Coors up front." Upon returning to the table, he stated, "Our pizza should be arriving shortly. Ida Kay had told me what to order when I got here."

Ida Kay had indeed played the matchmaker. Sara and Buck discovered they had a lot in common. They traded stories. Buck confided he'd lost his wife of four years about five years ago. She'd been killed in a freak car accident. Someone ran a red light, slammed on his brakes, and hit her car on the driver's side – at just the wrong angle to crush the side panel into her. It should've never killed her, just real bad luck. It was the first time in many years he'd told the painful story. Sara gently touched his arm in understanding. They'd both had their losses.

But, with the times of sorrow in their rearview mirrors, they also shared laughter.

Buck told of a crazy incident he'd had to investigate the previous day. "Some things you couldn't make up." Greeley Ross, up on Muddy Lane, came home to a 46-year old woman and her six children making themselves comfortable in his unlocked cabin. She was wrapped only in a towel, having just taken a shower. She told him the house had been her grandparents' and "God told her to reclaim it." Greeley called 9-1-1. Buck had questioned the interloper as he and some deputies took her family to a shelter. She told him that God had sent a flock of crows to guide her to the house.

In the same category of real life being stranger than fiction, Sara told Buck of a big rig driver at PAYNE's loading dock the same day. Half the boxes he was supposed to deliver were missing. The driver told Sara he had a problem with critters half-teenager and half-insect hiding in his trailers and stealing stuff. She got a couple of co-workers to search the trailer with her. "We couldn't find any of the mutants," she laughed, "and the trucking company told us to take his keys."

They quickly became comfortable in each others presence. Turville was never mentioned. Sara wondered how she'd overlooked the charm of Detective Fowler. Buck compared Sara's beauty to Evalina's. Two lonely people became unlonely that night. They talked until they were the only ones left at the pizzeria. They finally got the hint that Tony and Wanda wanted to close up when Tony sat down at their table. Their private conversation no longer was private.

Sara then admitted to Buck she needed to get home. "Possum is going to be upset. He hasn't been fed yet." But she didn't leave until they made plans to get together again.

On his drive home that night, Buck's mind focused on Sara instead of anodynol and the Turville murder. As his daddy would've told him: "Life is as unpredictable as a grapefruit squirt."

Chapter Thirty Two

DEATH, IN PART, BY ANODYNOL

In the absence of help from his own crime laboratory to confirm anodynol had been used to drug Turville, Buck once again reached out to Dr. Quinn Stanton. They'd become good friends. This time, though, Buck was subtly recruiting Q-Dawg in his attempt to connect the unknown substance in Turville's blood to anodynol.

Q-Dawg admitted it wouldn't be too difficult for him to analyze for anodynol, given all the time and effort he'd previously devoted in his research to synthesize, then to characterize, the drug. From his perspective in using GC/MS analyses as a tool to study the molecular structure of anodynol, he perused the results of the crime laboratory. He concluded the unknown and unidentified substance in the lab's analysis might be anodynol. To prove beyond a shadow of doubt, though, Q-Dawg would have to do some analyses on his own, so as to correct for apparent differences in instruments, solvents, and protocols.

Buck explained to Q-Dawg his theory for Turville's murder – why he needed proof that anodynol had been switched with Turville's other medication. If his premise was true, such would link the crime to BettyJo Burks, Turville's mistress who had motive, knowledge, and opportunity. Then, Buck pled poverty. The Sheriff's Department had no funds to reimburse Q-Dawg for any work done.

Q-Dawg was undeterred. He was interested and intrigued. No money needed to exchange hands. His only needs would be a couple of the anodynol tablets from PAYNE Pharmaceuticals, and eventually a small sample of Turville's blood from his autopsy. Buck readily arranged these accommodations.

○ ● ○ ● ○

In the first step in his analytical scheme, Q-Dawg calibrated the amount of anodynol in a sample to the signal intensity in a GC/MS analysis. From his past work, he already knew that anodynol, as a dipyrazole, readily dissolved in a mixture of methylene chloride and methanol. He injected a sample of this solution containing only a fraction of a milligram of anodynol into the GC/MS and obtained a measurable signal. The GC (gas chromatograph) portion of the instrument immediately vaporized the liquid. The interaction of the anodynol with the packing material in the GC column controlled the time needed for this specific chemical to be transported to the detector. Thus, the GC signal at the set time identified the specific chemical; its intensity provided the amount of the chemical. Then, to further confirm the identity of the substance, the MS (mass spectrometry) component of the instrument provided the fingerprint, in a sense, of the chemical for that specific GC signal. Accordingly, Q-Dawg first powdered the tablet that contained anodynol amongst other filler and binder chemicals. He then weighed a known amount of the powder to supply him with a sample of a target mass of anodynol. Afterwards, he extracted the anodynol into a constant volume of methylene chloride – methanol solvent. Finally, he injected the resulting solution via syringe into the GC/MS. Q-Dawg established, as he anticipated, the more target anodynol in the sample, a proportionately larger signal, always occurring at the time specific to anodynol. Meanwhile, the complementary MS signal confirmed that indeed that GC peak was due to anodynol. Thus, his procedure not only identified the GC signal specific to anodynol, but also calibrated the intensity of the peak signal to the amount of anodynol.

For the next step in his procedure, Q-Dawg used himself as a human guinea pig. The Q-Dawg swallowed an anodynol tablet and his wife, who had nursing experience, observed that he fell soundly asleep within about 15 minutes. Q-Dawg's wife then collected small samples of the blood of a sleeping Q-Dawg at a half hour, one hour, and two hours after tablet ingestion. She had also collected a blood sample before he took the anodynol tablet as a reference point (for a sample not containing any anodynol). After sleeping about four hours, Q-Dawg woke suddenly but fell violently ill for the next several hours. Q-Dawg described the sickness as one of the worst times of his life – a combination of an extreme case of stomach flu with the nauseating feeling of food poisoning. He rapidly purged his body by spewing from both ends of anything in his stomach as well as intestines. After about three hours, he once again felt fine. He had initially planned to do a duplicate trial ingesting anodynol, but thought otherwise. Q-Dawg was quite impressed by the power of anodynol to both put the victim to sleep and to sicken in sequence; but, unfortunately, not for the control of pain as originally expected. It seemed contradictory that a medicine with such great promise for the control of pain instead induced pain.

The next day, Q-Dawg extracted the anodynol, and its metabolic byproducts, from a specific volume of both his and Turville's blood samples with a constant volume of methylene chloride – methanol solvent. He then injected these samples into the GC/MS. The blank sample, of course, showed no anodynol; and with his own blood samples he calibrated the amount of anodynol still in the bloodstream to the time after ingestion. Other signals from the instrument were identified as metabolic byproducts of anodynol. His analysis of Turville's blood sample demonstrated conclusively that not only was anodynol present but also just a short time had elapsed after Turville took the anodynol. As Q-Dawg reported back to Buck, he surmised that Turville must have been killed only minutes, less than a half hour maximum, after the anodynol had put him to sleep. All in all, Q-Dawg completed the needed analyses and identifications within a month amidst his college duties of teaching, research, and committees.

○ ● ○ ● ○

Ida Kay was watching several squirrels from her folding chair next to the driveway when Buck and Sara arrived. The dogwoods and redbuds in the yard were blooming. Buck gave Sara a quick kiss before strolling hand in hand over to Ida Kay.

Without taking her eyes from her squirrel experiment, Ida Kay chuckled, "You know, you transferred eighty million microbes in that kiss."

"I'm shooting for a billion by the end of the day," Buck deadpanned. He glanced at Sara and smiled.

Sara blushed and playfully bopped Buck in the shoulder.

Ida Kay went on to describe her squirrel experiment in progress, regardless of whether such would interest her visitors or not. She put out peanuts, almonds, and walnuts at different locations in the yard. Earl, the big squirrel preferred the walnuts, while Pearl wanted the almonds, and Fuzzy tried to hoard as many of any he could carry. Elmo was cautious. He hid in the big oak tree until she went into the house.

Buck had called ahead. Ida Kay already had the hanging basket of flowers prepared for Buck. Once given to Sara as a present, Sara transferred many millions of her microbes to Buck.

On their walk back to the car, Buck turned to Ida Kay. "I'm concerned about Wilma Warren, AKA 'Winky.' She was arrested again yesterday."

Ida Kay kicked at the gravels and grumbled under her breath.

Buck continued, "She tried to pass a bogus $20 bill at the Millikan Grocery. It was a real bad photocopy. Monopoly money would've looked better. So the deputies raided the place she shares with her boyfriend, who's definitely not a good influence on her. They found lots of bad counterfeit bills. The boyfriend said he'd told her to use a better grade of paper. He threw her under the bus. The deputies also found a bottle of pain pills, Oxycontin. Boyfriend said Winky was hooked on them."

"Maybe you should've substituted anodynol for the Oxycontin," Ida Kay snarled. "That would've cured her of taking pain pills – putting her to sleep and making her sick."

"How'd you know that about anodynol?" Buck growled.

Ida Kay got tickled. "Word gets around."

Buck shook his head.

"I'm sure Winky will be calling about bail." Ida Kay sighed. "Fortunately, my apartment is empty. I'll put her back to meaningful work." She paused a moment. "By the way, talking about anodynol, how's your Turville murder investigation coming?"

"You know I can't discuss that." Buck rolled his eyes.

Ida Kay chuckled. "I hear you're zeroing in on BettyJo."

Buck shook his head again.

Ida Kay turned to Sara. "I bet you tell Sara tidbits about what's going on."

Sara smiled. "I plead the Fifth."

Ida Kay turned back to Buck. "It also seems like Shelley Turville and Reverend Einstein are becoming quite the item. He claims she was his inspiration to complete his mathematical analysis proving God and Quantum Christianity. Have you watched 'The Holy Event' lately?"

Both Sara and Buck nodded. Sara commented, "I've noticed the same. They seem smitten with each other." Buck remained mute, deep in thought.

"Oh," Ida Kay laughed. "You know – what's the difference between mathematics and the Bible?"

Sara and Buck stared at Ida Kay in wonder.

Ida Kay laughed louder. "Math isn't forgiving."

Buck put the floral basket in the car's rear seat and opened the door for Sara, then circled the car to get in as well. He started the car, but Ida Kay tapped on the passenger window for Buck to lower it.

She leaned in toward Sara. "I always heard – in fact maybe I heard it from Buck's daddy. You should always hope for enough happiness to make you sweet, enough trials to make you strong, enough sorrow to keep you human, and enough hope to make you happy."

Tears of happiness and hope clouded Sara's eyes.

○ ● ○ ● ○

A week later, the trees were half dressed for Sara and Buck's drive to Keaton College. It was springtime in West Virginia.

They arrived at Q-Dawg's home unannounced. There, they presented him with a bronze bust of Anton Vilsmeier, just like the one that had graced Turville's desk before being used in his murder. Buck said this duplicate was in appreciation for the police work of Q-Dawg. Q-Dawg was humbled. Evidently, Evalina's friend never destroyed the mold from which the original had been made. The artist created this replicate for Buck for just the cost of the bronze.

Chapter Thirty Three
CONFESSION, SOMEWHAT

Buoyed by a renewed confidence in the circumstances surrounding the murder of Dr. Mason Turville, Buck arranged for BettyJo Burks to meet him at the Sheriff's Office for further questioning. She arrived with her lawyer, Anderson Clay, a newly minted law school graduate who'd just set up shop in Colebrook. Buck was taken aback as he entered the spartan room by how terrible BettyJo looked. She appeared quite emaciated, having lost lots of weight from her already thin frame of a couple months ago. Buck contemplated what his daddy would've said: "She looked so thin, she had only one side." In this condition, Turville wouldn't even have given her a second glance, much less sweet talk her into becoming his mistress.

BettyJo couldn't sit still as introductions were made. She continually fidgeted with her hands, acting nervous and edgy.

Buck quickly put his cards on the table. He looked BettyJo square in the eyes. "Here's what you did. You overheard Adam Clarke threatening to bop your lover over the head with Vilsmeier's bust. You saw your opportunity to garner revenge on Mason – do what Pastor Clarke threatened, and blame it on him. Mason had just put the moves on Evalina and told you to get lost."

BettyJo stared at her shoes, squirming in her chair.

Buck talked with more force. "You knew Mason was due for his blood pressure medication. You also knew the anodynol tablets were readily available in his office and looked the same as his blood pressure tablets. And that anodynol would put Mason to sleep fast. You made the tablet substitution while Mason worked at his desk, then waited for him to fall asleep. You took the opportunity to smash him in the back of his head with the bronze bust of Vilsmeier. Your fingerprints are all over the –"

"I did the tablet switch, but I didn't kill my dear Mason," BettyJo whispered, while still staring at her feet. Despite the efforts of Mr. Clay to silence her, she continued, albeit louder and looking straight at Buck. "I would never do anything to hurt my Mason."

Buck felt buoyed, like a boxer who has his opponent on the ropes. "Come'on BettyJo, we know you did it. If you couldn't have Mason, Evalina certainly wasn't gonna. Mason kicked you to the curb. You did it!"

BettyJo confessed, once again, to using the anodynol to put her lover asleep. She kept talking as though, if she didn't let it all out, she would explode from her own personal pressure cooker. She'd planned to hit him over the head with the bust to hurt him, not kill him, just like she was hurting. Like Lum in the first "Death by Vilsmeier," she talked over her lawyer's advice to shut up in this next "Death by Vilsmeier." But she said she had second thoughts on her plan. She couldn't go through with it. She loved her Mason.

"Your fingerprints are all over Vilsmeier's bust," Buck increased the volume of his voice yet again. "You did it!"

Mr. Clay interjected, "So are a dozen other individuals'. The fingerprints don't prove anything. She admitted touching it earlier in the day."

BettyJo once again ignored her lawyer. She conceded to picking up the bust to whack Mason. But she threw the bust back down on the desk, and ran from Mason's office. According to her story, she retrieved her pocketbook from her office, ran to her car, and went home. The next she heard, the police wanted to ask her some questions about the death of her Mason. Just at the thought of her Mason being dead, she was mortified and overwhelmed with grief.

Buck shrugged his shoulders and stared at BettyJo. "Come'on BettyJo, let's come completely clean! You want me to believe you just ran away; that you planned to whack that sleazeball Turville over the head, but that you ran away. There was no one else there – you had to do it!"

BettyJo regained her composure somewhat. Knowing that Lum entered the office after she left, he must've finished his revenge on her lover by killing him. BettyJo stated matter-of-fact to Buck: "Lum must've done it!"

No matter how hard Buck pressed BettyJo to confess to the murder, BettyJo stuck to her story. She readily confessed to putting Turville to sleep with anodynol, but she wouldn't admit to finishing the "Death by Vilsmeier."

"So did you pass Lum coming into PAYNE as you were going out?" Buck asked harshly.

"Nope," BettyJo said, as she blinked her eyes uncontrollably. "I did pass, though, some other guy in the hallway. I'd never seen him before. He had long hair, not very attractive." She paused, then mumbled, "I think he wore a bright red cap. It had the letter 'W' on it and the picture of some animal. If Lum didn't kill my Mason, then he must've."

"So now all of a sudden, you create an imaginary man to give credence to your story," Buck growled. "Give me a break, BettyJo – just fess up. How many others are you gonna blame?"

BettyJo started to cry. "You know, Detective Fowler, before my Mason went to sleep, he apologized to me. He said he'd made a mistake, for me to forgive him. So why would I kill him?"

"Now you're really talking nonsense, making up more stuff," Buck snarked.

Mr. Clay gave her some tissues. After drying her eyes, she continued, "I told my Mason . . . if he didn't come back to me, I'd burn his papers he kept at my house."

Buck feigned interest. "Mason came over to your house outside Colebrook to do work. You expect me to believe that as well?"

"He didn't want Shelley to know what he was doing. She was always rifling through his papers on Quantum Christianity. She'd go through them when she thought he wasn't looking," she spat out with venom. "My Mason would work on his mathematical proof, 'new and improved' according to him, over at my place. He was brilliant." BettyJo smiled. "My Mason said he liked it when I massaged his back and neck as he worked differential equations. It helped him with his solutions and ideas." She paused and looked to the heavens. She grinned, "I was going to be the First Lady of his church."

Mr. Clay looked at Buck as though his client had lost her mind.

Buck, though, was now interested. "Do you still have the papers?" he asked casually.

"Nope," BettyJo grumbled. "I burned 'em. I was never gonna let Shelley have 'em." A smile then returned to her face, as if a pleasant memory struck a chord. "I did keep one page by which to remember my Mason." She pulled out a folded piece of paper from her pocketbook and handed it to Buck.

Buck tried to understand the writings and equations. Evidently, this saved paper must have been the first page in his analysis. It gave some rationalizations for what followed. As close as Buck could figure, Turville's previous work on Quantum Christianity was based on Euclidian geometry, normal x-y-z space – the papers Shelley collected from her husband's desk. But the space of our universe according to Einstein (Albert) and others is curved, not one with square corners. Turville was developing a new theory of Quantum Christianity based upon hyperbolic geometry. This more sophisticated math resulted in immense improvements from his previous theory. Buck stared at the corner of the room thinking. He mumbled to himself: "Shelley lied. The theory and math were all Turville's." He scratched his head. He continued to mumble to himself: "Not only the mathematical proof now in Shelley's possession, but also a supposedly improved proof hidden from Shelley."

Buck told BettyJo he needed to keep the page as evidence. BettyJo went hysterical. She snatched the paper from Buck's hands, ripping the page in the process. Then she attacked Buck, flailing and kicking, trying to retrieve the rest of the page. Buck's arms bled from the resulting deep scratches. Both Mr. Clay and Buck had to physically restrain her, taking several minutes to do so. Once back in her seat, she refused to talk anymore. She sat and sulked.

Buck left the room and consulted with the Sheriff and prosecutor, both of whom had been watching the proceedings. He returned to the room and announced BettyJo would be charged with murder. BettyJo regained a relaxed but defiant look. She'd unloaded from her heart what she had planned to do in the passion of the moment.

"Y'all are jumping the gun," Mr. Clay complained. "You just have a circumstantial case. You have my client's admission that she put him to sleep, but no confession or any shred of evidence to support the murder." He smiled. "Look at BettyJo, just a wee thing. Would any juror actually believe she had the strength to whack Turville with enough force to leave an indention of Vilsmeier's face in his skull?"

Buck turned his arms to Mr. Clay to reveal the still bleeding cuts. He pulled up his shirt to show several bruises. "These will be photographed. Her outburst, which was as vicious as a cornered bobcat, was captured on videotape. I think the jurors will believe when they see the pent-up energy of a woman scorned." Buck chuckled, "As my daddy used to say, 'Lettin' the cat outta the bag is a whole lot easier than puttin' it back in.'"

○ ● ○ ● ○

A half hour later, Buck sat at his desk working on the case's paperwork. The Sheriff had been happy, congratulated him for solving the case – and for being willing to sacrifice his body to show BettyJo indeed had the strength to whomp Turville. Buck sat back in his chair and took a deep breath. He was pleased with himself. Perhaps he could convince BettyJo to face off with Reverend Einstein in his "Pastor in a Box." Maybe, she'd give a full confession, just like Lum.

The phone rang. The fingerprint expert in the state crime lab said the feds identified a set of fingerprints on Vilsmeier's bust, the murder weapon in the Turville case. "They belonged to a guy by the name of Shelton Smith."

"Who's he?" Buck yelled, as he threw his pen against the wall of his office.

PART 4

FINAL REVENGE

Chapter Thirty Four
DIFFERENT CLOAKS

While Buck Fowler investigated Turville's "Death by Vilsmeier," Lum was serving his prison sentence for Ron Austin's "Death by Vilsmeier." At first, Lum simply languished in prison. He felt overwhelming remorse. He sought forgiveness from everyone involved. Lum realized he'd done evil and needed to pay the price to society for his wrongs. He deserved his punishment, and more. Of more concern to him was the near-destruction of his spiritual well-being, no longer thinking he was worthy of God's love and mercy. Many days, Lum simply sat in his jail cell and read his Bible, most times focusing on the Apostle Paul's letters. In particular, he seemed drawn to the 12th chapter of Romans in which Paul wrote –

> *Romans 12:17-21*
>
> Do not repay anyone evil for evil. Be careful to do what is right in the eyes of everybody. If it is possible, as far as it depends on you, live at peace with everyone. Do not take revenge, my friends, but leave room for God's wrath, for it is written: 'It is mine to avenge, I will repay,' says the Lord. On the contrary:
>
> "If your enemy is hungry, feed him;
> if he is thirsty, give him something to drink.
> In doing this, you will heap

burning coals on his head."
Do not be overcome by evil, but overcome evil with good.

Lum reasoned he'd been overcome by evil and, worse yet, a misplaced evil. Instead of leaving this evil for God's judgment, he sought revenge on his own. Lum often pondered why, on that fateful night in his rage, the Bible didn't spill open to these verses in Romans instead of the ones in Genesis directing him to Jacob's sons seeking revenge on Shechem. He shook his head and stomped his feet. He kept trying to rewrite history, to skew his memories. He'd actually searched the Bible for a justification for revenge. He would've ignored the passage in Romans. One of the prison guards told him a saying that kept reverberating in his mind – "A moment of patience in a moment of anger saves you a thousand moments of regret." If only he'd waited several days to seek his revenge, he'd have realized the folly of his thoughts.

Lum was especially remorseful for his sins against Ron and Sara Austin. Due to his own selfish and misplaced revenge, he unwittingly took the life of Ron. His financial reparations to Sara could never fully right this wrong. Once released from prison, he vowed to make further amends by sacrificing his needs to support her earthly needs. He knew in his heart, though, such would always fall far short of replacing her loss.

Lum still felt little advancement in his spiritual well-being. He seemed to be stuck in a pattern. He prayed to God for forgiveness, but kept questioning, "So what? What would be next for me to do in God's world? What can I do – I'm a sinner and a convicted felon?"

○ ● ○ ● ○

For the first week after Turville's murder, Lum's most frequent visitor at the prison was detective Buck Fowler. He kept pestering Lum about the events surrounding the murder. Buck accused him of bonking his nemesis over the head with the bust of Vilsmeier, thinking it would be just as easy for Lum to kill twice in the name of Vilsmeier as it was once. Sometimes, Buck played "bad cop" on him, pressuring him to confess. Then, other times, Buck played "good cop" and sat down with Lum in his cell. Often, Buck discussed Reverend Einstein's "The Holy Event" from the previous Sunday. They had both become regular viewers.

Lum sat glued to the television screen set to the HTN network every chance he had, in particular beaming with pride when Evalina sang. Evalina, as his personal messenger for hope, visited every other month or so. Like her appearances in "The Holy Event" spread joy to millions of television viewers, her appearance at the Millikan prison always provided unabashed cheer to Lum.

And Ida Kay Hall didn't toss Lum aside. He'd tell her not to come, that "she had better things to do." But she claimed she needed someone to tell her stories, that she had a captive audience in him.

Besides telling Lum of her experiments with crows and squirrels as well as the latest animals being rehabbed, Ida Kay told stories of giraffe weevils and rhinoceros beetles. In both these cases, the small guys outsmart their bigger rivals to get the female. She'd tell him of red-billed oxpeckers, a type of bird, living in a symbiotic relatioinship with rhinoceruses; of certain spiders mimicking ants; of slime moulds being able to learn; and of female wrens judging the singing ability of their male suitors; amongst many others. She always occupied her visitation time with interesting yarns. The prison guard would usually laugh at her telling of the stories, while Lum always responded with "crazy woman."

After a few weeks, Lum mellowed. He'd found an intriguing fact in a magazine in the prison library. On Ida Kay's next visit, he asked, "Where does the smallest possum in the world live?"

Ida Kay eye's opened wide. She was astounded. No words came from her mouth.

"Australia." Lum's grin covered most of his face. He knew something about possums that Ida Kay, the Possum Lady, didn't. "At ten grams, or a fraction of an ounce, the pygmy possum is one of the world's smallest mammels."

Lum would then scour the prison library looking for animal trivia to try to stomp Ida Kay. For example, he discovered chickens exuded a natural misquito repellant, pill bugs have green blood, the hagfish's only bone in its body is its skull, and slingshot spiders accelerate almost a hundred times faster than a cheetah. Ida Kay and Lum would then continually kid and tease each other. They became more comfortable in each other's company.

It was hard to determine who was more disappointed when the hour for Ida Kay's visit had expired. The prison guards were rapt not only with interest but also enjoyed the back-and-forth banter. They often volunteered for the duty, saying "such was the best entertainment in the prison." They also knew the two posed no threats, looking the other way when the visits started to end with a parting hug or kiss

○ ● ○ ● ○

About two months into his prison sentence, Lum was visited by Pastor Barney Bennington, complete with long hair, scraggly beard, blue jeans, and tie-dyed shirt. In a weak attempt at humor, Pastor Bennington told Lum he was visiting the "shut-in's" of Goose Creek Lutheran Church, and that Lum was definitely "shut-in." Pastor Barney, as he wanted to be called, also tried to provide a spiritual message of redemption and hope. But Lum remained combative and angry. Lum couldn't get past the pastor's appearance. Lum never heard what the pastor said, just envisioned him as someone whom Turville had foisted upon the congregation. Finally, Lum spewed vehemently to Pastor Barney that he really didn't want to talk to a "hippie-lookin' preacher."

About a week after that visit, Lum was called to the visitor's lounge. There a distinguished gentleman in a blue pin-striped suit with a clergyman's collar stood waiting for Lum. Lum immediately imagined this man as the reincarnation of Billy Graham, back when Reverend Graham was in his prime. Lum further felt this man's holiness radiating in all directions. He ran in excitement to this new preacher. When they finally faced off and shook hands, Lum realized the hand he held was that of none other than Pastor Barney. Lum shook and cried with raw emotion. Pastor Barney explained that if it took a change in his appearance to communicate with him, then so be it. The congregation had been equally shocked when Pastor Barney led Goose Creek's Sunday service clean shaven, with neatly-trimmed hair, and dressed in ministerial garb. Even the young people of the congregation thought the change in the pastor's appearance was a hoot. His sermon that Sunday on whether anyone would recognize Jesus if they passed by him on the street – that is, whether Jesus would have a beard or be clean shaven; or whether Jesus would be dressed in robes or a suit; or whether Jesus would have long hair or neatly trimmed – was a total success in communication to both young and old alike. Everyone's picture of what constitutes a godly appearance was different, but yet the message of what constitutes godly behavior should be the same.

At that moment in time, the line of communication between Lum and Pastor Barney opened. Almost immediately Lum unconsciously wanted to discuss with the pastor the biblical reunion of Joseph with his brothers who years before had sold Joseph into slavery. Like Joseph's brothers, who neither recognized Joseph's physical appearance nor his inherent goodness upon their reunification in Egypt, Lum overlooked Pastor Barney, simply because of appearance. But Lum's eyes, like Joseph's brothers', were jubilant in their new-found glory. Lum grabbed his Bible and instantly turned to chapters 42 through 45 of Genesis, reading aloud several of the verses as he encountered them.

> *Genesis 42:3-8 and 45:1-5*
>
> Then ten of Joseph's brothers went down to buy grain from Egypt. But Jacob did not send Benjamin, Joseph's brother, with the others, because he was afraid that harm might come to him. So Israel's sons were among those who went to buy grain, for the famine was in the land of Canaan also.
>
> Now Joseph was the governor of the land, the one who sold grain to all its people. So when Joseph's brothers arrived, they bowed down to him with their

> faces to the ground. As soon as Joseph saw his brothers, he recognized them, but he pretended to be a stranger and spoke harshly to them. "Where do you come from?" he asked.
>
> "From the land of Canaan," they replied, "to buy food."
>
> Although Joseph recognized his brothers, they did not recognize him.
>
> . . . Then Joseph could no longer control himself before all his attendants, and he cried out, "Have everyone leave my presence!" So there was no one with Joseph when he made himself known to his brothers. And he wept so loudly that the Egyptians heard him, and Pharoah's household heard about it.
>
> Joseph said to his brothers, "I am Joseph! Is my father still living?" But his brothers were not able to answer him, because they were terrified at his presence.
>
> Then Joseph said to his brothers, "Come close to me." When they had done so, he said, "I am your brother Joseph, the one you sold into Egypt! And now, do not be distressed and do not be angry with yourselves for selling me here, because it was to save lives that God sent me ahead of you."

Lum proclaimed that God, through Joseph, saved Joseph's brothers not only from the famine but also from their selfishness. And now, furthermore like Joseph's brothers, he too felt he'd taken another step away from his spiritual famine and selfishness. Lum wept so loudly with joy that the prison guards stared wide-eyed at Lum and Pastor Barney.

Lum hugged Pastor Barney. Lum repeated over and over his appreciation to the pastor as one willing to completely change his appearance to save the soul of just one individual. Lum then thought how selfish he'd been in wanting a pastor and a message that fit his mold. His mind wandered back to the battles he'd fought at Goose Creek Lutheran Church to have the worship services his way, even when Pastor Clarke, now his son-in-law, tried to warn the people of Paul's message that it was selfish to think that worship services had to be that one way. Lum mused about his inherent selfishness all those years. Pastor Barney finally opened Lum's eyes to seeing through God's eyes. God's message could come in many packages, not just wrapped in Lum's way of thinking. Now that Pastor Barney had changed his looks to satisfy Lum's desires, Lum quietly felt an immense guilt for having the message his way!

Pastor Barney visited Lum every week in prison. Most often Pastor Barney spoke of the Apostle Paul. In his early years, Paul readily admitted he was a nasty person, rounding up Christians for persecution. He then saw Jesus, and became the voice of the early Christian church, and eventually jailed in Rome for his beliefs. Many of Paul's letters were written and distributed throughout the Christian world while he was in jail. In fact, Paul wrote a letter to his protégé Timothy that summarized his past and conversion –

> *1 Timothy 1:12-17*
>
> I thank Christ Jesus our Lord, who has given me strength, that he considered me faithful, appointing me to his service. Even though I was once a blasphemer and a persecutor and a violent man, I was shown mercy because I acted in ignorance and unbelief. The grace of our Lord was poured out on me abundantly, along with the faith and love that are in Jesus Christ.
>
> Here is a trustworthy saying that deserves full acceptance Christ Jesus came into the world to save sinners – of whom I am the worst. But for that very reason I was shown mercy to that in me, the worst of sinners, Christ Jesus might display his unlimited patience as an example for those who would believe on him and receive eternal life. Now to the King eternal, immortal, invisible, the only God, be honor and glory for ever and ever. Amen.

Pastor Barney encouraged Lum to model his life after that of Paul – to truly find Jesus in his heart after having done evil, to use the time in prison for reflection, and to spread the goodness of Christianity. During one of his visits, Pastor Barney also indicated to Lum he'd stumbled upon a quote that summarized Paul's life. In the words of the author Maria Robinson, "Nobody can go back and start a new beginning, but anyone can start today and make a new ending." Indeed, Lum evolved into a humble and reverent man, starting anew on the path to seeing God in His true light, not the light predicated on Lum's prior stubbornness and foolishness.

With the aid of Pastor Barney, Lum started a Bible study group in prison. Pastor Barney supplied a poster for this group that was then copied many times and found its way into most of the cells.

YOU ARE NOT TOO DIRTY FOR GOD TO CLEANSE,
YOU ARE NOT TOO BROKEN FOR GOD TO FIX,
YOU ARE NOT TOO FAR FOR GOD TO REACH,
YOU ARE NOT TOO GUILTY FOR GOD TO FORGIVE,
YOU ARE NOT TOO WORTHLESS FOR GOD TO LOVE.

Pastor Barney indicated he'd copied it as well from someone else, who in turn copied it from someplace, so many times no one knew its true source.

Many of the prisoners also watched the worship services telecast on the HTN (Holy Trinity Network) with Lum, then discussed the spiritual ramifications of Reverend Einstein's sermons and presentations. The other prisoners envied Lum once they discovered that the beautiful singer for "The Holy Event" was Lum's daughter, Evalina. It was as if such gave Lum extra credibility in their mind.

Every now and then, Pastor Barney teased Lum by calling him "Paul," in honor of Lum's somewhat analogous conversion in following and spreading the teachings of Jesus Christ.

Chapter Thirty Five
ALL IN THE FAMILY

"Shelton Smith was arrested ten years ago for robbery and assault. He evidently beaned a so-called friend with a baseball bat. Then he took the guy's wallet, claimed he owed him money," explained the fingerprint expert at the state crime lab. "He served a couple years in the pen. Then he got nabbed in Peru for, of all things, trying to smuggle protected frogs out of the country. Just got released from their hole of a prison a week or so before Mason Turville's murder."

Buck cringed. He didn't look forward to telling this development to the Sheriff. His boss wouldn't be happy. Mr. Clay, on the other hand, would be thrilled. He'd be getting his client out of jail without doing anything.

The crime lab technician continued, "I don't know how the feds, but not us, picked up these fingerprints. The prints were probably mixed with the muddled mess of them on the bust. The feds claim Smith's fingerprints were positioned on opposite sides of the bust, just like someone using it to smash Turville's head. But the one thing I can't figure out is why Smith wasn't on your list of possible suspects."

Buck closed his eyes. He put his elbow on the desk and used it to prop up his head. He stewed for a few moments before he mumbled, "Willie Mudrick."

"Now, you wanna hear the real shocker," the technician snickered.

Buck just grumbled. He snapped in half a pencil laying on his desk.

"Smith's last reported address, probably several years old, is 314 Birch Lane in the Hickory Grove subdivision. Sound familiar?" He broke out laughing.

Buck hit disconnect with a vengeance. He growled, "Turville's place."

○ ● ○ ● ○

That night, Sara came over to Buck's house to treat his wounds, both to his body and to his ego. The bruises were turning black-and-blue and his muscles becoming sore. Buck also suffered from one of BettyJo's kicks to his right calf. He could barely limp around – not only sore but now also stiff. Plus, Buck remained out of sorts from the revelation of the crime lab, then the subsequent angry outbursts from the Sheriff and prosecutor. BettyJo had been released from custody soon after.

Sara made dinner of hamburger steak and gravy with mashed potatoes and green beans. Buck only picked at the meal. Then, they snuggled on the couch and relaxed by watching some game shows on television. Little was said. Buck's eyes were getting heavy by nine o'clock that night.

The phone rang. Buck looked at the caller ID – Central Dispatch. He sighed; the last thing he wanted to do that night was go on a call.

Central Dispatch apologized for telephoning. They'd just received a 9-1-1 call from Belle Hagan. She seemed flustered and out-of-breath. She insisted that Detective Fowler needed to call her immediately.

Buck turned to Sara and shrugged. He grimaced, even the shrug hurt his sore muscles. "Belle – she used to be Turville's secretary – wants something."

Belle reported she'd just watched a re-run of Reverend Einstein's "The Holy Event." The date of its original airing was about a month prior. She was stunned to see a man who looked like Willie Mudrick sitting next to Shelley Turville. She replayed over-and-over the scene when the camera panned the congregation. She swore that the person was a cleaned-up and clean-shaven Willie Mudrick or his twin.

Buck looked upward in shock, once off the phone. He internally fomented, “The case floundered along for months. Now, within hours of the time I put the last piece in the puzzle of Turville’s murder and thought I closed the case, it explodes in a different direction. What luck? Why didn’t all this information come out yesterday?”

Sara snuggled into Buck’s chest. He held her tightly and immediately felt better.

Sara helped Buck access the re-runs of past programs on the Quantum Christian Church’s website. He saw the man sitting next to Shelley Turville and her children. Indeed, he looked like the picture of Willie Mudrick – minus beard and long hair – drawn by the sketch artist from Belle’s recollections. And sitting next to Shelley, the family resemblance was obvious.

Sara and Buck went on a late night stroll through the neighborhood. He needed to clear his head, even though his leg hurt. Limping was better than sitting and stewing. And Sara wanted to be with him, to console him.

Buck was lost in his thoughts. Perhaps he initially jumped in the wrong direction, thinking the murder was all about Turville’s boorish behavior. It always bothered him that Shelley Turville hadn’t been pushing for a resolution of her husband’s murder. In fact, she never even called him. He always called her with an update or report. He’d called that afternoon. BettyJo had been arrested and charged with the murder. She was emotionless. He’d assumed such was Shelley Turville’s own unique way of grieving, that of escapism without anger. Her attitude was nothing but totally apathetic. There was also her move to Dallas, happening only months after her husband’s death, seemingly to be with Reverend Einstein. He remembered his Sheriff basically implying, “So what? It may be scandalous; but is it relevant?”

Shelley had flagrantly lied to him, claimed her husband’s mathematical papers to be hers. Buck kicked at a stick on the sidewalk. His leg thumped. He turned to Sara. “My daddy always said, ‘There’re three types of memory – good, bad, and convenient.' Shelley Turville's memory clearly fits into the last category."

Shelley Turville had appeared to be the clueless wife. She claimed not to know what her husband did at work. She seemed oblivious to his romantic affairs and wandering eye. She just took care of the kids and was a stay-at-home wife with very few friends.

Buck thought out loud: "What if it all was really an act on her part?"

Sara nodded. She gave a squeeze to his hand.

"Shelley seems like the central figure in the case, even though Lum inadvertently gave her an alibi," he spouted. "What's her relationship to Reverend Einstein? What's her connection to Willie Mudrick, or rather Shelton Smith?" He gritted his teeth and spewed, "It's mighty relevant!"

The time approached midnight when the two returned from their moon lit walk. Sara, once again, aided Buck in his internet search – this time on Shelley Turville's background. They quickly discovered she'd earned both a Bachelor's and a Master's degree in Applied Mathematics. She clearly would've understood the relevance of her husband's mathematical papers. And according to BettyJo, she probably knew about his proof for the quantum mechanical basis of the Holy Spirit.

"Did she also know he was trying to market such to Reverend Einstein?" Buck queried, deep in thought.

"I'd say yes." Sara smiled. "But did she find out through her husband or through Reverend Einstein?"

Buck nodded, "Key question." He finally laughed for the first time in several hours. "The Sheriff may hire you to replace me."

Upon further investigation, they discovered that Shelley Turville, nee Smith, had a twin brother by the name of Shelton Smith. He'd graduated from the University of Wisconsin with a double major in Spanish and Field Biology.

"Shelley and Shelton – definitely names for a set of twins," Sara observed.

"The color for Wisconsin is red," Buck scowled, "and its mascot is a badger. Shelton Smith, Shelley's brother, is definitely

Willie Mudrick – seen by BettyJo going toward Turville's office to garner his revenge."

○ ● ○ ● ○

Early the next morning, the Dallas police arrived at Reverend Danny Einstein's guesthouse, home for Shelley Turville and, at least on probation records, for Shelton Smith as well. Shelley greeted the police as a very concerned and helpful citizen. She politely gave the officers another address, a townhouse several blocks away, where her brother had moved a couple weeks previously.

The police then reported back to detective Buck Fowler: "It looked as though the suspect left in a hurry moments before we appeared. He skedaddled. We suspect his sister gave him a head's up. The coffee pot was still warm. They'd keep the place under surveillance, but didn't think he'd return."

○ ● ○ ● ○

Buck canvassed the ex-neighbors of Mason and Shelley Turville on Birch Lane in Hickory Grove. One person disclosed there appeared to be a man hanging around the Turville house with Shelley the day of her husband's murder. That man didn't seem to be intentionally hiding his presence, but on the other hand wasn't making his presence known either. According to the neighbor, "It was just odd!" But no one had inquired of the neighbor previously.

Buck hit the jackpot in an interview with Mrs. Naomi Tingler, the widow of Roland Tingler who'd been the police chief in neighboring Colebrook. She lived across the street and one house down from the Turvilles. The frumpy, gray-haired lady had made it her mission to keep track of all the comings and goings at Hickory Grove. She opened a notebook she kept next to her front window and turned back to 12 February. She said the Turville house had a revolving door the day of Mason Turville's murder. Shelley had a visitor who arrived an hour after Mason left for work. He drove a real beater of a car, an old and dirty gray Chevy. She opined Shelley should've been embarrassed to have such a car visiting in Hickory Grove. Not only that, but the guy was dirty looking. He left mid-afternoon but returned about an hour later. He parked the car in the garage. Around dinner time, a handsome man in a spotlessly clean black Cadillac SUV parked at the *cul de sac*. The guy in the old beater car left a few minutes later. Two guys soon showed up in an old Dodge Ram pickup truck. The passenger, a short, stubby guy, talked to Shelley briefly in the doorway of the house. They left. The man in the Cadillac immediately pulled up to Shelley's. He parked the car in the garage. About a half hour later, the beater car returned. Then, both the Chevy and the Cadillac left within a minute of each other around seven o'clock, as the national news was ending on television.

"It was disgusting," the widow spilled. "She hugged the one guy, the one in the nasty car, as he left. I'd never seen him there before. But she got all kissy and huggy with the other one, just like all the other times." She turned up her nose. "I knew what was happening."

"What do you mean, just like the other times?" Buck opened his eyes wide.

"For the past year, the man in the Cadillac would show up every month or so – usually for only part of a day and usually when Mason was out of town." The widow grumped, "Does she think we're stupid, that we couldn't put two and two together?"

○ ● ○ ● ○

Buck stopped at the small Colebrook Municipal Airport. The owner of the airstrip initially didn't want to cooperate. But Buck convinced him otherwise. He'd have officers dropping by to check for drug activity every day for the next month and tie him up with paperwork. Evidently, Reverend Einstein wanted to keep his presence hushed up. He paid a pretty penny to do so. The owner opened his records to Buck – eight visits in the past year; it was just him with the pilot and co-pilot in and out the same day, except for the night of Turville's murder. A long-haired fellow with a red ball cap flew back with him to Dallas. The rental car agent wasn't initially cooperative either. He, too, relented after Buck explained such was in his best interests. He confirmed

Reverend Einstein rented a specially-ordered black Cadillac Escalade on the days of his visits.

Back at the Sheriff's office, Buck also corroborated his recollections. An old gray Chevrolet Malibu was recovered abandoned in the ditch on Little Spring Road the day after Turville's murder. It'd been reported stolen in Charleston the day before. And Little Spring Road was between Turville's house and the airport.

The Sheriff wasn't happy – Why hadn't Buck done this detective work previously? Why had Buck focused all his efforts on BettyJo? It was as BettyJo admitted. She put Turville to sleep, but Shelton Smith, AKA Willie Mudrick, arrived soon after to clunk his brother-in-law. Turville had reneged on paying him money. All evidence pointed to him. And, now, Shelton was on the run several states away. Buck had screwed up.

Buck visited Pastor Barney Bennington at the Goose Creek Lutheran Church to get his impression of Shelley Turville. Buck assumed incorrectly that Pastor Barney knew Shelley. But Pastor Barney only met Shelley Turville once. She never attended church with her husband, even though he was a leader in the church. Turville had told Pastor Barney his wife stayed home every Sunday morning to watch "The Holy Event" live. His wife seemed mesmerized by Einstein's worship services. Because of her college background, Shelley was fascinated by the use of mathematics to illustrate the analogies within the Quantum Christian Church. Turville, on the other hand, satisfied his interests by catching re-runs of "The Holy Event" later in the week.

○ ● ○ ● ○

All evidence now pointed to Shelton Smith as his brother-in-law's murderer. Buck's current obsession, though, fixated on whether Shelton operated alone or in concert with his sister and/or Reverend Einstein. That night, Buck remembered one of his daddy's favorite sayings when he couldn't figure out how to solve something: "Remember to make time to think quietly about the problem. It seems obvious to do so, yet it's so easy to forget." Buck connected this advice to Lum thinking quietly about his spiritual problems in prison, before finally coming to grips with them. Q-Dawg also related he went for long quiet walks in order to think about his pressing chemistry problems. Buck thought to himself: "If it worked for problems in faith and science, why not also for detective work?"

For the first time in many months, Buck took a day off work. He went fishing at a lake near Millikan. Indeed, Buck was alone with his thoughts in the quiet of nature. When he slipped some salted peanuts in his freshly opened and ice-cold bottle of coke, such thoughts drifted to remembering that was exactly what his daddy always did when fishing. Afterwards, in the midst of one of his casts, his thoughts drifted to Shelley Turville.

Shelley must've known lots more than she'd admitted. One example – through her brother, she had to know about her husband trying to smuggle frogs out of Peru to gather more natural anodynol. Her husband also let her brother rot in jail when he'd been caught by the customs agent. Perhaps, then, Shelley even knew all about the synthesis of anodynol. After BettyJo left Turville's office, Shelton could have slipped into Turville's office at just the right time to perform the deadly deed before the arrival of Lum. Shelton had the obvious motive – money and revenge. Buck wondered whether Turville even knew Shelton was his wife's brother, that perhaps Shelley controlled Turville's actions more than he even realized.

Buck's mind spun to other possibilities. Perhaps, Shelton hadn't worked alone to kill Turville. He might've acted in concert with his sister. Shelley might have found out about Turville's affairs, even about his most recent attempt to pick up Evalina that same day. One thing for sure – Buck had discovered long ago, gossip and gossipy events spread like wildfire at PAYNE Pharmaceuticals. It wouldn't be improbable for Shelley Turville to have had her sources around her husband's office. She definitely would've known about BettyJo Burks.

Buck's imagination whirled at fast speed to incorporate this new information. The line on his rod pulled taut. Buck failed to react. A large bass, enjoying a worm, swam away to live another day. Instead, Buck's mind filled with wonderings: "Did Shelton

Smith act on behalf of his sister? She may have wanted revenge because of his affairs. Or, maybe, she wanted out of the marriage because of her own affair with Reverend Einstein. Then, did Reverend Einstein have any role in the murder? He may have conspired with Shelley's brother because he wanted Shelley for his own. Or maybe he wanted Turville's mathematical proof of the quantum behavior of the Holy Spirit, and thought if he didn't get it directly through Turville, he could get it through Turville's wife." These options saturated his thinking. The motive might not have been work-related, but related to the quantum proof. It was even possible that the three individuals, Shelton, Shelley, and Einstein conspired for all this to happen on 12 February. Maybe it was just their good fortune that the anodynol rejection by NuDRUG as well as BettyJo's antics happened on that same day.

A loud boom quaked the lake's shoreline and shook the thoughts from Buck's mind. Big black clouds were approaching. A lightning bolt lit up the horizon. He'd better call it a day. He reeled in his line – no worm on his hook. No fish, nor case resolutions, had been on the menu for that day.

Chapter Thirty Six

ANODYNOL, REMADE

To someone unversed in the intricacies of organic chemistry, that person might think it'd be easy to tweak the molecular structure of the PAYNE Pharmaceuticals' produced anodynol in order to synthesize the real structure of natural anodynol. However, literally thousands, if not millions, of different ways exist for assembling the atomic components of a large, complex molecule such as anodynol. Even if one assumes that some structural units such as the dipyrazole core remain the same, the organic chemist might be left with hundreds of different variations for the chemical's molecular structure. Then, the synthetic chemist would have to construct each of these molecules, any one of which might take years to design and develop its own proper synthetic scheme. All of the chemists in the pharmaceutical industry recommended their respective companies refrain from even trying. They concluded the odds of hitting the right molecular structure without the guide of having a sample of natural anodynol were virtually hopeless.

In Dr. Quinn Stanton's mind, the demise of anodynol might have been a bit premature. Q-Dawg had experience with anodynol. He realized the constraints in identifying a new target molecular structure for natural anodynol. The molecular structure of this natural anodynol had to have a GC/MS signature and NMR spectrum very similar to those of the incorrect synthetic anodynol. In fact, the two anodynols were similar enough so that, when Turville and he made their synthetic anodynol, they thought these analytical fingerprints were close enough to be matches. Q-Dawg established that the original discoverer's GC/MS and NMR results might be a sufficient guide to aid an expert, such as him, in anodynol and organic synthesis to project some good guesses as to how the original discoverer mischaracterized the reported structure. And, having had a career in the ways students misidentify the structure of compounds through their interpretation of GC/MS and NMR results helped guide Q-Dawg in his guesses. And, he had lots of experience in the quirks of synthetic anodynol, spending many months in the laboratory synthesizing and characterizing a molecule which was, at least, close to the real thing.

Even before Q-Dawg performed the gratis analysis of synthetic anodynol in blood samples for Buck, he imagined possibilities. Could he narrow down the possible options to likely molecular structures? He hoped to define a handful of target structures based on the original discoverer's characterization, or rather mischaracterization, and his knowledge of the anodynol system. He spent lots of time doing structure doodling as well as embraced his free time thinking about which of these structures might be possible. Some of this doodling happened when he sat through boring committee meetings, uninteresting seminars, and laboratory supervision. Most valuable was quiet time, in particular he seized the chance to take a half-hour walk every day at lunch. The combination of being alone in his thoughts and mild exercise energized his brain.

About eight months after Turville's death, Q-Dawg had already eliminated all his possible structures as unlikely except two. Both were dipyrazoles, but their substituents were arranged in just a slightly different way than the anodynol he and Turville had previously synthesized. He further determined that the general synthetic scheme for both possibilities shouldn't be too dramatically different than the previous scheme used in Turville's laboratory. The key step for each synthesis would once again be the control of the Vilsmeier reaction to generate the desired reaction intermediate. According to his best estimates, the syntheses of the two possibilities wouldn't be too onerous or time-consuming, especially based on his experiences in the PAYNE Pharmaceuticals' research and development laboratory.

○ ● ○ ● ○

Q-Dawg presented a proposal directly to NuDRUG. He introduced himself as one with a unique perspective, straddling the two worlds of academic and industrial chemistry. He professed to the NuDRUG executives and scientists he had expertise in the analysis, properties, characterization, and preparation of anodynol-like structures. In fact, with the death of Turville, Q-Dawg might be considered the world's sole expert in the very specialized field of dipyrazole synthesis. He told NuDRUG there were only two possible target structures, which of course would remain confidential, for natural anodynol. In order to prepare adequate supplies of these two structures to NuDRUG for testing in terms of their pain-relief properties, he would only need funds for salaries – those of his and a full-time laboratory technician – for nine months, some materials and supplies, maintenance of instrumentation already available, and overhead to Keaton College. The total tally was $175,000. Q-Dawg argued to NuDRUG such an investment was "small potatoes" for a major drug company. Although he agreed with other scientists the project was high risk, it also had the potential to produce spectacular yields if one of those two structures were indeed correct.

If he weren't successful in producing a compound that had the properties of natural anodynol, Q-Dawg rationalized the only loss to NuDRUG would be $175,000, their initial investment. If, though, Q-Dawg were successful in producing the correct structure, he would sign over the patent rights for this new structure to NuDRUG for $100 million or 25% of NuDRUG's future profits on anodynol. That is, if Q-Dawg did produce anodynol, NuDRUG might have a potential block-buster drug as a pain killer. NuDRUG would get to choose their desired pay-out option within a half year of Q-Dawg providing his samples. If NuDRUG reasoned the anodynol might eventually make billions, they could buy out Dr. Stanton for cash up front. If they inferred anodynol might only be a minor drug, they could opt for 25% of the profits. The final contract negotiated between Q-Dawg and NuDRUG provided the $175,000 up-front research costs to Keaton College with Dr. Stanton as principal investigator; and, if the synthesized structure generated the pain-killing property of natural anodynol, in exchange for eventual patent (or trade secret) rights, NuDRUG would agree to a cash settlement of $20 million or 8% of the drug's profits with Dr. Stanton. The settlement option would be finalized within the first year after discovery.

○ ● ○ ● ○

Buck Fowler called Q-Dawg to bemoan the status of his investigation into the murder of Turville. Buck somewhat jokingly related his daddy would've said that his mess of the murder probe was just a "bad situation!" With Q-Dawg's analyses, he was able to prove that BettyJo Burks put Turville to sleep by switching his blood pressure tablets with the synthetic anodynol, so that Turville was basically "knocked out" and sleeping with his head on his desk. In fact, BettyJo admitted as much. Unfortunately, BettyJo wouldn't confess to the actual murder. But, then, it really wasn't her. She chickened out in doing the deed. Shelley Turville's brother, now hiding out in parts unknown, actually did the deed. Usually talking to the Q-Dawg stimulated Buck's thinking on his next step, but such did not happen this time.

On the other hand, Q-Dawg announced to Buck he'd just gotten support from NuDRUG to make another attempt at the synthesis of the real anodynol. He proposed to NuDRUG to complete this work in nine months and had planned to hire a recent chemistry graduate, who had not yet gotten a job, from Keaton College to help him on this short term project. The student, though, just received a full-time job offer. He was no longer available for the synthetic effort. So, Q-Dawg bemoaned to Buck he hadn't been able to find any competent person to hire as his laboratory technician. The nine months had started to tick away, with Q-Dawg needing to make immediate progress.

"All I need is someone to take orders, with good hands, able to follow directions, shoot injections into instruments, and wash glassware," Q-Dawg lamented. "A high school graduate could do the work. I'll be doing all the chemical reactions myself."

"Maybe I should apply," Buck kidded. "The Sheriff hasn't been happy with my performance of late."

Q-Dawg chuckled, then continued to complain. "It's hard to get a good person for a position that goes away in nine months. I need someone full-time, not a Keaton College student or several students coming-and-going to the laboratory at their pleasure."

"How 'bout Lum Baumgartner," Buck joked. "He's getting released early from prison – in fact, in a couple days." He laughed. "Lum's heard about the Vilsmeier reaction, anodynol, and related chemistry from Evalina for several years."

"Are you serious?" Q-Dawg wasn't sure what to think of the possibility.

Buck hesitated, transitioning from something said to be silly to the same being a definite possibility. "Well, Lum is a very competent worker. He's familiar with mechanical operations at PAYNE Pharmaceuticals. He can fix anything."

"Hmmm." Q-Dawg thought out loud.

"Lum has nowhere to go after his release," Buck offered. "You know, he gave his house and all his assets to Sara Austin before he went to jail."

"Yep," Q-Dawg responded, "a real gesture of atonement." He then teased, "I think someone else has given their heart to Sara."

"Well . . . yeah," Buck stumbled on his words. He quickly recovered, "By all accounts, Lum seems to be a good person who did a bad deed. His intense desire for revenge overtook his good sense. Lum at one time was a suspect in Turville's death. But he just happened to be at the wrong place at the wrong time."

"Sounds like an interesting candidate for the job," Q-Dawg mused.

Buck continued, "In fact, the warden and jailers don't want Lum to leave the prison. He has a calming effect on the other inmates. He started Bible studies and religious education programs there. And Lum seems to be at peace. Sara and I had visited him in jail last week. I told him that my daddy would've said he appeared 'too blessed to be stressed; no longer too stressed to be blessed.' Maybe he would be a good candidate."

"Indeed," Q-Dawg concurred, "it seems he has all the right attributes and more."

○ ● ○ ● ○

Q-Dawg contacted Lum the next day. Lum began work at Keaton College the day after his release from prison. Lum's only reservation had been his separation from Ida Kay. He'd planned to move into her apartment. But Ida Kay told him it'd, and she'd, still be there in nine months. He shouldn't forgo the opportunity that came a-knocking at his door. She'd visit him, just like she visited him in jail. But, this time, he could also visit her.

Q-Dawg and his wife kindly "rented" Lum their small guest house, basically a one-room apartment over their garage. No money exchanged hands. Lum agreed to do repairs on Q-Dawg's house in return for staying at the apartment. Lum also rode to-and-fro work at Keaton College some days with Q-Dawg. As long as the weather cooperated, though, Lum found it just as refreshing to walk the mile to campus. Evalina telephoned her old adviser numerous times in the course of the next few months to vocalize her appreciation for giving her dad a second chance at life.

In response, Q-Dawg told Evalina that hiring Lum was the best decision he'd ever made – that her dad was a quick learner, did four times the work of most students or recent graduates, and had the nimble hands of a born chemist. Furthermore, Lum anticipated Q-Dawg needing certain maintenance on equipment and accomplished tasks before he'd even mention them. Lum was never idle in the laboratory. The proposed reactions proceeded twice as fast as he'd expected, once Lum had come on board the project. He admitted Lum was the perfect laboratory technician. For the first time in his career, his laboratory was actually organized, which was a rarity for an organic chemist. The lack of chaos was due to the presence of Lum. And the Keaton College students loved him. They flocked around him for stories and counseling sessions with "grandpa," as they called him. He, on the other hand, preached to them about the power of the Vilsmeier reaction to make neat substances every chance he would get. Q-Dawg kidded Lum he sounded just like Evalina. In addition, Lum convinced many of the students to start watching "The Holy Event" to see his daughter, who also had been trained by the Q-Dawg in Vilsmeier reactions.

Q-Dawg got on the schedule doing, with Lum assisting, the next iteration of a Vilsmeier reaction for synthesizing anodynol every Monday, Wednesday, and Friday afternoons. Lum did the preparation work, characterization work, set-up, and clean-up on Tuesdays, Thursdays, and most Saturdays. Q-Dawg also did other related syntheses on these off-days as well. Q-Dawg boasted to Evalina that the Q-Dawg – Lum team performed like a well-oiled machine!

○ ● ○ ● ○

Lum finished the listed repairs and updates to the Stanton house within the first month of living in their apartment. That is, Lum was just as efficient at their home as he was at work. In fact, after the first few weeks there, he started to cook dinner every other night for the Stantons and himself. Like Lum's dinnertime conversations of past with Evalina, these dinnertime talks centered also on the power of the Vilsmeier reaction, until Mrs. Stanton finally put an end to any mention of Vilsmeier in "her" home.

Then, the discussion often centered on what would happen to Q-Dawg and his wife if he succeeded in making anodynol. Such would be the equivalent of winning a lottery. Lots of money would descend upon them. Q-Dawg actually feared the destruction of their life as they knew it. They might become one of the many examples of people who were less happy after winning lotteries. Both he and his wife enjoyed the quiet life of a small college professor. Q-Dawg couldn't imagine retiring with lots of money at a vacation resort and not teaching or doing research with students. Lum, conversely, approached the subject from a different point of view, using the parable of a rich man getting to heaven as an analogy –

> *Matthew 19:16-26*
>
> Now a man came up to Jesus and asked, "Teacher, what good thing must I do to get eternal life?"
>
> "Why do you ask me about what is good?" Jesus replied. "There is only One who is good. If you want to enter life, obey the commandments."
>
> "Which ones?" the man inquired.
>
> Jesus replied, "Do not murder, do not commit adultery, do not steal, do not give false testimony, honor your father and mother, and 'love your neighbor as yourself.'"
>
> "All these I have kept," the young man said, "What do I still lack?"
>
> Jesus answered, "If you want to be perfect, go, sell your posessions and give to the poor, and you will have treasure in heaven. Then come, follow me."
>
> When the young man heard this, he went away sad, because he had great wealth.
>
> Then Jesus said to his disciples, "I tell you the truth, it is hard for a rich man to enter the kingdom of heaven. Again I tell you, it is easier for a camel to go through the eye of a needle than for a rich man to enter the kingdom of God."
>
> When the disciples heard this, they were greatly astonished and asked, "Who then can be saved?"
>
> Jesus looked at them and said, "With man this is impossible, but with God all things are possible."

Lum urged Q-Dawg and his wife that they should never let the love of money taint their goodness. Lum argued for them to give away the money, upon the assumption they actually succeeded in synthesizing the anodynol.

Another favorite Bible verse of Lum in this regard was from the charge of the apostle Paul to his student Timothy –

> *1 Timothy 6:6-10*
>
> But godliness with contentment is great gain. For we brought nothing into the world, and we can take nothing out of it. But if we have food and clothing, we will be content with that. People who want to get rich fall into temptation and a trap and into many foolish and harmful desires that plunge men into ruin and destruction. For the love of money is a root of all kinds of evil. Some people, eager for money, have wandered from the faith and pierced themselves with many griefs.

Lum emphasized that Paul wanted Christians to understand that money could not purchase spiritual happiness. And that a Christian's trust in God trumped the false security of perishable wealth on earth. One's love of money doomed that person to suffer many problems by trapping him or her into seeking satisfaction from ever-increasing amounts of money. Christians should not allow money to become the focal point of their lives or, in a sense, the idol that they worship instead of God. In this fashion, Lum confirmed Q-Dawg's fear of accumulating instant wealth, for bad things might then happen.

Ida Kay also supported Lum's way of thinking. She often joined Lum and the Stantons for dinner on weekends. She used to play the Powerball lottery every week. She expected to beat the odds and win. But she stopped playing after she'd read a study showing the long-term happiness of lottery winners didn't improve. The sudden wealth actually prevented the winners from enjoying simple things like hearing a good joke or watching television. And the wealth came at the expense of personal relationships. She brought up the example of Jack Whittaker, a West Virginian who won a then record $315 million Powerball jackpot on Christmas night in 2002. His life became rife with setbacks and tragedy. He fell victim to scandals, lawsuits, and thefts. He endured constant requests for money, leaving him unable to trust others. His wife left him. He struggled with drinking, gambling, and the deaths of a daughter and granddaughter. He was quoted numerous times as saying "He wished he had torn up the winning ticket."

○ ● ○ ● ○

Q-Dawg quickly discovered there were two places to find Lum when Lum wasn't at work or at the house talking on the phone with Ida Kay. Lum attended the local Lutheran Church only a short walk from the college campus. His spiritual mentor, Pastor Barney Bennington, was a seminary classmate of this pastor. Lum would do home repairs, miscellaneous fixings, and cooking for the widows, needy, working poor, and elderly in the church. Q-Dawg realized that Lum never had money left from his meager paycheck, as he would oft supplement the inconsequential social security or disability checks of these people with his own funds. Lum also sent money to Sara Austin, but such was always returned with the note "Thanks, but others could put the money to better use. I have enough for my needs."

Q-Dawg and his wife, impressed by Lum's example, started to attend the church.

The other place Lum frequented was the county jail. A phone call from Detective Fowler was sufficient for the warden of that jail to allow Lum to start a Bible Study and to pray with the prisoners. As Lum had once been an inmate like them, he gained instant credibility among the jail's population. Needless to say, Lum did not allow grass to grow under his feet either at work or at Q-Dawg's home.

The professional team of Q-Dawg and Lum worked so well together they produced sufficient quantities of the two target compounds within seven months, beating the proposed nine months. Subsequently, Q-Dawg sent the hoped-to-be substitute for natural anodynol to NuDRUG for testing.

Chapter Thirty Seven
PASTOR IN A BOX, SECOND ACT

Reverend Danny Einstein prospered in his mission, bolstered by the use of Turville's opus as his own. His church services at the Quantum Christian Church continued to relate quantum properties in the atomic world to happenings in the spiritual world, as well as to employ "his" new Theory of Spiritual Relativity. "His" mathematical derivations for waves in an infinitely large space had successfully described the heavenly realm of God, Jesus, and the Holy Spirit.

The current focus of his sermons highlighted the miracles of Jesus Christ. After the end of "The Holy Event" each week, Reverend Einstein always acknowledged Shelley Turville, his personal assistant, for help in developing the underlying mathematics. He never referenced her murdered husband.

Although much of the science and mathematics of these quantum connections were beyond the understanding of Buck Fowler, he was intrigued by the teachings of Reverend Einstein. Buck, along with Sara, taped or watched Einstein's televised worship service each Sunday morning and became regular viewers of Einstein's other shows. There was also the lure of listening to the melodic and captivating music of Evalina and Adam, mostly Evalina. Buck would hear a song they sang. It would stick in his mind. He'd hum the tune to Sara. She'd put her hands over her ears. His daddy used to say his humming "sounded like a chorus of drunken bumblebees." When he'd hum or whistle, his daddy's dog whimpered in pain.

○ ● ○ ● ○

Reverend Einstein's sermon that Sunday dealt with Moebis strips. He picked up a foot long strip of purple cloth, an inch wide, from a box on the pulpit. He gave it a twist of 180° and stapled the two ends together to form a continuous circular band.

He held up his construction for all to see. "It's quite simple to make. And it has some interesting properties. For example, even though it's three-dimensional, it has only one side and one edge."

Reverend Einstein took a scissors and cut the band lengthwise. He, once again, held the resulting structure up for all to see. "Not two strips, but still one band," he announced. "Its circle has expanded to twice its original diameter. And from one twist to four. Interesting!"

He put his Moebis strip aside. He transitioned to telling about chemists making a molecule in the shape of a Moebis strip. These molecules possessed peculiar quantum mechanical properties, directly opposite those observed for molecules shaped like a normal ring.

"For the past few weeks," the pastor preached. "We've been talking about Jesus' miracles. One of the most astounding is Jesus feeding the multitude." He read from the Scripture –

> *Matthew 14: 15-21*
>
> As evening approached, the disciples came to him and said, "This is a remote place, and it's already getting late. Send the crowds away, so they can go to the villages and buy themselves some food."
>
> Jesus replied, "They do not need to go away. You give them something to eat."
>
> "We have here only five loaves of bread and two fish," they answered.
>
> "Bring them here to me," He said, And He directed the people to sit down on the grass. Taking the five loaves and the two fish and looking up to the

> heaven, he gave thanks and broke the loaves. Then he gave them to the disciples, and the disciples gave them to the people. They all ate and were satisfied, and the disciples picked up twelve basketfuls of broken pieces that were left over. The number of those who ate was about five thousand men, besides women and children.

Reverend Einstein then used mathematical equations to relate the quantum mechanical properties of molecular Moebis strips to this miracle of Jesus Christ. Just like breaking a Moebis strip increased its number of twists, so too Jesus breaking the loaf of bread increased its number of loaves. As he neared the end of his sermon, he smiled broadly, satisfied with himself for another stunning example in Quantum Christianity. Any attribution to Mason Turville had long been buried in his mind.

At the end of "The Holy Event" for that Sunday, Reverend Einstein heralded, "Next week's Sermon and Pastor in a Box will be ones y'all don't want to miss. The sermon will deal with the miracle of forgiveness. And I will face off against one claiming he's been falsely accused of murder – maybe with some bombshell revelations."

Buck, snuggled next to Sara on the couch, looked into her eyes. He thought a moment about the pastor's teaser. He shook his head, then mumbled, "Would he, or they, be so brazen?"

○ ● ○ ● ○

Late the next day, Monday, Buck received a phone call from the owner of the Colebrook Municipal Airport. He reported Reverend Danny Einstein's plane had flown into the airport at 11:05 am and departed at 3:56 pm. The owner had the rental car agent next to him as he spoke. As usual, Einstein had rented a black Cadillac Escalade. And the pastor had come alone, just with the flight crew who stayed with the plane the entire time. Buck was furious. They were supposed to let him know upon Einstein's arrival, not departure. Before ending the call, the owner stated the pastor tipped generously – he tried to keep everyone happy.

"Oh, and one more thing," the owner mumbled, "the pastor had visited for a few hours Tuesday the previous week as well."

The next day, Buck checked with the Dallas police – still no sign of Shelton Smith. His calls to Reverend Einstein were intercepted by the pastor's secretary. She informed Buck the pastor wouldn't be taking any of his calls. Shelley Turville likewise refused to talk to Buck. She gave him the phone number of her lawyer; he didn't return any of his calls.

Thursday of that same week was a beautiful day, sunny and unseasonably warm. Both Buck and Sara took well-deserved vacation days. They strolled hand-in-hand along a trail that circled Little Foggy Lake. They enjoyed their peaceful excursion through nature, not meeting another person all day. They chatted. They laughed. They shared their dreams for the future over a picnic lunch of sandwiches and chips. Afterwards, Buck nervously gathered a ring from his pocket, got down on a knee, and proposed. Sara said "Yes" for the second and final time in her life.

The next night, Sara and Buck invited Ida Kay and Lum to join them for a prime rib dinner at Big John's Steakhouse in Colebrook. They revealed their joyous news. Both Ida Kay and Lum celebrated with them. Ida Kay was proud as a peacock, having been the one to put the two together for their first date.

Ida Kay turned her attention to Lum. She provided mock outrage. "Well, when are you gonna take the lead from Buck?"

"Kinda expected that," Lum groaned with a smile on his face. "Are you gonna tell a story about the mating behavior of an animal to spur me on?"

All shared a laugh.

Ida Kay gave a sly grin to Lum. "Did you know that peahens are very particular about what they look for in a peacock?" Without pausing, she answered her own question. "They search for the one with the most spectacular plumage. On the average a peahen evaluates three males before she chooses her mate. By the way, Lum, I'm impressed by your red shirt tonight."

Lum rolled his eyes. Sara and Buck chuckled.

Ida Kay looked over at the bar. "See the guy with the green shirt. He's the first." Then she pointed at a neighboring table. "Not gonna be that guy either." She smiled at Lum. "Just like peacocks and peahens, the third one is a charm."

Lum's face turned a bright red, matching the color in his shirt. But his face also had a beam of satisfaction.

○ ● ○ ● ○

Reverend Einstein described a new form of matter, the time crystal, in his Sunday sermon. He compared such to the church's crystal model of salt in its courtyard. In the salt crystal, sodium and chloride ions repeat themselves in a perfect pattern in space. A time crystal, on the other hand, possesses atoms that move in a pattern repeating in time. They flip back and forth in unison, like a crystalline clock. Something in perfect cadence continuing for all time. This theoretical time clock had been demonstrated by scientists using ten ytterbium atoms flipping regularly. And this exotic new material is supposedly the basis for the memory in quantum computers.

Reverend Einstein then posed a rhetorical question: "How far out in time does the perfect time crystal keep repeating? In a different way, this question was also posed by Peter to Jesus" –

> *Matthew 18: 21-22*
>
> Then Peter came to Jesus and asked, "Lord, how many times shall I forgive my brother when he sins against me? Up to seven times?"
>
> Jesus answered, "I tell you, not seven times, but seventy times seven."

The pastor preached the "seventy times seven" is another term for forever, for infinite time. God's grace and forgiveness is like a time crystal, it repeats itself time and again in response to our sin. In fact, Einstein's mathematical equations for spiritual forgiveness had an eerie similarity to the quantum equations for a time crystal. Once again, no attribution to Turville. To end his message, the pastor chuckled, "Quantum, once again, repeats itself – pardon my pun – in a perfect pattern in spiritual affairs."

As the "Pastor in a Box" segment started, the camera panned onto Reverend Einstein sitting in his assigned chair in the box. As usual, the man facing him sat back to the camera. A red baseball cap hung on the support for his folding chair.

Reverend Einstein calmly spoke, "A couple years ago, right here in this box, an individual confessed to accidently killing another. That person thought God told him to seek revenge, just like Jacob's sons sought revenge on Shechem for the same reason. His victim met his fate via 'Death by Vilsmeier,' an explosive chemical reaction. Today, our guest also stands accused of committing a murder whose victim suffered a 'Death by Vilsmeier.' This time, though, the person died when the murderer smashed the back of his head with a bronze bust of Anton Vilsmeier. Tell us your story."

"I'm falsely accused," Shelton Smith whined. "I've been hiding from the cops who want to pin the murder on me. I have no life anymore. Why would God allow this to happen to me?"

"Why do the police think you did it?"

"I argued with Mason, 'er the victim, earlier in the day," Shelton confided without emotion. "He did me dirty. He owed me money. I threatened him. I returned a couple hours later to talk to him after I calmed down. But, once I got there, he was sound asleep at his desk. I couldn't wake him. Unfortunately, before I left, I picked that stupid bust up off the floor and put it on the desk. My fingerprints were all over it."

"Did you tell this to the cops?"

Shelton started to get agitated. "I ran. They wanna pin it on me. Why would God let them do it to me?"

Reverend Einstein sat back in his chair. He rubbed his chin. After a few moments, he growled, "So you're not gonna confess?"

"Of course not. I didn't do it!" Shelton became more animated, flailing his arms chaotically. "As I was leaving Mason's . . . "

The pastor quickly talked over Shelton's response. "Remember John 8:32 when our Lord, Jesus Christ, said 'the truth will set you free.' Just tell the truth, you'll feel the freedom."

"What are you talking about? I am telling the truth. I didn't do it."

The pastor smirked. "Just tell your story like you told me on the plane back to Dallas that night. You were sorry. Anger and revenge got the best of you. Ask for forgiveness for what you did to Mason Turville."

Shelton stood up. He slammed his right fist into his left hand. "Aren't you listening to me? I have no need for forgiveness. You know the truth."

"In the Gospel of John 18:37, Jesus said, 'Everyone on the side of truth listens to Me.'" The pastor continued with a smug look of sincerity. "If you tell the truth, I'll listen."

"You self-righteous charlatan," Shelton yelled. He picked up his folding chair, raised it over his head, and jumped at the pastor.

The pastor instinctively put his arms over his head to ward off the rapidly descending chair to his head. The congregation could hear a bone in the pastor's left arm snap. Shelton threw the chair on the floor and burst off the stage.

As Reverend Einstein held his arm tightly against his body to stem the pain, an irate Shelley Turville came up behind him.

"You set him up," she screamed. She slapped him across the face with all her strength, then raked both his cheeks with her fingernails. Blood flowed profusely. Several men from the camera crew tackled Shelley, bringing her to the ground.

Reverend Einstein stood, albeit in pain. The camera focused on his battered, bruised, and bloodied face. His arm hung at an odd angle to his side. As if he were in total control, he spoke, "From 1 John 1:10, the Word says, 'If we claim we have not sinned, we make Him [Jesus] out to be a liar and His word has no place in our lives.' We pray that our guest today will eventually confess his sins and bring Jesus Christ back into his life."

The camera panned back out to conclude "The Holy Event."

Sara and Buck had been watching the show intently along with Ida Kay and Lum. All were flabberghasted.

"Did I just watch 'The Holy Event,' or part of an upcoming Jerry Springer show?" Sara wondered, as her eyes opened wide.

Buck was deep in thought, after which he spoke, "I wonder what Shelton was saying when Einstein intentionally talked over him."

Chapter Thirty Eight
SLEEPING DOGS

Buck visited the crime lab with his recording of "The Holy Event" for that past Sunday. He wanted them to determine what Shelton Smith was saying when Reverend Einstein loudly talked over him. His words were just background noise in the soundtrack. The camera had been on the face of the pastor, his mouth pursed with surprise written on his eyes as if Shelton had gone off script.

Shelton clearly started with: "As I was leaving Mason's . . ." The crime lab could only flesh out a few words – ". . . office, . . . passed . . . woman."

○ ● ○ ● ○

Buck made another trip to Dallas, hoping the catch Reverend Danny Einstein and Shelley Turville off-guard.

He first dropped by the Quantum Christian Church and was greeted, once again, by the twin busts of Albert and Danny Einstein in the vestibule. Buck contemplated whether worshippers might construe these busts as religious idols. And whether, if Moses visited this church, Moses would destroy the idols like he did the Golden Calf many millennia ago. To refresh his memory, Buck flipped open a nearby Bible to the book of Exodus.

Exodus 32:1-8, 15-16, & 19-20

When the people saw that Moses was so long in coming down from the mountain, they gathered around Aaron and said, “Come, make us gods who will go before us. As for this fellow Moses who brought us up out of Egypt, we don’t know what happened to him.”

Aaron answered them, “Take off the gold earrings that your wives, your sons and your daughters are wearing, and bring them to me.” So all the people took off their earrings and brought them to Aaron. He took what they handed him and made it into an idol cast in the shape of a calf, fashioning it with a tool. Then they said, “These are your gods, O Israel, who brought you up out of Egypt.”

When Aaron saw this, he built an altar in front of the calf and announced, “Tomorrow there will be a festival to the Lord.” So the next day the people rose early and sacrificed burnt offerings and presented fellowship offerings. Afterward they sat down to eat and drink and got up to indulge in revelry.

Then the Lord said to Moses, “Go down, because your people, whom you brough up out of Egypt, have become corrupt. They have been quick to turn away from what I commanded them and have made themselves an idol cast in the shape of a calf. They have bowed down to it and sacrificed to it . . .”

. . . Moses turned and went down the mountain with the two tablets of the Testimony in his hands. They were inscribed on both sides, front and back. The tablets were the work of God, the writing was the writing of God engraved on the tablets.

. . . When Moses approached the camp and saw the calf and the dancing, his anger burned and he threw the tablets out of his hands, breaking them to pieces at the foot of the mountain. And he took the calf they had made and burned it in the fire; then he

> ground it to a powder, scattered it on the water and made the Israelites drink it.

Buck imagined burning the Einstein busts in a fire, grinding them to a powder, and presenting the ashes to Reverend Einstein on a gold plate. After all, did Reverend Einstein want his followers to worship God or to worship Einstein's "The Holy Event?" Such thoughts almost made Buck wonder whether Turville had worshiped his bust of Vilsmeier on his desk as his personal scientific idol. His evil behavior would've indicated he certainly didn't act like a practicing Christian. And yet he wrote scientific treatises to explain the Holy Trinity?

Buck burst into the pastor's office, walking right by the secretary who said "You can't go in there." Reverend Einstein, sitting at his desk, was not near as smug and arrogant as the last time they'd met. In fact, Buck sensed a bit of humility in the air about the pastor. Or maybe, such was only the outward effect of the pastor's pain pills. His arm was in a cast. Scratches and bruises were still clearly visible on his cheeks.

Buck remained standing in front of the pastor's desk. Without any attempt at greetings, he snarled, "Where's Shelton Smith?"

"How am I to know?" the pastor snarled back. "Ask his sister."

"Why'd you visit Millikan the past couple weeks?"

"Private matters," Reverend Einstein smirked. "Not any of your business."

"Just like it was a private matter when you used to visit Shelley Turville there." Buck slammed his hand on the pastor's desk for effect.

Reverend Einstein would not be provoked. He simply smiled. "I visited Shelley periodically. She was a friend who needed spiritual guidance."

"Was it also just a coincidence that you and her brother both happened by for a visit on the same day as her husband's murder?"

"Coincidences happen," the pastor said calmly, as he sat back in his chair.

"And coincidentally the same day you discussed Mason Turville's mathematical treatise, the quantum basis for the Holy Trinity, only a few hours before his murder," Buck sarcastically added.

"Coincidence," he nodded.

"Why do you use Mason Turville's work without attributing such to him?"

"Shelley told me it was her work, not his." Reverend Einstein chuckled.

"And I guess you believe that?"

"No reason not to." The pastor's chuckle evolved to full-fledged laughter.

Buck readily admitted to Reverend Einstein he couldn't prove any conspiracy among Einstein, Shelley, and her brother. But it certainly didn't "smell" right. He could, though, plant suspicions throughout Einstein's world – that Einstein's actions could be interpreted as those of another power-hungry, sexually-charged, and soon-to-be-fallen tele-evangelist.

Reverend Einstein calmly responded that was not who he was or is. He went into a rant. Among other things, he claimed, "It was Mason Turville who had done evil things leading to his own death." Shelley and he had been quite willing to bide their time until her husband self-destructed through his perilous professional and personal affairs. Einstein quoted the apostle Paul as saying –

> *Ephesians 4:2*
>
> . . . Be completely humble and gentle, be **patient**, bearing with one another in love.

He emphasized the word "patience." Then, he added, "How rotten to the core could a man like Mason Turville stoop, especially one who professed to be a leader in a Christian church?" At that moment, Reverend Einstein buzzed his secretary and stated, "Call security. Detective Fowler needs to be escorted out."

Buck simply shook his head. His daddy probably would've told him in this situation, to just let "sleeping dogs lie." And that's what Buck did, at least for the time being.

○ ● ○ ● ○

An hour later, Buck found Shelley Turville packing her possessions, obviously moving out of Reverend Einstein's guesthouse next to the mansion.

Buck asked the obvious. "Moving?"

"Relocating to the Florida coast with the kids," Shelley responded without emotion. She placed a handful of plastic toy trucks in a box. "A beautifully furnished beach house with its own private beach."

"I assume compliments of the good pastor," Buck snarked.

Shelley smiled. "I won't have to worry about money for the rest of my life."

The conversation stalled, as Shelley went about packing more toys.

"Where's your brother?" Buck asked.

Shelley hesitated, stared at Buck for a moment, then went back to her task at hand.

"Don't know, or not gonna say," Buck added.

Shelley once again looked up at Buck, then ignored the question.

"What was your brother saying about leaving Mason's office when the good pastor cut him off?" Buck fired back.

Shelley half-laughed. "You wouldn't believe me if I told you."

"I suspect I just might." Buck smiled. "Do you know who the woman was? The woman coming in as he was going out."

"You wouldn't believe me if I told you," Shelley repeated.

"I suspect I just might," Buck smiled.

○ ● ○ ● ○

Pastor Adam Clarke substituted for Reverend Danny Einstein the next few Sundays on "The Holy Event." Sermons focused on music and Christian worship, instead of quantum physics and the

Holy Spirit. Evalina sang a solo of a traditional hymn each week. Television ratings for the services actually increased.

After a two week hiatus, Reverend Einstein, with his arm in a cast, walked onto the stage at the end of the Sunday morning service. He made a few announcements and thanked his congregation for their prayers of recovery. The camera then panned to the front row of the sanctuary, onto a woman who looked like a beaming Tammy Faye Bakker with extra make-up, if such was possible. Everyone in Millikan, though, recognized her as BettyJo Burks.

Reverend Einstein proclaimed, "Let me introduce y'all to the future First Lady of the Quantum Christian Church."

Chapter Thirty Nine
JACKPOTS

After two months, a married Reverend Danny Einstein made a triumphant return to "The Holy Event" with his new bride in arm. He proudly announced God showed him a vision, a vision of His universe much like his namesake Albert had of the scientific universe. The universe existed in curved space, not in normal space with 90° corners. His new derivations of the mathematical equations in both the quantum and spiritual worlds had resulted in amazing revelations about the world of the Holy Trinity.

Sara turned to Buck sitting on the couch next to her. She snickered, "Looks like he hit the spiritual jackpot, just like his namesake hit the scientific jackpot with his theory of relativity."

"Vision, my foot." Buck scowled. "Theft is a better description."

Sara looked at Buck with confusion. "Whatcha gonna do about it?"

"As the good pastor told me himself . . . patience." Buck chuckled, as he put his arm around Sara, drawing her closer.

○ ● ○ ● ○

Dr. Quinn Stanton called together detective Buck Fowler, Lum, and Evalina for a meeting with him and his wife. First, Q-Dawg formally announced he hit the scientific as well as financial jackpot. One of the synthetic anodynols that Lum and he had prepared was indeed the replica molecular structure of natural anodynol. And, by all signs, this chemical compound would be a blockbuster medication for the treatment of chronic pain. Talk in the pharmaceutical community boasted of anodynol replacing most of the opiates in the next few years, after NuDRUG's production facilities and FDA approvals fell into place. Experts predicted a new era in pain relief without major side-effects. Furthermore, the key synthesis step in the anodynol preparation was indeed the Vilsmeier reaction, as previously championed by Evalina in song many years ago.

> ". . . As they shouted out with glee;
> Vilsmeier the Heterocyclic Reaction,
> You'll go down in history!"

In a sense, Q-Dawg finally succeeded in relieving, instead of causing, people's physical pain via Vilsmeier. With a sigh of personal relief, Q-Dawg broadcast that the paperwork for the patent rights for the correct structure of anodynol had been finalized for their purchase by NuDRUG for $20,000,000.

Q-Dawg said he spent many, many hours with his wife discussing potential problems caused by too much money, in a similar fashion as conversed previously with Lum over dinner. They worried the influx of money would drastically alter their lives. They wanted to continue to live the life of a small town college professor undisturbed. In order for them to live comfortably but not lavishly, they kept only $500,000 of the $20 million for their own as retirement savings. They planned to tell no one of the sale of patent rights and to keep it as quiet as possible. They already donated one million dollars anonymously to Keaton College for the Evalina Vail Chemistry Research Fund. Evalina had agreed to the name, with the college thinking the money came from the Quantum Christian Church, for the support of undergraduate students doing chemical research.

With the remainder of Dr. Stanton's financial windfall, which was over $18 million, he created the "Life by Vilsmeier" Foundation. Q-Dawg used the following analogy. Whereas anodynol prepared via the Vilsmeier reaction will be treating physical or chronic pain, the "Life by Vilsmeier" Foundation will be treating or comforting life's spiritual and/or emotional pain.

Q-Dawg recalled a dinnertime discussion with Lum about the possibility of millions of dollars coming into his life. Lum warned him about the dangers of money as Paul similarly warned Timothy about the love of money. Q-Dawg admitted he opened his Bible and read what came next in 1st Timothy. After the verses about the love of money, came the following chapters as to what men of God should practice in lieu of love of money –

> *1 Timothy 6:11-12*
>
> But you, man of God, flee from all this, and pursue righteousness, godliness, faith, love, endurance and gentleness. Fight the good fight of the faith. Take hold of the eternal life to which you were called when you made your good confession in the presence of many witnesses.

Lum had set the example at that time by putting into action these words. He did repairs for the needy, provided groceries for the cash poor, and helped the elderly living on their Social Security checks. Q-Dawg further explained that he was also drawn to the admonitions of Paul in his letter to the Colossians when Paul described the rules for holy living –

> *Colossians 3:12-17*
>
> Therefore, as God's chosen people, holy and dearly loved, clothe youselves with compassion, kindness, humility, gentleness, and patience. Bear with each other and forgive whatever grievances you may have against one another. Forgive as the Lord forgave you. And over all these virtues put on love, which binds them all together in perfect unity.
>
> Let the peace of Christ rule in your hearts, since as members of one body you were called to peace. And be thankful. Let the word of Christ dwell in you richly as you teach and admonish one another with all wisdom, and as you sing psalms, hymns and spiritual songs with gratitutde in your hearts to God.

> And whatever you do, whether in word or deed, do it all in the name of the Lord Jesus, giving thanks to God the Father through him.

Q-Dawg announced the foundation's motto would be "Love weighs more than gold." Buck's eyes sparkled – one of his daddy's sayings – as Q-Dawg gave him a wink.

The plans of Q-Dawg for his foundation were to distribute one million dollars, or more, of the foundation's funds each year throughout West Virginia and Appalachia. The money would be dispensed directly to the people in need of treatment for the pain of just living. For example, needy people with too much land to receive governmental assistance, veterans unable to work, people too proud to take money because others are more needy, widows slipping through cracks in the system, individuals just getting out of jail and needing a second chance, a single parent struggling with their children's welfare, grandparents trying to raise their grandchildren, and the like. The funds would be distributed as cash in anonymity to avoid people or groups actually lobbying to get money from the Foundation.

Q-Dawg already had plans in place to identify the needy people as recipients of the cash. Q-Dawg, his wife, Evalina, and Buck would be unpaid officers for the foundation. Ida Kay and Lum would travel as undercover missionaries through the small towns and hamlets with a particular focus on rural churches. From the pastors and people of these parishes, they would pinpoint the struggling families or individuals. Instead of working through governmental agencies, they would work through the churches, much like the churches operated in the communities before being overtaken by the welfare system of the government. Accordingly, they would focus on those truly in need of additional money, especially those living meagerly from check to check. They would not only supply cash but also contract getting a leaky roof fixed, installing a new heating system, purchasing a new stove or refrigerator, or filling a freezer with groceries. Q-Dawg indicated the concept would be like the movie "The Sting" in reverse. Instead of conning someone who doesn't realize they are being conned, Lum would be helping someone before they realize they are being targeted as being helped. For obvious reasons, Lum didn't like that analogy. Lum preferred a comparison to the "Lone Ranger" – to spread Christian love and leave with no trace of him and Ida Kay having been there.

Buck added, "Sort of like a modern 'Johnny Appleseed' spreading the seeds of Christian hope amongst those hoping for a miracle."

"Sort of like your daddy might've said." Q-Dawg laughed.

Chapter Forty
EVOLUTION

Reverend Danny Einstein had returned to the pulpit of the Quantum Christian Church several weeks previously, fully recovered from his injuries. He was effervescent with excitement, continuing his new series of sermons. He'd been systematically exploring the ramifications of using "his" hyperbolic or curved space model for God's universe – both at the atomic level and for the spiritual world. He emphasized the physical and spiritual worlds embody a primordial mathematical beauty which connects the physical world's foundation with spiritual harmony. He claimed, once again, a vision from God. In his new revelation, he'd been addressing spiritual truths that could not be addressed by math previously, only with his novel approach. He'd been applying his hyperbolic equations to detail living things.

One of his results generated the equation,

$$\pi = 2[\{2 \cdot 2\}/\{1 \cdot 3\} \text{ x } \{4 \cdot 4\}/\{3 \cdot 5\} \text{ x } \{6 \cdot 6\}/\{5 \cdot 7\} \text{ x } \ldots]$$

This result is an infinite series used as an approximation for π, or 3.14…, the ratio of a circle's circumference to its diameter. The approximation is an interesting as well as a beautifully symmetric mix of numbers. The series was first formulated by a mathematician in 1655, then also resulted from equations for quantum physics in which one molecule transforms to another. But in the pastor's treatise, the conclusion highlighting this one set of equations from this hyperbolic universe was related to a circle, but this time to the circle of life.

Reverend Einstein proclaimed this equation was fundamental to not only explain evolution but also provide consistency within the context of Quantum Christianity. Its meaning was that evolution, the Creation, and intelligent design were all one and the same. They are all the same mathematically. There is no contradiction. The pastor preached, "It may seem wacky, but it's true."

In this mathematical series, use of the next term brings the product to a closer approximation of the actual value for π. Likewise, the next step in evolution is a closer approximation to the final form of the creation or design event – things become closer and closer to perfection. Just like classical physics is a special case of quantum physics, one can consider evolution, guided by the Holy Spirit, to be a special case of the Creation. The pastor ended his sermon with the teaser: "Many of the details will become apparent in the next few weeks of sermons."

○ ● ○ ● ○

The "Pastor in a Box" segment started that same week as every other. The camera panned onto the face of Reverend Einstein on the stage, past the person's back facing him. That person was in obvious disguise, wearing a curly-headed wig.

Reverend Einstein smiled. "The person in the box with me today wants to be called Mr. Darwin. He wishes to remain anonymous, as he's a professor at an Ivy League University. His question fit in perfectly with my sermon. Our guest submitted, 'How can a person consider himself educated and believe in the Creation. The moron might as well believe in magic.'"

Reverend Einstein laughed. Audible snickers echoed throughout the congregation.

After a pause, Reverend Einstein continued, "Do you still ask this question – even after my sermon today?"

Mr. Darwin didn't speak. He squirmed in his seat. Then, looking straight at Einstein, he spoke, "I have a question for you. Do you have any trouble sleeping when your bride BettyJo is around?"

Reverend Einstein was caught off-guard. He sneered, "What's that to you?"

"You, of course, realize that BettyJo killed her previous lover as he slept," Mr. Darwin stated matter-of-factly.

"What are you trying to do here?" Reverend Einstein growled. He looked around at the cameraman and the producer standing nearby. He motioned for them to cut away. Several stern-looking uniformed police officers stood next to them.

"The cameras will keep rolling," Mr. Darwin stated. He stood, removing his wig, beard, and some of his make-up, before sitting back down.

Reverend Einstein immediately recognized Detective Fowler. He scowled, "You've hijacked my show. You . . you . ."

"So are you gonna answer my question?" Buck calmly continued.

"You know as well as anyone that Shelton Smith confessed to that murder on this show weeks ago," the pastor flippantly espoused.

"No," Buck was emphatic. "You said he confessed. He didn't. Your bride murdered Mason Turville. I suspect you were just trying to provide cover for her."

"That's not how it happened. Shelton Smith did it."

"You've told so many lies, you wouldn't know the truth if it smacked you on the face," Buck responded. "Shelton wouldn't kill someone as that person slept. He'd wanna look you straight in the face so you'd know it was his revenge."

"You think you're so smart, but you're not," the pastor confidently replied. But the pastor's actions spoke otherwise, sweating and becoming fidgety. "I speak the truth. My God shows me right from wrong."

"You say your hyperbolic treatise appeared to you in a vision. The Holy Spirit showed you the mathematical derivations and meanings."

Reverend Einstein nodded.

"You sure you don't want to modify that assertion." Buck chuckled. "Perhaps your vision appeared when BettyJo showed you the treatise of Mason Turville on the same topic."

The pastor sat mute and stiffbacked. He had the face of a pouty child.

Buck chuckled some more. "I take that as a yes. Did you –"

"BettyJo is my messenger from the Holy Spirit," Reverend Einstein interrupted. "She told me God is pleased with my work and message here. The Holy Spirit wants me to spread God's Word, giving me the papers as a personal revelation."

"So it's only coincidental that both BettyJo and Shelley were involved with Mason Turville, and both supplied you with personal revelations from the Holy Spirit." Buck paused, but no response was forthcoming. He then sarcastically added, "I saw portions of both these revelations. I guess the Holy Spirit gave me a preview."

The camera showed Reverend Einstein clenching his teeth, every face muscle tense. He appeared ready to explode.

"It's a shame BettyJo used a bad copy of the first page of what you claim is God's message to you as an unsuccessful get-out-of-jail trump card. I suspect BettyJo never admitted this part of the revelation to you. She also told me she burned the rest to keep Shelley from having 'em. But she knew that Shelley didn't even know the papers existed. She lied. She even starved herself for a few months to make me think she was grieving for her previous lover. And you lied. Both of you lied with your words but not your actions."

Reverend Einstein wiped some moisture from his forhead with a sleeve. He shot lasers at BettyJo sitting in the front pew with his eyes. BettyJo jumped up and ran down the main aisle toward the exit.

Buck continued, "At one time I thought BettyJo killed her lover because he cheated on her, his mistress. How ironic? But not anymore. She saw it as her opportunity – leveraging her lover's treatise to money and a life in luxury and limelight."

"She did it, not I," grumbled the pastor. He saw his own opportunity – to cut his losses before accusations of his involvement.

"As my daddy would've told you, 'it's easier to get older than wiser,'" Buck sarcastically kidded, as the allotted time for the "Pastor in a Box" segment ended.

Chapter Forty One
LIFE BY VILSMEIER

After watching the showdown of Buck with Reverend Einstein on "The Holy Event" that Sunday morning, Ida Kay and Lum sat next to each other on the couch in Ida Kay's living room. Lum quietly got up. He'd planned to make lunch for them.

Suddenly, he turned to Ida Kay. "You know. The male cockerel gives off a unique clucking sound when he finds food. Its purpose is to attract females. Hens are always on the lookout for food. They –"

"What are –" Ida Kay tried to interrupt. Lum shushed her.

"The hens come a'runnin' to check him and the food out. If the male cockerel can't offer what he said he could, the hen moves on. If he can, she stays."

Ida Kay looked confused.

Lum got down on one knee in front of the couch. He pulled a ring from his pants pocket. "If you say 'yes,' I promise not to make false promises. My actions will speak as loud as my words."

○ ● ○ ● ○

In the course of the next year, Evalina and Adam made surprise appearances at local churches after sweeps by Ida Kay and Lum as undercover agents for the "Life by Vilsmeier" Foundation. They provided a worship service of singing to generate a sense of community and hope fulfilled. The two of them had taken over the operation of the Quantum Christian

Church, at least temporarily, perhaps permanently, as the image of its founder Reverend Einstain was being rehabbed. Ratings soared in their format emphasizing music and Christianity. Music was probably a better draw than mathematics or quantum physics.

One goal of Q-Dawg had been to just go about business without trying to draw attention to the "Life by Vilsmeier" Foundation, to give away money to the needy without making a fuss. They would not solicit any more money or entertain requests for grants. The only grants would pass through Lum and Ida Kay as cash on the front line of Christian giving. They discovered one particularly successful approach. They'd stand outside payday loan facilities and surprise those needing cash with cash before they entered the business to pawn a car or the like.

○ ● ○ ● ○

After the first year, at the annual Board of Directors' meeting at the home of Q-Dawg and his wife, Lum and Ida Kay reported great success with their quiet mission. Indeed, the "Life by Vilsmeier" Foundation had been making a difference spreading hope and joy throughout Appalachia.

Q-Dawg then asked Evalina whether she knew anything about the one million dollar donation to the "Life by Vilsmeier" Foundation by the Quantum Christian Church. It had been given, quietly and anonymously without any public fanfare, for the support of the missionary work of the foundation. Evalina sat there puzzled. She commented that she hadn't even told Reverend Einstein about the work of the "Life by Vilsmeier" Foundation.

Buck smiled and calmly remarked that the foundation might expect it to become an annual contribution. He confused everyone with his analogy to his daddy saying, "every now and then, you had to wake those sleeping dogs." Then he added, "Maybe Reverend Einstein is making good on his second chance at doing God's work. Everyone deserves a second chance."

Lum nodded with a tear in his eye.

EPILOGUE

BILL MEYER

Lum had just finished directing a Lowe's delivery truck to the front door to drop off and install a new refrigerator, freezer, and oven. The previous day, a contractor completed the replacement of a decrepit and leaking roof. The team added insulation to the attic with the coming of winter. Ida Kay had also filled the pantry with canned goods, flour, sugar, and food staples to supplement the canned green beans, pickles, and jam.

The 85-year old Widow Putnam had been hanging onto her small house, but just barely, built by her great-grandpa many years ago. Owning this shack and an acre of land disqualified the widow from governmental assistance. She would've been too proud to accept such anyway. The previous month, her fellow parishioners at the local Baptist church helped her plight by fixing the termite-infested floor.

Ida Kay entertained the widow with animal stories. The widow was astounded to discover baby robins ate fourteen feet of earthworms every day. And that the bar-tailed godwit flew 7500 miles non-stop in eleven days during its migration . . . and that sixty-five percent of the water in wood frogs freezes during the winter. Ida Kay continued to fascinate her with a tale about toads eating bombardier beetles. In a flick of its tongue, a toad can catch the beetle and gulp – down the hatch. But the beetle gets the last laugh. While in the toad's tummy, the beetle shoots hot steam and noxious chemicals from its back end. The toad spews the beetle out before it's digested. The beetle goes on to live another day.

A chill had already descended into the hollow. It was that time of the year sweatshirts and jackets were needed to go outside. The widow complained about the stink bugs being particularly bad. And the wooly worms she'd seen were mostly black – a cold, snowy winter was on its way. Ida Kay gave the widow hope. She'd picked a ripe persimmon from her tree the previous week and cut it in half. The seeds in its core formed a fork, meaning no snow. None of them had a spoon shape, which would've meant you would be shoveling snow that winter.

The widow grabbed Ida Kay's arm as she got up to leave. "I can't thank you and Lum enough. Ya-know, my mamma always said, 'Kindness is like snow – it will make beautiful anything it covers.'"

Ida Kay smiled and gave the widow a hug. She and Lum headed to the doorway. He contemplated the widow's thoughts when she discovers that her electric bill has been paid for several months in advance, and she finds the cash in the envelope on the end table in the living room. He had worried the previous day he'd accidently breached anonymity by telling the widow that the changes in her life were financed by Vilsmeier.

The phone rang before they exited.

Lum became choked with emotion as he overheard a tearful phone conversation of Widow Putnam with her elderly child, living in a shelter a day's drive away in Ohio.

"An operation – I think its name is Bill Meyer – delivered hope and Christian love to me!" She paused, catching a glance of the vase on the table. "And a bouquet of beautiful pink carnations."

TOPICS FOR DISCUSSION

1. Another one of the sayings of Buck Fowler's daddy might have been "as nervous as a long-tailed cat in a room of rocking chairs."

a. Share bits of country wisdom that have been passed down in your family.

b. What was the most relevant saying of Buck's daddy to you?

2. Scientists readily accept seemingly impossible results from quantum physics. For example, Schrödinger's cat can be both alive and dead simultaneously.

a. Why might so many scientists then not believe in the Holy Trinity?

b. Would you attend the Quantum Christian Church?

c. What do you think Lewis Carroll (pen name of Charles Dodgson who was not only a writer {*Alice in Wonderland*} but also a mathematician and theologian) meant when he said, "Sometimes I've believed as many as six impossible things before breakfast?"

d. Can you think of a time in your life when the impossible became possible?

3. Evalina kept the secret of a romantic affair from her father. One might think of many reasons to keep secrets. Do you think Evalina was justified in keeping her secret from Lum?

4. A primal reaction of most people when another wrongs them is to seek revenge. Some might say "Revenge is sweet," while others say "Revenge is wasted time."

a. Provide an example of a time when you sought revenge, and whether or not such was justified in retrospect.

b. An old saying is "forgive your enemies; it messes up their heads." What's easier – revenge or forgiveness? What's more effective? More satisfying?

5. Lum took a biblical passage out of context to justify his revenge. Have you ever taken a biblical passage and twisted such for your own purposes?

6. In this story the reader follows several characters pursuing happiness. People might state they're happiest when they give happiness to others, when they're comfortable with their own conscience, when they're rich, or when they have freedom, among others.

a. Do you have a particular recipe for happiness?

b. Can there be happiness without sadness?

7. Idols are objects of worship. Compare and contrast the busts of Anton Vilsmeier, Albert Einstein, and Danny Einstein to the Golden Calf of the ancient Israelites.

8. Maria Edgeworth (1767-1849) said, "A straight line is the shortest in morals as in mathematics." Do you think Reverend Danny Einstein, knowledgable in both theology and mathematics, would accept this statement in both his words and his actions?

9. Do you think Ida Kay Hall was a "crazy woman?"

10. Three pastors – Adam Clarke, Barney Bennington, and Danny Einstein – gave sermons in this story.

a. Which of the three would you like to have as the preacher in your church?

b. Which of the three not only preached but also lived their sermons?

11. If you won $20 million (after taxes) in a lottery, what would you do with your windfall?

12. Lum was described as a man with a good heart who got caught up in the moment and did a bad deed.

a. What showed he had a good heart?

b. How can one get beyond a bad action in an otherwise good life?

c. Who do your think was the character with the best heart in this story? The most flawed heart?

13. Some animals have, at least, an awareness of death, while others have feelings of awe and wonder. For example, elephants "mourn" their dead by smelling and touching deceased relatives, magpies place "wreaths" of grasses next to dead individuals, and chimpanzees "dance" at the sight of waterfalls. Ida Kay Hall might consider these observations indicative of animals worshiping their God. Do you agree?

14. In quantum physics, mathematical equations describing wave-like states provide depictions of real things (matter). Reverend Danny Einstein and Dr. Mason Turville were analogously convinced that mathematical equations describing spirit- or thought-like states can result in the reality of God. Both approaches argue the background of the universe is mind-like and such underlies the real world.

a. Do you think the foundation of the world is non-material?

b. Do you believe God can be described by mathematics?

c. Immanuel Kant, the German philosopher, said, "Science is organized knowledge. Wisdom is organized life." Could this quotation likewise be a tenet of the Quantum Christian Church?

d. Would Reverend Danny Einstein argue that God delivers His gift of hope through mathematical probabilities?

ACKNOWLEDGEMENTS

I hatched the concept for this novel, as well as its title, while attending a student seminar in the Virginia Military Institute (VMI) Chemistry Department. The student reported on undergraduate research done under the supervision of Dr. Stanton Q. (Quinn) Smith, a colonel in the Virginia Militia (unorganized), a professor of organic chemistry, and an expert on Vilsmeier reactions. I thank Dr. Smith for providing helpful and useful information on the chemistry of Vilsmeier reactions.

I greatly appreciate Dr. Ron Miller, Dr. Martin L. Stokes, Jr., and Nancy Grace for reading early drafts of the manuscript and providing valuable comments and encouragement. I also thank Helen Irvine, Florence Connors, Karen Duff, Dr. Ron Miller, and Barbara Plott for their constructive criticism of later drafts.

The "Possum Lady" was based on an article describing Karen Brace ("A passion for possums," Cathy Dyson, *The Roanoke Times*, 24 June 2019, p. V1 & V4). Many of the animal facts and mating behaviors were reported in *Science News*, *Discover*, and *BBC Science Focus*.

My late mother instilled in me a love for reading novels, while my late father provided a unique sense of humor and a flair for story-telling. And, as with all my writings, I gain inspiration and wisdom from the Holy Spirit.

I am grateful to Dr. C. Buckley Gillock and Dr. Kelvin Raybon for diagnosing and for successfully treating my lymphoma over the past two years, as well as to the infusion team – Michelle, Susan, Peggy, Greg, Jennifer, and Darin, among others – at the Augusta Health Center for Cancer and Blood Disorders.

I cannot give sufficient thanks to my wife Helen Irvine, who's my most ardent supporter, most honest critic, prime encourager, ray of hope, and muse. She has indeed been a joy and a blessing to my life, from cheering me as I chase my dreams to instituting a holistic therapy in keeping my cancer at bay.

ABOUT THE AUTHOR

Henry Schreiber is professor emeritus of chemistry at VMI (Virginia Military Institute). He retired in 2014 after 38 years of teaching and research at VMI as the Beverly M. Read '41 Institute Professor in the Arts and Sciences and with the rank of Colonel, Virginia Militia unorganized. His teaching focused on courses in general chemistry, physical chemistry, botanical chemistry, and writing about science. His research spanned the gamut from the nature of the hydrogen bond, to the chemistry of lunar and terrestrial magmas, to chemical constraints on the incorporation of nuclear waste into glass, to coloration and bubble elimination in commercial glasses, and to the development of uniquely colored inflorescences (blooms) in hydrangeas – resulting in the publication of over 130 articles in professional journals.

He received a B.S. in Chemistry from Lebanon Valley College and a Ph.D. in Physical Chemistry from the University of Wisconsin - Madison. Honors during his career include the State Council of Higher Education in Virginia Outstanding Faculty Award.

He lives in rural Rockbridge County, Virginia, with his wife Helen Irvine. As Buck Fowler's daddy would say, "Helen and Henry are like peas and carrots – good in their own right, but paired together they're even better!"

Made in the USA
Middletown, DE
20 March 2022

62953426R00179